MARKED BY FATE

COVEN OF SHADOWS AND SECRETS

CROWNS OF MAGIC UNIVERSE

ASHLEY MCLEO

MERAKI PRESS

* *Abscondita* Coven - a coven hidden in the woods of England tasked with keeping information about the *Vindix* and *lapis caelesti* safe.
* *Arcacustos* - the eight members of the ultra secretive *Abscondita* Coven.
* the Beinecke - a library at Yale
* the Covenant - the supernatural ruling body of the human world. It's made up of three individuals from each supernatural order (example: three vampires, three witches, three phoenixes and so on).
* the Darkborn - people in the human world who follow the Princes of Hell. Some are Hellblooded, but not all.
* Eyes of Darkness - one of seven portals linking the human world and Hell. All were closed until the events of *History of Witches* transpired.
* Hellblooded - individuals with demon blood. They are usually born in the human world and are forced to register by the Covenant.

GLOSSARY

* Hellborn - individuals who were born in Hell. Nearly all of these creatures are demons.

* Isila - another realm where magical beings live. It's comprised of nine kingdoms (four fae kingdoms, mage, dragon shifter, elf, vampire, and wolf shifter). Many characters in the Coven of Shadows and Secrets have direct ties to Isila's courts.

* *Lapis caelesti* - the sacred stones made by angels thousands of years ago and given to seven witches to protect. They are great sources of power that can defeat the darkest evil.

* Luxiter - an orb that allows its holder to light-travel. Few can make these items.

* Ordo Aeternum - Also known as the OA, Ordo, or the Order. An elitist group of supernaturals who believe those of magical blood should rule the world (many believe they should enslave humans too).

* Ouroboros - The symbol of the Coven of Shadows and Secrets. It is a snake, formed in a circle, eating its own tail.

* Wolvea - royal wolves of Isila

* *Vindix* - the chosen seven individuals who can claim and use the *lapis caelesti* to their highest potential. The *Vindix* all have witch blood in their line.

* *Volar* - the spell that activates a luxiter

* Vow of Intent - an vow between supernaturals where the person loses their magic if they break it

FOREWORD

To see character art of the characters in the Coven of Shadows and Secrets go to the author's website.

This book is part of the Crowns of Magic universe. In this universe, characters and storylines cross over, but the series and standalone can be read independently from one another. The reader just gets a fuller picture of the world by reading all of the books.
Other series in this expanding universe include:

The Winter Court Series - start with A Kingdom of Frost and Malice
Curse of the Fae Prince - a standalone

CHAPTER ONE

HARPER

THE STENCH OF SULFUR WAFTED INTO MY ROOM ON AN AUTUMN wind, drawing a shiver up my spine. It smelled like demons and reminded me of Wrath.

Immediately, I halted my ritual and turned away from the flickering candles atop my altar. Though I sat on a velvet floor-cushion, and could see nothing of the neighborhood outside, exploring was easy. I'd cracked the window to allow smoke outside, and my shifter sense of smell was keener than most, allowing me to monitor the area. Even so, searching for it now, I couldn't detect the sulfur at all.

Had I imagined it? Or was the stench really a threat?

Goosebumps pebbled my arms, but I fought to master my fears before they got out of hand. It was the middle of the day. I'd probably just smelled a skunk. Or maybe a neighborhood kid had set off a stink-bomb. There was no evidence that the funk pointed to trouble and no need to find trouble where there wasn't any. Matters were dire enough without me inventing new problems.

Two of the seven *lapis caelesti* were on the loose, and a

Prince of Hell walked free in this realm. Worse, he searched for the other five sacred stones—artifacts with the power to change the world.

Then, another option that explained the smell came to mind; a much better one. With the idea, my hopes lifted.

Was my ritual working?

I'd never successfully called the Old Ones before, but Mom had done so a handful of times. In each occurrence, she claimed the signs had differed. Perhaps because she had called different wolves—ancestors—each time. That was our working theory, though there wasn't enough data to be certain.

A snort escaped me. That would be just my luck to call the most rotten smelling Old One.

But it would still be an ancestor . . .

I resolved to try again. Stinky or not, the lure proved impossible to resist. With a deep breath, I turned back to the altar covered in red velvet and brimming with symbolic objects.

Three long, slender tapers ended in wildly dancing flames. The bowl of dirt adorned with three rocks from my pack's land in California sat before the candles, right next to a cup of water from a nearby river. Witches might consider the ritual to be elemental, but that wasn't the intention. The inclusion of earth, water, and flame signified a wolf's connection to their past, present, and future. Of course, they were all connected by one thing—the pack. The way of the wolf.

I honed in on my intention, trying to achieve that perfect balance Mom always spoke of, but after two full minutes, no one appeared. I exhaled a long breath.

No such luck this time.

Disappointed, I bowed my head to finish the ritual. "For

the Mother Wolf in all her nurturing and wisdom." A breath took the life of the center candle.

"For the Alpha Guardian." I blew out the taper to the right.

"And for the pack. I bleed. I love. I live." Pursing my lips, I extinguished the last flickering flame.

Immediately, another breeze soared in through the window, this one colder than before. A chill drew shivers up my spine. The wind was clean, with no stench, but it still felt wrong. A bad omen.

Taking no chances this time, I stood and crossed to the window, opened it all the way, and leaned outside.

In the neighborhood—an upper-middle class area of New Haven—everything seemed normal. Kids recently returned from school played outside. Bikes littered the yards. If not by name, then by face, I recognized every child running amok. A middle-aged woman four houses down raked leaves into an enormous pile of reds, oranges, and yellows. I knew her, too.

No one even vaguely resembled Prince Wrath, the Ringmaster, or any other enemy of my coven, Shadows and Secrets.

I frowned and slipped back inside, pulling down the glass behind me. My imagination was running away with me.

Too whimsical for her own good.

My father's words rushed back as if he'd just uttered them, but it had been years since he accused me of being whimsical or soft. To Alpha Mace Ferenz, the most cunning alpha on the West Coast, those qualities equated to weakness.

I didn't agree. More than that, I wasn't weak. Dad had trained me to fight in my wolf and human forms since I was thirteen. I was intelligent—as cunning and calculating as my father. Everyone agreed I was a fine replacement for him and would one day be Alpha of the Midnight Pack. As Dad required, I'd trained, what he referred to as, 'the fluff' out of me.

Mostly, anyway.

I crossed the room to the door, only to stop at the threshold and turned to look at the altar once more. Growing up, my quiet meditations with Mom were a treasured part of our secret life. A softer part. Dad always looked down on them, but it was one thing I hadn't been willing to give up. As ever, I wished my father understood my pull toward the past, to the mystical side of the wolves.

"No point asking for miracles," I muttered. "The world needs those for Wrath. And Mer needs them—"

A loud rumble from my stomach cut me off, and I looked down at my belly, astonished by how much noise it could make.

So, I was hungry. *Finally.* I'd barely been able to eat since the battle in New York, so the fact that I was hungry now had to be a good sign. I'd grab a snack and then get to studying.

The floorboards creaked beneath my slippered feet, the sound of home, though it didn't feel that way with my nephilim and witch roomies gone. Hell, I even missed Meredith's feline familiar.

Actually, no. I didn't miss the talking fleabag for a minute, but I *did* miss knowing that if Benedict traipsed about, then Meredith was home, too. The house was full. Alive. Wolves, even more introverted ones such as myself, enjoyed having others around. We didn't go on about it like more sociable wolves, but it was still true.

The stink of Shay's forgotten Thai leftovers assaulted me when I opened the refrigerator. That girl was the worst at throwing out old food. After a few minutes of perusing, I settled on a strawberry yogurt and string cheese when my phone rang.

I gasped and bolted out of the kitchen, back to my room. Was it Shay? Meredith? Would they call me before Luca?

It might even be a spam call, but I hadn't been able to completely shake off my alertness. Something deep inside told me it wasn't spam, that I had to answer, that something in the world had shifted, and this was important.

I threw open my bedroom door. The wood cracked against the wall and the sound of it echoed through the empty house. My phone lay charging on the nightstand, and I rushed over, sucking in a breath when I saw the name on the screen.

Mom.

I snatched up the phone and answered. "Mom?"

My mother exhaled. "Harper. You're okay."

A chill dashed down my spine. "Why wouldn't I be? You called me. Are *you* okay?"

"I'm fine, baby." She exhaled. "I just felt wrong."

My fist tightened, and only then did I notice I still held my snacks awkwardly between my fingers. Thank the Old Ones the yogurt was sealed, else I'd have had a hell of a mess to clean up in the hallway. I set the food down and perched on the edge of the bed.

"Mom, have you communed recently?"

"Actually, I was just in the Moon Room." She paused. "Why, baby? Were you?"

The tone in her voice told me that this was why she called. Something *was* up and, all the way across the country, tucked up against the Santa Cruz Mountains, Mom had felt it too.

"I've been stressed and needed to calm down, but it didn't work. I felt something too, Mom. Smelled sulfur."

"I did too."

My heart rate kicked up. "What does it mean?"

"I'm not sure, but it can't be a coincidence."

I squirmed because I agreed and had a hint that it had to do with Wrath, but I couldn't tell my mother that a Prince of Hell was Earthside. That he'd been the one to attack New York.

The attack was common knowledge among supernaturals, but the person behind it was not. Most put the blame on the Ordo Aeternum, which, from their history, was believable. What the OA wanted and what the Darkborn and the demons wanted were not so different.

Only once the Covenant was sure they had things under control in New York would they release more information to covens, packs, clans, and any other gathering of supernatural creatures. Until that happened, I was bound not to speak of the Prince of Wrath, nor his followers, the Darkborn. At least not to anyone outside of my dark artifact hunting coven, Shadows and Secrets.

"You know something," Mom said slowly.

"Lots of things."

"Don't be sassy with me, Harper Mace Ferenz."

I cleared my throat. "I can't say anything, but I can tell you that the pack needs to be on the lookout for *outsiders*." The demons and every creature serving Prince Wrath were certainly that.

"We rarely welcome visitors."

No. My pack didn't, and that was by design. My father controlled large swathes of California, but he kept his pack, those he protected, tucked away in a safe community. When they had business to do, he traveled with his betas and a few other trusted wolves.

"Stay safe, Mom. I know you'll keep a watch on Henley, but tell the twins to chill." The thought of my younger identical twin brothers, Ethan and Elijah, caught in the crosshairs of demons or Darkborn, made me want to punch something. But they were nineteen and, unlike my thirteen-year-old sister, the twins would have a harder time staying in and keeping calm. Male wolves of that age were usually itching to show their dominance. I worried that if a demon or Darkborn challenged them, they'd rise to the occasion. "People shouldn't travel right now. Even Dad and the betas, if you can stop them. You'll learn why soon."

"From you?"

"I can't be sure."

A pregnant pause filled the miles between us.

"The Covenant," she stated finally.

"Yeah."

"It's bad?"

"It's not great."

By the moon above, what an understatement. The entire planet was in mortal danger.

"I'll tell your father."

"I'm guessing Elijah is at school in LA, but Ethan is still at home, right?"

I had half a mind to demand that Elijah leave UCLA and drive home to be with the pack. That would look pretty two-faced of me, so I kept that to myself for now.

"I'll tell everyone, baby girl. Now, it's your turn to promise. Will you stay tucked away, too?"

My silence was all the answer she needed, and Mom sighed. "Call me daily, okay? To check in? At least until this is over?"

"I will. And when I get the go-ahead from S&S that I can talk to you about it, I'll call." My stomach rumbled again, and this time, Mom heard it.

She laughed, and the sound eased the tension I carried in my shoulders. "You'd better eat. I wouldn't want you lunging at poor Shay."

I didn't say that 'poor Shay' wasn't home. Rather, she had left for DC with Hans to be used as bait for Hans's insane sister. I hadn't heard a word from her and was worried about how the mission had gone.

In a practiced manner, I forced a smile into my tone. "Yeah, I'm starving. Talk to you later, Mom. I love you."

"Love you too, baby."

We hung up and, grabbing the yogurt once more, I went to get a spoon. I didn't even make it to my door when another whiff of sulfur drifted through my room.

My mouth dried up, and I ran to the window. Again, nothing obvious was amiss.

But I didn't buy it. A wolf shifter knew that appearances deceived. Out there, in the vast world, something waited to pounce: a hunter, a predator, a breaker of worlds.

I couldn't see them, but I could read the signs. Trouble was coming for us again, and I would be ready for the next attack.

CHAPTER TWO

MEREDITH

A CHILL HUNG IN THE EVENING AIR, BUT ADRENALINE SHOT through me, keeping me warm. On my finger, the moonstone ring marking me as a *Vindix* was a touch hotter, like it did not want to be ignored. Although the piece was largely unpredictable, at that moment, I understood what it was saying. The ring was warning me.

If that was true, then there was only one possible explanation. The Ringmaster, my old boss, had to have been the one to set off the wards surrounding the *Abscondita* Coven's land in rural England. She was finally coming after me—demanding that I pay my debts with blood and magic.

"Breathe," Tobias whispered, and only then did I realize that I had stopped breathing.

"Nothing is nearby," Benedict said. The cat was climbing a tree and peering into the English woods with intense amber eyes, ready for anything.

I should have taken comfort that my vampire mate and my familiar could see, hear, and smell far better than me. They'd anticipate my enemy before she got close to me, but I felt anything but comforted. The woods were dense and the Ringmaster had already abducted me once. That time had been in a city, and I'd had far greater visibility. I shivered, but repressed any more emotion. I tried not to think about it, but I suffered PTSD from that night in New York City.

"Gloria says that Jon-Jon saw nothing!" Miriam Black, leader of the *Abscondita* Coven—a group that protected information on the *lapis caelesti*—cried out from my right, visible only by the glow of the moon in the dark woods. "He's on alert now, though and will give the signal should he find anyone."

"Nor did Rygor. He's searching too," Stuart called from my left.

So, the resident giant and wyvern hadn't seen the Ringmaster arrive. How? She wasn't coming alone. Why go to the Ordo Aeternum and strike a deal, if she would not use their might?

The OA was a radical faction that believed supernaturals should rule the humans, and my old boss had information on the *lapis caelesti* that the organization desperately wanted. Normally, the OA might balk at dealing with a human, but the Ringmaster was powerful in her own way and persuasive as hell. Plus, once she absorbed my magic—her goal—she'd be one of them, and the OA wouldn't have to compromise their screwed-up morals. The alliance was a win-win for both parties, even if I had a hunch that the Ringmaster would ultimately screw the OA over later.

Prince Orien—Wrath—was much more powerful than the OA, and my old boss would want to be in his good graces.

"Stay close, Meredith," Tobias growled at my side.

"Do you scent anyone yet?"

"I don't smell the Ringmaster," he assured me. "Nor Josiah, or my maker. I would be able to scent Giselle first."

For the first time, I worried about what would happen if Giselle had to go up against Tobias. We both knew his sire would have to make the fight look real. She was spying on the OA and couldn't blow her cover. As his maker, I guessed she'd be even stronger than Tobias.

"But," Tobias's voice yanked me from my growing dread over what might happen to him. "There is something different out here. Hot."

"Hot? Like fire?"

"The OA has fire elementals. Witches certainly, and perhaps those of other orders too."

Another type of fear gripped me. Fire in a forest as vast and remote as this one would be devastating.

"Let's keep going," I said. We needed to stop this fight before it could begin.

Side-by-side, we trudged forward. Occasionally, Tobias would glance left or right, and I suspected the guardian witches of the *Abscondita* Coven searched in the distance. No one had released magic to give away their position.

I swallowed. Ten of us prowled the woods. Not counting Jon-Jon, Rygor, and Benedict. How could an army of OA be hiding so well? Was it possible that they'd run after they set off the wards?

I wished my seeking powers worked on finding people, not just things. But no, all I had was a sense of dread and a warm ring around my finger. The heat it gave off was steady and pleasant, unlike when it had tried to burn me in the Beinecke library a few days ago.

"Hey! You!" a raspy voice screamed in the distance. I

pivoted in time to see fireballs streaming through the trees. "Arggh!"

"Gloria!" Claire's Irish lilt rang out as the sounds of thundering footsteps tramped through the thick underbrush.

Tobias, Benedict, and I broke out into a sprint too—but toward the attacker—now weaving through the trees to get away from Gloria. I could just see the person's outline, small and curvy, through the moonlight.

The stout, iron-haired witch seemed indestructible, even at seventy-something, but judging by the stream of colorful curses ripping from her lips, something had happened to her.

"This way." Tobias herded me to the right.

"How many?" I asked Tobias.

"Just the fire elemental still." He shoved a branch out of his way as we ran by. "The scent grows stronger. They're—"

Twenty feet ahead, a short figure leapt out from behind a robust tree, their hands ablaze, fire shooting erratically from their torso in a way that resembled wings.

"Stay back!" The person, a young woman, maybe a year or two younger than me, shouted at us in a Scottish accent. Her arms trembled violently in the orange glow of the flames. "I don't want to hurt you!"

I blinked. "Y-you don't? Then, why are you here?"

"Are you alone?" Tobias demanded, and the woman shifted her attention to him; the bigger, more obvious threat.

"Who else would coom all the way oot here?" Fire fanned around her hourglass figure, brighter than a second ago. She glanced down at the flames spreading and fleeting fear dashed across her face.

She couldn't control her magic, but she was trying to hide it. I needed to proceed with caution.

Stepping forward slowly, I held out my hand, creating a

barrier between this woman and Tobias. "We thought you were someone else. You haven't seen anyone in these woods?"

"No." She inched backward. "That old hag leapt out at me. Scared the piss out of me."

Gloria had probably taken joy in it, too. The caster of the *Abscondita* Coven had spunk.

"She lives here," I said, barely aware of the rustle in the trees. Benedict continued to watch from above in case something went wrong. "Clearly, you have magic. Did you feel the wards when you walked through?" I had to be certain that she had been the one to break them.

"I think so." The girl shuddered. "It was like walking through a fridge."

My shoulders loosened, and I dropped my arm so that it fell at my side. In response, the other woman seemed to relax a touch, but when Tobias shifted slightly, she tightened once more.

"Tobias." I looked at him and took in the rough edge of his jaw and the coldness of his emerald eyes. "Maybe take a step back?"

"You're my mate and you're requesting I stand down when she looks like a bloody phoenix? Their kind can ignite an opponent in seconds, my love."

"I'm no' a phoenix!" the young woman spat out, as if the idea offended her, though I couldn't say why. Being a phoenix sounded pretty cool to me. "I'm a witch."

A witch. And a fire elemental.

My gaze swept over the young woman. When I spotted a bracelet on her wrist and quickly counted the stones, my knees buckled. Tobias caught me a second before I would have saved myself.

"You're trembling." he growled, tightening his grip on me

as if his touch could calm me down.

"Look at her wrist." I whispered, righting myself. It wasn't exactly like my ring, but the piece was close enough. Miriam had mentioned offhandedly just days ago that each *Vindix* would have a talisman, and I was certain the bracelet was such an item.

"What are you two talking aboot?" The girl narrowed her eyes and the flames around her fanned higher.

"Sorry," I said, walking closer to her. "Your bracelet. Is it old?"

"*What?*"

"I'm Meredith," I said. This girl didn't know me, perhaps didn't know what I believed her jewelry meant. "And I can't help but notice your bracelet. It reminds me of my ring." I extended my hand to show her. We were still about fifteen feet apart, so she had to lean closer to view it.

She shrugged. "Don't see how."

"There's a large moonstone and seven other stones. Yours are just all red."

"My Mum gave it ta me as a graduation gift." She shook her head. "But what's yer point? Yer freaking me oot and I've already had a hard couple o' days." At the end of her sentence her voice broke, and sorrow flitted across her face before she buried it.

"Is the bracelet warm?" I softened my tone. It should have been. Her bracelet and my ring were made to tell us that we were one and the same.

"A wee bit, but I was playin' with fire—in case ye hadn't noticed."

"Has it been warm this whole time? When you were walking through the woods looking for . . . " I trailed off, leading her to what I hoped would be an answer.

She gaped before she caught herself and her features rearranged into one that gave away little. "A feelin' brough' me here 'n then my bracelet, my da's mum's, got warm. I dinnae know wha' it was doin'."

I exhaled and lowered my hands. "I do. There's a reason you're here. What's your name?"

"Tana."

"Fire or star goddess," Tobias whispered, making me whirl on him.

"What?"

"Her name." The vampire looked to Tana, studied her dark hair, amber eyes that caught the firelight, and olive skin tone. "You're Greek?"

"By birth. My family moved to Scotland when I was a wee girl. Da got a job at the uni."

"No other reason?" I asked.

She shrugged. "They said coming 'ere felt like coming home, but th' job instigated th' shift."

No. Fate had done that. I looked at Tana in wonder, almost certain a *Vindix* stood before me. This young woman had to be the keeper of the Ruby of Flames.

She had a bracelet that acted like my ring—a sort of talisman, she had the right type of magic, and she had the pull to be here, to seek us—me.

Had my appearance on this island prompted her arrival?

All those things swayed in her favor, but there was only one way to know for certain if she was a *Vindix*.

"We need to find Miriam." I turned to Tobias. "Or someone else who can take us to the pool."

"A pool?" Tana asked.

"This is going to sound weird," I started, "But I'm going to ask you to submerge yourself in a small pool of water."

Her nose wrinkled. "I don't like water."

Of course not. Fire and water didn't mix.

"Well, if you want to know why something brought you here, you're taking a dip, nonetheless." Out of the dense foliage, Miriam Black approached with a stern tone. Her blue eyes narrowed as she took in Tana. As always, she reminded me of an iron-haired, strict English Headmistress.

"I did it," I offered, when Tana glared at the woman and her eyes seemed to burn from within. "It's magical. And, more importantly, it's the only way for us to know for sure why you're here."

I didn't need it. I recognized my bond with Tana in my heart—my blood, my bones—but the pool would be confirmation for others. It would also make Tana believe. She, perhaps, was the most important person to convince because, while Tana knew how to use fire magic, I got the sense that that was all she knew.

Had all the stone-guardian families lost the knowledge of the *Vindix*? Of the incredible power and responsibility that ran through their lines?

"Dinnae hurt, did it?"

"It's cold, but it wasn't painful. I promise."

She studied me and, for a moment, I was certain that she'd turn tail and run again. If she did, what would I do? Chase her? That might result in disaster. Though she'd been drawn here, she seemed scared . . . and not great about containing her magic, especially in such a thick forest.

After a minute that seemed to stretch into a decade, her arms dropped and the fire wreathing her body disappeared on a phantom wind. "Fine." Her tone said it all; she wasn't happy about this, even if she had agreed.

"We can show you to it now." I kept my voice soft and gentle, so as not to offend her further.

"I would hope so. I dinnae have a bloody week."

An unexpected snort escaped me. "Follow us."

Miriam didn't have to be asked to lead the way. The coven leader turned and strode through the woods, around the vast manor that her coven called home. All the while, Tobias walked at my side, closer than necessary. Benedict rustled through the foliage, apparently still unsure about the girl and unwilling to reveal himself.

Tana trailed us as we passed by other coven members, each throwing intrigued looks our way. I didn't speak to her. If I were her, in this odd place, watched by so many strangers, I'd want a moment to mull things over.

When Miriam reached the crypt-like entrance to the underground enchanted pool, Tana sucked in a loud breath.

"That's it? Why is it a door 'n a wee room? We cannae even all fit 'n ther'!"

I'd asked a similar question when I'd been shown this place. The door that popped up from the ground only to lead down a set of stairs into a cavern was creepy.

"The pool is underground. That's the entrance to the stairwell, so it doesn't need to be large," I explained, watching fear tighten her features. "When I first saw it, I thought it looked like a crypt."

"Why is the pool underground?" Tana peered at the door skeptically.

"I—I'm not sure. It's natural, so I guess it was just there? Miriam?"

"Aye, that's the measure of the pool," Miriam nodded stiffly. "Now, I'd like to get moving. It's getting cold out and my old bones don't take to the chill as well as they used to."

"Tobias, will you wait up here?" I turned to face my mate. He wouldn't like the request, but Tana didn't seem comfortable at all.

"Yell if you need anything," he said firmly.

"Why's he staying?" Tana asked, clearly not trusting my motives.

"You'll have to undress to get in the water," I answered. "I thought it might make things more comfortable for you."

She paled. "Get naked?"

"Something will happen on your body and your skin will need to be bare for you to see it. That's how we'll know for certain that you are who we think you are."

Tana stared at me for a moment. The girl was practiced as hell at intense eye contact. "Only ye, then. The auld lady kin bade up here too. Save her knees."

Miriam scoffed. "I'm coming, girl."

"I only want her." Tana pointed to me. "She's done it, so she kin come. I dinnae trust anyone else." She cast me a suspicious glance. "Nae even sure why I trust ye a little. But I do."

At that, I laughed. "I'm flattered. Miriam, I can tell you what happens. It will be the same thing that happened to me, right?"

"It will be." The elder's lips pursed, and I sought to soften the blow.

Gently, I touched her arm. *"Trust me.* You're going to have to do so for much larger matters soon."

Her expression softened ever so slightly. "That I will." She opened the door wide. "Go on, then."

I nodded to Tana. "There's a railing. The staircase is steep."

Without another glance back, I descended the steep steps. One. Two. Three. Four. Finally, a creak of wood behind me told me that Tana followed. I exhaled.

I understood Tana's resistance to trusting others. As far as I was concerned, trust needed to be earned—especially with a demon prince on the loose.

"Why is it so . . . musty?" Tana asked after a moment.

"That's the water." I waved my hand in the direction we were going, taking care on the narrow steps. "The cavern isn't very large and I don't think there's much ventilation."

"I don't see it."

"Just wait," I glanced back at her as the rock ceiling lifted enough for her to see the pool, and Tana's footsteps faltered.

"That's the pool. It looks—"

"Like magic." When I got to the bottom, I turned to her with a smile. "It's gorgeous, isn't it?"

The small blue pool of water spread before me, tranquil yet cloudy. The cavern took my breath away. We stood beneath a dome ceiling embellished with natural yellow crystals. Mica shimmered in the walls, reflecting the glow from the larger gems.

"'Tis," Tana said, eyes raking over the space. "But dae I really have to get in tha'? I dinnae like tha' I cannae see the bottom."

I wasn't about to tell her I wasn't sure about the depth. The pool might have been ten feet deep or a thousand. I suspected neither of us wished to find out.

"You do."

She huffed. "You lot are quite secretive."

"You don't know the half of it," I said, thinking about the manor's library, all the mysteries hidden there, secrets that the *Abscondita* Coven had been guarding for thousands of years. "Can I ask you something?"

"I guess." Tana moved closer to the water and undressed.

"How *exactly* did you know to come here? Did an event

instigate it? Or have you been feeling the need to move this way for a while?"

She turned white as a sheet. "I—I felt a pull 'n started driving." As she spoke, her eyes darted from the water, to the ground, and the crystal-crusted walls. They lingered anywhere but at me.

Whatever had happened hadn't been good, but I didn't need to learn about her past yet. I'd learn, in time.

"Turn around," she said, already in her bra and underwear.

Unlike how Miriam had refused me, I did. Only after a splash telling me she'd jumped in and the sound of her sputtering for air did I turn again. Her back was to me, and the moment I laid eyes on her, I smiled.

The glowing white swirls were there. Gleaming otherworldly tattoos climbed her arms to cover her shoulders and plunged down her back. Most prominent was the glowing white full moon on her back.

And there was more, too. It was difficult to see her bracelet in the water, but I swore I spotted a flash of green and purple that had not previously been present in the circlet of rubies. Just like my ring had changed when it became whole in the Beinecke, this water had washed away whatever enchantment was on her bracelet, revealing its truth. Tana's destiny.

"What th' hell is all this?" She shrieked and stared down at her arms, her hands, and her chest.

"Get out," I answered, heart thundering in my chest at the implications of what had happened.

The glowing white swirls and symbols were proof, marking Tana as a *Vindix*. Most likely, the keeper of the Ruby of Flames. "I hope you're not tired, because girl, do I have a story to tell you."

CHAPTER THREE

HANS

MILES OF SLEEPY ITALIAN COUNTRYSIDE FLASHED BENEATH ME SO fast that the trees blurred. And yet, we were still not flying swiftly enough for my liking.

The problem was, I couldn't speed up. My midnight black wings, born just hours ago, ached from use. They were already being pushed to their limits, and I feared that soon, they'd fail me.

For the millionth time, I glanced behind, but as before, only the starry night sky stared back. So far, no one had followed us. I released the breath I'd been holding and turned to the other distracting feature of my travels.

Archangel Uriel currently still passed out in my arms.

Since Shay, her father, and I had escaped Lake Como, I'd had hours to notice that Shay did not resemble her father. Instead, she favored her mother, Angelina Ramos, Covenant Seat, Mexican smoke-show, and business tycoon. However, the magic rolling off the unconscious Uriel resembled his daughter's. Strong. Radiant. Unmistakably angelic.

That last quality was quickly becoming an issue. Because

Uriel was a large being, I couldn't see my forearms, but where the archangel touched me, my skin felt irritated.

"Hans!" Shay called out. "Are you okay?"

I looked up from her father to find her flying backward, watching me. I envied the graceful way she soared.

"I'm tired," I admitted.

"I can try to take him?" Shay offered, sizing up her father, all two-hundred and fifty pounds of muscle.

I wasn't doubting that Shay was strong, I'd seen her athleticism plenty of times. But, like me, Uriel was a big guy and even though I worked out religiously I was having trouble holding him. Had we not been fleeing for our lives, I would have stopped to reposition him a long time ago.

"Or we could rest?" I arched an eyebrow, hoping she would agree. "Perhaps you can try to wake him?"

Shay looked down. Quiet forestland spread below us, and Lake Como had disappeared hours ago, but I understood her hesitation. Wrath had wings, as did many of his minions. Technically, they could appear at any moment. And yet, I really needed a break.

"We don't have to stay in one place for long," I added, desperate to touch the ground, to stop flying.

"You're right." Shay nodded. "I bet they would have already come for us if they were going to do it. We have a little time."

They were the seven Princes of Hell: Orien, Lucifer, Bale, Asmodev, Belhor, Levi, and Mon. All, save for Orien, the Prince of Wrath, had recently exploded from a newly opened gateway linking our world to Hell.

A shiver ran through me at the memory of last night, of how the waters had parted and the earth had fallen away to reveal fire and evil before the princes rose. If someone would have told me that I'd watch an Eye of Darkness open, I would not have believed them. But I had, and there were six more such portals somewhere in the world.

I hoped that only one Eye of Darkness had burst open and not all seven.

I swallowed, trying to banish the image of those dark figures rising from the usually quiet water, but it was impossible. When I thought of the princes, specifically Lucifer, another person came to mind.

Lilith. My mother.

Had she risen with them?

"Whatever you did to Orien must have them thinking twice." Shay's tone sounded nonchalant. Fishing.

But I wasn't ready to go into what I'd done to Prince Orien to stop him from tormenting her father. Nor what I had done to those spectators on the lakeside who had watched the demons battle Shay, Archangel Uriel, and me. I'd ignored my vile Hellblooded gifts for so long, but now, with my wizarding magic bound to fucking Richard Brons, the blackest of powers were all I had at my disposal.

"How about there?" Shay added when I didn't reply. She pointed below. "There's a stream to wash in and get water from."

I followed Shay as she descended into the thick trees. Touching down was new to me and it showed as I stumbled on legs that hadn't been used in hours. Lunging forward, I lost control of the archangel, but Shay was there, ready to catch her father.

In doing so, her hands landed on mine, skin-on-skin. Demon on nephilim. She sucked in a breath and jerked back ever so slightly before she realized I might not yet be stable, that I might drop the archangel. Stiffening, she maintained our connection.

"I've got him," I assured her, hating that I made her uncomfortable. "I'll set him over there." I gestured under the trees.

"Thanks." Shay dropped her arms to her sides and clasped her hands behind her back, as if she didn't know what to do with them now that she was sullied.

I edged to the side of the woods and, finding a softer stretch of ground, laid down the archangel. My arms thanked me, but the relief proved short-lived.

My forearms were worse off than I'd imagined. The rare stretches of uninked skin glared back at me, red and irritated. Some parts blistered from where strong angel magic met more sinister powers. Deeper still, gray veins so dark that they were almost black taunted me. How long would this take to fade?

My heart raced, and for the first time, I became aware of how the back of my shirt had split open to accommodate my wings. Were the veins back there gray, too? I ran a trembling hand through my hair.

Nearing a breakdown, I forcibly pulled myself together and turned to my S&S partner. Shay was already on her knees, checking her father for injuries.

"Uh," I started, feeling shitty and useless and about a million other negative emotions. "Let me know if I can help."

"Thanks," she replied, and this time she gave me a small smile. "I think he's okay. He just—"

The archangel jolted up, his sword of fire and light flaring in his hand, his chest heaving.

"Dad! You're okay!" Shay placed her hand on the sword's hilt, steadying the weapon before it could cause harm. "I'm here. You're safe."

Uriel's gaze traveled between his daughter and me, running momentarily over my black wings, which hadn't been a thing when he saw me last, before Wrath wrapped him in a cocoon of darkness. "How did we survive Wrath's attack?"

"Uh, well . . ." Shay swallowed.

"You, tell me." Uriel gazed at me again, his expression serious. "Leave nothing out."

Fuck me. The last thing I wanted to do was talk about what had happened. How, not only was Wrath walking the Earth, but now six more Princes of Darkness were too.

But people don't deny archangels, not even Hellblooded souls like me, so I began the tale. When I got to the part when Shay gave me her sword of fire and light, her father blinked and turned to her. "You did that?"

"There was no other way," she said. "I don't give it out all the time though. Almost never." Her cheeks flushed and her eyes dropped.

"You misunderstand." Her father cupped her shoulder with his large hand. "I'm pleased you did so. And proud, daughter. I'll admit, I wouldn't have guessed you would give it up, but . . . " Uriel's penetrating stare caught mine, "you chose a worthy soul to hand it to."

A faint breeze could have knocked me over, I was so stunned. I wasn't the only one. Shay looked as if someone had slapped her, which both hurt me and made me feel somewhat vindicated. Not enough to say it out loud. My self-worth issues had not disappeared at the angel's word, but it helped. His belief in me made a difference.

Would it last, though? When he learned what I'd done? How I'd gotten us out of there?

"Now, please continue with your story . . . What is your

name?" Uriel spoke as if he and his daughter hadn't just had a moment.

"Hans." I glanced at Shay as I spoke. She dragged her eyes from her father and nodded.

"Once I had Shay's sword, and learned how to fly with these," my aching wings rustled at my command, "I used the weapon to cut you free from Wrath's bindings and caught you before you fell." I paused.

He wouldn't have fallen into the lake. No, the archangel would have plummeted much farther. But did he know?

"Before I fell into Hell," Uriel said. "I'm aware. I can feel them. The seven princes are all here." He rose, the movements fluid, as if he hadn't just been attacked by a dark equal and unconscious for two hours. "That is what you mean, correct?"

"Yes," I said.

"Why did Wrath not stop you?"

My muscles tensed with dread. "I used magic against him."

The archangel studied me. "I sense a bind within you. If I were able, I would cut you loose, but that is not within my scope. I can only assume you did not use wizarding magic but your Hellblooded powers? Those of Lilith?"

An exhale parted my lips. "How did you know she's my mother?"

"Her power signature is unmistakable. Now, answer me." Uriel raised his head to stare at me.

"I did," I admitted. "I used my demon magic for the first time in a very long time."

"And what is your black gift?"

Gift? I shuddered. That was something Nicoleta would say.

Uriel came closer, his sword vanishing into the aether. "The Princes of Hell were once angels."

"Yes," I replied, uncertain where he was going with this.

Behind her father, Shay watched us quietly.

"You might disagree," Uriel said, "but that means we are not all that different. Our shades of power vary. The intensity of our magics. But what really divides us, even myself and the dark princes, is choice. They made a choice and paid for it. However, your mother is different. She was never an angel, never had a choice in what she is, and yet, I sense she has stronger, more heavenly morals than the princes." He paused. "I sense that you differ from the fallen, too."

"I do," I blurted. "But my dark gift, as you call it, is to cause others pain. I can torture them if I want to."

A soft gasp came from Shay, and I forced myself not to meet her eyes. It wasn't the first time I'd revealed my demon magic to non-family members, and I knew the look of horror she'd wear. I'd rather not see it.

"And that is what you did to Wrath?"

I gulped. "It was."

"He did not expect it, though certainly, he deserves it."

"*Father!*"

"Angels are not perfect, Shaylina." Uriel looked at his daughter with love in his eyes, but his jaw was firmly set, as if he knew what she needed to hear. "No matter what your lovely mother says."

Her shoulders loosened, and I felt her relief swelling. Angelina Ramos was a real piece of work. She placed heavy expectations on her daughter's shoulders. Not that Shay couldn't accomplish whatever she set her mind to, but I'd seen how Angelina pushed and pushed and pushed. Most would break under such pressure. Shay's mother also, notably, hated Hellblooded people.

"You should learn to harness that gift." Uriel caught my eye. "Do you possess other dark gifts?"

I shook my head, struck by how this conversation was taking a turn. "No. That's the one I had before I stopped using my demon magic."

"At what age?"

It was hard to say. Officially, I stopped at thirteen when I'd decided I was done terrorizing others. But for a few years after, there were still moments when I slipped. And when I'd taught Nicoleta about her power, I'd accessed my wellspring of magic too.

"I haven't used it for a decade," I settled on.

"Things might have changed."

I hoped not. I didn't wish to have more demonic powers.

"Don't discount what you have, Hans." His stare, much like his daughter's, penetrated me before dropping to his arms and hands. "I am covered in blood and wish to wash. Would you two mind giving me a moment?" The archangel gestured to the stream.

So, as Uriel washed up, Shay and I entered the woods, silent as the grave for a few paces before she turned to me.

"Thank you so much, Hans."

"For what?" I asked. "Bringing you to DC and getting us both abducted and used by Wrath? You should be furious with me. With my family."

I hadn't forgotten that my sister was responsible for so much of this pain. For luring me and Shay into her trap so Prince Wrath might use Shay to release his brothers from Hell.

"I don't blame you for your sister's mistakes." She released a long breath. "I mean, do I think you need to stop redeeming her? Hell yes, I do. But she's making her own choices, and anyone can see you don't agree with them." Her lips pursed.

Though she was right about Nicoleta, I wasn't sure I deserved any trust. Anytime I'd been presented with my sibling, I'd made the wrong choice. That had to stop.

The girl who'd loved running wild in the woods, the girl who made me play tea party with her dolls and who adored the ground our father walked on, was gone. When I saw Nic next, I didn't think I'd be able to forgive her. Or save her.

Once, Luca had offered my sister salvation, a place in S&S, but no longer did I consider it a real option. She did not care to choose the right path. My little sister wanted power and a place in the pantheon of dark gods. If she wed Wrath's son and heir, Rikel, then she'd likely get it, too. As if being Lilith's daughter wasn't impressive enough; once she produced Rikel an heir, Nicoleta would cement her place among Hell's royalty.

"But you saved my father," Shay continued slowly. "I was failing. Without you, he'd be gone and . . . that's something I can never repay. So, thank you."

"I would do it again," I said.

Shay's gaze strayed back to the stream, before she looked at me again. "You flew well enough to escape, but as a token of my gratitude, what do you say I teach you a few tricks? We don't have passports or anything on us, so we might have a long journey home. Flying would be easiest, if you can manage."

I hadn't considered that issue, but Shay was correct. We hadn't had our passports on us when Wrath had smoke-traveled us from DC to Italy. The idea of flying from wherever we were in Italy to New Haven, Connecticut with my new wings exhausted me all over again.

"Luca can overnight our passports," I said. We didn't have our phones either, but I had the coven master's number memorized for emergencies.

"Sure, but he can't send them here." Shay gestured to the woods. "We'll have to get to a major city, and flying is better than walking. Plus, I don't know how quickly you'll learn how to hide your wings. If you can't, the passports won't help, anyway." She bit her lower lip.

For fuck's sake. My demon side caused more issues by the second.

"Can you show me how you do it? Maybe it's the same way you do it?" I suggested.

She blinked, taken aback that anything about us would be the same, but I didn't take offense. I hated my demon magic too.

"Sure. We can try," Shay recovered with a small smile. "I can't guarantee it will work, but if it doesn't, maybe my dad has tips?" She beat her white feathered wings and lifted into the air. "What do you say we begin by you trying to catch me?"

"I followed you here." I stretched my wings and tried to shake the ache from them. "With your father in my arms."

Shay's lips curled up in a genuine smile. "As much as I wanted to, I wasn't going anywhere close to my full speed. Not with you and Dad behind me. Someone had to be prepared to defend you." She winked. "But I will go faster while we're putting those bad boys to the test." With that, she took off and zipped away, showing me that she spoke the truth.

I watched, stunned by this turn of events, before soaring after her.

CHAPTER FOUR

SHAY

I PULLED BACK MY HAIR, DOING MY BEST TO TAME THE DISASTER
that had resulted from flying lessons.

"You did well," I said as Hans landed next to me, his pale
cheeks pink from the wind. The color made the white scar
running the length of his jaw stand out against his skin. "You
need some work on your barrel rolls," I added teasingly, only
to realize I might sound like I was hitting on him. "Still . . . " I
infused more seriousness into my tone so he didn't get the
wrong idea. "For a newbie, I'm impressed."

"I had a good teacher." He smiled.

Maybe. He'd made progress in a short amount of time. We
had been at it only for about a half hour, when my father sent
up a gold spark—a signal that he'd finished bathing, and
doing whatever else he'd been up to—and I'd ended the
lesson. More than anything, even getting out of the ridiculous
white dress Prince Orien had put me in to ridicule the
nephilim order, I wanted to get back to Dad. To talk to him. I
didn't get that chance often, and he'd have to return to Heaven

soon to tell those above what had happened. Thankfully, Hans had understood why I wanted to cut the lesson short.

"The stream is this way." I set off through the trees toward where the water cut through the woods.

I spotted my father through the trees minutes later. Angels, even ones who are trying to dampen their essence, give off a golden glow. Humans could not see it, but all supernaturals possessed the ability, and as a nephilim, I was extra sensitive to the glow.

He turned to greet us as we exited the trees. "Good, you're back. We must talk."

"For sure," I said, elated that he was making the time for me. "Let me wash my hands."

"Of course." He leaned against a tree, white wings spread to an impressive twenty-feet, wingtip to wingtip.

Hans joined me and we washed in the cool stream. As we did so, I tried not to stare at the gray veins etched onto his red skin. They were a symbol of dark magic. That he'd used it, that he'd been at the mercy of it. Hours ago, that would have sent me into a total tailspin, but now . . . Well, I still didn't feel 100% right about it, but he'd done it to save my father. To save me.

Once I felt clean, or at least as clean as I could get, I rose and turned. Dad was still there, just watching and waiting. He held his arms out. I beamed, darted to him, and embraced him.

"It's been too long, little light," he said in my ear, his powerful arms wrapped around me. "Are you well, Shaylina?"

Though he'd used my given name, it didn't rub me the wrong way like it did when Mom used it. Coming from Dad, any acknowledgment was special. "As well as expected, given everything that's happening."

He loosened his grip, and I leaned back. "I used the time

while I washed to think. Now, I must ask you . . . Are some of the *lapis caelesti* loose?"

"They are, Father. You didn't know?"

"I did not. Wrath has them?"

"Exactly," I said. "He's been lying low for a while."

"Indeed. He is cunning."

I gazed at him intensely. "Do you know where the other sacred stones are?"

His face fell. "I do not. After they were entrusted to those in this realm, the angels did not track them. And only *one* archangel can speak openly of the stones. The rest of us are bound to silence to protect the stones."

Frustration built inside me. "Well, we know that the Opal and the Pearl are with Wrath. We're trying to find the others. My friend went to a woman who might have knowledge of them."

"There is a coven," my father said. "I cannot tell you much, but they will have all the answers. That is their lot in life."

"Are they in England?" Behind, footsteps sounded in the opposite direction. Hans walked away, to give my father and me space.

"The coven has traditionally been located on that island," he said. "I cannot say if they are still."

It had to be Miriam Black. That was the only thing that made sense.

"My roommate, my friend, is going there now. She's probably actually there by now. She's the holder of the Opal."

Understanding dawned on his face. "You should go too, little light."

My eyebrows narrowed. "Why?"

"All I can say is one of your kind will be needed. It is not a coincidence that a stone keeper found you and lives with you.

I cannot be sure. I've never been a seer, but I believe it is fate that brought her to you."

At first, Meredith had been hard to befriend, but when she opened up, a floodgate opened. She didn't hold back, even when sharing the ugly bits. We'd only known each other for a matter of weeks, and I had felt close with her. I was certain we were destined to meet one another, just as Dad said. And I got the sense I wasn't the only one in Shadows and Secrets that felt that way.

Tobias was protective of her. He'd known how to find her in New York. There was a bond between them. While I hadn't had time to ask him or Rooms much about it, I wondered if, somehow, they were fated too.

Dare I even say mates?

It had happened before—two different orders mating. My friend Kora, a fire witch, and a fae prince were fated mates.

Were Tobias and Meredith the same?

I shook my head and focused on my father. "We could fly, but it will take days. And Hans is so new to flying."

My father nodded. "That poses a problem. Logistics in general will, if what I fear comes to pass."

I was about to ask what he feared when my father's wings curled around him. From the right one, he plucked four feathers, then did the same from the left. "Take these and seek the Coven of Illumination in Paris. It's an ancient coven. Among them is a renowned alchemist, one who has perfected the art of imbuing items with the ability to light-travel."

"L-light-travel?" I blinked. "Is that like smoke-travel?"

"Precisely." My father nodded. "Angels can perform it as demons can smoke-travel. Perhaps you can do so? Have you ever experienced an inclination to . . . for lack of a more eloquent word . . . teleport?"

"Uh, no."

Not that I hadn't had the desire to do so. Who hadn't? I managed to get myself into tons of embarrassing situations and the ability to—*poof!*—disappear and go elsewhere was a dream.

"You are of my blood, and hence, you might have the ability," my father said. "Perhaps give it a try?"

I almost laughed, but remembered Nicoleta. *She* had learned to smoke-travel. Pure angel or demon blood was not needed.

I looked at the feathers. "If you think I can do it, then why give me these? For protection?"

An angel's feathers were sacred and when paired with angelic magic, could do many things. Like make soldiers to fight Wrath's peons, as my father's had done.

"You will need something precious to barter for an item that will give you the ability to light-travel. One feather should buy you one item. If I am reading the signs correctly, and the seven stone keepers are to come together soon, they will each need one. And as my daughter, I want you to have one for . . . " For a moment, his eyebrows screwed together until he struck the word "insurance."

"In case I can't manage," I said, taking the feathers with reverence. "Thank you, Dad."

"It is the best I can do. For now. Once I speak with those above, I might be able to do more." His eyes flickered upward, toward the heavens. "We have to work with a consensus. It is our way."

"But is there any question they should help? You came down from on high for me. Surely, they don't want pure demons running around on Earth!"

"You are my blood." His hand landed on my arm, soft yet

strong and reassuring. "Of course, I arrived for you."

While his answer made me all gooey inside, it didn't put an end to my questions. "And the demons?"

"We entrusted the stones to certain people for a reason, little light," my father said. "They are the ones who will see this to its end."

"Who?" I considered Meredith and the Opal of Heaven. "Is it the people who own the *lapis caelesti*?"

"In the beginning, they were all witching families and that responsibility passed through blood."

Witches? Of all the orders, why them? The witches accepted the common belief that the angels had created magical beings, but they didn't even revere the angels more than other orders. More often than not, they worshipped their Goddess, something I'd never understood.

"Is the witch Goddess an angel?" I asked, trying to make sense of the witches' beliefs.

"No, she was the first witch. Much like wolves revere the Mother Wolf and the First Alpha, the witches celebrate their roots."

"Do the angels above like that?"

My father smiled understandingly. "We do. The first witch was the most powerful of their kind to ever live. Angels gave her magic, but she proliferated it, created *more*, and spread it far and wide, as a goddess would. Her power still lives today." His blue eyes twinkled. "No angel begrudges the witches for worshiping her. She really was quite majestic."

Hmmm, interesting. And yet, I still didn't understand what was stopping the angels from helping.

"I have to ask, though, if angels can create magical orders, why can't they just destroy the demons?"

My father paused before a long sigh passed his lips. "We

cannot."

"But *why*?"

An expression, as though he were warring with himself crossed his face, before he took my hand. "This will come as a shock, but we cannot vanquish the demons, or any magical order, because the power that we used to create other orders is not wholly ours."

"*What*?!"

"The power angels used to create the other orders is not angel magic, but something else, something greater. A power we were gifted, subsequently used up, and have never been offered since."

My head spun. It was almost like I knew nothing about the world I'd been born to. Actually, it was like no one did. As far as I knew, everyone believed angels had created the other orders. Ancient, powerful angel magic that to this day they'd never used again.

I shook my head with a frown. "I don't understand."

"We used the magic of the *stars*, Shay. Such magic can only be harvested during a very specific cosmic event, and it is quite dangerous." He looked to the sky. "We lost two of our kind in harvesting the raw magic and creating the *lapis caelesti* from them, which is why we have not done so again."

"I had no idea." I blinked several times.

"Few in this realm do. Only the most ancient fae, vampires, and elves remember. Those who broke through the veil to create Isila."

"Why didn't you tell me before?"

"My kind holds their secrets tightly. It is a sort of power for us. A way to make certain that the world is balanced."

I nodded, knowing it was the truth. Knowledge was power, and not everyone was meant to wield power. "What do you think the demons' plans are? You said you had an idea before, but I got stuck on the light-travel."

"The princes rule the underworld," my father replied. "They will try to do the same here. Perhaps each will choose a continent. Or major countries or cities."

My blood froze.

"I see that frightens you. As it should." Father cupped my face. "But you have an advantage now, so seize it. You know they are here. Use all your powers, your tools, and send them back to Hell before they can get a foothold in this world."

"We will, Dad." A yawn escaped me before I could stop it. Despite the seriousness of our conversation and the revelations, I'd flown through the night. My body was shutting down. "I think we all need to rest. Are you staying for a while?"

He smiled down at me. "No. But you and your friend are safe and together. If you help one another, you're in good hands." He gestured in the direction my Shadow and Secrets partner had gone.

"You believe that?" I asked.

"I do."

Another affirmation. My father, an archangel, trusted Hans. Now that his secret lineage was out, few did in this world. I'd been taught not to and had been scared to do so in front of my mother and other nephilim. That my father didn't care about Hans's blood spoke volumes. It made me feel less stupid for never realizing what Hans was back when we used to hang out. And it also lifted a weight off my shoulders. I'd been fighting between an instilled prejudice and what I'd experienced of Hans personally. If Father, of all people, said he was good, then I believed it.

"Because one is born a certain way to a certain family

means little, Shaylina. It is our choices that matter most." My father looked down the stream to where Hans tossed pebbles in the water. "That man made his choice when he saved me."

"He chose before that," I said. "I was too pigheaded to admit it, even to myself. But I'm not anymore."

"Admitting your wrongs is only human—and that is in your blood, too." Dad's angelic light warmed my face. "I must go." He pulled me close, kissing the top of my head. "I might return soon. If I can."

"I hope so."

We separated and my father inclined his head. His honey blond hair fell into his eyes before he beat his wings and shot into the sky. A streak of gold followed until I could see him no longer.

"Bye, Dad," I whispered. The gold light dissolved as if the stars had absorbed my father's essence.

"He's gone already? Was he alright?"

I spun on my heel to find Hans standing a distance away, watching me.

"He has work to do."

"If it was me, I—"

"Don't," I started, not wanting to hear him dog himself again, even if I'd played into his self-loathing. "God, Hans, I'm so sorry," I blurted out in a single breath. "I've been treating you like crap and it was unwarranted. I apologize for my actions."

He stood there, frozen, as if he didn't quite believe my words.

"This seems like it's coming out of nowhere. But you did save my dad and, well, honestly, I've been wrestling with it for a while. I never got bad vibes from you before, but when you told me you were Hellblooded, I fell back on what I'd heard.

On what society, specifically nephilim society, drilled into my head. Sometimes my order thinks we're so much better than everyone else, but I—"

"It's okay, Shay. I understand." Discomfort flitted across his face. Yet another tell that no matter what I said, he wasn't okay with losing the wizard part of him and having only the demon half to contend with.

"You shouldn't *have* to understand," I pressed. "People should judge you by your actions. I should have done that."

"Is this because of your father? What he said?" Hans asked. "Because your mom won't agree."

"Well, screw her," I spat.

I loved my mother, but she was wrong about this matter. So many people were. "And yeah, Dad drove it home, but I also had been wrestling with it since your secret emerged. Ask Rooms and Harp. They tried to talk to me about it before, and I couldn't deal. So much weighed on me and I was lost."

He stared at me for a moment before he shook his head. "I don't have to ask them. I believe you."

An exhale parted my lips. I hadn't even realized I had been holding my breath. "Thank you."

Another long stare, but this time the air between us pulsed as if Hans verged on saying something, but couldn't quite bring himself to do so.

"Soooo," I drew the word out. "Should we try to sleep?"

"What about those?" Hans gestured to the feathers forgotten in my hands.

"We're going to Paris tomorrow to trade these for things that will help us light-travel."

"Excuse me?"

A dry laugh escaped me. "Have a seat. I'll tell you what Dad told me. Then, we'll rest for the journey ahead."

CHAPTER FIVE

GUNNER

After bein' confined for days and days in that old English manor house, bein' back home was a dream come true.

I loved having the sun shinin' on my face. Loved ridin' in my truck. Best of all, on my walk to the S&S tomb, the college girls smiled at me, and I always smiled back. The only thing that could be better was if I was with my pack, eatin' home-made biscuits and gravy, gettin' ready to go on a run.

But in a way, I was with a pack. The coven had become my second pack—one filled to the top o' the barrel with all sorts of supes. Untraditional as my choice was, Pa thought it was a good idea for me to hang with vamps and witches and all other sorts. It made me a more well-rounded man and leader. Of course, Ma thought it was stupid, but it didn't matter what she thought. Not here, anyway. I loved what I did and who I worked with.

The best of them all, Coven Master Luca, had called earlier this morning. Normally, I wouldn't be up at six and ready by seven, but I was still on England time. So, here I was, bright eyed and bushy tailed, lettin' myself into the tomb to learn what the mage wanted.

This early, the halls were empty and my footsteps echoed through the vast atrium as I crossed it to the staircase. I climbed the steps to Luca's third floor office two at a time. When I was down the hall, I heard a voice that didn't belong to the Italian mage. It only took a second of listenin' harder for me to place it.

Harper. I grinned.

The she-wolf wasn't as taken with me as most ladies, especially of the wolf-ish sort. It was an unfortunate fact 'cause I couldn't help but want to be around her. The wolf was pretty and smart, and got things done. She was a fine wolf, if there ever was one.

I stopped at the door to the mage's office and ran a hand through my hair. Good thing I'd showered and didn't reek like the plane.

"What are you waiting for? An embossed invitation?" Harper called from inside.

She'd scented me.

Couldn't help but preen over that, me. And preen I did as I opened the door and swaggered in.

"Miss me, Harper?" I asked, inhaling her inviting scent of apples and sun-baked earth.

"Almost as much as that cat I live with." She scoffed.

"Aw. Benny sends his love from across the pond."

Luca rolled his eyes. "Sit down, wolves. Gunner needs to be brought up to speed, and then I have a mission for you."

"Already?" I asked. Usually, we got a day or so to relax. "They locked me up, Luca."

The mage arched an eyebrow. "Silas already checked in last

night. I'm well aware that you had a king-size bed, a fireplace, and other plush amenities at the coven manor."

Damn, the fae couldn't let me have any fun.

"He coming?" I asked.

"Silas?" Luca sat and, with a cup of coffee in hand, he pointed to the leather chair across from him. Harper settled into the one beside him.

I nodded. "Yeah."

Luca shook his head. "No. After he caught me up, I told him what I planned, and he said he couldn't make it. Which is fine. Your noses are better, anyway."

"We searchin' for something?" I furrowed my eyebrows.

Luca held up a hand. "First, Harper? Tell him what you sensed last night."

"Yesterday afternoon, actually," she corrected. "Gunner and Silas would have been on the plane." Harper's green eyes brushed over me, all business-like. "But I was doing a ritual and got the strangest sensation. Then, I smelled sulfur. A couple of times."

"When Harper told me this morning, it struck me as curious," Luca chimed in.

"Why is that?" I leaned forward and placed my elbows on my knees.

"Because my morning skim of the news revealed there was an earthquake in Italy. It created a strong smell of sulfur, one that is spreading across Europe as we speak."

Now, that got me. One instance of rotten-egg stink was just that: one instance. But more than that?

Images of Hell came roarin' at me. It had stunk so badly down there I thought I'd never get that stench outta my nostrils. "You thinking this has somethin' to do with Wrath? Or Hell?"

Luca scrubbed at the five o'clock shadow on his jawline. "It might. I tried calling Tobias and Meredith, but their phones are off."

I sat up straight. "Yeah. Cause of the OA coming to visit."

Luca nearly spilled his coffee all over his lap. "The OA?" His voice rose in surprise.

My lips parted. "Silas didn't tell you?"

"Not a word." With widened eyes, Luca shook his head.

"Toby's sire messaged him from a burner, 'cause their phones might be tracked. That's why they haven't been in touch."

"What about the witches?" Luca leaned forward.

I paused at that. At the very least, Claire had a cellphone. I'd used it to ring Luca. "I guess we didn't consider that. There was a lot goin' on. Meredith was about to use the library and, even if we thought about it, I dunno if Toby would have gone for it. He didn't seem to trust anyone in the *Abscondita* Coven when I left."

Luca huffed out a breath. "Tobias has been losing his head lately."

"He and Stoney are gettin' cozy." I smirked. Their scents had mixed, and I had a feeling I knew why. "They might be mates."

"*What?*" Harper shot up. "But Meredith is a witch and Tobias is . . . " She trailed off, and I knew what she was thinkin' about.

"It happened before." I shrugged. "With a witch and a fae. All I know is they're smellin' similar, and that happens with mates."

"By the Old Ones," Harper murmured and lowered into her chair. "He is protective of her . . . and I've never seen him act like that before. I assumed it was because she is important to our cause, and maybe that he had a little crush too, but . . . shit, Gunner, you might be right."

Luca waved his hand to get my attention. "Be that as it may, I want to back up. The Ordo Aeternum is coming for Meredith and Tobias, and I need to get ahold of them somehow. Perhaps I should send others?"

"The witches probably won't let you, but I called you from Claire's phone, so you should have her number. I mentioned you. I bet she'll listen." Hell, if any of the *Arcacustos* were gonna listen, Claire would.

"Okay, I'll do that once you leave. Let's get down to the matter of why you're here." He rolled out his neck as if he'd had the longest morning of his life before he refocused on first Harper and me. "You two are a team now."

I didn't miss when Harper closed her eyes in annoyance. We didn't pair together often 'cause I talked too much for her. Annoyed her so much that she'd asked not to be put as a team. It had stung at first. Sometimes the truth hurt.

"I need you to locate Sara," the coven master said. "She's been missing for days now. While I believe she must be alive because she's all that the Ringmaster holds over Josiah's head, we need to do all that we can to save her."

"For sure," I murmured, feelin' bad for the sweet necromancer. Sara had always been a peach to me.

"What about the traitor?" Harper asked. "Who's on that?"

"I am," Luca said. "I've put it off for too long."

"The traitor might also be involved in taking Sara," I added. "Not just lettin' the shade into the tomb."

Luca gave a succinct nod. "We're dividing and conquering. You two have the best noses in the coven. If anyone can track Sara, it'll be you. Start at her apartment and be on the lookout for demons. There have been sightings again in the city and we're not far from there. Kill them, if you find them." He rose. "Now, I need to make that call."

And with that, the meeting was over. I stood. "Want me to drive, Harper?"

"I walked, so yeah."

"My truck isn't too far." I headed to the door. "You be the demon lookout on our way, 'kay?"

She didn't reply; she just breezed by me and out the door. I shot Luca a grin, and he shrugged, probably not quite sure what to make of the she-wolf.

I wasn't sure either, but I knew one thing. This was a chance to thaw the pretty wolf toward me, and Gunner Ray Bryant always made the most of his chances.

———

WE PULLED UP TO THE GARDEN-STYLE APARTMENT COMPLEX. IT was nice and roomy with an expansive yard area out front that all the renters could use.

"No space at all between units," Harper muttered as she hopped out of the truck. "How is it possible that her neighbors didn't hear Sara being taken?"

"If the abductor was a witch, they might have cast a silencing charm," I suggested. "Or maybe they snuck up on her and knocked her out. Necromancers don't have keen senses."

"True." Harper's green eyes scanned the area. Her pert nose wiggled, hintin' that she was already on the job. I followed her lead, sniffin' deep.

The apartment complex smelled like most others. Lots of humans. Spices in the air and the scent of cooked onions lingered from someone's dinner the night before. I didn't smell a supernatural around, which meant Sara was probably the only one in this complex.

"Her place is over here." Harper led the way to Sara's door. When we got there, we stopped and eyed each other.

"You do it," she said. "Your nose is better, and Luca has been here since Hans discovered she was missing. Mage scent is really strong, and might have covered up someone else's."

"That's it, though, right? Just those two checked it out?"

"Luca would have told us otherwise, so we didn't follow a false trail."

Undoubtedly, she was right. If Luca had sent someone before us, he would have mentioned it. I bet he even forbade other coven members who wanted to take a look. Dan and Gus came to mind. The bears were tight with Sara and her traitor boyfriend, Josiah.

I bent at the knees, bringing my nose closer to the door handle. Right away, I picked up on Hans's faded scent. As ever, he smelled like a wizard, sorta earthy but with honey, and the car oil aroma that clung to Hans cause that was just who he was. It still surprised me that he hid his demon side for so long. Musta known a spell to dampen his *eau de demon*.

Luca's smell was stronger, almost overpowering Hans's, but there was nothin' else. Whoever had abducted Sara had been sure to wipe their tracks. At least right here. We'd see if they were as diligent on the inside.

"Nothin'. Anyone behind us?"

"No," Harper said.

I took a step back and kicked open the door that Luca had locked behind him.

"Damn. They coulda cleaned up." I moaned as the rot of vegetables assaulted me.

"And you could have gone through a window!" Harper hissed. "Sara is going to be pissed when she gets back."

"We'll cross that bridge when we get there, toots," I drawled. I added the last bit to get a rise out of her and it worked. Her pale cheeks reddened, and the air perfumed with her scent as her inner wolf snarled and green eyes flashed.

"Don't call me that."

"My bad." I bit back a grin. "Ladies first."

She scowled as she stalked into the home, and I couldn't help but think she was even prettier when she was riled. It thrilled me. Few wolves spoke to me like Harper did. They wouldn't dare. But her pa was as influential as mine—though not of wolvea blood. Alpha Ferenz simply had a reputation for being ruthless.

"I'll take the bedroom and bath," Harper said. "I doubt Sara would appreciate a guy rooting around back there. We should leave the door open to air it out. You got the living spaces and kitchen?"

"Stickin' me with the stinky spots, I see." The apartment smelled like rotten food.

"Luca didn't want to clean up in case we needed to bring in Covenant officials. Obviously, that's undesirable, so let's hope we find her." Harper had spoken over her shoulder as she made her way to the back rooms.

I stalked deeper into the apartment. A cat had been here, and if that wasn't enough, it had shredded the back of Sara's sofa. Luca musta taken it, though, because I saw neither hide nor hair of the critter.

Slowly, I circled the living space, inhaling, tasting the air and moving on when all I scented were mage and wizard and rotten food. Upon entering the kitchen, I saw it wasn't the lettuce that was bad. Luca had left everything intact and a spaghetti sauce handprint now grew mold. My fingers itched to wipe it up. Sara shouldn't have to come back to this.

I barely refrained from tampering with the evidence and prowled deeper into the kitchen, my gaze scouring the white countertop, the appliances, and the knife block in particular. Each blade was there. Would Sara still be around if she'd grabbed one? I got to the end of the small galley kitchen and performed a slow turn, determined to find something that could be of use.

That was when I saw something that made the skin on the back of my neck tighten.

A thread of fishing line glinted along the back wall of the countertop, barely noticeable in the early morning sun coming in through the window.

My eyebrows screwed together. Did Sara fish? Even if she did, what a weird place to keep line. Inching closer, I examined the line, but only when I stood right in front of it did I realize I'd misidentified it.

That was hair—long, silver-white hair that had been trapped in place by a few stray drops of tomato sauce.

My blood went cold. I knew someone with flowing silver-white locks.

I bent, brought my nose to the counter and drew in a long breath. The scent of fae wasn't fresh; there wasn't even that much of it, but I'd spent days traveling with one who smelled exactly like this.

"Si, my man," I whispered.

A scream ripped from the back of the apartment. "Gunner! They're here!"

I spun to help, only to find a hulking brute of a winged demon walk into the kitchen and bare his teeth at me.

CHAPTER SIX

HARPER

THE DEMON MIGHT HAVE PASSED FOR A HUMAN, IF NOT FOR HER glowing red eyes and the faint smell of sulfur wafting off of her.

"You shouldn't have come here, wolf," she growled from the entrance to Sara's dusty pink and cream-colored bedroom

My jaw tightened. "Screw you."

There was only one reason for this demon to be here. They'd been watching the property, waiting for another Shadows and Secrets member to show up.

"Where's Sara?"

The demoness barked out a cruel laugh. "You should forget about her. She's nothing. Not like you, little wolf."

"You don't know a thing about me." I transferred my weight from one foot to the other, ready for an attack.

"We've learned more than you could imagine. Like who to leverage."

She lunged toward me, knife in hand. My wolf simmered under the surface, but I wasn't fast enough to shift and attack, so I spun, snatching up Sara's bedside lamp on the way. When the Hellborn came at me, I was ready and cracked her over the head with the lamp. I hit her just right too, because she fell to the ground. Not about to play around, I kicked her in the side once for good measure. No reaction.

From the kitchen, a growl rang out. Gunner.

Every instinct told me to shift and go to him, but first, I had to check something. I turned the woman over, pried her eyelid up. The irises that stared back at me weren't red any longer, but brown. There was a good chance this woman wasn't a Hellborn. Maybe not even a Hellblooded, but rather a possessed human. The demon remained inside her, waiting until the body could rise.

"Dammit," I murmured. With Shay gone, we'd have to call in the Covenant to deal with this. A nephilim would have to arrive quickly to save this human from possession.

Another growl shifted me from one issue to another. Gunner still hadn't kicked his adversary's butt.

I called on my wolf form, my physically strongest aspect, and my senses heightened even more. I bolted out of the room, down the short hallway, and into the living room to find not one but two male demons of the brutish, animalistic variety.

This pair proved unlike any creature I'd ever taken on. Winged and horned, they did not hide their true nature, which meant they were probably invisible to humans.

Gunner, the largest wolf I'd ever set eyes on, was cornered and snarling. One demon bled from the chest, so Gunner had gotten in one good attack, but he was also bleeding from the side.

Luckily, I was light of foot and the demons didn't hear me coming. Not until I launched into the air and landed on one's back, right where the wings connected. He roared as my teeth dug into his neck, ripping it to shreds.

Blood filled my mouth, vile tasting as all get out. I spat, but went in for another chomp to be sure he was good and dead. The demon shrieked and frantically flapped its wings, hurling me off, but the damage was done. I slammed into the far wall as the brute fell to the floor to die.

I shook and prepared to go in again, but Gunner had already struck, tearing into the other adversary's abdomen first, then the neck. That demon fell too, spilling innards all over Sara's floor.

The tension in my muscles loosened as Gunner prowled closer. We weren't in the same pack, so we had no mind-link to fall back on. It was a disadvantage, but normally I didn't mind. Mind-linked wolves were valuable, and if we had shared that connection, Luca would have denied my request not to be partnered with Gunner. Like this, we were any other set of partners and could work with others as well as together.

There was something about Gunner that set me on edge, something more than his excessive chatter. I told myself the weird vibe was the wolvea blood—but I didn't think that was all of it.

When he was close enough, Gunner sniffed me, looking for injuries. I remained still, allowing the posturing. We were both alphablood, but he was even stronger than me. It was in his nature to want to make sure those he perceived as under his protection were safe and, as much as he frustrated me most of the time, I understood that need. Had experienced it myself among those in my pack back home. Once Gunner assured himself that I was fine, he shifted. I did the same.

"Thanks, Harp," Gunner said, using the nickname Shay liked to fling around. "How many did you take on? Before him?"

I checked him over before answering. His wound was already healing, thank the Old Ones.

"One," I answered. "She might be a possessed woman. Not like these two."

"Aw, damn. Shay's not back home yet, is she?"

"No." It worried me she hadn't checked in yet, but the whole point of using her as bait was so that Hans could go undercover. Maybe he'd succeeded, and they'd already gathered new information on Wrath and the Darkborn? "If she doesn't get in touch soon, we'll have to call in a nephilim."

"Should we take the possessed to headquarters?" He hooked a thumb at the back room.

My teeth dug into my bottom lip as I briefly considered. "I wish, but getting her out of here will be hard. We'll need an illusion, or a glamour, to hide her. Maybe Silas can help?"

Gunner's face hardened. "I found a silvery hair in the kitchen."

"And?"

"Silas is the traitor." Gunner spat out the words that made my stomach sink. "Didn't get another scent. Did you?"

"No." I shook my head. "Nothing in the bathroom or the bedroom."

"Fae can cover their tracks, and as much as I don't want to think of Silas doin' it, he's a smart guy. Good at magic. I wouldn't be surprised if it's in his repertoire."

Hurt flashed in his eyes, making me feel bad for Gunner. He just looked so struck. It was clear Gunner liked Silas. For that matter, I did too. He wasn't one of my best friends, or even someone I talked to weekly, but he'd always been polite and interesting.

"Did you know he was a refugee from the Winter Court?" Gunner asked.

"I didn't."

"I wonder if this has something to do with that?" He loosed a long exhale. "Si had to pay someone off to get here, and I don't think that would come cheap."

"That's a potential clue," I said with a slow nod. "We need to call Luca, tell him about the lady back there," I gestured to the bedroom, "and go to Silas's house."

"Luca told him we'd be coming here."

My lips parted. "So, you think that Silas fled?"

"I think he knew I'd spent a lot of time with him and was familiar with his scent. He wasn't sure that whatever magic he did to hide his presence would be strong enough. I betcha when we go to his place, he won't be around."

I swore under my breath. First, Josiah. Now, Silas. Were they the only two traitors in the coven?

Josiah's reasoning enraged me, but it also made sense. From everything I'd heard about her, the Ringmaster was brutal, and Josiah was trying to save Sara.

Silas had no family here. No romantic partner, either. Was it really a matter of repayment? Or was it something more sinister? I looked around the living room, my gaze falling on the hallway leading to the bedroom, and the memory of what the possessed woman said came rushing back.

What in the world did the demons want with me? I could see the other side wanting Meredith so she could find the sacred stones, but I was a wolf, a dime a dozen in the supernatural world. I had a good nose but not good enough to find the *lapis caelesti.*

"Did those two say they came looking for you, Gunner?" I asked.

"Nah, I expect they were watching the place." He took a step toward the bedroom. "Let's tie that demon in the back up, so she won't go anywhere until someone exorcizes her, and then hit up Silas's place." Unaware of my inner turmoil, Gunner lumbered down the hall.

I kept quiet as I followed, still deep in thought.

I STILL HADN'T FIGURED OUT WHAT THE DEMONESS MEANT WHEN we turned on to Silas's street. Before arriving, Luca and Gunner had both called the fae, only to be sent right to voicemail.

Things weren't looking good.

My partner pulled over a few homes away and put the car in park. "Feels like I'm tryin' to ambush him."

"We called," I assured him. "It's the best we could do."

Gunner nodded, but the conflict that had riddled his voice was still reflected in the tension in his shoulders. "Didn't Kora live around here?"

"A bit farther out of town with her Mom. In a small forest. Why?"

"Was there a faerie portal by her place? Maybe the prince put one there so her ma could visit?"

I swallowed, understanding what he meant. What if there was and Silas knew about it? Fae portals were the most common ways in and out of Isila and one needed to either pass through with a fae or follow close behind a fae. If there was a portal, and Silas disappeared through it to one of the otherworldly kingdoms, we wouldn't be finding him anytime soon.

"Let's hope not," I said. "Check the house first."

"Yeah, right." Gunner exited the car, and I followed right behind him.

Together, we walked toward the home, which was a single-family cottage surrounded by a double lot lush with trees.

"I scent him." I walked down the flat-stoned path, sniffing the air.

"Same. It's strong too. Like he was just out here."

"Maybe gardening?"

By the Old Ones, I felt idiotic saying it, but I didn't want to think of the fae as a traitor. Was there some other explanation for the hair on Sara's counter?

"I sure hope so, Harp."

We reached the door, and sensing my partner's hesitation, I knocked. Seconds passed, too many, so I tried once more.

And again, no one answered.

A sigh gusted out of me. "Guess we're breaking in."

"My record for the day," Gunner said, though instead of preparing to kick down the door like he had at Sara's, he reached out, tried the handle.

It opened.

"Weiiiiird," I whispered. "Why'd he leave it open?"

"I bet Si knows we're coming and figured, why make it difficult? Either way, it's a bad sign." Gunner swallowed.

A pit opened in my gut. That rang all too true.

Gunner pushed open the door, and we walked into a home that struck me as unapologetically fae.

The colors befit someone from the Winter Court. Silver-blues, whites, grays. Images of snowy landscapes lined the walls, places that must have reminded Silas of his home. Thick furs covered the couch and chairs in the sitting room, and the largest one was used as a rug. Magic hung in the air too, not wards, but enchantments that made the place different from any home I'd ever been inside.

"What do you think that feeling is?" I asked, twirling my

hand through the air.

"I betcha he was trying to mimic the Winter Realm." Gunner's answer shocked me. "Isila feels different. I bet the courts do, too. From each other, I mean."

Having never been there, I hadn't known that about the other realm. I was envious of what Gunner had experienced. He rarely talked Isila up. In fact, quite the opposite. He claimed the other realm was a hard, cruel place. Yet, I still hoped to go one day, to see it for myself and visit Wolf Island, the home of the most powerful wolf shifters.

"He was homesick," I whispered.

"I guess so. He left his family there, so I can understand."

Our eyes met. Gunner and I didn't see eye-to-eye on many things, but family and a pack was one thing we agreed on. Wolves needed their packs.

"Let's see what we can find," I said after a moment. I wanted to find information related to Sara, but if we discovered that Silas was sad and homesick, I'd take no joy in that.

"We should stick together," Gunner said. "Fae have powerful magic. Who knows what we might find here?"

Defensive wards. Curses to harm someone who touched anything Silas wanted to keep private. Traps. I wouldn't think any of that was weird. After all, we worked for a secret society that had no shortage of enemies.

Plus, the fae was a very private person, and for good reason. He'd either somehow duped Luca's test to ensure that new coven members were good and true and did not want to harm the coven, or he'd turned on Shadows and Secrets later. Whatever the case, Silas had things to hide, so Gunner was right. We had to stay alert.

"Together," I agreed, and we began our search.

The living room came up as a bust. As did the kitchen, the

downstairs bathroom, and a bedroom.

When we climbed upstairs, though, things changed. If the downstairs screamed otherworldly, up here was ten times as much. Fake snow flooded the hallway up to my knees and Silas kept this part of the house cold as heck.

I shivered. "Where to first?"

Gunner opened the door to his right. "This looks like his room."

"Not much in there," I mused, taking in the fur-covered bed and the heavy wooden chest of drawers and side tables. On a whim, I opened the door next to me, and my eyes widened. "His office."

"And the library," Gunner agreed, scanning the area. "Seems more promising."

"Cramped too." Drawn to the bookshelves, I entered, scanning his leather-bound titles. "Portal magic." I lowered my voice to a whisper. "He's obsessed with it, Gunner."

"Not just that. He had an interest in necromancy, too." Gunner pointed to a stack of four books with several stickies poking out of the pages. "Seein' as he's a fae, he can't do this."

"This is looking more and more like it's connected to the Ringmaster," I murmured, moving down the shelves. One thick, leather book caught my eye, marked 'ledger'. I pulled it from the shelf and flipped to the front page.

Silas had purchased property. Two lots, to be exact. One was in Ireland, in a small town named Doolin. He'd owned it for years and as his accent was slightly Irish, I suspected he'd lived there when he first arrived in this world. The other property was a hunting cabin in upstate New York. I noted the hunting property with interest.

Silas didn't seem the type to go toting guns in the wild. That might be a lead. Trying not to get stuck on it though, I turned the page, and another new piece of information leapt out at me. Written in an old-fashioned scrawl, a name I recognized made my stomach tighten.

Raphael Laurent.

Laurent . . . Tobias's family. Who was Raphael? A sibling? Cousin?

"Whatcha find?" Gunner asked.

"Silas owed money to a man named Raphael Laurent," I said. "Have you met him?"

"Nope. But Toby's one of 'em."

"Yeah." Tobias had tried to hide it, but after Wrath ousted him, the secret spread among the coven members. Before she went to DC, Shay had confirmed the rumor. Tobias had confided in her.

Cold stomped down my back. I hoped that this information did not point to Tobias being a traitor too. "Apparently, Silas owed him money. It looks like he's paid it off."

"Hmmm," Gunner said. "Ya think this Raphael might have helped bring Si here? It would be a pricey ticket. 'Specially from the Winter Court. And the Laurents got the cash."

I gazed up from the book and caught Gunner's eye. "The fae courts control the portals, right? And the Winter Court isn't letting anyone from our world through?"

"There's one on Wolf Island," Gunner corrected, "But they had to pay the fae out the ass for that. Far as I know, the rest are in the fae territories. Unless another of the courts has a hidden one. Wouldn't put that past the Laurents in the Blood Court. They do what they want."

I furrowed my eyebrows and peered back at the book. "Sure, but why would a vampire care about Silas?"

We stared at each other, neither having the answer, but I knew somehow this was all connected.

CHAPTER SEVEN

HANS

WE WOKE EARLY AND TOOK ADVANTAGE OF THE CLOUDY SKIES, flying for miles over mountains and fields of wildflowers before the sun rose. But as we crossed the Swiss-French border, I felt depleted. Hours in the gym and a good diet did not prepare me for so much flying. While Shay was more experienced, I could tell our journey taxed her too.

"There's a town up ahead," I pointed. "Time to rent a car? Get new clothes?"

My shirt had been ripped in the back by my wings, and the jacket I'd worn when Wrath abducted us was still at Lake Como, along with my phone and personal effects. If we were to go anywhere public, I needed a fresh shirt. And I wasn't alone in wanting a change of attire.

Shay still wore the white dress Wrath had forced her to wear. As she flew, the material fluttered around her long legs. Prince Orien might have meant it as a slight, but I couldn't help but think that Shay made the dress look good.

"That town looks big enough to have a rental agency and a hostel," Shay replied after a moment.

"You're sure your plan will work?" I measured the hesitation in her tone. It seemed she was not quite convinced.

"Getting a passport and money will be easy and if the person we deal with at the rental agency is human, then no problem. But if they're vamp, witch, shifter, or any sort of magical, the use of my influence to manipulate them will depend on the strength of *their* magic. Like, I'm not influencing someone as strong as you, or anyone in Shadows and Secrets anytime soon. But a hedge witch, I can manage."

"I'm not so strong anymore," I said.

"You're not strong in the way you *want* to be. But you took down Orien, so you're no weakling." She gave me a pointed look. "Let's land at the edge of those woods. Judging by the signage, it's probably where tourists go, so we have a better chance of snagging a passport."

I didn't enjoy the idea of stealing passports, but we had to do it. We had no identification and car companies had to scan ID to rent out a car. Once we had the car, we'd ditch the passports somewhere they could be found, but we had to use them first. There was no way around it.

We descended quickly to avoid notice, and when I landed in the trees, I stumbled before catching myself.

"No one saw us." Shay looked around the wooded area. "I was watching."

"Let's hope that's true." My legs wobbled after being in the air for so long. "Now comes the genuine test."

Shay snorted, but there wasn't malice in it like there would have been two days ago. "Some would say that flying over a whole-ass country was the hard part."

"Have those people dealt with vanishing their wings? Because I can tell them that bringing out wings is easier than getting rid of them."

The act was difficult, and if I couldn't do it now, Shay would have to go it alone.

"How did you feel when you did it before?" Shay ignored my negativity, and snapped her wings in at her side. They vanished into the aether surrounding her. "Think back, Hans. You need to do this at will."

"I realize." I stuck out my tongue. Instantly, I regretted the gesture. It was so reminiscent of the old us, the pair of friends who sometimes flirted when we had drinks.

But Shay didn't seem to mind. In fact, she surprised me by grinning. "I have faith in you. My father did, too. You should as well."

Her father. If it wasn't for the archangel's compassion, I wasn't sure where we'd be. Tension would still riddle the air between us. But things were different now.

"Let me think." I considered the one time I'd been successful in hiding my new appendages with magic. I'd been exhausted, but also elated after flying around and trying out a few new tricks.

Digging deep, I brought that memory to the forefront of my mind, trying to mimic it when I felt so far from elation.

"Uh, are you okay?" Shay asked, slicing through my introspection.

I huffed out a breath. "I need silence."

"Well, you looked like you were trying to poop your pants or something."

I gaped, which made the nephilim laugh.

"Sorry! But maybe don't try *so* hard. Take the feeling and you can use any memory that mimics it, maybe? Something not so strenuous."

There was merit to that. What made me happy? Elated, even? I closed my eyes and thought back.

A memory came to me right away; the moment my father and I fixed our next-door neighbor's car together. It was my first, and I'd felt so a part of the process. Father had been so proud.

Recalling the day, my chest warmed. I latched onto the sensation, digging deeper, seeing my father's smile in my head, while willing my wings to be gone.

Shay gasped. "You did it!"

My eyes opened, and I craned my neck around. My heart skipped a beat. "I did!"

A laugh tinkled from the nephilim. "You didn't feel it, did you?"

"Not at all."

"That's a good sign. I bet if you use that method a couple of more times, and pay attention to your wings during it, you'll master vanquishing soon enough."

"I hope so." I turned to the town, barely visible through the thick trees. "Shall we find a hostel?"

We trekked through the trees, her in front and me trying not to notice the tempting way her hips swayed. Shay was a beautiful woman, and I'd always seen that, but I'd also always known what I was—that I wasn't good enough for her. So, I'd flirted a bit, but dated other women, witches mostly. A nephilim was simply off limits.

"Wish we had our phones," Shay said. "We would find a hostel so much faster."

"We don't have to." When she turned and shot me a bewildered glance, I gestured toward the town. "The sign."

Visible through the trees, on the edge of the town, was a grouping of buildings. One proudly displayed a sign proclaiming that they were the oldest hostel in the Jura region of France.

Shay's eyes widened, and she pointed. "One room has a balcony! I bet I can get in there with no issue. That bypasses the front desk."

I swallowed. "Good plan."

I hesitated because of what I might have to do for her plan to work. As Shay's eyes swept over my face, it was obvious that she understood that.

"We need to be as invisible as possible. Think of what we saw on the lake, and the demons who know what we look like now. And, obviously, I need to change. No one wears this toga shit around town." She gestured to the dress, and as hot as she looked, she was right.

"We're sticking with it." I hoped no one would be around when Shay snuck into the hostel.

"Okay, so come on!" Shay peeked out of the trees and when she saw no one was coming, she emerged on the sidewalk that led into the heart of what appeared to be a quaint downtown. "How about you sit on that bench? It will mostly hide your torn shirt, and you can see people coming from both directions."

I did as she said, hoping no one walked by. After sitting, I took in the area and shot her a thumbs up. "I'm good."

She gave the area a thorough once over before her wings unfurled and Shay launched herself into the sky. A mere second later, she stood on the balcony. Before I could blink, she looked human once again. I exhaled, studying the area to ensure no one was coming.

A flash of light in my periphery told me that the nephilim was working her light magic. This wasn't as flashy as the wings, but it could still draw attention from passersby. Thankfully, no one was coming, and when Shay managed to break the lock with her magic and slip inside, I felt a million times better.

How fucked up was that? We intended to steal passports, and I was *relieved*. It told me a lot about the state of my life at the moment. Father would not be pleased.

And what would Mother think?

Though, most probably assumed my mother, Queen of Hell, only taught us vile things, it wasn't true. Mostly, she was kind and soft toward us. Lilith knew how to laugh and make Father and her children happy.

But there were *other* times. Lessons when she instructed Nicoleta on manipulation and taught me how to use my powers of pain. She said they would protect us. Perhaps I'd proven her right using my demon magic on Wrath.

A whistled tune caught my attention, and I twisted to find an older gentleman wearing a bowler cape and holding a cane strolling down the street. My throat tightened.

Turn around, I pleaded.

But he didn't. The man kept whistling and walking down the path, right toward me. Soon, he'd be able to see the hostel.

My gaze went to the balcony. She hadn't finished yet. What was taking so long?

As if my thoughts conjured her, Shay appeared dressed in new clothes and with a smart trench coat, just as the old man got close enough to see the hostel. I held up a hand, warning my partner, and she leaned against the railing, as if she were a traveler taking the air.

"Beautiful morning, isn't it?" the man called out and I turned to find him waving at me.

"It is." I stood and wiped my hands on my pants to get rid of the sweat.

"A tourist?" His French was thick and intrigued. "Where are you from?"

"I live in the United States." I hoped he wouldn't want to talk about it, but his expression lightened. Fuck. He was a rare type of Frenchman who wanted to swap a few stories.

"Where in the States? I've been to New York. What a city! Great walking there. Have you been?"

Behind me, Shay coughed. That was the signal that someone was in the hostel and we needed to leave.

My stomach pitted. This man had to go. And there was only one way I knew for certain that would clear the area.

"I have been to New York," I replied as I reached for my demon powers, which came far too easily for my liking. "It's great."

Shay coughed again, more urgently this time, which earned her a look from the inquisitive Frenchman. My mouth dried up, but I had to think of my partner first.

So, putting the conversational niceties aside, I struck, and the man doubled over in pain. Wincing, I pulled back and made it so that instead of feeling excruciating pain, like I'd done with Wrath, he merely had a stomach ache.

"Are you alright?" I took a step toward him, as if concerned.

"My stomach." The man gripped his belly as I loosed another wave of pain within him. "I think I must go home. Have a good trip."

With that, the old man turned and hobbled off. I allowed my magic to stay within him until he was out of sight. Then, I spun and waved for Shay, but she already stood on the ground, dressed in baggy jeans, a black t-shirt, and a trench jacket.

She handed me a bundled up white t-shirt. "Someone tried to get into the room!"

"Did they see you?" I ripped my tattered shirt off and slipped the new one on, not missing the way her gaze dropped to my abs as I did so. My lips curled upward. Poor timing, but any man liked a compliment—even one unspoken.

"I put a chair under the doorknob, so no, but we need to leave. Once they get in, the proprietor will know something is wrong. We need to be out of town by then."

"You'd better be able to work your magic," I said, and we set off into the town. Once we were a fair distance away, we inquired as to where a car rental agency was. The shop clerk gave us directions to the only agency in town, and we were off again.

Then, the sirens sounded.

"What the hell?" Shay shouted over the noise.

A passerby noticed her confusion. "American? You should be on the lookout. Someone broke into the hostel and stole two travelers' passports. The police are patrolling."

"Oh, no." Shay blanched.

"As you're not from here, they might stop you," the person said. "But don't worry. They're only looking for criminals."

"Of course. I hope they find them," I said and pulled Shay away.

"Hans, I have the passports in my pocket. If they search us we're screwed."

"You can use your influence."

"True, but this is leaving quite a trail. And I don't think I'll be able to run fast if needed." She gestured to her flip-flop clad feet. "They were the only thing I could find that fit. I think they're shower shoes." She wrinkled her nose, disgusted by that tangent.

She was right, and I worried the rental agency might not work with us. Or that the passports might already be in the system as stolen and give us away. We needed to pivot.

I scanned the area, searching for an idea, or a place to hide, or anything. When my gaze landed on a rundown, filthy car that clearly had not been driven in months, an idea struck.

"How about a joy ride?"

"What?" she squeaked.

I went to the car. As I suspected, it wasn't even locked. Who would bother with such a heap?

As long as it ran, that was all we needed.

"Oh no, Hans." Shay approached, her tone thin, worried. "What are you doing?"

In answer, I dropped to my knees and ripped the faded paneling off to search for the wires I needed. They were covered in cobwebs, but after a little manipulation, I grasped the correct ones. Hot-wiring was something every mechanic should know how to do and I sure as hell did. Seconds later, the car roared to life. Quickly, I checked the gas. Half a tank. It would be enough to get us out of town fast.

Sirens blasted closer. I turned to Shay. "Get in."

Her mouth hung open so wide, a bird could have flown in. "Are you insane?"

"The rental agency might not give us a vehicle anyway, Shay. Not without calling the cops first."

"Like you said, I can influence them."

"Sure, if they're human. What if they're not? Besides, no one will miss this piece of junk for a few days." I slammed my hand on the cloth seat and dust flew up.

Shay wrinkled her nose. "Ew."

"Get in."

A hesitant expression rippled across her face, but the next

thing I knew, the nephilim strode around the car and slipped into the passenger seat.

"Don't draw attention in town, but once we're out of here . . . put the pedal to the metal," she said, eyes wide and round and uncertain. "I want to be far, far away."

I smirked. "You're going to wish you hadn't said that."

CHAPTER EIGHT

SHAY

Signs for Paris proclaimed we were only a few kilometers
away. Thank the Heavens.

Already, it was getting dark, and I was ready to get out of
the stolen car. Though the drive had passed quickly, only in
the last forty-five minutes had I stopped looking behind to see
if a cop was trailing us.

I shook my head. Hans had hot-wired this hunk of junk
and driven it across France.

I snorted. Mom would be *so* pissed if she found out. Especially if others did. Her daughter's automobile theft would
screw with her next campaign for reelection.

"You okay?" Hans shot me a sidelong glance.

"I still can't believe we did this." I slammed my hand on
the dashboard and the glove box popped open. The angel
feathers, our bargaining chips, popped out onto the floor,
making me laugh. I picked them up and straightened them,
placing the plumes alongside my leg. "Then again, maybe
we're doing the owner a favor. Do you think they can get paid
for their stolen property?"

"If so, they can buy a bottle of wine with their compensation," Hans joked. "I'm shocked it got us this far."

At that, my stomach swooped. What would we have done if it hadn't made it to Paris? Stolen another car? Tried the passports I had on hand? No . . . those had surely been reported as stolen by now. They were worthless.

I chewed on my bottom lip. Would the ring and bracelet I left behind at the hostel be enough to make up for the fact that the travelers would have to be inconvenienced? Both had been gifts from my mother, and Heavens knew that she always chose expensive jewelry. I hoped it would be enough.

"Where to?" Hans asked.

"What?" I swam out of my whirlpool of thoughts.

"Where do we need to go?"

I shrugged. "Dad just gave me the coven's name. He might not have even known where they are in Paris."

"You're kidding."

"No, but they're called the Coven of Illumination."

Hans swore in Romanian, which made my lips curl. He caught me and arched an eyebrow. "Usually, people are not happy about a cursing demon."

"You sound so cute when you do it." The moment the words left my mouth, I wished I could pull them back inside and swallow them. Heat dashed across my cheeks, and Hans couldn't seem to look away.

"Uh, the road," I croaked as brake lights flashed ahead.

He cleared his throat, and continued to drive with his eyes firmly on the highway. For a moment, no one spoke and the air thickened.

Why was I such a flirt?

"Do you have any connections here?" Hans asked after a full two minutes of tense silence. "I don't."

I was about to deny having any connections, when I remembered Mom had brought me here once to do business. She'd mostly left me to my own devices, but one afternoon we visited one of her friends, a prominent French nephilim.

"Yes, I know someone. And I even remember where she lives." A person didn't forget an apartment as memorable as the one we visited. "She's one of my mother's friends."

"Angel blood?"

"Uh, yeah."

Hans swallowed. "I can stay out of sight."

It might be smarter, but after coming as far as I had in accepting the man next to me, I wasn't about to stand for it. I laid a hand on his shoulder, trying to ignore the tingles at our contact and how much I appreciated the look of his tattooed arms. Why did I always love a bad boy?

"We'll approach her together. We're partners and she knows about S&S. That should be enough."

Hans glanced at me warily. "You're sure?"

I wasn't, but I also wasn't about to let Hans wait in the car. He'd saved my father, and saved our asses from a French jail cell by stealing this vehicle and driving it like a wild man out of Jura. It was my turn to contribute to our mission.

"Go toward the Eiffel Tower. She lives close to it."

Hans's eyebrows shot up, but he followed the signs into the city and then toward the famed tower. When we were close enough, I directed him to park and stopped the first Parisienne on the street. Thankfully, they spoke English since I was fluent in a handful of languages and passable in others, but French wasn't on that list.

A few minutes later, I knew where to go. I directed Hans to the street and, once parked, placed my father's feathers in the pocket of the khaki trench coat I'd stolen before slipping out of the car.

"This has to be a pricey area." Hans nodded to the chic shops we passed.

"One of the most expensive in the city. She's done a lot of business with my mother."

"Enough said," Hans muttered.

Others knew Angelina Ramos not only for being a nephilim Covenant Seat but a business tycoon.

"I'm pretty sure it's this building." I stopped in front of a nondescript white door and rang the bell.

A male voice answered with a, "*Oui?*"

"Hello. Do you speak English?"

"*Oui.*"

"Oh, great." I exhaled. "I'm here for Celine Durand. My name is Shay Ramos." I paused and then added, "my mother is Angelina Ramos, a friend of Celine."

"Do you have an appointment?"

"I don't," I said. "But I need to ask a favor of Celine."

"One moment, *Mademoiselle.*" The intercom clicked off, and I exhaled, only to have the man speak again before I could do anything else. "Ms. Durand says welcome. Proceed to the elevator and press the penthouse suite. She will wait for you."

A buzz sounded, and I pushed the door open, trying not to laugh at Hans's expression as we entered a foyer of such extreme opulence, I would have felt bad touching anything. Every surface was white or gold and gleaming. The aesthetic was minimal but not to the point of being stark. It was too rich for that.

"Who else lives in this building?" Hans's tone was barely above a whisper, as if they'd throw him out for asking.

"There's one family on each floor, so three families or individuals. I don't know who they are." I shrugged.

"You don't think this is insane?" He gestured to the gold-plated elevator doors as they opened. Chopin played as we stepped inside.

"My mother's place in Paris is similar."

And her one in New York and Milan and . . . well, all of her properties were lavish, save for the one I now owned. The Victorian home, while nice by most standards, was what Angelina considered a starter home, suitable for college students only.

Hans's eyes stayed wide. "I bet the mortgage on this place could have fed my village for a month."

The elevator stopped, and the doors opened with the chime of a harp. I rolled my eyes. Nephilim were so extra sometimes.

"Shaylina!" Celine swept into the frame, voice lyrically French, and a smile swept across her round face. Her dark skin glowed as though she'd had one hell of a facial. I was envious. Hans and I looked so dirty and disheveled—a thought that was confirmed when Celine's hands flew to her mouth.

"My girl! Are you quite alright? You seem . . . " She trailed off, unable to even bring herself to speak about how filthy I appeared.

"Shay, please," I told her, though I was sure she'd insist on using the horrible name my mother did. "And I'm fine but we've traveled a long way. Thanks for seeing us, Celine." I stepped into the penthouse, and the fresh scent of lavender filled my nose.

"But of course. Angelina's daughter is always welcome at my home." Her intelligent, dark eyes went to Hans.

"This is my friend and partner at my work, Hans."

Hans stepped out of the elevator, but did not offer his

hand. I had a feeling he thought Celine might sense what he was and didn't want to complicate matters.

"Work?" Celine asked. "Is this a business call? I had hoped to make an *apéritif?*"

"I'm afraid so. We can't stay long, but I hoped that you might help me locate a group in the city?"

"What group is that?"

"The Coven of Illumination."

Celine's eyes widened. "What do you want with them?"

The priceless archangel feathers burned in my pocket. If I told Celine about them, she'd try to buy the feathers off me. At least one of them. I couldn't mention them.

"Shadows and Secrets business. You understand." I smiled, and Celine studied me, before gliding over to a bar and fixing herself a drink.

"What would you like?" She lifted a martini. "Remi can make anything."

"Tequila," I blurted.

Judging by the look of shock on Celine's face at my preference, I'd said the wrong thing. Apparently, ladies didn't drink straight tequila. Well, screw being a lady.

Hans cleared his throat. "A whiskey. Neat, please."

Celine clapped her hands. "Remi!"

A gorgeous man with long black hair pulled back into dreads and snow-white wings appeared. I sucked in a breath, which prompted an unimpressed '*humph*' from Hans.

"Yes, Ms. Durand?"

"Please give Shay a tequila cocktail," she said, "and Hans here a neat whiskey. Our best."

Remi set to making the drinks. Once done, he handed the libations to us, and Celine, once again, studied our attire.

"I think you two should clean up before we get down to

business." Celine's nose wrinkled as her eyes swept over me and then her white furniture. "There is a restroom down that hall and one that way. Do you recall where the hallway one is, Shay?"

"I do," I said, conflicted. I wanted to be clean, but I also wanted information and to move on.

Still, many nephilim considered cleanliness holy—closer to God—and I should respect my host, a valued member of our order. Mother had taught me as much.

"Remi, show Hans to the other one. There are towels in both restrooms. Use as many as you need."

We acquiesced, taking our drinks with us. The moment I shut the restroom door, I took a quick shower, leaving my long hair unwashed. I had to admit that even though I wanted to get this show on the road, it did feel amazing. Even better, after a few sips of my drink, I was much more relaxed. Good thing too, because the moment I opened the door, Celine was there.

"She's finished beautifying herself, Angelina. Here she is." Celine shoved a phone at me, and I exhaled an annoyed breath.

The restroom charade had been a ruse to speak with my mother, perhaps get more information from her. Nephilim were not only obsessed with cleanliness, but nosey as hell too.

"Hey, Mom." I turned my back to Celine and walked straight back into the restroom, shutting the door behind me. If she was going to bombard me, she could try and listen at the door.

"Shaylina! We've been so worried You're in Paris? But how?"

In a low voice, I gave her the rundown of how well our trap for Nicoleta had gone, which was not well at all. I dropped my tone to a whisper when I told her about Wrath being in league with Tobias's brother and the seven Princes of Hell rising.

When I was done, my mother didn't speak—a first.

"Mom?"

"That Hellblooded? He had nothing to do with it?"

My jaw tightened. "No. And Dad said he's good. So, lay off."

She sucked in a breath, and I could feel the anger coming at me through the airwaves, but ever the diplomat, my mother's tone was calm when she spoke again. "I'll inform the Covenant about what happened and the new dangers in our world. Is there anything else?"

"No." I wasn't about to mention the feathers or anything else Dad said. Not until I spoke with Luca.

"Very well. When will you return?"

"I'm not sure. How about I call you when I find out?"

She paused for a long time and then released an exaggerated huff. "Very well. Give Celine my regards. And Shaylina?"

"Yeah?"

"Be safe, okay?"

A lump lodged in my throat. I was often as hard on Mom as she was to me, but she did love me. In her own twisted way.

"I will." We hung up, and when I opened the door again, Celine was still there, looking haughty and holding out her hand for her phone.

"If you don't mind, I think Hans will want to call our coven master?" I asked sweetly, knowing after what she'd done she wouldn't say no.

"Fine," Celine drawled. "I wish to learn about why you want to visit the Coven of Illumination."

"Sure," I said, letting her think I was going to share that information as I sashayed into the living area, right toward Hans, who already perched uncomfortably on a chair. I pressed the phone into his hands. "Call Luca. Tell him what happened. My mom already knows, so he can contact the Covenant too, if he needs. Actually, make sure he does, 'cause I mentioned Stiff's brother."

He rose. "Might I use a private chamber?"

Celine instructed Remi to take Hans to another room. Once they left, I turned to my mother's friend, prepared to bullshit my way into getting some answers, while Hans caught the coven master up to speed.

<hr>

"Excuse me, but what?" I slammed the car door shut, unable to fully comprehend what Hans had told me.

"Luca says Gunner and Harper found confirmation that Silas is the traitor. Since the fae was in England, where Meredith and Tobias are now, Luca wants us to go there too." His tone lowered. "Using light-travel, if we can. To stay under the radar."

"I didn't see that coming. Did you tell him about Tobias's brother?" I leaned back in the seat, somewhat exhausted from fending off Celine's questions while Hans spoke to Luca. She knew about New York and that something magical had happened there, but nothing more. It was tiring to discern where to draw that line. Especially since Celine was good at probing.

"I told him all I knew about Raphael and the castle, and he's certain that Tobias doesn't know," Hans answered. "Apparently Tobias and his brother have had issues for years.

And, of course, Luca freaked out over the Princes' rising. He actually asked me the time that happened."

My eyebrows pinched together. *"Why?"*

"Harper had some weird feelings around that time. With the time conversion, basically to the hour."

"Huh."

"How do we get to the coven?" Hans asked, moving on.

I gave him the directions Celine had given me. The coven's headquarters was across the river, but not too far, and to hear Celine tell it, someone was always there. Unusual, but not unheard of in a grouping of magical beings.

We were silent for most of the trip, so when Hans parked and turned to me, his voice rang in my ears. "Thanks for not telling Celine about me."

"It wasn't her business," I replied. At the very least, since I'd learned what he was, I'd been consistent with that belief.

Hans had felt the need to come clean to everyone about his lineage, whereas I had wished he kept it within Shadows and Secrets. Maybe it was more for my comfort, but I didn't think so. S&S members stuck together. It was a cardinal rule of our organization.

"True, but she's in your order."

I snorted and opened the car door. "Even more reason not to tell her. Nephilim are so nosy!"

He let out a dry laugh.

"Come on, Hans. Let's meet the Coven of Illumination."

CHAPTER NINE

HANS

Shay confused me.

First, she wanted nothing to do with me. Now, we seemed on better terms, but there was still hesitation there. I couldn't read it.

Were we friends? Or was she still a little ashamed to be friends with me? My own issues with my heritage made that last question entirely possible.

"This is it. The Coven of Illumination's headquarters," Shay stopped before a door that looked just like all the others on *Rue de Montmorency*. The only thing that stood out on the street was the stone facade of an old restaurant, but the apartment we approached was typical of a Parisienne home.

"Ready?" Shay asked.

I straightened. "As I'll ever be."

She knocked. Seconds passed, then a minute, and I was sure no one would come when the door squealed open. An elderly man with flyaway gray hair and dark brown eyes stared out at us.

"*Comment puis-je vous aider?*" the man asked.

Shay cleared her throat. *"Parlez vous anglais?"*

"Oui." The man's eyes narrowed. "Quite well."

"Oh, good. My French is very lacking. I apologize." Shay exhaled on the back of a breath.

"What can I help you two with?" The man looked from Shay, to me, and back to Shay again.

"I'm Shay Ramos, and this is Hans Novak. We're here to visit the Coven of Illumination. Are you a representative?"

The man took a half step back. "I am. You have need of my organization at this hour?"

Shay nodded. "I'm afraid it's urgent. We work for the Coven of Shadows and Secrets. Perhaps you've heard of them?"

The man studied her for a moment before opening the door to us. "Come in."

We stepped inside and the aroma of roasted meat filled my nostrils. This man had clearly been in the middle of dinner. I hated to interrupt, but wasn't about to deny that our need was great.

The sooner we got to Tobias and Meredith, the better. They needed to hear what happened, to prepare.

After we bypassed the sitting room and main staircase in the front, the atmosphere changed. I stood in an elaborate hallway, gilded and polished to perfection. This far back, the apartment appeared to expand. Rooms materializing on my right that, from the outside, I was sure shouldn't have been there.

"This is excellent charm-work," I murmured. "You have a skilled caster."

I'd never done such work, wouldn't risk it in an apartment that was connected to so many others. One wrong inflection and the spell might destabilize the entire building.

"Well, I've had a few centuries to learn," the man said. "Come, come."

Shay and I exchanged glances. Had that man said *centuries*? Witches and wizards might live a touch longer than humans, but not for centuries.

"I'm sorry, sir," Shay said. "Are you the caster?"

"I am." The man didn't look back.

Shay shot me a confused look as we kept following him, all the way to a large lounge area filled with books and tabletop games, through it, and into a workshop of sorts. The scents of herbs and earth hung in the air, and in the back corner, a cauldron bubbled away.

"Did you say you had centuries to learn how to expand such a home?" I asked. "As a caster myself, I'd be envious of that lifespan, if it were possible." I gave a half smile, as if to make light of his misspeak. "My lexicon of spells would be unrivaled."

"Ah, I see you know little about our coven." The man had a twinkle in his eyes. "Or who created it. Ever heard of Nicolas Flamel?"

"Of course." I waited for how this connected to him.

"Well, now you've met him too!" The man grinned. My heart stopped at the implication. "I organized this coven in 1410. For a while, it was in the home I designed, just a few doors down in the restaurant, but we had to move. When we returned, the location was not for sale." He shrugged. "One day, I'll get it back."

"You—wha—you're the famed alchemist?" Shay gasped and exchanged a glance at me. "Holy crapamoli! Do others know?"

Nicolas, the most well-known alchemist in history and creator of the philosopher's stone, barked out a laugh. "Many in the magical community of Paris are aware."

Shay scowled. "Celine didn't tell us. Or my father."

"No matter. You are here now." Flamel positioned his tall, thin body behind a table littered with flasks, powders, and other implements for potion making. "And on urgent business, or so you say. What can I do for you?"

Shay seemed frozen for another second, but it passed, and she stepped up to the table. I followed just as she pulled out the angel feathers.

Flamel's eyes widened and he held out his hand. Magic poured from his fingers as he sensed the feathers with his power. "Are these what I think they are?"

"They're archangel feathers," Shay answered.

"How can I be sure these are not from some powerful nephilim and not an archangel?"

Shay jerked back, possibly struck by the lack of respect for her kind, but recovered quickly. "Because they are from my father, Archangel Uriel. If you look me up on my order's database, I'm listed as his daughter. My mother is Angelina Ramos. I believe our photos are somewhere on there, too."

They were. It was no secret who Shay was related to, though, of course many did not know; why would some wizard on the other side of the world care? Flamel, however, was not one to trust blindly and offering the information proved a good move. The man stared at her before pulling out a laptop from a drawer and firing it up.

Shay and I waited, and the instant he'd landed on Shay's photo and the information of her lineage, his shoulders straightened.

"I'll be . . . he was here? Uriel?"

"He was. I can show you my wings if you wish to be

certain I didn't pluck those feathers. And my father's are much larger."

"I believe you," Flamel breathed. "These are valuable. What could I give you to acquire them?"

"My father told me your coven is gifted in creating something that allows a person to light-travel from one place to another."

Flamel nodded. "Ah, yes. We call them luxiters. I came up with the formula myself."

"Can you make eight?" I asked. "One per feather."

Flamel sucked in a sharp breath. "I can, and that is sufficient payment, but it will take time. When do you need them by?"

"As soon as possible. How much time are you thinking?"

"I can have them ready within a week."

I looked at Shay. "We need to be there much sooner."

"What about one?" she asked the alchemist. "We can come back for the others."

"One . . . If I focus, they only take four or five hours, but do understand, it's quite draining to focus on creating something for that long. Do you have a specific location in mind?"

My heart sank. "They only go to one place?"

"The simplest luxiters do. Others can go wherever you speak. Or to whomever. For all of my luxiters, I apply the use of a password. That way, if an innocent gets their hands on it, they won't find themselves in a new place without any idea as to how they arrived there."

"We need the kind that goes anywhere and everywhere," I said, knowing that was how smoke-travel worked, so doing so by light should be similar and possible. "The best. We need to speak a place and be there in an instant. Or a person's name and find them." That would be extremely helpful in finding

Meredith and Tobias. "And when I say anywhere, I mean anywhere. They will need to be able to go through wards too."

"It will cost more," Flamel said.

"You said the feathers were valuable and there are eight!" Shay exclaimed, pink rising to her cheeks.

Flamel glowered. "The luxiters are valuable too. And to make them, I give a large part of myself. I will need something on par with the feathers to rush the order along. What else have you got?"

"I have money," Shay said. "Lots of it. I can call my mother to transfer however much you need."

Flamel laughed. "Child, I have been alive for centuries and possess more money than I could possibly spend. No, in this coven we deal only in the rare. The items only we will have. That which cannot be bought."

Would information be enough? We had loads of that. Though I'd have to call Luca before I told this old man anything. Lost, I scanned the alchemist's workshop. The shelves were indeed lined with interesting objects.

Wings that I was sure had come from a fae hung high on the wall. A unicorn horn lay on a shelf alongside a scale that I'd bet my beloved Jeep had come from a dragon. Most striking, however, was a bottle of something dark red and glittering. Light from the fire heating the cauldron played upon the clear bottle, revealing a peeling piece of tape on the container.

I squinted and inched toward it. The instant I got close enough to read what was on the label, I froze. Orien's blood.

"Why do you have that?" I pointed to the bottle. "And when did you get it?"

Did Flamel know that the demon prince was Earthside? And if so, were they in league with each other?

"Ah, the blood of a Prince of Hell." Flamel crossed his thin arms over his chest. "I've had that for some time. Since before they were banished. Wished I could have gotten the lot of them, but only Orien needed a trade."

I didn't ask why that was. I didn't care. But when Shay met my gaze, what we'd offer to trade next became obvious.

"What about Lilith's blood?" I asked.

"The Queen of Darkness? As far as I'm aware, no one has ever done a deal with her, let alone gotten her blood. I'd give practically anything for it." Flamel eyed the bottle of Orien's blood wistfully.

"I'm her son," I said.

The alchemist whipped his head around. "What did you say?"

"I'm her son. Part of her direct line." I paused, unable to believe what I was about to do. "Part caster witch, part demon royalty. Would my blood be valuable enough to ensure the luxiters work how we want them to? So that we need only the name of a place or a person to travel?"

"You . . . Are you certain?" Flamel's eyes narrowed. "The Eyes of Darkness have been closed for years."

"I'm aware." I stuck out my arm. "And I'm sure you have a way to test it, so if you must, do it."

He studied me. "The moment I open your vein, I'll know."

He turned and went to another, smaller, battered wooden table on the far side of the room, opened a drawer, and began extracting vials from its depths. "I will take four vials, and in return I will make the luxiters as you wish. They will respond to names and places and be able to breach any ward—go anywhere. Is that fair?"

My gaze met Shay's.

"It's up to you," she whispered.

We were in a race against time, and while I was sure that

my blood could do vile things in the wrong hands, I couldn't consider that right now. There was only one choice.

"It's fair," I said.

"Sit, young man." Flamel pulled up a chair next to the wooden table. "I will sterilize the needle."

CHAPTER TEN

MEREDITH

I HURLED MY BODY ONTO THE BED AND HEAVED A HUGE SIGH.

"It's been a long day." Tobias stopped and leaned against the doorway.

"The hours since dinner have lasted *years*." I sat up and looked around. "Where did Benedict go?"

My familiar had come out of hiding long enough to meet Tana before Miriam took her to the coven's library. There, the leader of the *Arcacustos* began to teach the newcomer about the seven sacred stones and her place in this wild web as the holder of the Ruby of Flames. I joined them for a few minutes and learned that Tana knew nothing of the *lapis caelesti*. While I had been in the same camp, that was frustrating. Would we have to start at square one with every *Vindix* found?

I glanced down at my ring. Along the base, seven tiny stones represented the *lapis caelesti*: the Pearl of Hell, the Opal of Heaven, the Diamond of Souls, the Emerald of Earth, the Sapphire of Seas, the Amethyst of Air, and the Ruby of Flames. The largest center gem was a moonstone. It symbolized the full moon that the ancient holders of the stones danced beneath at festivals long ago—before we separated and forgot our place in the world. This ring was a signifier and identifier. It was going to be even more useful than I'd thought. Besides binding me to the other *Vindix*, it announced them to me. I just had to get close enough to sense them.

"While you joined Miriam and Tana, Benedict went hunting." Tobias's voice was a soft, inviting rumble that drew me back to the present. "I expect he won't be around for a while."

Goosebumps sprang up along my arms. That meant no interruptions from the cat that was the biggest cock-block I'd ever met. My body yearned to take advantage of this moment, to find relief in Tobias's arms, but before I could lose myself in that pleasant dream, my brain stopped me. There were unresolved matters between us, and I couldn't deepen our connection until we talked them out.

"We still need to discuss the soulmate thing," I said, inwardly cringing at how awkward that sounded. "We never had time to finish before Tana arrived."

"No, we didn't. What are you thinking?"

I swallowed. "I don't know what to expect. I need to understand *all* the reasons you were so hesitant to mention that we might be fated mates."

He'd told me some of them. I knew that being with a Laurent was dangerous. And of his last love, Cecilia, a human woman that his enemies had attacked. They'd done so viciously, too, and Tobias had been forced to turn her into a vampire—which she hadn't wanted at all. Days later, Cecilia had met her final death at her own hands. That was about all I had to go on, but there had to be more.

"Shall I?" He gestured to the door, waiting to be invited inside.

Sitting up, I patted the bed as he shut us in, trying to lighten the mood a touch. "Join me, ancient one."

"Hardly ancient." He said, blurring over with vampiric speed. The moment he stopped in front of me with a smoldering smirk on his lips, my heart gave a hard thump. "That's reserved for those who have lived a millennium, like my sire and the original, born vampires. A few others, too."

"What?" I blinked at him.

"The honor of being called ancient," Tobias purred. "Are you going to be able to focus, witch? Or are you vampire struck?"

I rolled my eyes as if he wasn't exactly right. "Sit down, already."

The bed groaned beneath his weight. "Keep in mind I'm not sure there's ever been a pairing like this before."

"See *that*," I started, "what does that even mean? Vampires and witches have never been soulmates?"

"I cannot say ever. That's a long time, and tales get twisted or lost to the years, but generally soulmates came from one's own magical order. And only there."

"So, if you had a soulmate, she, or he . . . " I trailed off, unsure.

Tobias shrugged. "I'm attracted to females, but I've heard of soulmates of the same sex."

"They would just have to be a vampire?" I finished.

Tobias nodded. "Precisely."

"You mentioned another witch, though. And a fae was her fated mate?" My brow furrowed as I tried to piece the information back together.

"Kora is a fire witch and she found her soulmate in the Prince of the Spring Court. A different order and a different realm."

"Do you know of others?" I tilted my head.

"No. I considered Kora an outlier, but now I'm not so sure."

"What does it mean? How will this affect us?"

Tobias swallowed and turned to face me. "For me, my desire and emotions toward you have been getting stronger the longer I know you. Is it the same for you?"

I nodded.

"Then, I expect by the time the bond snaps in place, we will have fallen in love, or be falling in love. That's what others always say about their soulmates."

My throat went dry. *Love.* It had always felt so out of reach, but my body told me that he was right. My feelings for Tobias had changed remarkably since we first met. From hate to . . . affection, maybe already teetering on love. I swallowed, trying to come to terms with it.

"That's what my maker said it was like with her blood-bound," Tobias added, possibly to fill my stunned silence, though as he did he looked uncomfortable.

"Is he gone?" I asked.

"Centuries ago. Before Giselle turned me."

"That's so sad." What an understatement. That someone had lost their one true love and then had to keep living for forever was soul-crushing.

"Giselle claims she hasn't been the same since." He swallowed, eyes boring into me as if to say he couldn't imagine losing me either. "There's something more important that you should know about being bonded to me, Meredith. A few things, actually. They are among the reasons I was hesitant to accept our fate."

His evergreen eyes looked pained, and instead of comforting him, I waited. If there was one thing I'd learned about Tobias, it was that he'd give information when he was good and ready. "I will grow protective of you."

"That doesn't sound so bad," I whispered, even if a small part, the old, hyper-independent me, recoiled at the idea.

Used to be, I relied on no one except for my partner during gigs. But day-by-day, I unlearned that old habit. I'd discovered I enjoyed relying on others and knowing that they had my back. As long as I liked and trusted them as people, teamwork was satisfying. Tobias absolutely fell into the camp of people I liked.

He, however, didn't seem to agree that a little protectiveness wasn't so bad. His lips flattened and turned white before he added. "My level of protector might astonish you. Vampires can become . . . there's no other word for it—*feral*—regarding their mate. Especially in the beginning, when the bloodbond is fresh and all-consuming. But there's more than that. Something I'm sure will occur and put you in danger."

A long silence passed and finally, I could take it no more. I placed a hand on his shoulder. "What is it, Tobias?"

"Once the bond forms, we will change and there will be no going back. It will bond us for life."

My life, he meant. Tobias was a vampire, and unless he was killed in very specific ways, he'd remain immortal. I, on the other hand, was completely mortal. If I was lucky, I'd reach a century. A lump rose in my throat as I looked him over. The dark hair, the emerald eyes, unlined and shining, struck me in a place I hadn't felt before.

He'd look the same then, but I wouldn't. Could I handle that?

A frantic laugh nearly burst out of my lips, but I pressed them together. I was worried about a distant possibility of looking old and haggard, when it was growing more likely by the day that a demon prince, the Ringmaster, or maybe a sunny team of both, would murder me. Vanity was a real bitch.

"What do we do if we want to form the bond?" I asked, trying to dismiss my fears and focus on the issue at hand. "Or if we don't? How would we even avoid it?"

"The latter would involve us staying away from one another."

"No." I shook my head vehemently. Just the idea made me feel ill.

He paused. "I wouldn't like that either."

"What about forming it?"

"I don't know how our bond will snap into place." He arched his eyebrows.

"Oh, it just happens?"

"Not really." He took my hand and rubbed my thumb thoughtlessly. "If we were of the same magical order, it would be easy. Vampires seal their bonds with blood. Witches with magic. Wolves perform a ritual with their packs and then run beneath a full moon as a couple. But there is one consistent aspect to every order's way of doing things."

"Which is?"

"True intimacy. In it, the pair must be open-hearted, and if they are, the bond occurs."

So, if we had sex, it happens? Is that what he meant? Or would there be magic and blood involved?

My questions were at the tip of my tongue when a knock came at the door. I wished I could tell the person to go away, that whatever it was could wait, but the truth of the matter was that it might not be able to. I rose and found Claire in the hallway, holding out her phone.

My eyebrows furrowed. "What's this?"

"Your coven master needs to speak with you."

That must mean Gunner was home and had told Luca we suspected the OA had hacked our phones. Smart of Luca to use Claire as a workaround. The OA didn't know she existed, so the risk of her being hacked was negligible.

"Thanks." I took the phone. "We'll get burners soon."

The elder witch shrugged. "I don't mind. We've debriefed Tana, but Miriam called a meeting because there was more to discuss, and she thought your presence might be helpful. The girl seems more open with you. Are you up for it?"

"Sure," I said. Claire was right. Tana hadn't wanted me to leave her at the library, but I thought it best. Though I'd studied a bit, the *Arcacustos* were the best people to tell her about the *lapis caelesti*.

"Join us in the meeting room after your call. The one with the wee tree on the table."

"We'll be there."

The witch turned and made her way down the drafty corridor. I shut the door and brought the phone to my ear.

"Hey, Luca."

"Meredith, is Tobias with you?"

Taken aback, I cleared my throat. "He is."

"Put me on speaker phone."

Even though Tobias could have heard the conversation without the aid of technology, I did so. "Okay, we're both here."

"I'm on a hunt, so I'll make this brief," Luca said. "We've discovered the traitor."

I gasped. "Who?"

"Silas." Luca growled, and my stomach pitted at the name.

"No way," I breathed. Yesterday I'd sat with Silas in front

of a fire. We'd talked, and he'd seemed so keen to help the coven. Not once had I gotten traitor vibes from him.

"We're nearly certain of it. If you see him, take him into custody. And Shay and Hans will join you as soon as they can. They—" He choked on his next words, and I threw an alarmed look at Tobias. Luca was smooth. He didn't falter. What had happened?

"Are you alright?" Tobias asked, concern lacing his voice.

"No. And neither are you. Shay and Hans failed in their mission in DC. They ended up in Italy."

"Uh, how?" I asked, confused.

"It seems Prince Orien can travel by smoke. Supposedly, it is like how angels and some nephilim can use light to travel, but that's not the most important thing."

What could be more important than learning that the Prince of Wrath had a very useful and powerful magic?

"He used Shay's father's blood to raise his brothers. The seven Princes of Hell are all Earthside."

My knees buckled. "No."

"I'm afraid so." Luca sighed. "It's why I want Shay and Hans with you, Meredith. We need to find those other stones and we need to find them fast. And that's not all . . . "

My head spun. The hallway we strode down was nothing more than a blur as we made our way to the meeting room. The others needed to know what we'd learned.

After a mere ten minutes on the phone with Luca everything, was upside-down and topsy-turvy.

Silas was a traitor.

The Princes of Hell were here.

And Tobias's brother, a vampire named Raphael, seemed to be on their side.

I swallowed at that last one. My mate had practically exploded when Luca told us. Even now, he vibrated with anger.

Guilt I had no business feeling raged through me, filling my every cell. I couldn't control his brother, but that didn't stop me from hating what he'd done to Tobias or from how my mate was furious, betrayed, and hurt.

Acting on instinct, I slipped my palm into Tobias's colder, drier one. "I'm sorry."

He squeezed my hand. The pressure reassured when so little managed to. "You did nothing."

"I know." And it was so unlike me to apologize for the actions of others, but I couldn't help myself. Whatever I had to do to ease his pain, I would. "I hate that he did this. That you feel this way."

My mate stopped walking and pulled me close to his chest. His gaze was soft, though the tension in his shoulders and jaw lingered. "My brother is his own vampire. We have been at odds more often than not, particularly of late." His eyes closed briefly, as if trying to reign in the fury raging through him. "I visited him. He said things I found . . . disturbing, but did not press upon. I should have. Should have reached out to him more. If I had, perhaps Raphael would not have opened his home to the Prince of Darkness. We might not be here."

My fingers unwound from his and my hand traveled to cup his cheek. "I won't let you think that. We're not responsible for the actions of others, even those we love."

His lips curled. "A woman who believes she has the power to sway a vampire. A Laurent, at that. Audacious."

"Are you surprised?" My thumb caressed his jawline, hard as granite despite my efforts to relax him.

He barked out a laugh. "Hardly. If anything, it drives home the fact that we are well-matched."

"And we'll always be in each other's corner," I added. "From here on out, Tobias, it's you and me against any enemy. Against the world, against this realm and Isila, if needed."

Even as the words left my lips, it shocked me how much I meant them. We had a support system. We weren't alone.

But even if we were, we'd survive. Together, we'd ride out any storm.

"It pleases me to hear that," he whispered, his lips drawing closer.

When they met mine, I sighed and my body relaxed into his, which was still hard as rock. I suspected Tobias wouldn't be able to loosen up until he faced his brother, made him answer for how he'd wronged the world.

But all that worry disappeared as my mate's tongue swept over mine. In response, my hand inched up, teasing into his hair, pulling him closer.

He did the same and as our bodies pressed together tighter, heat pulsed in my hips.

Damned this meeting. I wanted him here. *Now.* I wanted more than stolen seconds with Tobias and to give myself to him. For our bond to solidify.

"The meeting," Tobias rasped, his lips breaking from mine for a second and traveling down my neck.

"But do I care?" I breathed.

He chuckled. "Unfortunately, we do." His kisses inched back up, to my lips, my cheeks, and a final one landed on my forehead. "There will be time for us later."

"Dude, I'm a modern woman. I can't be waiting years here."

Not now that I knew what I wanted, how badly I wanted it. Not now that I knew who we were to one another. I craved a bond like the one he spoke of, even if I didn't understand every aspect of it.

"One." He pulled back, eyes gleaming with amusement. "I am not *your dude*."

I rolled my eyes.

"Two, it won't be forever. A mate bond is cherished and if you wish to seal it, I want it as well. But at the right time."

I brushed off the 'if' comment. The bond would be sealed. I had no qualms about that, and he knew it too. His eyes burned with a promise of passion, and it took everything I had not to drag him back to the bedroom.

Perhaps sensing my weak moment, Tobias took a step back and slipped my hand in his again. "Come, love."

I allowed him to lead me to the meeting room, and breathed deeply, methodically, to calm myself. By the time we got there, I hoped my cheeks were no longer pink. No matter how much I wanted to bond myself to Tobias, I didn't need everyone else knowing our business.

All eight members of the *Abscondita* Coven and Tana sat around the large circular table. In the center, the small tree adorned with stones that symbolized the *lapis caelesti* twinkled back at us. Tana had been positioned between Miriam and Falak.

Among the *Arcacustos* there were two whom I had not spoken more than five words to—Aya and Falak. Aya hailed from Nigeria and wore the most spectacular bright clothing, which initially made me think she'd be extroverted, but really, she was very quiet. The witch spent most of her time meditating, which she seemed to be doing at that moment.

Falak was even more reserved. I'd barely seen the old Indian witch during my stay at the manor. According to Claire, she spent most of her time outside, in the garden. Seeing as their gardens out back were prolific, I suspected Falak might be their resident earth elemental.

"Do you feel like your head is about to explode?" I asked, careful to keep my tone light. I'd left the library before Tana and wouldn't be surprised if the other witches had just released her.

"I expect my head tae pop off any minute now," Tana replied. "I guess I made yer job easier, didnae I?"

"A bit," I replied as Tobias and I took a seat at the table. At my right, Hannah smiled. She looked beat too. Once we got to sleep, no one would wake for hours.

"But there are still five more *Vindix* for me to find. I'm not getting off *that* easily." I leaned forward. "Which brings me to a few questions—like, how trained are you?"

In the library, we'd only gone over *Vindix* stuff, and I'd seen her fire magic before, but I was curious. As the Keeper of the Ruby of Flame, she should be able to create full-fledged infernos. Against the Princes of Hell, that would be incredibly useful.

"I've nae used my stone, but I'm okay." Tana shrugged.

"Like how okay?" I pressed. "Claire said there were things to discuss, and Luca, my coven master, just shared some pretty important news with Tobias and me."

"How about I show ye in the morn?" Tana's face turned red as she averted her gaze to her folded hands. I figured pressing wouldn't do much good.

"What's the news, then?" Miriam piped up.

The rest of the coven looked at me with interest and I told them about Silas and the Princes of Hell escaping their realm. Once I was done, half the table was no longer sitting but paced the room. The other half looked like they might collapse from their chairs.

Tana was in the latter category.

If we were closer, I'd go over to her, help ease the shock. But we'd just met, and the girl seemed more reserved. It was best to let her process and then answer questions that might arise.

"Who else knows this?" Miriam asked. She'd been pacing but now stopped, her gaze leveling me.

"Luca, Hans, and Shay, for sure," I said. "I assume those in S&S who need to know do know."

"The Covenant too," Tobias added. "Shay and Hans were on a mission that included that ruling body."

"Bloody everyone in the world will learn our secrets soon." Miriam tipped her pointed chin to the ceiling and closed her eyes.

"I don't think that's a bad thing," I ventured. "With seven devils on the loose, people will need to protect themselves. You didn't see New York, but—"

"I don't care about New York," Miriam spat. "I only care about *this coven* doing their job. And we are woefully behind. You need to seek the other stone keepers. Tana, you require training, specifically with the Ruby of Flames. Olga is our coven's fire witch and will help train you, though with the power the *Vindix* are rumored to have, you'll surpass her soon."

The old Russian witch nodded. "Goddess willing."

Tana didn't reply. Instead, her chin tilted down, and her gaze landed on her hands, folded together on the table. I shot a sidelong glance at Tobias. The newest *Vindix* looked scared—a reasonable reaction, but there was something more there, too.

"Hey, Tana?" I asked. "Are you okay? I know this is a lot but we can help you take it in."

"I—no, 'tis me. It's—," she croaked out. "I didnae want to say this earlier, but I dinae *have* my stone."

"What?" Gloria's raspy voice shook the room, but the rest of the *Arcacustos* remained quiet as tension filled the room.

"It's lost?" My stomach plummeted.

Mine had been locked away in a supernatural bank, but we'd known it was a possibility that other stones were lost. Whole families had been, and stones were much easier to displace than people.

"Maybe not." Tana shook her head. "But I cannae be sure."

"I'm going to need more to go on than that," I replied to keep the *Arcacustos* from talking. They looked about ready to jump out of their skin. Only Tobias radiated true calm, and I suspected that was all a front.

Finally, Tana's eyes met mine, shining with tears. "I think I might have held it. Might have . . . Och my Goddess, I can't!"

"What can't you do? Tana, we're here to help you. Let us." I stood to go to her, but fire burst out of her palms and climbed up her forearms. She darted a few paces back, away from the table.

Flames licked the skin of her bare arms, and from the terror in her eyes, she wasn't controlling them all the way.

"You cannae help me!" she wailed. "No one kin! I only hurt those I get close tae!"

My stomach pitted. What in the ever-loving hell was she talking about?

"The thing is, child." Claire stood now, her voice soft and reassuring. "We must learn to live and trust one another. This group here, perhaps with a few others, are going to save the world from the monsters that rose. So, please, tell us what's the matter?"

"Besides the obvious, of course," Stuart said dryly. "Demon princes running amok. I'm gonna have to call me Mum. Tell her to go into hiding." He paused. "Then again, maybe the princes should be scared of *her*. Wicked with a wooden spoon, that one."

His attempt at humor cracked the tension in the room, and the moment Tana's flames dimmed, her chest sank in.

"Tana, please. You're not sure you've held the stone, but you might have," I said. "Can you explain why you think that?"

A shuddering breath left the fire witch as she met my stare. "The night before I came 'ere, I argued wi' my parents. It was stupid, but I wanted tae go tae a costume party and they would no' let me. Seein' as I'm an adult, I did as I weel pleased." She gulped and the sound filled the otherwise silent room. "I used one o' Mum's necklaces as part o' my costume— a scarlet witch. The necklace had a large ruby and wi'oot asking I stole it right from her jewelry box and went tae the party. When I got back, they were pissed. Laid into me richt good, they did. We fought, and I ran upstairs, vowing tae never come home from uni again."

Her hands flew to her face and her knees buckled. On trembling legs, she lowered herself to the ground, careful to keep her flaming hands away from her clothing. Unable to stop myself this time, I knelt in front of the witch.

"What happened?"

"I was angry 'n," she choked *out a sob*, "I was so stupid, and now I'll ne'er see them again!"

"I don't understand," I whispered, dread washing through me at the haunted look in her eyes. "What happened?"

"I'd taken the necklace off before bed, but twas close tae me, on my nightstand. It musta been the stone felt how mad I was because it . . ."

"The ruby is in the necklace and it started a fire, didn't it?" Olga asked. Tana didn't reply, but Olga pressed on. "That's the truth of it, right, girl? The Ruby of Flames responded to you and, now, your previous life is no more?"

"Aye," Tana croaked out. "I didn't know twas the necklace! I ne'er would have touched it, if I knew!" She sniffled and wiped her eyes. "The house was ablaze and went doon fast. Only I survived." The instant the words left her, she broke down crying.

Hannah and Olga were there in an instant, and though it was selfish of me, I left them and retreated to Tobias's side. He met my gaze, his pale face whiter than usual.

"She doesn't have it on her, only the bracelet," he said. "The talismans, as you call them, are only so that the *Vindix* can recognize one another. But the actual Ruby is in the ruins of her home."

"Let's hope it's still there," I replied.

"We must go and find it. Before Wrath does," Tobias added. "With the Pearl and the Opal in his hands, the other stones will call to him."

"I agree." My teeth dug into my bottom lip as I studied Tana, still weeping and trembling from her reveal. "We need to learn where she lives and get there as soon as possible."

BY THE TIME WE ARRIVED IN THE SMALL TOWN OUTSIDE OF Edinburgh, the moon hung high in the night sky.

In the passengers' seat, Meredith twisted Tana's bracelet on her wrist, hinting at her nerves.

After reliving her trauma, losing her home and family, and the overwhelming instinct to flee to a place she did not know, the fire representative of the *Vindix* was simply not emotionally well enough to join us. However, my cunning Meredith had convinced her to part with the bracelet.

My mate figured that between her own ring and Tana's heirloom, she had enough for her seeker magic to find the Ruby of Flame. I prayed she was right. And that we wouldn't run into trouble.

Would the fire have drawn the Darkborn's attention? The article we'd found online had made it sound like it was far more than a house fire—the tunnel of flames had reached for the sky in a way that screamed magic.

Now that we had learned all seven of the Princes of Hell had risen and they had the backing of powerful people, such as my brother, the game had changed. My fingers gripped the wheel tighter as anger washed over me.

How could Raphael do this?

Not only did I not understand my elder brother, but I felt betrayed. Lost. Had I ever truly known him?

During my time at Castel Romono, he'd dismissed humans so harshly that he'd reminded me of an OA member, but his deception was far too complete for that. The Ordo Aeternum was no place for my brother. No, he'd gone a step further. In siding with a Prince of Hell, Raphael was not just saying supernaturals should rule humans; in my mind, he was saying a small sect, the vilest, should rule over *all*.

I shuddered. Luca had relayed what Shay's father told her —that the princes would claim vast swathes of the Earth. That those locations would be their new kingdoms. I hated to think what the world would look like then.

"Please calm yourself, vampire. I can smell the tension on you," Benedict drawled from the backseat.

Since Tana and Meredith first disappeared into the library, the feline had been hunting. However, the moment my mate and I proclaimed we would drive to Tana's home in Scotland to retrieve the Ruby, Benedict appeared and announced he would join. How he knew to return, I wasn't sure. I chalked it up to familiar magic.

"Many things might have happened in the time that she was away," I said, not about to admit what I was really thinking about. "Expect the unexpected when we reach her home."

"Speaking of . . . the GPS says take the next left," Meredith replied, looking up from the phone we'd borrowed from Claire and leaning forward in her seat. "Riiiiight there!"

A dim street lamp illuminated the turn a few seconds

before we passed it, and I swung the rental down a one-car lane. Immediately, my eyes adjusted to the darkness. No lights illuminated this road, and every home appeared dark inside.

"Cozy neighborhood," Meredith said politely, taking in the small homes that were well-kept but clearly in need of maintenance. "Looks like their place is at the end of the lane. Hopefully, you'll be able to turn the car around down there."

"We'll deal with that bridge when we get to it."

I slowed as we drove down the street, which was longer than I'd imagined. Finally, we reached the end, on which an empty lot stared back at us.

Tana's fire had burned so hot that most of her family home was nothing but charred rubble. The police tape was still up, but we all knew no one would be able to pinpoint the reason for the blaze. Even the best fire forensic teams did not know about enchanted gems with the power to set entire city blocks ablaze.

I edged the car to the side of the street and parked. Meredith reached for the door handle, but I stopped her. "Wait."

"We've been traveling for hours. I want to get out and get this done."

"Just let me sense the area for danger."

Her eyebrows pulled together, but she leaned back in her seat. "Okay."

I started with my eyes closed, scenting and listening for any sign someone might be here. With Wrath possessing a sacred stone that could, theoretically, sense another *lapis caelesti's* usage, we could not be too careful.

But there was nothing but the faint scent of burnt wood and plastic in the air, a mercy considering Tana's parents had perished in the blaze. And when I opened my eyes once more, nothing leapt out. Still, being extra cautious, I turned to the cat. "Do you feel anything amiss?"

"Except for the distinct lack of rats and mice in the area, no." His nose twitched. "That might be a good sign. Maybe they sense the pulse of the Ruby and fear another fire."

"We can only hope." I opened my door. "Don't forget your flashlight, Meredith."

She snorted, but the glove box fell open. Confident she'd be prepared for a thorough search, I approached the place where the home had once stood.

"You're bossier than usual," Meredith grumbled, coming up behind me.

"We're mates. I told you I'd be more protective. That includes ensuring that you have what you need to remain safe." I arched an eyebrow at her.

She didn't respond, just turned the flashlight on and began sweeping it over the wreckage. Now that we were closer, I could better make out the few items that remained: a warped metal sink, a fireproof safe—unopened and left behind—and a steel filing cabinet.

However, most of the family home was not but charred beams and ash. The Ruby of Flames had, in Tana's words, demolished her life in ten minutes.

That boded well for the power of the stone—if its wielder learned to control it.

I swallowed. The girl had raw power, but according to Olga and Miriam, she required intense training. Despite them being a witching family, her parents had forbidden her from using her magic, so she'd only begun playing with magic when she attended uni. Perhaps it was best if Tana kept the stone outside the *Abscondita* Coven's manor? We did not need a repeat of the scene before us.

"Anything?" Benedict asked Meredith, who scanned the remains.

"Her bracelet is warm, so I'm sure it's here. The Ruby and this bracelet should be connected and I can use that connection with my power."

"Walk about," I suggested.

"*Dude.*" Meredith flung the deplorable moniker at me as she arched an eyebrow in annoyance. "Chill on the commands."

"I'll try." And I would, but I recognized commands as a side effect of wanting to keep her safe.

The witch moved through the rubble inch by inch. Benedict and I followed, using our keen senses to assess the area. Aside from the stench of burned debris and rubble, nothing leapt out at me—certainly not a sparkly red gem.

However, when Meredith froze, I did too. "What is it?"

"I think—I think it's around here," she replied. "The gems on the bracelet lit up for a second and my magic yanked at me, like it has before. It's a tell." She shook her head. "The bracelet is not burning me like my ring did though. Tana got a way more humane trinket. And she's a fire witch!"

"And what of your ring?" I asked, stepping closer to her. We did not know what to expect, but if Meredith's ring sensed not only other *Vindix*, but the items that belonged to other *Vindix* that would be a boon, indeed. We needed to use this opportunity to discover the full range of its powers.

"It's warm, like when Tana approached us in *Abscondita* land. Not hot, though. Not like when we had to find the missing stone. That was really hot, almost like it was insisting upon something."

"That seems to indicate that being whole was very important to it." Benedict spoke of the ring as if it had thoughts and a mind of its own. "If not, then it gives more subtle hints."

"Whoa . . . Yeah, I guess so," Meredith breathed. "I haven't found information on the talismans in the library, but I think you're right. At least for now, that's what we have to go on."

"Speaking science," I rumbled. "Sexy."

"Please, no," Benedict hissed. "I understand that you two will be all over each other for the foreseeable future, but try to refrain while I'm around." He shook his body as if he could shake off how we made him feel. "Thank goodness, I've already toured the manor and found a new bedroom that suits me."

Ignoring the feline, I gestured to the mess at our feet. Most of the items were too blackened and warped to be distinguishable. Only a bathtub and a half a metal stand that had likely once been used for towels stood out. "Around here is where you feel the Ruby?"

"I think it's under the tub."

"Let's dig around it first," I said. "Just to be safe."

Tana had told us the necklace holding the Ruby was in her room before the catastrophe. While I wasn't surprised to find it might have moved—whether by fire crews or by an explosion throwing it elsewhere in the ravaged home—we needed to be careful when searching. If we weren't, this could take far longer than necessary.

Kneeling, I searched the area around the blackened tub. Meredith did too, and Benedict prowled around, sniffing and turning things over with his paws. Once we'd cleared the area and my hands were sufficiently covered in ash, I stood. "It appears it really is beneath the tub. Stand back."

"Do you need help?" Meredith asked. "That looks heavy."

Seeing as it looked old, undoubtedly it was heavy, but vampires were strong, and I was no exception.

"I can handle it. Be ready." I squatted, reached under the lip, and lifted. The bathtub rose with me, and though the tub was awkward, I lifted it over my head.

"Now, *that's* hot," Meredith flashed me a grin. "You're not even breaking a sweat."

Benedict groaned. "I should never have come with you two."

"Oh, shove it, Benedict." Meredith twisted the bracelet around her slender wrist and beamed the flashlight on the ground as she squinted down at the remains. It didn't take long for her to kneel and begin to dig.

"Might I assist?" Benedict came closer. Setting her light down, my mate nodded.

Together, the cat and the witch dug into the ash and bits of charred wood with such shared intensity that had I ever doubted their bond, I could no longer. Seconds passed, then minutes. Sweat trickled down Meredith's brow and yet, she didn't let up. If anything, her focus increased.

I stood back with an enameled iron tub over my head, taking it all in. A seeker at work. Meredith's kind was rare, and to watch the witch use her magic, to hunt for a treasure only she could sense, was nothing short of mesmerizing. She seemed to be in a trance.

Suddenly, her hand plunged into the soot and when it came out, a flash of red caught the beam of the flashlight.

"Got it!" Meredith squealed. "It must have fallen to the first floor, and the tub fell over it 'cause it was deeper than I thought, but—"

"We'll be taking that," a male voice rumbled.

I spun, tub still overhead, and my entire body grew rigid as five male vampires prowled our way.

"Who are you?" I growled.

"That's of no concern to you, Tobias." The one in the center, the same who had spoken before, leered at us. He was a tall male with bronzed skin and burning red hair.

I didn't recognize him in the slightest, but he knew me. Bloody hell! Did he work for my brother? If so, how would Raph have found me?

"Come here, witch," the red-haired leader ordered.

"Hard pass," Meredith snapped back.

In that instant, I saw everything that would happen before it did. The men on the far sides of the line prepared to dart forward. One would grab Meredith, take her. Thanks to the Ringmaster, they surely knew she was a seeker. The other three would assault me.

Before any such thing occurred, I hurled the tub at them. They split, but it gave me time to do what I'd intended: defend my mate.

I lunged in front of Meredith, fangs bared as a vitriolic hiss rolled out of me.

"You will stand down. Freeze and do not move an inch further." I roared at them and my voice was thick with compulsion.

The two on the edges stopped, frozen in place. That marked them as weak vampires. However, the center three were closer to the original Blood, and though their pace slowed, they kept stalking toward us.

"Tobias!" Meredith whispered. "Let me help!"

"Stay back," I warned, body going taut. "I can't control my instincts right now, Meredith."

"Do what he says," Benedict urged.

Footsteps sounded, reassuring me that my mate had listened to her familiar.

"Someone is protective of the witch," the leader taunted. "You getting a piece of that ass, Laurent?"

My teeth ground together. "Who do you work for?"

"Wouldn't you like—"

I struck while he was still speaking. My compulsion drilled into his mind, extracting the thought at the forefront—the unspoken answer to my question.

These fuckers were OA, and had worked out that Giselle was acting as a double agent. My sire's information, that the OA had been in Edinburgh and left, was incorrect. A contingent had stayed behind.

Bloody fucking hell.

I retreated from his head in time for another one of the trio to strike at me, zooming forward, hands aimed for my neck.

"Watch out!" Meredith screamed, but I was ready for him, and the moment the idiot was close enough, I beat him to the punch.

My hands gripped his neck, snapped it, and ripped his head clean off.

"Oh, *sick.*" The sounds of retching followed Meredith's gasp, though I didn't have time to comfort her. The other two were upon me, fists flying, fangs extended.

"I'm going to take your little witch to our headquarters," the red-haired leader said. "And once she's done her job, I'll ask for dibs on her. Such a sweet looking thing shouldn't—"

I lunged, but before my attack struck, a blinding light blasted through the night, blinding me and everyone else. I roared in pain.

"What the hell?" the leader yelled. He spun and shielded his eyes.

"Stiff! Get down!"

Rather than question why I was hearing her voice and how she got here, I did as Shay commanded and dropped to the ground.

The next second, the sound of heads being split from necks by a sword of fire and light made me all too glad I'd followed through. Blood sprayed on the burned down debris, bright red from freshly feeding.

"I'm holding two more!" Hans called out, and I shot up.

"Stop! I need to question them."

I spoke not a moment too soon. Thanks to her wings, Shay had already been zooming over, ready to strike. Instead, she landed and turned to me. "What the hell is going on?"

"I'd like to ask you that!" Meredith squawked. "Why are you here? And how?"

"Do not get distracted. Not yet." I prowled toward the remaining OA vampires, still frozen from compulsion. I charged toward the closest. My hands gripped his chin. "Who sent you?"

"The OA. We've been watching this area for weeks."

"Since my sire was in Edinburgh?" It was no use covering for Giselle now. I'd have to tell her the moment we left so she could flee.

The vampire nodded in my grip. "Yeah. We heard the Greek family moved here. That the girl lit shit on fire all the time."

"What?" Meredith was at my side.

A second later, Benedict joined her, amber eyes narrowed in feline hatred. "How do you know that?"

"Been looking for the fire stone for a long time. It's the one that leaves a trail that's easiest to follow," the vampire said.

"You followed it here? From where?" My voice was thick

with the power of my blood. I would wring every secret out of them that I could.

"Found articles in Greece about fires popping up everywhere. Figured that had to be it. Went there and learned the family moved. They came here but their last name is common, so it took us a while to find this place. That, and the girl stopped playing with fire for a couple of years. Only recently started again. By the time we figured that out, the house was gone. We thought of the stone too, but we were on the lookout, just in case the seeker came looking."

"Who figured that out?" Meredith asked.

The vampire did not reply, but one snarl from me changed his mind.

"I don't know. The Ordo is huge, and only a few know everything that happens within the organization. We were stationed here to look out for fires. There have been a few recently, and we just learned of this one. When we saw you here, we recognized the Laurent and knew we were on the right track."

So, the Ordo did not keep everyone in the loop. They compartmentalized their knowledge.

"Do you know where my sire is?" I asked.

I knew, but did they? Was she in danger right now?

"No idea." The vampire grunted as he tried to break free from my hold.

"Good." I looked at Meredith. "Anything else?"

"Not that I can come up with. But we can't let them go."

We were in complete agreement there. They'd only return to the OA and tell others we'd found the stone. Already, there was a target on Meredith's back and according to Giselle, the Ringmaster was working with the Ordo Aeternum.

"I can handle it." Shay unsheathed her sword.

I took a step back, allowing the nephilim to behead the vampires as she had the others. They fell unceremoniously, and I found it impossible to pity them. These vampires had been given the world, *immortality*, and they wanted more.

It was too much. The Blood of Isila had proven that to me, and they only reigned in one of the nine kingdoms of the other realm. Too much power corrupted, and the OA was rotten to the core.

"Do we just leave them?" Meredith asked.

"We do," I replied, taking her in my arms. She trembled, but only slightly. My mate was strong. "Depending on their age and how recently they fed, they'll eventually turn to ash."

"And fit right in here." Hans gestured to the ruined house. "Wherever that is. What are you two doing? Where the hell are we?"

"We retrieved a *lapis caelesti*. But the better question would be, what are *you* doing here?" I gazed at him.

"And how the hell did you get here?" Meredith pulled away from me and turning to her roommate. "A light blinded me and then—*poof*—you were here. Is that a spell, Hans?"

The wizard's gaze dropped to the ground, and my eyes widened. What had happened?

"Did I say something wrong?" Meredith asked, picking up on the same cues I had.

Hans shook his head. "I made a mistake and now it is costing me." The wizard inhaled deeply. "I performed a Vow of Intent and unintentionally broke it. I did it to save my sister, but in doing so, my wizard magic is now under someone else's control. I can no longer use it."

These were dire implications.

"Who?" I asked.

Hans gulped. "Richard Brons."

My fists clenched. Brons was a friend of Egor Drago, a vampire I despised. Both men were disgusting, though some circles of supernaturals liked them as they were both elected officials. "You can't be serious."

"He is," Shay spoke up. "And he doesn't need us to make him feel bad about it. Hans only has his demon magic now."

I swallowed, knowing full well the agony Hans's darker powers could inflict upon a person, even a vampire. I'd seen it once, in his blood.

"I thought you couldn't use that," Meredith piped up again. "I'm so confused."

"It turns out that even after many years of disuse, I can call demon powers. I used them once in New York, before we saved you. And I did again in Italy."

"He saved our butts with it too." Shay's voice held pride in it.

"From the princes when they rose?" I inquired.

"Yep. And he held those vampires in place with his demon magic too."

Silence fell upon the ruins of the home. I was certain we were missing much more of their story. The way Shay regarded Hans, rather than glaring at him, spoke volumes. But those were tales best left for later.

"Okay, but seriously," Meredith broke the silence, "how did you get here?"

"Oh, right." On her hip, Shay wore a bum bag, and from its depths, she pulled out a glowing ball no larger than a grape. "This is a luxiter."

My mouth fell open. Those were immeasurably valuable. "Few can make those. Fewer still can afford them."

"The maker was someone you might have known, Stiff," Shay teased. "Nicolas Flamel ring any bells?"

"What." Meredith's eyes widened. "He's real?" Her voice rose in surprise.

Real and very much so alive. I had, in fact, met the ancient alchemist before, but had not seen him in nearly a century. Wisely, the man kept his head down. "He's real," I assured my mate. "So, you met him and he made that?"

Shay nodded. "Pretty much. Hans and I had to do some wheeling and dealing to get one—and we have more coming; seven more, in fact. But this brought us here."

"You bought eight?" I gaped. "How? They are priceless."

Shay came from money, but even so, I wasn't sure cash was enough to obtain a luxiter. Creating one cost the maker too much. As the holder of the philosopher's stone, Flamel was uniquely qualified to rejuvenate his life-force, but it would still be an arduous task and he was a very, very old mortal man.

"My father paid me a visit. He gave eight feathers. One for each luxiter. We had to pay extra to get them fast and for us to be able to use names to locate who we needed to find."

"You said my name and," Meredith's closed fists rose and her fingers splayed open wide, "you were here?"

"Basically. Yeah." Shay shrugged and replaced the luxiter in her bag. "Yours will be done next, Rooms. My dad told us to have one for each stone keeper, and then I'm keeping one too."

"It seems you've found another stone keeper?" Hans nodded to the necklace, still clutched in Meredith's hand. "May I?"

She handed it over, the red center stone gleaming in the moonlight as she did so. "There's lots to tell, but yeah, we found the fire elemental—part of the *Vindix*, the group for the stone keepers. She's a girl about a year younger than me. This was her home." Meredith kicked at the ground.

"Oh . . ." An uncomfortable expression crossed Shay's face. "How awful. I—"

A phone rang, cutting Shay off. I looked at the pair who had joined us and they shook their heads.

"We lost our phones in Italy," Shay explained. "Still need to pick up new ones."

"Oh my God. It's got to be Claire's. In the car!" Meredith shot me a look laced with fear. "Something must have happened at the manor."

I darted over to the sedan, flung the door open, and snatched up the phone. "What's wrong?"

"Tobias?" A voice I recognized as Miriam's filled my ear.

"Yes?"

"You need to return. The wards have been activated."

"By who?" I asked.

"We can't be sure, but there were multiple breaches, so we think it's the OA," Miriam said and, try as she might, she could not hide the trembling in her voice. "They're here and they've brought enough power to level our protections, which means we need you two. *Now.*"

CHAPTER TWELVE

MEREDITH

Tobias whirled to face us, his jaw set in a hard line as he shoved the phone into his pocket. "Everyone get in the car."

My heart had been hammering since the moment the phone rang and sped up to a frenzied pace. "What happened?"

"The OA has made their move. They're at the manor."

Shay shot Hans a confused look, but we didn't have time to explain.

"Shay, you said that a luxiter can get you anywhere with a name?" I asked.

"And a password, but yeah, that's the basics. From Flamel's place, I spoke the magic word to activate it, then gave it Meredith's name and specified she was a seeker witch, just in case your name is popular, and *zap!* We were here."

"There are no usage limits, correct?" Tobias asked, latching on to my idea. "We need to use it again."

"Flamel said nothing of the sort," Hans replied. "But this manor . . . It's where Miriam Black lives?"

"Yeah." I nodded. "She's part of the *Abscondita* Coven. They're all older witches, except for two—a red-haired man and a female witch in her forties. Tobias." I turned to my mate. "How many did the OA bring?"

"Miriam didn't say, but enough to level their wards."

"Which they recently reinforced," I murmured. "So, whoever they brought isn't messing around. Shay, we need to move!"

"Hold hands." My roommate held out her hand.

"Benedict, let me hold you."

Without so much as a sassy remark, the cat leapt into my open arm. I pulled him tightly to my chest.

"We're seeking Miriam Black, but can you give me a relative location?" Shay asked.

"They are a few miles from the Lake District National Park in England," I answered.

"Or you could say the *Abscondita* Coven manor," Tobias suggested. "Surely, there is only one."

"Right." Shay replied. "I'll try the coven, then. Hold on tight to Benny, Rooms."

Once Shay saw we were secure, each person attached to the other by a grip of the hand, she fished the luxiter from her bag again. "Hang on to your tits, guys." She squeezed the magical item. "*Volar.*"

It glowed, and Shay held the ball slightly aloft. "Take me to Miriam Black of the *Abscondita* Coven!"

The Scottish town we'd been standing in disappeared. All that was left was blinding light and the nauseating feeling of being squeezed through a tube meant for mice. In my grasp, Benedict hissed and squirmed, but I kept a one-armed vice grip around the cat. Who knew what would happen if I let go? Where would he end up?

As the question occurred to me, the light lifted, slamming me into the night once again. My feet hit the ground, and I teetered, toppling until Tobias caught me.

"Steady," he said, as Benedict leapt from my arms. "Gather your wits. The wards are down."

A high-pitched, whooping alarm confirmed it. I shook myself, trying to pull myself together when my stomach violently rolled and twisted.

"It was better that time," Shay said.

"It was." Hans agreed.

Shay beamed at him, and I gaped. When I'd seen them last, they'd been so at odds. What had happened?

"*How* are you here already?" a stern English accent barked.

I spun to find Miriam ten paces away in the trees. The lights of the manor were not far behind us. "We thought you'd take hours to return. Granted, I'm glad because they've already broken down the wards, but it's unsettling."

"Tell you later," I replied. "Give us the scoop. How many?"

"Rygor flew overhead," Miriam replied.

That she didn't demand answers on how we'd gotten here so fast spoke volumes as to how worried she was. Everyone understood that the OA was here for me, but if they searched the coven manor, they would raid it of *everything* precious. There were volumes in that library that did not exist anywhere else on the planet.

And Tana . . .

"The wyvern counted fifty, but there might be more." Miriam waved a wrinkled hand above. "The trees obscured his sight."

"Wyv—isn't that a dragon!?" Shay squealed.

"His name is Rygor," I said. Knowing the wyvern's name might help them if we got separated. "There's a giant too."

"Okay . . . Wow. For once, I don't know what to say."

A dry laugh left my lips. "His name is Jon-Jon. If you see them, don't hurt them."

"Girl, I'm not heading into a fight without you." Shay snorted. "You're crazy."

"I'll stick close, too," Hans said. "I wouldn't want to accidentally inflict pain on anyone fighting for us."

As there were only eight *Arcacustos*, Tana, and us, that was a smart choice.

"Benedict, go inside." I nodded my head toward the manor. The Ringmaster needed me alive until she took my magic, but she wouldn't blink at killing my familiar out of spite. "Maybe stay with Tana. Is she in there, Miriam?"

"Aye." She gave me a knowing look. "The girl is no fighter. Not yet, anyway."

Seeing as Tana possessed enough raw power to light half this forest on fire, I was glad Miriam had seen that in the newest *Vindix*. I hoped she stayed put.

"I don't want to go inside," Benedict piped up. "I'm your familiar. Not hers."

"She has no one," I replied. "I have Tobias, Shay, and Hans. Please, Benedict. I need to be sure Tana is okay and you're good at looking out for others."

The cat let out a huff. "You deserve an Oscar for that one." He turned around, giving me a view of his butt. "Fine. I'll watch the girl. Stay safe."

"Thanks, you too."

My familiar darted through the woods toward the manor. Two less beings for me to worry over, and I suspected Tana, who'd been through enough trauma of late, would appreciate having someone with her.

"We do not want the invaders getting close to the manor. You lot take the northeastern bit of the woods." Miriam took that moment to dole out instructions. "I'll separate my people so that we all protect a bit of land. If you need help, send up a ball of light. You can do that, correct Meredith?"

"Yeah." I said.

"We're all capable fighters." A smug expression crossed Shay's face as she unfurled white wings and pulled her sword of fire and light from wherever she hid the thing. "Hans? Flying might really help . . . "

Hans hesitated, but Shay gave him an encouraging smile. The next thing I knew, massive black wings unfurled from his back.

I gasped. "You didn't mention those!"

My wizard mentor frowned.

"Don't have the attitude," Shay said to Hans. "We need any advantage and flight is totally an advantage. Are there weapons on the property?" She directed the question to Miriam, whose eyes widened at the sight of Hans's wings.

Miriam blinked several times before snapping out of it and gestured right.

"In the shed up that way. If you need something, break off the lock. I don't have time to open it." With that, Miriam turned and began walking through the forest. "Protect this land, protect the future."

Yeesh, if I hadn't thought this was ominous enough already, the old lady knew how to throw a dire veil over the night.

"Shay, what do you need?" I asked my roommate.

"Girl, I have my sword. You need a weapon. Or are your spells up to snuff?"

Aside from my seeking powers, there had been little time to practice my hedge magic—basic powers that all witches had and could stretch into protection. "A weapon would be good. Let's check out that shed."

We ran around the manor in the direction Miriam had pointed. The moment we rounded the corner, the shed presented itself. As did the enormous lock on it.

"Tobias?" I pointed at the lock.

He blurred to the door and slammed it open as if the lock was nothing.

"Whoa," I breathed. "That's hot."

Shay snorted. "And it begins."

My cheeks heated as I ran into the shed. Miriam hadn't specified exactly what would be inside, but the answer was weapons that I guessed were from the Middle Ages.

"Are these as old as they look?" I looked at my vampire mate.

"I believe so." He pointed to some of the swords. "It's confusing because the manor is newer, but then, weapons are mobile. Perhaps, once, the *Arcacustos* used these as defense."

A tale for another time.

"Which looks best? No swords. Or maces." I added, spotting a hulking spiked weapon I was sure I would only manage to impale myself with.

"A dagger, for close fighting," Tobias said. "You'll have to use magic for battle at range." His keen gaze swept a wall lined with axes, swords, daggers and other pieces, some jeweled, some plain, some still stained with blood.

My nose wrinkled, and I waited. Shay stepped inside the shed, and without hesitation, plucked a weapon from the wall. "This one is perfect for you." She grinned. "Made for supernaturals. One side is a dagger, the other is a stake for vampires. You hold it in the middle."

There were only three ways to kill vampires: by wooden stake, decapitation, or fire. Shay was spot on that this was my best option.

"And it has a handy halter." Shay tossed the halter at me. "Put it on."

I followed directions, looping the leather around my thigh, and cinched it tight.

"Now that you're settled, we need to get closer to the boundary line." Tobias herded Shay and me from the shed and stalked toward the woods. I followed, sheathing the dagger side in the halter as I walked. The stake portion was pointed upward, dangerous, but I'd have to deal. There were far more treacherous things in the woods tonight.

Beyond, darkness smothered the forest despite the moonlight and the stars twinkling above. In sync, we crept through the trees, on the lookout for anyone who did not belong on these hallowed lands. We made it no more than fifty feet when, to our left, someone screamed. The rasp in their tone hinted that it might be Gloria. Instinctively, I spun on my heel, but Tobias caught me at the wrist.

"We go this way."

"They might need us." I tugged against him.

"Miriam gave us a sector to defend and we will do that, Meredith. Running that way only puts the *Arcacustos* in danger."

"I cannot wait to understand what you're talking about with *Vindix* and *Arcacustos* and all these other words," Shay muttered. "But yeah, Rooms. I agree with Stiff."

"I despise that nickname," Tobias snarled in warning.

Shay smirked as if pissing off Tobias gave her the greatest

joy, which it probably did. Shay liked to get reactions out of people.

In the distance, a twig cracked and every one of us froze. The opposition was closing in.

"Lower," Tobias whispered, and as one, our group crouched.

Hans and Shay took the right, while my mate and I hung left. Strategically, we were close enough to be able to help the other pair, but not close enough to impede fighting. Or for me to hit someone with magic. Maybe Hans too. I wasn't sure how much control he had over his demon magic.

"Focus, Meredith," Tobias breathed.

"You, focus."

"I told you I would be protective," he shot back, not at all fazed. "This is a minor example. I cannot fight as effectively if I always have one eye on you."

"I can handle myself," I said, even as the memory of a demon snatching me up and flying me to an abandoned skyscraper filled my mind.

Shit. Could I? I'd known how to fight for a long time—but only against humans and not to kill. In the past, I'd fought to give myself enough time to escape. My training against supernaturals had not been as thorough as I would have liked. Time, or lack thereof, had dictated I spend my hours on other things —like reading about the sacred stones.

I needed to balance my time better.

"I'm aware that you have skills," Tobias conceded, although he had to be thinking about New York, too. "Stay close."

That, I could do. In fact, it was what I *wanted* to do, so I nodded as we continued snaking through the forest. We crept through the dense underbrush for so long I began to think we'd all imagined the snapping twig. Or that it had been an animal.

Of course, that was when they struck; two wolves and a gamut of other creatures exploded out of the darkness.

Three went for Tobias, fangs extended—vampires. One wolf targeted Shay, while the other came for me. I wasn't sure what the remaining adversaries were until magic spewed from the hands of three and the spells hurled right for Hans. One spell struck him square in the chest. Hans froze for a moment, and that was all it took for a vampire to fling his fangs into Hans's neck.

Shay screamed, but as the other vampire detached from his first assault and went for her, she couldn't go to Hans.

As for me, I slashed my dagger at the wolf I fought. It was clear as day this group knew who they were attacking and that they saw me as the weak link. Gritting my teeth together, I called my power, winding up my hedge magic in an effort to prove them wrong.

It built inside me, so potent I might burst. With one final swipe of the dagger to effectively ward off the wolf's sharp teeth, I stepped back. Then, I let it fly. It struck the shifter in the head, dropping the creature to the ground.

One down. I spun, trying to take in if the others were having any luck, and my heart lodged into my throat. Shay and Tobias battled enemies, but Hans was on the dirt, moaning with a gaping wound in his neck.

Why hadn't he used his magic? He was Lilith's son, and his sister was powerful, so I suspected he was too.

Had he hesitated on purpose?

I swallowed, hating the idea and its implications, and started toward him, to help if I could. But before I made it even halfway there, a hand wrapped around my arm.

"You're coming with me, witch." The deep male voice sent shivers up my spine, and not in a good way.

I twisted, blade raised, intent on taking down my new foe. "The hell I—"

The threat died on my lips as the person knocked the dagger out of my hand, swept me over their shoulder, and ran. Behind me, Tobias roared, but I couldn't locate him because the world blurred from the speed that my captor ran. A vampire had taken me.

Fuck me.

I considered thrashing, but if I freed myself that way, the speed at which I traveled would make that freedom dangerous. I'd be hurled into a tree and die on impact. My jaw tightened. Why was I always the one being abducted? I didn't care that Hans had no wizarding magic. When we got out of this, he was teaching me all the hedge magic he knew. No excuses.

My captor jerked, as if he had to slow for something, and a creak hinted he might have opened a door. Then, we headed down. A musty stink filled my nostrils, but the world still moved too fast for me to determine where I was.

"Ah, here we are," the vampire said, as if I could see anything more than his ass. "As you requested."

"Set her down."

I stiffened. That voice; I would know it anywhere. The Ringmaster hadn't even tried to find me on her own. She'd sent minions to do so. Just like in New York. The woman had balls, bossing around supernaturals the way she did.

The vampire thrust me off his shoulders and to the ground with such force my knees buckled. I sucked in a breath, trying to get my bearings after being transported at the speed of light and cast a glance around the room. I recognized the area.

We were down by the Enchanted Pool. Dread spider-walked down my spine.

The pool was secluded and deep underground. I'd have better luck attracting help in the thick of the forest. How these people had even found this area so quickly baffled me, but I didn't have time to think it over. Right now, all that mattered was gathering my wits and surviving.

The Ringmaster stood before me and a big burly man hovered beside her. A black wolf tattooed on his neck hinted at his magical order. Then, there was the necromancer I'd once counted as a friend. Josiah stared at the ground, his expression blank, but I studied him with every ounce of hate I could muster and saw he'd sustained an injury. His arm bled from a gash higher on his shoulder. I wished they'd struck him in the heart.

"Good to see you, Meredith," the Ringmaster cawed.

"Can't say the same."

She twirled her hand. "Lovely, isn't this place?"

A lump rose in my throat. "How did you find it?"

"Shifters can be quite useful." The Ringmaster smiled at the burly man next to her in a way that made me think something was going on between them. "One smelled water, but it didn't smell normal. He followed his nose to this place and left us to it. I feel like such a beautiful place is special. Ritualistic. Much more appropriate for our second attempt at magic transference, don't you think?"

While she wasn't wrong on two of those counts, the Ringmaster was dead wrong if she thought I was dying down here today.

"Vampire," the Ringmaster said, as though she hadn't asked me a question. "Guard the top of the stairs. I don't want you smelling my blood."

The male who had carried me here vanished as fast as he'd arrived, and I was in a nightmare once more. Stuck here with a random wolf, Josiah, and the Ringmaster.

"No dilly dallying this time, necromancer," the Ringmaster said. "Take her."

I was about to spin, but caught myself. What would be the point? Even if I outran the wolf shifter, I wouldn't be able to sneak up on the vampire at the top of the steep steps. Instead, I stood my ground as Josiah approached. I could knock him out to buy myself time. Without the necromancer, the Ringmaster would never get what she wanted.

The issue of Sara—who may or may not have been rescued by now—entered my head, but I shoved it out. At that moment, I had to think about myself.

So, I let Josiah get close, let him try to apologize with his eyes, yet again. When he got close enough, he reached a hand out to guide me, and I prepared to fight. But then, his hand bent upward, ever so slightly. Had I not been watching him so closely, I never would have noticed.

Metal glinted inside.

My eyes widened and met Josiah's.

"Don't fight it." He gave a slight nod, his eyes darting to his wrist

Fast as a flash, I reached into his sleeve. A blade *had* been hidden there. The metal cut into my hand, but I took it, yanked it out, and with my opposite fist, sent an uppercut to the necromancer's chin.

"No!" the Ringmaster screamed as Josiah staggered, and I rushed forward, blade at the ready, only to be stopped.

A barrel of a pistol stared me down. Locked and loaded.

"You don't think I'd rely on magical means, did you?" My old boss sneered at me. "If I didn't need your power, I'd put a bullet in your heart right now. But other parts will do—take one more step, if you want to test me."

I didn't. She'd shoot.

The Ringmaster looked at the wolf. "Tie her up. When the necromancer wakes—"

A groan filtered from the door above. Before I could even blink, a blur of motion raced past me. The huge wolf shifter slammed into the wall, hitting it so hard that his skull cracked, and a clatter of metal and the discharge of the gun had me dropping.

"You must be Meredith," a feminine voice rang out, French and musical. "I scent my son all over you."

I glanced up, and my mouth fell open. A blonde woman dressed in skin-tight jeans and a black top with lace sleeves stared down at me. She stood behind the Ringmaster, gripping the woman tightly with one arm. In her other hand she held the gun. Though my old boss struggled to get free, she barely seemed to move in the woman's vice grip. Only a vampire could be so strong. But who was she?

"I am." I rose.

"And I'm Giselle. Tobias's sire." Her lips were ringed ruby and mesmerizing as she spoke.

"How?" I gestured around at the cavern, at a loss for how she found me.

"I was not able to join this piece of trash's team, but I found the shifter she released. He told me where you were—right before I ripped his throat out."

The Ringmaster cried out, and Giselle's fangs popped out. "Quiet."

Wisely, the human silenced, though her eyes still burned with rage.

"I had hoped to find my son," Giselle continued.

"We were ambushed."

"He will be worried about you." Giselle's grip on the Ringmaster's neck tightened and she nodded down to the blade Josiah had given me. It lay on the ground, dropped when the gun had gone off. "Do what you need to do, Meredith, and then we'll find him."

I scooped up the knife, ready to end this for good.

CHAPTER THIRTEEN

SHAY

My sword of fire and light hissed through the air, finally hitting my evasive target. The vampire's head lopped off, and the body fell to the ground. Not wasting a second, I spun toward Hans, but Tobias's guttural roar had me turning yet again. Two more vampires lunged at him.

Shit! My heart leapt into my throat as I weighed the options.

Hans was breathing. Against all odds, he lived. I had to pray he had a few more seconds.

I sprinted for Tobias and didn't falter as my sword rammed through the center of one vampire. As it was made of fire and not a grazing flame, the body ignited, but to be sure, I decapitated the bloodsucker, too.

Tobias took advantage of my arrival and lunged at the last foe, ripping out his neck with a viciousness that both appalled and awed me.

Then, we were alone.

"Meredith," I breathed.

She'd been taken five minutes ago. Far too long. So much could have happened in that amount of time.

"I'll follow her." Tobias looked at Hans. "Does he need blood?"

"Please." I knew it had to be killing Tobias not to run after Rooms, but Shadows and Secrets had a credo. We did not leave people behind. We took care of each other. "Pour it on the wound. I'll do the rest."

Tobias darted over and, before I even joined, his vein opened and blood poured on to Hans's neck. A moment later, the vampire stood. "I must go."

The shifting of air indicated he was already on the hunt. *Please, let him find her in time,* I thought, knowing that wherever Meredith was, the Ringmaster would be too.

Hans groaned, and I dropped to my knees, rolling him closer. "It's Shay. I'm going to pour angelic magic into you."

The vampire blood sealed the wound slowly, but Hans had already lost a ton of blood. He needed any help he could get and my magic might stabilize him enough so that moving him wouldn't be risky.

"Okay, I'm going to start," I said, as much to myself as to him as I pressed my hands to his chest. One exhale, and I released my magic.

Hans cried out in pain and hissed in a deep breath.

"Stop!" Hans gasped, the effort of it tearing at me as much as it did him.

Tears sprang into my eyes. I'd hoped that wouldn't happen. Nephilim weren't healers, but our magic could repair the damage—a little. That combined with the vampire blood should have worked. I'd done it before to others, even Hans once. My magic had never harmed him in the past.

But Hans's demon side was growing stronger and that was changing him. He couldn't tolerate my power inside him. I swallowed the rising panic before it took me over.

Stop, I told myself. *Dad assured me that Hans was good. He is good. He's just . . . Different.*

I looked down to find him staring up at me, blue eyes bloodshot with pain. "No more. Please, Shay."

"I won't," I assured him. "But we're still under attack. I need to get you to the house. A vampire tore your neck open, and Tobias helped so the skin is sealed, but I can't be sure about the inside and—"

"What about Meredith?" he asked, putting an end to my verbal diarrhea.

"She's . . . " The words stuck in my throat. "Tobias went after her."

Hans tried to lift himself, the stubborn man.

"Hans, you can't go! You can barely talk. I won't have it. I —I'm taking you to the manor!"

Hans had at least fifty pounds on me, but there were no other options. I could do this. I simply *had* to.

I squatted and shifted my arms under his bulk, and then rose. It worked—until it didn't. I'd lifted him maybe ten inches off the ground when my arms gave out and Hans tumbled to the ground. I fell too and when I landed, our lips were inches from one another.

My hand had found its way to the planes of his chest, rock hard beneath my touch. Somehow, though we'd spent all day in transit, from Italy to France to England, he still smelled nice. Like mint with a hint of motor oil. Before I knew what I was doing, I inhaled deeply.

Hans's eyes widened. "Um . . . "

Oh my Heavens! What was wrong with me? I cleared my throat. "Sorry. Thought I might have smelled a wolf."

His eyebrows arched. "You can scent those?"

So caught. Nephilim weren't known for their senses, like vampires or wolves.

"I live with Harper, so I can distinguish wolf." I flailed for a semi-believable lie as I shifted away from him. "But I clearly can't lift you. I need help."

"You need to help the others. I'll stay here," he moaned again, hand fluttering to his neck. "I'll be fine."

"No, you won't, and I can't leave you here. There's still fighting. I—"

A rumble behind me had the hairs on the back of my neck lifting. I spun and gasped.

From the woods, a freaking giant was approaching. His lips were set in a hard line and his fists clenched.

This had to be the one who lived in the forest. What had Meredith called it? The anger on his face made me want to run, but I couldn't leave my partner.

"Hans? Do you remember the giant's name?"

"Johnny?" he guessed. "No . . . Not that."

I swallowed as the giant closed in on us. Not trying to anger it more by calling it the wrong name, I waved. "Hi! We're friends with Meredith and Tobias! The witch and vampire?"

Please, let this giant know what I'm saying.

"Jon-Jon know. Who you?" His fists clenched menacingly. "You hurt woods?"

"Never! Hi, Jon-Jon!" I smiled, even though I trembled inside. "I'm Shay and this is Hans." I gestured to my partner. "We're here to help."

"Help coven?"

"Exactly." I sounded breathy. Despite the fact that this enormous being appeared less menacing, I still wasn't sure. Never having met, or even *seen*, a giant, I had no idea how they acted.

"Why he no stand?" Jon-Jon asked after a moment.

"Hans is hurt," I replied, surer now that we stood on even footing. "I need to get him to the manor. A vampire bit him."

"Not friend?"

"No, a different one." I pressed my lips together before going out on a limb. "Can you carry him?"

"Shay! This is unnecessary!" Hans hissed.

I ignored his protest, not about to turn my back on the giant. Hans might not enjoy being carried, but he'd have to deal. I was doing this to keep him safe, and the manor house was probably the safest place at the moment. If it wasn't, they wouldn't have kept the other stone keeper there.

"I help." Jon-Jon lumbered forward.

I stepped aside as he approached Hans and my heart continued thundering. The giant didn't seem aggressive any longer, but I kept my guard up, and was ready to pull my sword from the aether should we need to.

"His neck was hurt," I said as the giant squatted. "Can you be careful of that?"

Jon-Jon nodded and scooped up Hans as if he weighed no more than a small child. My partner shot me a look, but I shrugged and fell into line with the giant as he ambled back toward the manor.

The giant was strong, but he sure as heck wasn't quiet. I figured it was only a matter of time before his crashing through the woods attracted a foe.

I was proven correct as the manor came into sight. A wolf lunged out of the trees, jaws extended and eyes on Jon-Jon, but I had been on guard.

I leapt forward and my sword hissed in the air, catching the wolf's fur on fire. It yelped and twisted, but not fast enough. The next second, I plunged the tip of my weapon into its side.

A whine left the creature's lips as it hit the ground and its body went slack.

"You save Jon-Jon."

I turned to find the giant staring down at me, tears in his huge eyes.

"We're a team." My lips curled up slightly.

The large man swallowed, and Hans cast an alarmed glance upward. "Shay, I don't want to drown in tears."

I snorted. "Jon-Jon, we need to keep going." I kept my voice soft because, even though the moment of vulnerability was sweet, Hans was right. We needed to move on.

"Okay," Jon-Jon croaked out. Though I was pretty certain he had a lot more to say, we rushed the rest of the way through the woods and only stopped at the door to the manor.

I tried it, but found it locked. "Crap."

It was possible for me to sear through the lock with my magic, but then the home would be insecure.

"Someone's inside. That girl," Hans said. "I saw a figure through the stained glass. It has to be her."

"That's not very smart of her."

"Would you be able to hole up in a room with a fight going on outside?"

Fair point. I'd find that impossible. "Okay. I guess I'll . . ." I lifted a fist and let it fall in a knock.

"Who's there?" a feminine voice called out. "I have fire at the ready."

"Good," I said. "Keep it up, but let us in. I'm Meredith's roommate. We work with her and Tobias in the coven."

"Prove it."

I scoffed. "How can I?"

"What's my stone?"

I reeled. Meredith told us this, but so much had been going on and we'd been catching one another up. What had she called it?

"Ruby of Flame," Hans called out. "You're the fire elemental."

The door swung open, and I thanked the heavens he had a better memory than me. My relief was short-lived though because the moment the young woman caught sight of Jon-Jon, she nearly slammed the door in our face. Thankfully, I had fast reflexes and stuck my foot in the jamb before the door could shut.

"Stop! The giant lives here. Hans lost a lot of blood and needs a place to recover. Can you help? Watch him?"

My partner shot me a look, but I didn't stop. Hans would be safe in the manor. Or as safe as anyone in these damned woods could be. I needed to pivot and help Rooms and Tobias.

"Sure." The girl looked at Hans, lingering on his tattooed arms and then his face. I hated that look, but understood it all too well. The bad boy image had major sex appeal, even to a nephilim.

"Shay—" Hans started.

"Jon-Jon, can you set him inside?" I pointed, and the giant reached inside, setting Hans down on a chair inside the entry-way. Not the best place, but as Jon-Jon didn't fit through the door, it would have to do.

The wizard slumped, still clearly beat, but he looked like he wanted to throw down with me as I gripped the doorknob.

I waved. "Stay put, Novak. You're safe here and the coven can get you a blood regeneration potion when someone returns. Right now, I need to make sure Rooms is okay."

Then, much to my partner's great annoyance, I shut the door and went to find my friend.

CHAPTER FOURTEEN

TOBIAS

Every part of me flamed with fury.

Meredith had been taken from me, not once, but *twice*! The moment I was sure Meredith was untouched, I'd rip into the offending parties.

No mercy.

But first, I had to find the fuckers.

The vampire who scooped her up was fast, even faster than was normal for my kind, which meant he left little trail. And Meredith, well, she must have been unable to move, let alone touch a branch along the way. Or perhaps she hadn't considered it. Had she marked a path, I would have already found her.

I stopped for the first time since leaving Shay and took in the night air haunted by screams and the sounds of battle. Blood tinged the woods, witching, shifter, and . . . My spine straightened.

Was that necromancer?

Josiah.

Again, I broke into a sprint. The necromancer would be

with the Ringmaster, and that woman was undoubtedly the one responsible for taking my mate. For bringing the OA here. For . . .

I stumbled.

In New York, the Ringmaster told Meredith that she'd traded Denz for a powerful assistant. Someone with magic, and I suspected that was the wizard S&S turned over to the Covenant in New York. But that wasn't what had me losing my footing.

When I visited my traitorous brother in Italy, I'd seen a pair of sunglasses. Ones that had not matched Raphael's posh style. A niggling thought assured me that I'd seen them before.

And I had.

On top of Denz's head when he attacked my mate in the New Haven museum. Raphael had needed a child that others did not know about. One to do his bidding in the shadows. Why they'd gone after Meredith, I wasn't sure yet. Was Denz simply set on revenge against the woman who'd left him in prison? Or had Wrath already known about her?

Impossible.

The wind raced in my ears, echoing the shouts for help and hissed curses flung at opponents. I ignored them all, making connections as I tracked Josiah.

The moment I rounded the vast manor, I knew where he was. In the distance was the vampire who had taken Meredith.

His body lay crumpled on the ground in front of the entrance to the Enchanted Pool the *Arcacustos* used to identify *Vindix*. His head was a good twenty feet away. Someone had ripped it clean from his body.

I sprinted forward, stopping short of his body, and knelt to study it. One sniff and the hairs on my arms raised.

I knew that scent. Three of them, actually. As I suspected, Josiah was here. As was my mate.

And my sire.

A groan sounded, and the tang of blood fresh from the vein caught my attention. My heart lunged into my throat as an image of Meredith, blood rushing from her body, filled my mind. I sprinted down the steps and when I got to the bottom, stopped short.

My maker stood before Meredith, a blonde woman at their feet—the Ringmaster. Blood pooled beneath the heinous woman who'd once owned my mate. She'd been stabbed. Not Meredith. And that wasn't the only corpse. Another man had been killed, his skull crushed against the cavern wall. Josiah was there too, but I saw no lethal injury on his person.

"Tobias!" Giselle called out, and Meredith spun, her eyes wide as they caught on me. "Good of you to join us!"

I didn't reply; just ran to my mate. The moment I reached her, I swept Meredith up in my arms and pulled her tightly to my chest.

"Are you okay?"

"F-fine," she stammered, but I felt the staccato beats of her heart, smelled the fear radiating off of her in waves. "She's gone."

"I see that." I pulled back, hooked Meredith's chin, tilting it up, and lowered my lips to hers.

Indecent, some might call the kiss, but as my tongue swept her mouth and her hands pulled me closer, I didn't give a damn. I'd almost lost her, my bloodbound mate. For the second time, I'd failed her.

Never again.

"I see that I was correct," Giselle sang. "Mates!"

We broke apart, eyes locked on one another for a second

longer. Meredith's gaze told me she truly was fine, and I hoped mine promised she'd never again be abducted.

"When did you learn?" Giselle placed her hands on her hips.

My bloody sire had always had a nose for gossip. She wouldn't stop until she had her fill.

"Recently." My hand slid into Meredith's smaller palm. "The bond is not in place."

"It will be soon." My sire arched her eyebrows.

Meredith cleared her throat. "Can we not talk about that?" She gestured to the ground where Josiah lay. "He's knocked out but he might wake up and I don't want him to overhear."

A low and dangerous growl rumbled out of me. "I should tear him limb from limb."

"Don't," Meredith said. "He still has crimes to answer for."

I snorted, wanting revenge even if it was against our laws. Back in New Haven, Josiah was an accomplice to murders and the Night Circle Coven of hedge witches would demand their due. That still did not make me care much. He'd harmed my mate and he would pay. In one way or another, I'd have a hand in it too.

"And," Meredith drawled, "what if he can tell us something about the OA that Giselle can't?"

The moment she mentioned the Ordo, I recalled what we'd learned in Scotland. I looked at my sire. "The OA suspects you. Did you realize they retained a team in Edinburgh?"

Shock flashed across her gamine face. "I did not but things have been off for weeks. I need to consider things."

"You shouldn't leave tonight." Meredith's grip tightened on my hand. "Once the fight is over, stay here. Even if you have to say we caught you, don't leave until we've figured everything out."

Giselle's lips twitched. "Your mate wants to get to meet the family, Tobias! How sweet."

Family.

"Have you already sent Serena to visit Raphael?" The words burst out of my lips with greater force than I could have fathomed.

"What?" Giselle's eyebrows pinched together in the middle.

"Serena? You asked her to visit Raphael. Where is she now?"

"Last we spoke, in Prague. She had a few things to take care of and then she was going to Italy. Why, Tobias?"

"She cannot," I said. "Raphael is a traitor. He is allying with Prince Orien." I locked eyes with Meredith. "I believe he is also Denz's sire. Why Raphael turned him, I'm not sure, but it might have been to have a new child with skills. One no one had met. Or perhaps to toy with you—should that prove beneficial?"

Meredith snorted. "Well, it worked. But Denz is the least of our worries." She twisted to my maker. "Raphael also helped bring all seven Princes of Hell Earthside."

Giselle paled. The Ringmaster either hadn't known that, despite having been linked to Wrath, or she hadn't told the OA. Nor had they learned from other channels—at least not yet. I had no doubt they would. In time, I suspected that Wrath or his brothers might even try to ally with the Ordo.

Giselle pulled her phone from her pocket and began typing. A moment later, she met my eyes. "I just texted her. Serena will not go."

"She'll have questions," I replied. "And I don't know how much more I can share. Especially if you leave tonight. I must speak with Luca and the *Abscondita* Coven."

For a moment, silence hung in the air. If my sire stopped spying on the OA, the Blood would call Giselle to Isila and inquire why. But if she remained as a spy, who knew what the OA would do to her? I wished for my sire to remain here, but I knew better than anyone that Giselle Laurent could only be commanded by the royal vampires.

Finally, a sigh parted my maker's lips. "I will stay. You must tell me what I can say to Serena."

"Of course."

"But first, we should go back up," Meredith said. "And finish the fight."

I'd almost forgotten that, above ground, a battle might still be raging. However, Meredith was right. We needed to drive the Ordo Aeternum from these lands and then decide what to do next.

"Shall we bring him?" Giselle toed Josiah, who didn't move. He was still knocked out cold.

"As Meredith said, he has crimes to answer for and he might know something of value." I stepped forward to carry the traitor, but Giselle waved me off.

"I have him. You care for your mate." She lifted the man up and over her shoulder as if he weighed nothing at all.

"Damn." Meredith shook her head. "Sometimes I wish I was a vampire."

"You're perfect as you are," I assured her. "Let us go."

With Meredith in the middle, we climbed the stairs, leaving the Ringmaster and the other body behind. The coven would determine what to do with their bodies. Josiah was the only one I cared about.

When we surfaced, Giselle spared a glance at the vampire's corpse on the ground. "I told him to stand down. Pity he was such an idiot."

"It's quiet," Meredith whispered.

"That could be very good or very bad." I listened hard. The sounds of fighting, so prevalent before, were nonexistent now. Had the *Arcacustos* beat off the OA? Or the other way around?

"Where should we—oh shit!"

Meredith jumped back, knocking into Giselle as a figure dropped out of the sky. One glimpse of white wings assured me that we were fine, though I still scowled at Shay. "A heads up would be ideal. Unless you wish to have your throat ripped out."

Shay rolled her eyes. "I can pull my sword on you so fast, you wouldn't know what hit you." Her attention drifted down the line. "Are you okay, Rooms?"

"Fine."

"She killed the Ringmaster." I could not keep the tone of pride from my voice, but as Meredith cringed, I feared I'd spoken out of turn.

I didn't get to ask why she'd reacted though, because Shay moved forward and wrapped my mate in her arms. "That's *heavy*. But I'm glad you're not in danger anymore."

"No more than anyone else, anyway." Meredith exhaled, and a whirlwind of emotions came out on the back of her breath. Later, I would dive into those. "Where's Hans?"

"I had to drop him off at the manor. He needs a blood transfusion."

Meredith's face paled.

"But aside from that, I think the fight is over," Shay said. "I was flying around and looking for you and only saw older witches and lots of bodies. You said that the people who lived here are all old, right?"

"Most." Meredith nodded.

"Well, they can still kick butt."

My mate smiled. "Let's see if they need help."

The backside of the manor proved deserted, but once we swept round the other side, two particular *Arcacustos* emerged from the trees.

"Bloody tossers!" Gloria rasped from where she lay in Stuart's arms. "I dare that wolf to come back. I'll finish him!"

"First, let's get you seen to," Stuart said. "That leg looks bad. It—hey!" He spotted us and picked up his pace. "You alright?"

"We are," I assured him. "The others?"

"All alive."

"What can we do to assist?"

Stuart nodded to the manor. "Rygor is performing a sweep of the woods. But I assume that one is a prisoner?" He pointed to Josiah.

"He is."

"Then, we should show him to a room. Well-warded, I assure you."

As they'd contained Gunner and Silas in such a space, I didn't doubt that.

CHAPTER FIFTEEN

MEREDITH

We threw Josiah into a room inside the basement, one slightly less comfortable than the ones Gunner and Silas had been confined to when they were—in Gunner's words—'tossed in the dungeons'. The necromancer deserved far worse, but the *Arcacustos* weren't jailers, so I had to settle for what they had.

Afterward, part of our group converged in a small infirmary where Hannah worked on Hans and Gloria, the two fighters who had sustained the worst injuries. Although, if you didn't see Gloria's leg, you wouldn't know she was injured. The woman wouldn't shut up about getting revenge, or strengthening the wards, or hunting down the wolf that had bitten her.

Leaving Gloria to those of the *Abscondita* Coven, I swerved toward Hans's bedside. Shay and Tana were already there, whereas Tobias and Giselle stood off to the side, whispering.

"How is he?" I asked. This close, the smell of herbs and something astringent was much stronger.

"Fine." Tana's eyes locked on Hans in a way that was not

dissimilar to how Hannah looked at Stuart when she thought the sole male *Arcacusto* wasn't looking. "He just took a potion. It knocked him out right away."

Shay's mouth flattened, and she side-eyed the fire witch.

Tana didn't notice. Instead, she looked at me. "You got it, right? The stone?"

The Ruby of Flame. Damn. I'd been through so much in the last hours that I'd forgotten a *lapis caelesti* was in my pocket.

"I do." I pulled out the necklace encasing the stone and handed it to Tana. Carefully, she stroked the gem, and the moment her skin touched it, the ruby gleamed brighter.

"You'll not be sleeping in the same room as your *lapis caelesti*," a stern voice barked as Miriam appeared next to us, her eyes on the Ruby. "Not until you've proven you can handle it."

The unsaid words hung in the air. Tana had accidentally burned down her family home, killing her parents in the process. Had she been better trained to wield the power of such a potent magical object, she might still have a family.

"I understand." Tana's face and voice were tight.

"Speaking of the manor," I started, desperate to cut the tension between the two, even if it meant bringing up another testy subject. "We should really leave this place. Clearly, the OA knows about the coven, and that I'm here. They also know I'm a seeker. They'll want to take advantage of that."

"They could not pick you out of a lineup, though," Giselle interrupted from where she stood with Tobias, reminding me that while vampires might not appear to be listening, they usually were. "They know the Ringmaster wanted you and your magic. That you are a seeker, but not that the Opal belongs to you, Meredith. Nor that you are my son's mate."

She pushed off the wall she had been leaning against. "Speaking of which, we need to talk."

I refrained from groaning. Was this going to be some parental 'you better treat my son right' talk?

"Just as well." Miriam huffed. "Whether we move is a decision for the *Arcacustos*. No one else."

"Uh, if I'm to find the other *Vindix* and bring them to the manor, I would prefer that the location is safe." I folded my arms across my chest and ignored Giselle where she lingered at the side of the infirmary, waiting. "Some are going to need time to learn. They might not even know they're witches—or have that bloodline in their ancestry. This place must be able to provide safety as they prepare."

"Let's bloody hope I'm the one furthest behind," Tana muttered, and while I agreed, I doubted it would be the case.

I hadn't even known I was a witch. Tana didn't know the Ruby and her family heirloom were far more than pretty baubles. The other five *Vindix*, whoever they were, were sure to have gaping holes in their knowledge, too.

"Leave it to us *Arcacustos*." Miriam did not budge one bit.

My jaw tightened, and I prepared to bear down for an argument when a light hand landed on my forearm. "Meredith? If you please?"

I twisted to find Giselle's green eyes watching me, her eyebrows arched.

"Fine." She wasn't going to be put off, and I was wasting my breath with Miriam, anyway. "Let's go."

Together, we left the room, but right before I was out of his sight, I tossed a glance at my mate. He nodded, approving whatever his sire wished to talk about. I sighed softly.

We strolled down a long, dark hallway. The manor was quiet; most people were in the infirmary, or the woods, patrolling for any lingering foes. I doubted they would find anything but bodies, of which there had been an alarming amount. To my knowledge, no one had yet told Miriam about the Ringmaster or the wolf shifter down by the Enchanted Pool. I'd have to remember to do that.

"It was your first kill?" Giselle asked suddenly.

"What?" I blinked, having been so lost in my thoughts.

"Your old boss. She was your first kill."

I swallowed. "Others might have died from my actions. In my old life as a thief I didn't stick around long enough to find out what happened to them. But hers was the first one that didn't feel completely in self-defense. How did you know?"

"The body has many tells. Live as long as I have, and you learn them all."

"I don't regret it, but I also never thought about it too hard."

For many years, I'd been a thief, a tomb raider, a criminal. And while I'd known being in S&S might mean I had to kill, especially in self-defense, I couldn't say that that was what had happened.

Giselle had held the Ringmaster in her arms while I ended her life. She'd been powerless against the vampire, and it had shown. For once, I'd seen true fear in the Ringmaster's ice-blue eyes. I'd been protecting future-Meredith, but I'd not been in danger.

Now, I was a real murderer until the end of my days. There was no way to sugar coat it. No way to turn back the clock. If I was being honest, I didn't want to, either.

With all that was going on in the world, that kill wouldn't be my last. I knew that, but it still hit me harder than I'd been prepared for. It would take time to come to terms with what I'd done and move on.

"Meredith, I realize that you're going through something." She gestured toward the door leading outside and ushered me through it. "But I do not know how long I will stay here and I wish to speak with you about something. It's rather important."

"I figured." I rubbed my hands against my arms. We hadn't been in the manor long, but a chill seemed to sweep the forest. "What is it?"

"You're my son's mate." She began walking down the gravel path.

"I am." As we walked, I tried not to notice the random pools of blood in the dirt, filling the spaces between pebbles.

"Do you understand what that means? To be fated with a Laurent?"

"Tobias mentioned a few things. Mostly that being fated mates within your family is dangerous."

"He speaks true, and in this climate, it might be more dangerous than ever before."

I cocked my head. "How so?"

"King Vladistrica of the Blood Court in Isila is searching for the sacred stones. He set me to find information on them. Now that I have failed and can no longer return to the OA, I must face him." A muscle in her neck fluttered and annoyance that had nothing to do with me flickered across her face. "He is a born vampire and, as such, can compel anyone who came after him. That is, all vampires, but one; his queen and mate."

"You think he'll compel you?" I asked. "But you're close family, right?"

"In the Blood, family means both everything and nothing. You'll soon see that first hand." Giselle swallowed thickly. "For once he learns of Tobias and how he is mated with a witch, you both will be called to the Court of the Blood."

"Is there any way that we can deny it?"

"Not if you wish to live a long life." Giselle stopped. "But you can take a cohort, which I'd suggest."

I stopped and turned to her. Something about Giselle made me trust her. "Could you come?"

"After my failure as a spy, I think it would be best if another came. My daughter, Serena, would be an excellent choice." She leaned closer, and though the vampire smelled of old pennies, there was also a hint of flowers and musk, like an expensive perfume. "Serena is the smartest and most charismatic of all my children. She has talents that compliment Tobias's and would be an asset."

I chuckled. "I won't tell Tobias you called her the smartest and most charismatic."

Giselle laughed freely. "*I* have told him and you can bet his sister has too many times to count. He doesn't mind. Tobias has always liked strong women. You are a testament to that."

Heat flooded my cheeks. I didn't blush often, but there was something about Giselle that made the compliment seem so much more.

"Perhaps taking one or two more would be good too," she said. "Someone with command and power."

"Shay is an archangel's daughter, and Hans—"

"He is of Lilith's blood," Giselle interrupted. "Tobias told me. Both would be excellent choices. There is a wolvea in your coven as well?"

"Gunner. So, you think having a squad of powerful people with a distinguished bloodline would keep us safer?"

Giselle pursed her lips. "Indeed. In Isila, power is everything. A force of varied supernaturals might be what King Vladistrica responds to best. I hope you take my counsel when you are called."

I paused before nodding. "We will. Thank you for looking out for us."

Giselle took my hand in hers. "I love my children. I want them to be happy and will do almost anything for them."

"Even Raphael?" I asked.

Her exquisite face fell. "If it meant saving him from the mess he is in, yes. But will I join him with the devils? No. I love him and hope we can save him."

For Tobias's sake, I wished the same.

"Perhaps we should head back?" Giselle asked. "My son will not want to be parted with you for long. The mate bond grows stronger by the second."

"How can you tell?"

"Mostly, I sense it in my son." She swallowed. "There will be no going back for him, though I would be remiss not to say this, Meredith. Should you two bond and you perish, Tobias will never be the same."

I stared at her, not having expected that, but I knew it was what she'd wanted to say all along. And why not? Tobias had mentioned Giselle's mate had died—how she'd been a shell afterward. She wouldn't want that for her children.

"I have no intention of dying."

"None of us do." Giselle's voice broke, and she turned to hide her face. "No one ever sees it coming."

It was almost dawn when Tobias and I ducked back into the manor. For hours, we'd helped comb the forest, searching for OA stragglers or bodies.

Only two bodies remained.

The Ringmaster and the wolf, down in the sacred pool.

I still had yet to tell Miriam where they were because the leader of the *Arcacustos* wouldn't like the idea of the dead being down there. Though, as Tobias and I entered a dark parlor next to the breakfast room where the others had gathered for a fortifying cup of tea, I could put it off no longer.

I approached the circle. "Miriam, can I have a word?"

"Make it quick. I'm about ready to fall over from exhaustion, child."

With her dark circles, she looked like it, too. Then again, I was sure I didn't look much better, so I did as she requested, unsticking the words from my throat and flinging them at her along with my nerves. "The Ringmaster's corpse, and that of a wolf shifter, are still down by the Enchanted Pool."

"What?" she squawked as I'd known she would. "Why didn't you say anything before? That's *sacred* ground."

"I-I couldn't think about it," I replied, shakily. "Sorry."

Miriam studied me, her chin tilted up, before nodding. She was about to say something else when Tana appeared.

"I can burn the body if you want, Meredith."

I looked at the fire *Vindix* with my eyebrows arched. "Uh, sure?"

"It's . . . . I didn't help during the fight and I don't know what's up with this woman, but I can tell that you want her gone." Flame burst into her palms. "I *can* help with that."

"More training is always a good idea." Olga, the fire witch among the *Arcacustos,* shuffled over with a handkerchief tied tightly over her head.

I cleared my throat, surprised by her offer. Olga had taken her to burn other bodies, but she hadn't seemed at all enthusiastic to do so. Who could blame her? Burning bodies sounded awful.

I cast a glance at the girl and noted the resolve on her face.

But she did seem to want to do this . . . Was the bond of the *Vindix*, some fabled concept I'd read about in the *Abscondita* library, working on Tana, encouraging her to ease my pain? "Thanks, Tana."

"No problem." The fire witches left and once they were out of earshot, Miriam released a sigh.

"Olga told me that Tana's flames lack control and that they could be far more powerful too. That child will take weeks to learn."

Weeks. We might not have that long. Not with the devilish princes in our realm. Suddenly, exhaustion washed over me. More than anything, I wanted to go to my room and lie down.

A hand cupped my lower back. "We should retire," Tobias said. "The manor is secure, if only for the night."

Miriam sniffed, taking offense, but unable to deny that whatever the Ordo had done to render the *Abscondita* Coven's wards useless had worked.

"Giselle, are you staying in the manor?" Tobias asked.

"If I'm welcome." The elder Laurent looked to Miriam.

"I'll ask Stuart to show you to a room."

"One not so close to my son." Giselle had a twinkle in her eye. "I do not want to hear any noises."

Yeah. Right. As if I had the energy for that. More importantly, I needed to consider our bond before acting.

"Let's take our leave before my sire makes any more inappropriate insinuations," Tobias murmured, though there was no anger in his voice, just protectiveness.

I allowed him to lead me to bed.

CHAPTER SIXTEEN

GUNNER

 Silas might have stashed Sara was the very same one Harper found in the fae's ledger. Once Luca gave us the go-ahead, my partner and I hit the road and traveled to the remote cabin in upstate New York. After hours of drivin', we were closin' in on the property.

"Creepy out here, isn't it?" Harper peered into the woods flashin' by.

"You didn't grow up in the woods?" I teased, knowin' that she must have. She was a wolf, same as me. Our kind didn't do well without nature, and her family was well-off enough to have purchased land.

"Forests and mountains surround our pack's property." Harper nodded. "But there's something about being out *here*." She shuddered. "I've felt off since that night the earthquake happened. Not sure why—it has me kind of worried."

I shot her a sidelong glance. Harper wasn't like most wolves. She tended to be more solitary. Sometimes, I thought it had to be because she lived with Shay, and socially the chatty

158

angel gave Harper what she needed—maybe even wore the she-wolf out.

Then, there were other times that weren't as easily explained. Like when she felt something off during the earthquake that coincided with the same time the Princes of Hell rose to Earth.

I shivered. Luca had told us the news—that the earthquake in Italy was way more sinister than the human news had even known. I couldn't believe that Shay and Hans had seen six more princes rise from a lake. One had been bad enough!

Harper squinted down the road. "There's a side lane. I think that's the turn."

Our GPS had long since stopped workin' out here, but I thought she was right about the turnoff and slowed down. I took the curve gently in case there was a fence hidden in the thick trees. There wasn't. All that stared back at us was a ribbon of dark road disappearin' into the woods.

"Roll down your window a smidge. Take a whiff." I put the truck in park and leaned toward the window to scent. Pretty quick, I could tell that nothin' was weird. "Anything?"

"Nothing that I can pick up," she said. "Trees. A bit of autumnal rot, but that's all."

"Same here. Still, we don't know who else Silas might be in league with. Or maybe the Ringmaster is here too. Can't be too careful." I shifted the truck into drive again and got on with it.

The driveway was long and rocky. My truck jostled in a way that told me I needed to take a gander under the hood. Or maybe ask Hans to. That man knew how to make a truck purr. That train of thought lasted until we got to the end of the lane and my headlights illuminated a cabin. I parked and killed the engine.

"Looks like a dump." Harper got out and shut the door softly behind her. "I can't see Silas owning this."

"Me either, truth be told." I followed my partner, eyes takin' in the scene.

"Anything now?" Harper scanned the woods.

"Not a damned thing," I replied after taking a few deep whiffs. "Should we shift?"

"Not yet. At the first sign of trouble, I'll shift, but you should wait on it. You're a better fighter than me in this form."

"Girl, you're gonna make me blush." Harper rolled her eyes, and I couldn't help but smile harder. Compliments from this chick were rare as hens' teeth, and I ate them up when I got 'em.

We inched closer to the cabin. No lights blazed from inside, though I could tell someone had been here. Footprints in the dirt marched the same way as us. They weren't made that long ago, either.

"I'll open the door and you barge in?" Harper whispered when we got to the threshold. "I have your back, if you need teeth."

"Got it."

"Ready?" Harper placed her hand on the knob.

I shifted into position, ready to scoop the knife from my boot. "Waitin' on you."

Without hesitatin', she flung the door open. I ran into a pitch-dark room and nearly bowled over from the awful stink.

I gagged and stopped moving. The room was dark, so I couldn't see anything yet, but I heard nothin' and only smelled the rot. When my vision adjusted, I scanned the room, assessin' it in a second. "Empty."

"Go deeper," Harper urged, her tone tight—probably 'cause she was trying not to breathe in the rotten stench. She shut the door behind us, trappin' us in with whoever or whatever might be inside. "Judging by the size, this is a three-room shack."

I agreed and trekked forth slowly. Below my feet, the floorboards groaned and one bent. "Watch your step."

"This place is a death trap waiting to happen," Harper replied. "Do you smell her?"

"Too scared to breathe deep?" I retorted.

"Honestly, yes. This is rank."

I took one for the team and inhaled, nearly puking as the rot filled me. Maybe if I was a wizard or fae, it wouldn't be so bad, but I doubted it. If Sara was here, I felt bad for the girl, having to live in this.

"Nothing still," I said as we approached a door that, most likely, led to a bedroom and opened it.

No one leapt at us, or attacked, and when the door creaked open enough for me to slide on in, I did, but only made it two steps before I froze.

"Those fuckers," I growled, taking in the figure on the bed.

Sara had been tied up so that she couldn't move and left on a dirty mattress covered in filth. She seemed to be sleepin', though how she managed I had no idea.

"By the Old Ones," Harper breathed. "She's so thin."

The girl was already slender, with not a lot of reserves to use up, and now she'd gone and eaten through most of those reserves. Had they fed her at all since she'd been captive?

"You wake her," I urged.

"She knows you too, Gunner."

"I'm a big dude. That might scare her, first thing."

Harper nodded and approached the bed. Sara didn't stir, and Harper's lips spread into a thin line as she stood over the necromancer, studying her more closely. Slowly, she reached out her hand and laid it on Sara's boney shoulders.

Our covenmate's eyes flew open, and a cry left her throat before Harper could release the young woman.

"It's me, Harper. We're here to save you!"

A strangled sound that made me want to punch whoever had hurt Sara left her lips.

"This isn't a trick?"

Hell on wheels, what had they done to her?

"No trick," Harper whispered. "Gunner is here too."

Sara cut a glance at me and a little tension left her face, only to be replaced with a mortified expression. "I'm so sorry, you guys. I stink. They only came once every couple of days and I had to . . . and they never let me clean up."

The assholes who took her didn't even let Sara use the toilet.

"It's fine." Harper waved off her comment.

"It's not. You're *wolves*." Her cheeks went scarlet.

"We don't care," I affirmed. "We need to get you outta here. Let me help."

The shame didn't leave her face as we untied the ropes around her arms and feet, and that only made me angrier at whoever had treated her this way.

"Sit up slowly," Harper said once the ropes fell to the floor. "The room might spin."

Sara nodded and did as Harper said. She'd just sat up right, when I caught the first whiff of trouble.

Sulfur. That scent was burned into my mind from Hell, and I'd been reminded of it when we checked out Sara's place. Now that I knew all seven Princes of Hell were on Earth, it was easy to believe demons were all around us, all the time. Even here, in the middle of nowhere.

My jaw tightened, and I cut a glance at Harper, but my partner was so focused on Sara she hadn't noticed.

"Ladies." I kept my voice soft, not sure where exactly the reek came from. "We need to get outta here pronto. Someone is coming."

Harper stiffened, her nose lifting into the air. The truth registered almost instantly. "Demon?"

At that Sara went white as the moon. "No!"

"Do demons check on you?" Harper helped Sara off the bed and caught her when her knees buckled.

She'd been locked up for days and given little food. Still, should she have been so weak? Or had they been doin' other things to hurt her?

"A Hellblooded witch did. She's not powerful, but she's always armed. After Silas took me, demons brought me here, though."

"Well, I hate to break it to you, but there are *more* demons in this realm now, so they might be taking over for the witch." Harper said, and together the girls took a few steps. "We—"

The door to the shack flew open to reveal a hulking, horned beast straight from the underworld. I'd seen this kind before. It was one of the big ones that worked the fields in Hell.

I spun and threw the truck's keys to Harper, who caught them with her free hand. "Run."

"We can't leave you!" Harper retorted. "The code!"

My fists tightened as the enemy approached. S&S decreed we left no member behind, and normally I followed the rules. But not today. Not with Sara bein' so frail.

Even on the best of days, the necromancer wasn't a great fighter. While I'd take Harper's help in fightin' off a foe any day of the week, Sara would slow us down. And who knew how many more monsters lurked in the woods?

"You gotta," I said, and as if to prove my point, Sara fell to the floor, limp as a wet dishrag.

My partner scooped her back up, a frantic look in her eyes. "I can't even mind-link with you! How will I know if you're okay?"

"Run!" I yelled as the demon charged. "Drive back. I'll be fine."

"*Dammit*, Gunner," Harper shouted, but I didn't have time to argue with her about how things should be done.

The demon roared again. It was almost upon me, too close for me to shift, though that would be the best way for me to fight. Instead, I pulled out the knife hidden in my boot and slashed at the monster.

My blade struck gold, slicing across its neck. A dying roar burst from its lips and five other cries echoed it in the woods. Dammit. Just our shitty luck that there were others close by.

"Go!" I hollered. "I'll cover you."

Harper released a frustrated sound but did as I asked, runnin' past me with Sara in her arms. I followed, all my senses on high alert. The moment we burst outside and two more demons appeared, lingering on the edge of the woods, I wasn't at all surprised.

"I've got 'em," I growled as Harper threw a concerned glance my way.

"Luca is gonna be pissed!" She charged the truck and extended the fob. The truck lights flashed on, and I prayed Harper would get Sara inside to safety.

The next second, the bi-pedal monsters were upon me, and I swore. Blade clutched tightly in my hand, I stabbed at the closest monster first. The attack was effective enough for him to back off, but the other one kept on comin'.

Too bad for that ugly sucker, I was ready for him, too. I

ducked under an oncoming claw, twisted, and sank the blade between his eyes. Like a ton o' bricks, the beast fell.

The other demon roared, its eyes wild and wide. In that instant, fur sprouted on my arms, legs, everywhere, and I fell to all fours as a wolf. A deep, predatory growl rumbled out of me.

In this form, I was much shorter than the other monster, but my teeth and claws made up for that. Baring the weapons of the wolf, I prowled forward, and the demon took a step back.

A honk sounded. Harper backed up, telling me she was leaving, callin' out my chance to join her.

But as the demon turned tail and ran into the woods, I loosed a howl and laid chase. I wasn't backin' down tonight. Or ever. I'd track this demon to the edge of the world, and Harper would have to go on without me.

'Cause tonight my wolf was runnin' free and huntin' for blood.

CHAPTER SEVENTEEN

HARPER

THE SOUNDS OF CLANGING METAL STARTLED ME AWAKE, AND I jerked up with a groan. My back ached. My neck too, and I soon learned why. Apparently, I'd fallen asleep as I'd watched Daphne heal Sara and the chair I was in was not the most comfortable.

"Should have scooted my butt to one of the empty beds." I rubbed a tweak from my neck.

"What was that?" Daphne bustled out of one of the back rooms where the healers brewed potions, concocted salves, and did whatever else they had to do to save the lives of S&S.

"Just sore. Should have laid down."

"I doubt you expected to stay the night."

I hadn't. Old Ones, I hadn't even expected to sleep, but somehow the adrenaline from leaving Gunner to his own devices against demons and then driving through the night must have worn off, and I'd crashed.

"Is Luca in the tomb?" I asked, ready to get down to business.

"He arrived last night, shortly after you fell asleep. Asked me for a wakeful potion." Daphne shook her head. "I don't think the man slept a wink, nor did he intend to. He's in his office waiting for you."

A wakeful potion . . . What was going on? Had Luca heard from Mer and Tobias? Or Shay and Hans? I shook myself, trying to stay on track.

"And Sara?" I gestured to the bed where the necromancer slept. "Has she woken?"

"Not since we washed her." Daphne's nose wrinkled. The job of bathing Sara had been atrocious and made me want to punch in faces. Her captors had neglected her, and she'd been covered in filth. "But I did give her an IV last night. It had a potent sleeping potion mixed in because she needed *real* rest, so she'll probably be out most of the morning."

"Have you done a scan?"

"Yes. I'll perform a more thorough one when she wakes, but she's fine. Dehydration seems to be the worst of it."

"Glad you had those bags on hand." I stood and stretched.

Daphne snorted. "Some healers eschew modern medicine, and to be fair, some of it *is* complete shit, but it has its good points. Just like witchery."

"I'll go see Luca, then. Holler if you need me to help with anything else."

"You've done enough." Daphne's pity-filled eyes fell on Sara. "I'm glad she's not in danger anymore."

"Me too." Before things got too emotional, I ambled to the door. "See you later."

Entering the hallway, I listened. The coven tomb was quiet. I hadn't asked Daphne for the time, but I guessed very early, which was good. I might feel like hell on wheels, but I had classes today, and even though my enrollment at Yale was largely a cover, I hated falling behind. It grated against my perfectionist nature.

With each step, my legs and arms came to life a little more and the kinks in my back worked their way out. By the time I reached Luca's office, I almost felt normal.

The door was shut, so I knocked.

"Come in," Luca called.

When I opened the door, my mouth fell open. Luca stood at his espresso machine, making an Americano, but he wasn't alone. Gunner sat in one of the leather-bound chairs, his shirt in tatters, and a red welt on his cheek.

"How did you get here so fast?" I exclaimed, relief sweeping through me.

Before I'd passed out, I'd been so worried about Gunner, but every time I'd called him, his phone had gone to voicemail.

"Just got back," he drawled. "I hitched a ride back from a wolf in one of the local packs."

Ah, of course. We were both alphablood, but he was also wolvea and the moment most wolves met him, they recognized that distinct power from the other world. It was hard to explain to those who weren't wolves, but he sort of vibrated on a different level.

"Please never ask me to leave you again." I crossed the room and slipped into one of the four leather chairs Luca used for less formal meetings.

Gunner leaned forward and the scent of him, woodsy, musky, totally male, mixed with blood of the night before and dirt, filled my nostrils. The mixture made something deep within me warm, but I shoved it down before it could rise. Gunner was hot, no denying it, but he was also . . . a lot.

I didn't need that. Or want it. My lady bits might sometimes proclaim otherwise, but it wasn't happening. Not if I had anything to say about it, which I did. Alpha Ferenz was hard as nails and traditional in a lot of respects, but my father didn't believe in arranged marriages for pack gains.

"It couldn't be helped, Harp." A crooked smile crossed Gunner's lips.

True. There was no way I could have fought and saved Sara, but leaving him still pained me. I hated letting others down.

"Never again," Luca reiterated, as his espresso sputtered into a cup. "You two broke code, You had a good reason, and Gunner got out okay, but we have rules for reasons."

"Okay? I *annihilated* six more demons!" Gunner shook his head and leaned back. As he did so, the tears in his shirt shifted, gifting me with a stunning display of abs.

I averted my eyes, feeling hot all over again.

"It's concerning that there were so many." The machine finished and, with a cup of espresso in hand, Luca joined us. Only then did I notice the dark circles under his eyes. "And that's not the only thing that concerns me."

Thankful for something to focus on other than the hot wolf —who surely must be giving off pheromones because I wasn't usually so susceptible to him—I turned to Luca. "What's that?"

"Silas."

"He's still MIA?"

"Yes, but that's not what I'm worried about. It's the vow all members make when they join S&S."

The one to not harm anyone in S&S, which Silas had done by abducting Sara.

"While I am not the best potion-brewer in the coven, I consider my skills to be quite good," Luca said. "And knowing what we know of Silas's arrangement with Raphael—how he owed the elder Laurent money—presumably for smuggling him into this realm, Silas might have been sent here to watch Tobias. Spy on him, even. How did the potion I create not detect that the fae had less than pure motives?"

I'd seen the potion the mage spoke of, drank it myself, and I'd also witnessed when others ingested the brew and it exposed their ill intentions. That had not happened to Silas.

"I wouldn't know about the potion workin' or not," Gunner said. "But regardin' your idea 'bout him spyin' on Toby. Why would he do that?"

"To hear Tobias say it." Luca sipped his espresso. "He and Raphael have not been close for years. Perhaps his elder brother wanted to know why. Or perhaps he was already on a downward spiral and knew the coven to be powerful and, therefore, wanted to keep tabs." Luca took another sip of his coffee. "But right now, I'm more interested in how Silas tricked the potion. There are potions that might inhibit it, but the one I use is quite strong."

"Could a fae glamour do that?" I asked. "One that would have allowed him to hide his motives?"

Luca's eyes widened. "I suppose it's possible. Usually, glamours are physical, but perhaps one might tweak their intent. I'll have to research that." He shifted his body toward me. "As there's no way to figure that out now, let's move on. Is Sara alright? I popped in a few hours ago, but things might have changed."

I gave them the rundown on Sara's prognosis, reciting what Daphne had told me. Both men appeared pleased by my update, and by the time I finished, Luca was smiling.

"You two did well. I—"

My phone rang, the sound loud and shrill in the relative

quiet of the tomb. I rushed to pull it from my pocket and silence it, but one look at the screen and my heart dropped.

"It's my mother. And it's so early in California . . . I should get this." I stood and rushed to the door.

"Of course." Luca nodded.

I let myself outside and picked up the call before it went to voicemail. "Hey, Mom." I shuffled down the hall for privacy. "What's up?"

"Oh, baby. I'm so glad I got you. You weren't sleeping?"

"I was already awake, but why are you? It's the crack of dawn there. Something is wrong, isn't it?"

A long pause followed, telling me I'd hit the nail on the head.

"*Mom.*" I dragged out the word.

"It's your father," she said. "He was attacked."

"*What?*"

No one in their right mind would attack Alpha Ferenz! What in the world was going on?

"I told him to be careful, baby, but you know your father— he's not one to take a challenge lightly."

The pit that had formed in my stomach when I saw her name on caller-ID deepened. "What do you mean?"

"A group approached us, Harper."

"Who?"

"They call themselves the Darkborn."

"Fuck!" I roared.

On the other end of the phone, my mother gasped and muttered, "Harper! Language!"

Behind me, Luca's door squealed open. I turned to see both Gunner and the mage poking their heads out.

"Are you okay?" Luca's dark brown eyes widened.

I shook my head, but motioned for them to leave me alone.

This was pack business. And S&S business too, I supposed, but for now I could think only of my family.

"What did they say, Mom? And what did Dad do?"

"They—they're looking for wolves to join them, baby. They didn't tell us much, but I get the sense that they want a fight. A big one."

She was right that a fight was coming. A whole damned war was. Though I hadn't expected the Darkborn, followers of Wrath, and probably the other Princes of Hell, to act so fast.

My father was legendary. An alpha that others did not cross. And though I hated to dwell on it, he was sometimes cruel in a way I was sure the princes would *love*.

That begged another question. Had they approached Gunner's father, too? I'd ask as soon as I figured out what was going on. "What did they do to Dad?"

"When your father said we wouldn't help—"

"Wait, he did?" My voice rose in surprise.

"I told him about your warning and . . . " She trailed off for a moment. "Baby, I need you to come home. We need to talk."

That stunned me.

"Your father is badly injured. He—he might not make it." Her voice broke.

"What the shit, Mom? Why didn't you say so sooner?"

My insides were a mess. This was the worst time to leave the coven, but we were talking about my family here. My father was, apparently, so injured that Mom feared for his life. Considering he was an alpha wolf with heightened healing abilities, that had to be really bad. Not only that, but the Darkborn had been to see the pack.

The two dominant aspects of my life were colliding, and I despised it.

"I'll come," I said. "I'll book a flight today. But I have to go tell Luca now."

"Of course, baby. I'll be waiting." She drew in a long breath. "I love you."

Why did I get the sense that she was hiding something else? I shook my head. It didn't matter. I'd be home soon enough, and I'd wring all the information I could from the pack then.

"Love you too." I hung up the phone and swallowed down the lump rising in my throat.

The last few hours had been an utter shitshow. I returned to Luca's office, and the moment I entered, I had both guys' attention.

"My father was propositioned by the Darkborn. He denied them—only because I said something a few days ago. I guess they beat the crap out of him. I have to go home. My mother isn't sure he'll make it."

Gunner let out a low whistle. "I should call my pa."

"You should." Luca nodded. "If they went for Alpha Ferenz, there's no reason why they wouldn't go for Alpha Bryant. But I think you should go with Harper, Gunner."

"What?" I froze where I stood. "Why?"

Was Luca crazy? Gunner was from a rival pack, one that was the only competitor to my own in the country.

"Two reasons. The first being, if the Darkborn return, you will want backup. Someone who knows what's happening. The public knows that New York was under a magical attack, but largely, they do not know why. We cannot speak on any matter relating to the demon princes until the Covenant makes the announcement, but it will be easier with Gunner there," Luca explained.

"I can take care of myself." I blinked, still confused.

"The backup isn't just for you. Family is the most important thing." Luca's voice dipped, revealing emotion that he rarely showed. Then again, he never spoke of his family. Only recently did I learn he had a twin sister who lived in New York, a woman that, among the coven, only me, Tobias, and Meredith knew about. The city was only a short drive away and after what happened Luca must have been thinking of his twin more often. "Take the extra protection, Harper."

"And the second?" I pressed, even though the first reason was more than good enough.

"You come from a smaller city, correct?"

"Yeah, mostly supernatural. My pack was designed in that way."

"If the Darkborn found such a place and already targeted a prominent alpha, don't you think they'd explore more? Look for powerful witch covens or lone vampires who might be swayed to their side. The demons are here, there is no doubt, but the more backing they have, the better for them. There's no telling where they will need assistance to maintain power—if they get a foothold, which I'm sure we can all agree is their plan."

Of course. Why leave one kingdom if you did not wish to expand? In the underworld, the Princes of Hell had everything they needed. They *wanted* to come here, to rule over others, to expand their power to the human world. It was not a necessity, but a desire. And after they'd accomplished that, then what? Maybe they'd try to take Isila?

"But what about demon hunting around here?" I asked. "And learning more about Silas's past?"

"The coven is large and others will hunt demons. Sara is safe, so the most important task is complete. I will soon be traveling to England, so I'll ask Dan and Gus to help. I'll have them hack into cameras in the city and surrounding airports. Soon enough, we'll have a location for the fae."

I stood there, stunned. "Is everyone okay across the pond?"

Luca nodded. "They are. I spoke with Shay in the small hours and things are under control, but I do wish to monitor the situation. I can't share more now." Luca's voice stayed calm and smooth.

I had to take that for what it was.

Mer, Tobias, Hans, and Shay were fine. Luca wouldn't lie about that.

"Well, let me call my pa and make sure he's okay," Gunner said. "If they're fine, I'm happy to go with you, Harper."

"I have to admit, I'm a little worried to bring you to the pack."

Luca looked stricken. "Your packs are competitors, but surely it won't be bad?"

"It'll be alright," Gunner replied.

Uneasy, I shifted my weight. Mom would be okay with it. She'd trust me and understood the ways of S&S, like my siblings and Dad's betas did, to some extent. But the rest of the pack? They didn't know much, if anything, about my coven. They thought I was at Yale for an education only.

In fact, considering the pack alpha was injured, and I'd be coming home with a wolvea, I had a terrible feeling about all of this, but it also appeared I didn't have a say.

CHAPTER EIGHTEEN

HANS

I OPENED MY EYES AND GRABBED AT MY ACHING NECK, ONLY TO flinch when I touched it. What the fuck had happened? Had someone throat punched me a dozen times?

"You alright, there?" asked a woman, making me jump in shock.

I twisted to find that I was in a bed. But not one I recognized. The girl sitting in the chair next to me was unrecognizable too. Dark hair, amber eyes, and . . . who was she?

"Have we met?" I blinked rapidly and took in the young woman's amber eyes. They were mesmerizing, alight somehow.

"Hit yer heid too, did ye?" The woman set a book she'd been reading aside and stood. "Tha' angel girl said ye got a vampire bite but dinnae mention a bump on the heid'."

Vampire bite. Angel girl. I sucked in a breath as the memories of the night before came rushing back. I'd been out of it, but I remembered the giant transporting me and Tobias pouring blood on my wound. That was why the skin on my neck seemed fine. Someone must have given me one hell of a sleeping potion for me to forget all that.

"Her name is Shay," I said. "But I still don't remember yours."

"Hurts me to the quick, too. I took care of ye when she dropped you on the doorstep." She smirked, hinting that she was playing around. "But I suppose it's not too unthinkable. Ye were a right mess." She paused, and I arched an eyebrow, which made her chuckle. "Och right, I'm Tana. I'm also a *Vindix*, 'n holder of the Ruby of Flames, which, in case ye forgot, means I 'ave tae help Meredith save the world." She shrugged. "That's what they tell me, anyway."

I took in everything she said, and the pieces clicked into place. All except one.

"Why are you here, Tana? Are you a healer, too?"

Her cheeks turned pink. "I got up early and had nowhere to go, but I knew this area, so I came here."

I cast a glance around the room filled with potions and herbs hanging from the ceiling. Healing areas weren't my first choice of places to hang out, but to each their own.

Slowly, I sat up to lean against the headboard. Only then did I realize I had no shirt on, a fact that Tana seemed to latch on to.

"You have a lot of tattoos." Her eyes lingered on my chest where ink traveled down from my sleeves.

"I do."

"Do they mean anything?"

"Some. Others I got when I arrived in America because I was young and stupid and play acted like a man." I shifted and my neck twinged, making me wince. The rest of me felt fine, so I hoped my neck would soon follow.

Tana smirked. "Once, I pierced both eyebrows and my nose at the same time. Came home and me mum had a fit. Threw a bowl of stew against the wall. You should have seen the stain."

At that, I laughed. The girl was so random and chatty.

The fire witch smiled. "You have a nice laugh. Glad the vampire didn't wreck your vocal cords."

"He does, doesn't he?"

I jumped to find Shay standing in the doorway to the healing room, a cup of coffee in both hands and a scowl on her face.

"Am I interrupting?" Her voice held an icy tone.

"Uh, no." My brow furrowed. Why did she look so pissed? "I'm glad you're here, actually. I want to be caught up."

At that, her face softened and Shay stepped up to the side of the bed. "Let me look at your injury."

"Are you a healer now?" I teased.

"I can tell if a mauling from a vampire looks better or not." She set the coffees on the side table and leaned over me.

The scent of roses and something sharper, citrus cut with ginger, filled my nostrils. It was delicious.

Before I could lose myself in the aroma, she turned my chin and laid soft fingers on my injury.

"That okay?" she asked.

"Yeah."

She exhaled, and I knew why. Last night her magic hurt as it spread through me. She'd probably assumed a touch might twinge too. I had.

But no . . . Her mere touch didn't burn or irritate my skin. Not like skin-to-skin contact had irritated me when I carried her father from Lake Como. Was it because her father was a pureblooded angel and Shay had some human in her?

The question disappeared as Shay's fingers trailed the line

of my neck, almost as though she were caressing me, though I knew she was examining the wound. But when her hand stopped and moved on my jaw, stroking it, I wondered if I was wrong.

"I think you're good." Shay cleared her throat. "The skin seems healed, not thin or anything. And I'm not using magic, but I don't sense any corruption."

"Hard to compete with a half demon." I flinched when she cringed.

Why had I said that? We were working on mending our differences, and Shay was trying to be gracious. Why let my own self-worth issues get in the way?

Uriel's talk of accepting myself flitted to the front of my mind. It was something I needed to work on, for sure. Especially seeing as Richard Fucking Brons hated me and I was never getting my wizarding magic back, this was my new normal.

"Here." I shook myself and found Shay holding out a steaming mug that appeared to be handmade. "I can get you something else if you don't like it—personally, I'd kill for some oat milk—but I was pretty sure this was how you took your coffee."

"Or I can get something," Tana piped up. "I'm a great barista!"

Shay's jaw tightened. The reflex was so small that, had I not been watching her, I might have missed it. What was going on here?

"Unnecessary." I took a sip of coffee, touched that she remembered what I liked to drink. "This is great."

"Good." Shay brought her cup to her lips.

"Tell me what happened after that giant dropped me off."

Shay filled me in, and when she got to the part where

Meredith killed the Ringmaster, tension lifted from my shoulders. That was one enemy down. Too bad that, by all measures, the Ringmaster was the least powerful.

"Where's Josiah now?" I asked when she stopped.

"Locked up downstairs," Shay replied.

"I want to see him." I moved to get out of the bed, but Shay stopped me and pressed her hand against my shoulder.

"You sure you're okay?" She didn't remove her hand.

The heat of her sank into me, warming me even though I hadn't felt cold. As if just noticing her lingering touch too, Shay's cheeks turned pink, and she withdrew. I regretted her absence immediately. "Maybe I'm moving too fast. Should I get one of the older witches to check on you?"

Now that I'd been sitting up and moving about, I felt better. Mostly normal, so I shook my head. "I want to question him."

"Can I come?" Tana asked.

Shay and I exchanged a look.

"Not a good idea," I said. "This is Shadows and Secrets business and we'd have to clear it with our Coven Master. Sorry."

She looked dejected but not confused. Someone must have told her about Shadows and Secrets—that she wouldn't be privy to all that we discussed.

"I'll go to that library then." She threw a wave. "See you later, Hans. Maybe we can 'ave lunch together?"

"Uh, sure," I said, somewhat shocked.

Tana brightened and let herself out of the room. She couldn't have gone far before Shay snorted. "She likes you."

"What?" I blinked at her in confusion.

"The girl, well, I guess she's like nineteen or twenty, so not a girl, but still. She has a crush on you." Shay's nose wrinkled as she spoke.

Did Shay not like Tana? Why? She seemed alright to me, charming and light and fun.

"I think she has no friends," I replied, checking that I had boxers on before I stood, stretched, and searched for a shirt and pants.

"Here." Shay glided over to a dresser and pulled a robe out of the drawer. "Your clothes are in the wash. They were covered in blood. Put this on."

She handed me a long, white robe that made me feel silly, but I did as she said, glad we were off the subject of Tana.

"Just so you know," Shay added, "the witches here saw your wings. Miriam saw them while you were awake, and the rest while you were passed out. Somehow, maybe because your body was uncomfortable laying on them, you banished them while you slept, but not before the coven saw them."

I stiffened. "And? What do they think?"

"That you can conjure wings." She shrugged. "We only told them that you're a wizard. And there's no reason for them to think you are anything else. Certainly no one will guess the truth, not when S&S didn't for years."

I exhaled. "Thanks."

In time, I'd have to tell this coven the truth, but I far preferred to ease my way into that.

"It's your tale to tell. Also, I didn't mention it earlier." Shay leaned against the wall as I tied the sash around my waist. "But I already spoke with Luca, before everyone went to sleep. He wants me to come get him later and then to go see Flamel. He wants his own luxiter, which is a pretty good idea."

"Guess Flamel will get more demon blood," I muttered.

"Luca said he'd bring something of value. No idea what, though."

I tensed. "Nothing from his vault?"

The most dangerous items that S&S found were put in a vault that only Luca and one other person could open. Another mage. I'd never met the person, but had personally unearthed some of the items in the vault. They were valuable as hell, and most were just as terrible.

They had nothing on the Pearl of Hell, of course, but I still didn't want to see them in the wrong hands.

"No way!" Shay assured me. "He'd never do that. He took a vow never to harm."

I believe that, believed in Luca. But I still couldn't fathom what he'd bring . . .

Shoving down my curiosity, I joined the nephilim at the door. "Lead the way, Shay."

Though I'd been in the manor all night, I hadn't been conscious for any part of that, so everything was new to me. The place was dark, like the S&S tomb, but much older. Paintings of deceased members of the coven that lived here hung on the walls. The images went back a couple of hundred years.

"They've been here all this time?" I murmured, awed at the history of it all.

"I guess." Shay gazed at me and the pictures on the wall before she shrugged. "I haven't had time to learn who they are or anything. Meredith called them the *Abscondita* Coven. Do you remember that?"

"Vaguely."

She looked worried, and I aimed to lift her spirits. "I'm fine. Sore, but okay. I'll be ready for another battle by tonight."

She groaned. "Let's hope not. I'm kind of glad we're

getting Luca 'cause I want to bring him back here too. He can help with warding—I can too, like we did at my place."

Smart. Mage magic was rare, as was nephilim magic, and few people knew how to break their enchantments. When used together, the chances of someone breaking the wards were even smaller.

"Do you think the witches will be okay with that?" I asked.

"They probably won't like it 'cause it means they have no control, but what are they going to say? 'Please don't keep us safe?'" Shay arched her eyebrows. "They tried to ward their property, and it didn't work. Now, the OA knows where they are located, so the protections have to be stronger. I might even ask Luca if he can make this place unfindable to all those except the people with markings. Or a password. Something."

That left one niggling issue. There was always the option that stone keepers would come here and be drawn to this place. After all, lore told us that the stones wanted to be together. How would the guardians find the manor if it was so well warded?

Shay led me down another corridor and stopped suddenly. "I'm lost," she announced. "Sorry, I thought I—oh shit!"

A door swung open behind her and out popped an old witch with a red kerchief over her head and a scowl on her lips. "What are you doing out of bed?"

"I'm healed."

"Says who?"

"Uh . . ." My voice trailed off.

"You should have stayed in bed!" Her eyebrows knitted together as she studied me. "Where are you from, boy?"

"Romania," I said and, as her face softened a touch, I sensed a weakness, so I sought to take advantage. "Listen, we're looking for the necromancer your coven locked up. I need to speak with him."

"The traitor?"

"Yeah," I replied.

The woman cocked her head, seeming to think it over. "I will show you the way. You shouldn't be lurking around our halls, anyway. Most of the manor is off limits to you."

I cut Shay a glance, but she shrugged.

"Okay, thanks," I replied as the woman shuffled from her room and waved for us to follow her. "What's your name?" I only remembered Miriam Black because that name had been burned into my mind since Tobias went to *Le Bastion*. Had I met the other witches?

"Olga. I'm the fire witch training the new *Vindix*." She looked back at me. "You're a wizard?"

My heart stuttered. Should I tell her? I studied the harsh lines of Olga's face, trying to discern how she'd react.

Not yet. I wasn't ready to tell them who I really was yet.

I nodded. "I am."

"I've never seen our kind conjure wings." She paused. "You must be powerful."

"Years of practice," I replied lamely. I'd tell them the truth, just not yet. I wanted to get the measure of this coven first.

Olga seemed content to lead us the rest of the way in silence. We followed her through a couple of dark corridors and then down a set of stairs.

When we reached the bottom, I sensed the wards on the hallway. Josiah must have been close.

"He won't attack and try to escape?" Olga asked.

"No," Shay said. "I don't think so."

I didn't either, though if I had my way, Josiah wouldn't be in the room for long.

"Alright, then." The witch took a key from her pocket and stuck it in the lock to the closest door. My eyebrows shot up, and she caught the gesture. "It's no normal key, boy. Filled with enchantment."

"I wasn't going to say anything."

"You didn't have to." Olga swung the door open. "I'll be back in my room. Shut the door when you leave. The enchantments will reset. They're specific to necromancers, so you two will be fine should you need to use magic."

The OA had broken through their wards, but I was still impressed. Order specific protections were advanced.

"Thanks," Shay said, assuring Olga that we had it from here. The fire witch left us, and we stepped inside.

My nose wrinkled. Though the room was pleasant enough, it smelled of stale dirt, probably because Josiah was lying asleep on the bed, covered in mud.

"Why is he so filthy? They should have thrown him in a dungeon, not put him in here."

"They don't have one. And found him knocked out in a cavern," Shay replied.

Fucking hell. I had missed so much thanks to the damned vampire attack.

We approached the bed, and still, Josiah didn't wake. Fueled by anger at what the necromancer had done to the witches of The Night Circle and Meredith, I didn't care to wake him up gently. I slammed my fist on the bed, right next to his head, and Josiah yelped and shot straight up.

When he saw us, his dark brown eyes widened, and he pushed back, as if Shay and I were going to attack him.

"Chill." Shay's tone was hard. "We want to talk."

"You're not—not going to kill me?" Josiah asked, voice incredulous.

"What good would that be to anyone?" I shot back. "You have crimes to answer for. People who deserve justice. Plus, I have questions and you *will* answer them."

"Anything." Josiah held up his hands innocently. "I'll answer anything. I didn't want to do what I did. I—"

"Shut it!" Shay screamed, her face turning red. "Unless you're answering a question, I don't want to hear a word from you. Got it?"

Josiah's umber skin paled slightly, but he nodded vigorously.

"First off," Shay started, "Did you know about Silas?"

"Yes." Josiah sat up and nodded.

"Uh, more please."

"He didn't work for the Ringmaster, but for someone else, but they're still connected in a way. I think they did a deal and Silas was part of it. He actually took Sara—" At the mention of his girlfriend, Josiah's voice broke.

"You know they found her, right?" Shay asked, and when I shot her a shocked glance she added, "Luca told me when I called about the luxiters."

"Are you serious?" Josiah's eyes widened and filled with hope. He looked about ready to break into tears. "Was she hurt?"

"A little." Shay's eyes softened. "Dehydrated and covered in filth because she was left alone for a long time. It's still early, but Luca said she'll be okay. She's with the coven."

A tear slid down the necromancer's cheek. "Everything I did was for her. Did you know they took her first because her necromancer magic is stronger? I bet the Ringmaster made Silas take her and not me, even though he had to have told her about how Sara wouldn't harm a fly. Everyone knows how she is. I'm still pissed that he did that."

"And when Sara didn't use her powers, then they hung her life over your head," Shay finished.

"Did Silas let the shade into Shadow and Secret's tomb?" I asked, already moving on. Sara was safe and that was all that mattered on that score. Here, there was information I needed before I got to the point.

"He did. I don't know how he got it in there. It's not typically a fae power, but he has talents that we didn't know about."

"S&S you mean," I corrected. "You're no longer a part of us. There is no 'we'."

Josiah cleared his throat noisily. "Of course. The coven."

"How much time did you spend with the OA?"

"Not too much. I saw one of their headquarters, though. We stayed the night there while the Ringmaster told them about Meredith, and they figured out where she was."

"Using tech?"

"Yeah. They have a system that's," the necromancer let out a long exhale, "it's vast, man. Bigger and better connected than the one Shadow and Secrets has built. They can track almost anyone on the planet."

Fuck. The OA knew where we were, anyway, but this information meant that moving wasn't necessarily an answer. Then again, staying in one place might have been worse. We'd talk to Luca about it.

Among other things. Like the liberty I was about to take. "Could you get back into their headquarters? Without the Ringmaster?"

Josiah's lips parted. "They seemed interested in my magic."

"Good," I said, "because that's one way you'll be earning your penance. You, Josiah, are to act as a spy in the OA."

At my side, Shay stiffened.

"What? But if they learn, they'll kill me!"

"Then you'll have bought days, weeks, even months of freedom. Life too, maybe, considering how angry The Night Circle was that you killed their witches."

"I didn't!" Josiah's eyes widened.

"They don't care," I said. "They demand justice, and they'll be given it. So, that's your choice." I paused so it could sink in, "Spy on the OA for S&S. Or we'll deliver you to the hedge witches in magical chains."

He stared up at us, eyes pleading, but neither Shay nor I flinched. Finally, Josiah opened his mouth. "I'll do it."

"We'll be back later. Expect to undergo a Vow of Intent so we're sure you can't back out."

I turned and Shay followed. The wards on the room acted as Olga had said, not stopping us as we saw ourselves out. When we were in the hall, Shay waited until we were out of earshot before turning to me.

"Luca didn't approve of that, but I think you did the right thing. Tobias's sire was a spy in the OA and feeding Stiff information. Now, she can't do that anymore, so Josiah might be one of our best options. If they let him back in."

"I'm sure they'll want him. A necromancer is hard to resist," I said. Being one of Luca's right-hand men had certain privileges, and Luca would see how valuable a spy would be. I was certain of it.

"Sure. Meredith is gonna be super pissed, though."

I cringed. Tobias would be, too. I didn't look forward to being on the receiving end of either of their reactions, but I'd deal. "If Luca agrees, and he will, everyone will fall in line. Josiah will give us valuable information. And when he does, maybe we'll have a fucking leg up against what's coming."

CHAPTER NINETEEN

MEREDITH

stretched, arching my back, only to have my butt hit something hard. I froze.

"Forget where you are, love?" Tobias's voice rumbled with laughter and the tension left me at once.

I *had* forgotten where I was and *who* slept next to me. The vampire had refused to let me be alone last night and while I wasn't ready to deal with the mating bond, I'd wanted the company. After killing the Ringmaster, being alone sounded horrible. Just the memory made me shudder.

"Hey." Tobias gently placed his hand on my back and trailed down the lines that the Ringmaster had made there. "Are you alright?"

"I am." I turned to face him. My gaze dipped to his muscular chest, bare and lickable. Tobias hadn't slept, but he sure had made himself comfortable in my bed, stripping down to tight, black boxer-briefs.

"What happened?" His green eyes filled with concern.

I drew my attention back to his face and forced a smile. "I remembered the Ringmaster."

"A kill is always a hard thing to deal with. Whether it's your first or your hundredth."

Hundredth? The question of how many people he'd killed was on the tip of my tongue, but I stifled it.

Tobias wasn't a man, but a vampire. That order had different rules, and they were often more draconian. No matter what his number was, it wouldn't change anything between us.

"And that woman was a monster." His hand snaked around me, landing again on my thin scars, and a low growl rose in his throat. "I studied the marks she left this morning. If she wasn't already in Hell, I would have loved to send her there myself."

I hummed, not sure what to say to that. The Ringmaster was dead by my hands and, while I had trouble with some aspects of that, I wouldn't have wanted anyone else to do it, either. She'd been my monster to slay. "Is anyone else up yet?" I changed the subject.

"It's late morning and Shay awoke some time ago. I heard her walk down the hallway and she has not returned. I expect that she's gone to check on Hans," Tobias said. "Benedict has been padding around outside for an hour, too."

I rolled my eyes.

"If he wants to be closer to you, he can have my room, instead of the one he claimed earlier," Tobias said. "I don't plan on using it any longer."

That got my attention, and I sat straight up. "You're inviting yourself to share *my* room?"

He smirked, rising as well. "Is there a problem with that?"

Had he been any other man, I'd have played it cool. Told

him I needed space. But with Tobias, what was the point? The soulmate bond hadn't even snapped into place, yet day by day, I grew more attracted to him, more in need of him. I didn't want to be apart, so why play like I did?

The world might end at any moment. I didn't want to see my end, not having been truthful to the literal man fate made for me.

"No," I said. "But *asking* would be nice, you cocky ass vampire."

"If I wasn't a touch cocky, I wouldn't be the man you know, now, would I?"

The question wasn't meant to be answered for the next moment. His hand cupped my face and he leaned in. Our lips met and mine burned beneath his touch. The heat traveled downward, sizzling through my body and lighting me up inside.

A soft sigh left me, and Tobias took that for what it was, an invitation.

His hands threaded into my messy hair, making my heart beat erratically and my breath thin. When he pulled me closer so that the hard planes of his chest pressed into me, a surge of desire washed through me.

"Allow me to relieve you of this, Miss Stone." Tobias's voice all gravel and grit and desire as his hands dropped to the hem of my t-shirt. My skin simmered where his slender fingers touched it, taking his time as he dragged the material up.

"Bit drafty in here," I murmured as my nipples puckered in a way that had nothing to do with the chill.

My body hungered for him, had for a long time. My soul did, too. The prospect of getting what I wanted was enough to send my magic flying through my veins, energizing me in an unfamiliar way.

"You're chilled?" He arched an eyebrow, taking his time to revel in my naked torso as if I was the most beautiful creature on the face of the planet. His attention burned so intensely and his naked desire so mirrored my own. I couldn't hold back a second longer.

"Hmmm, warming up." I leaned in, kissing him again, biting his lower lip and pulling until he groaned. I smirked, enjoying getting the upper hand for once, and released.

"Let me see if I can't warm you up then, love."

I was about to remind him I wasn't quite ready to go all the way—and perhaps snap our mating bond into place. Not yet. I needed time to process everything that entailed. The good parts and the dangers.

But Tobias wasn't about to push me. Instead, his hands slid down, fingers slipping under my panties.

Deft fingers found my center, already drenched for him. A low rumbled, pleased sound parted his lips as he slid inside.

I tilted my head back, a foolish move, considering he was a vampire, but no fangs came. Lips, soft and insistent, covered the expanse of my neck instead, moving from jawline to shoulder bones as his fingers found a rhythm inside me that made my back arch into him.

"You're *mine*, Meredith," the vampire whispered. "Always remember that. I will protect you at all costs. Do anything to please you."

I swallowed as his words swelled to fill the room. An epic promise if there ever was one. The bond between us had been strengthening, but when it formed what would change? How would we feel differently? Already, I was his, and he was mine, and the feelings were intense. Far more intense than anything I'd ever felt for a man before.

Again, I reminded myself that Tobias wasn't a man. Not a

human one, anyway. And I wasn't a human woman. Whatever happened between us would be far more intense than what I'd shared with other lovers.

The idea both thrilled and terrified me.

"And you're mine, Tobias," I breathed. The power in the words filled the room, charging it. "All mine. I—"

My breath was stolen from my lungs as Tobias's thumb slid to the nub at my center and circled.

Vampires are far superior to human men, I thought as the pressure inside me built. The tension between my thighs coiled as Tobias's fingers played me like a damned fiddle.

"Come for me, witch." He snarled, lips going to my ears, whispering in them, biting just enough to be dangerous but not drawing blood. "I need to feel your pleasure, to smell it, to taste it."

My heart rate, already racing before, spiked. It was as if my body could not help but follow his command. Stars filled my vision as I came and leaned into his body, short on breath and clawing at his back.

"Good girl," he purred, maintaining his rhythm until I stopped shuddering, until I could see straight.

I peered down his back, a limp noodle of a woman. A tattoo of a snake, coiled and ready to strike, stared back at me. I lifted my fingers, tracing the snake.

And to my surprise, Tobias stiffened and pulled back to stare into my eyes. "It's the sign of my royal house. All Laurents within three generations of the natural born vampires are branded with the house crest."

I swallowed. After my talk with Giselle, the House of Laurent was now a source of anxiety for us. Eventually, the royals would demand that Tobias and I come to them, and in their world, they held all the power.

Well, not here. Not between us, I thought, my fingers digging into my mate's skin possessively. If those royals thought they might frighten us, or even tear us apart, they had another think coming.

"Fuck them," I murmured. "Fuck them if they try to tear us apart. If they try—"

His fingers pressed against my lips. "Forget them for now. Please."

Looking deep into his eyes, I could tell that Tobias didn't want to think about the havoc the Court of the Blood might wreak on our relationship. How they might use me to force him to do something he didn't want. I kissed him again.

A low growl came from him. "Honey."

"Hmm?" I asked, our tongues dancing together, our skin sizzling where it met.

"You taste so strongly of honey, love," Tobias's eyes met mine and crinkled at the corners with mischief. "I wonder, are you sweet everywhere?"

Before my orgasm-addled brain could come back with a remark, he dove beneath the covers. I sucked in a thrilled breath. "So much attention. A girl could get used to this."

"You haven't seen the half of it, my mate." He hummed. "We can do without these."

Two hands landed on my hips and spread. A ripping sound filled the morning quiet as he literally tore my favorite red lace cheekys off.

I gasped and my skin tingled where his fingers danced along my upper thighs. Good god, I was on fire!

"You owe me new panties."

"I'll buy you a bloody truck load."

I gasped as Tobias's tongue met my center, soft and teasing. "Oh, shit."

"To your liking?"

Liking? It was as if the floodgates of lust had opened between us. Would we even get out of the room today?

"Good god, yes. I—" I stopped as his tongue trailed the line of a very prominent artery in the inner thigh. "Tobias?"

"I'm in control." He ripped the blanket off, allowing me to watch him. His eyes were alight with lust, but seeing him eased the trickle of anxiety that had spiked inside me. "As delicious as your blood smells, I won't bite unless you allow it. Until then, I only want to worship you."

Oh, good God. I'm a fucking goner.

"Relax, Meredith," Tobias urged. "Let me know you."

So, I did. I leaned back, and again, he caressed me with his fingers and tongue. Second by second, my body loosened.

Below, Tobias's green eyes flashed upward, locking with mine, and a rough chuckle left his busy lips. He was smug as hell and he damn well should have been. Never, in all my twenty-one years, had I felt like this. So alive. My every cell sang.

Then, the song built, nearing a crescendo, and I couldn't fucking believe it. I'd had multiple orgasms before, but this fast? Never!

But the body wanted what the body wanted, and as the wave of euphoria washed through me, I let go, wrapping my hands into the vampire's hair.

"Tobias!" I screamed, and stars filled my vision once more.

Slowly, the wave of pleasure died, though my heart rate remained fast and my breath thin. When Tobias pulled back, I sighed and closed my eyes as my mate lay next to me. When I opened my eyes again, he was there, propped on one elbow, smiling down at me like the devil himself.

"How was it?"

I snorted. "You know you're amazing. By now, other people might have heard too." Heat rose in my cheeks. I'd screamed. Surely, Giselle had heard us. What about the others?

"We can't worry about them. But I love to hear how amazing I am from your perfect lips. Tell me more."

I grabbed a pillow and aimed it at him, but the vampire stopped me before the pillow made contact. He leaned in, brushing his mouth with mine. "You tasted as I thought you would. Sweet and spicy and perfect. My perfect mate."

My heart fluttered. Would I ever get used to that word? Mate? It was supernatural, of my new world, not my old. Plus, it was so much more than a girlfriend. Even heavier than wife. It was a word that, before a few days ago, I never would have considered using for a romantic partner, but it fit him, *us*, so perfectly.

I cupped the side of his face, my fingers tingling as his sharp cheekbones pressed into my palm. "Time for me to plea-sure you, my *mate*." My hand twisted through his hair, pulling him closer.

"Meredith," Tobias whispered, stopping my lips an inch from his. "Not today."

My mouth fell open. "You don't want me to?"

"Oh, I want you to very much." Tobias's voice dripped with desire. "But more than that, I want you to be sure, to know that after a release, a vampire is almost certain to bite their partner. As for a mate, it is how we seal our bond. Of course, I am not sure we can say the same for our specific bond —you being a witch, and all—but it might be. You need to be ready for that."

I paused. The time Denz had attacked me rushed to the forefront of my mind. That had been terrifying and it hurt, but surely when Tobias bit me, it wouldn't be the same, so I pushed it away. Tobias was not a newblood, even if he had, in his own words, exhibited bloodlust during the early days of our relationship.

So much had changed since then. Unlike when we first met, when he'd tried to dominate me again and again, I trusted Tobias, trusted that he could stop. Back then, he'd only lusted after my blood and it would have overridden any attraction, which was all we'd had. Now, however, I knew he wanted me, as his mate, not just for my blood.

"I understand." I nodded. "I'm prepared."

Tobias cleared his throat and placed his hand on mine. "I'd also prefer my first release with my mate to be when we are making love. For that, I can wait."

Oh. I looked down, not sure what to say, but Tobias hooked my chin, dragging my eyes back up to lock with his.

"You're coming to terms with what we are and how a vampire will act. I have lived a long time, and now that I've found you, I'm in no rush. You, Meredith, will be worth the wait."

My throat tightened. I'd had a few lovers, none of which were ever serious; it was hard to have a relationship with a professional thief. The men I'd been with had all been respectful, some more than others, of course, but they weren't dicks.

And yet, Tobias was in a class of his own. He put them all to shame. If I wanted to wait years, he would.

Not that I wanted that—not at all, but having the option made me feel all kinds of things. Valued. Safe.

Loved.

I threw my arms around him, pressed my lips to his, claiming this man for mine on this very day.

When we broke apart, I smiled. "Thanks, Tobias. For everything."

The words 'I love you' flitted through my mind, but I wasn't ready for that either, so I squeezed his hand and hoped he felt the love growing within me.

CHAPTER TWENTY

TOBIAS

The hour neared noon when Shay pounded on Meredith's door and announced a meeting. In truth, though I was accounting for the late night and the healing of others, it surprised me that calling a gathering had taken so long. I was surprised, and yet, I could not find it in myself to regret the stolen hours with my mate.

As Meredith and I entered the large dining hall to find the others already gathered, I prepared to put pleasure aside for a few hours, perhaps even days, if things had already taken another turn for the worse.

"Sorry to keep you waiting." Meredith's voice rose.

I squeezed her hand, and she threw me a soft smile that had me licking my lips.

While I'd always found Meredith to be beautiful, the attraction was growing stronger. Now, the witch was not simply lovely to look at, but appealing beyond my wildest dreams. She tasted of honey and her every mannerism, glance, and breath seemed designed to appeal to me. Once I'd started worshipping her body, I'd found it difficult to stop.

She hadn't seemed to mind. My lips curled in a self-satisfied smirk as I recalled the expression of ecstasy on her face, the way she'd screamed my name the last time she'd come. My cock twitched, and I forced myself to pivot to pure thoughts. It was nearly impossible. That was until Giselle cleared her throat.

I caught my sire's eye, and she arched a knowing eyebrow. Bloody hell, I probably reeked of Meredith, and the moment we were free of this meeting, my maker would have a million questions.

My family was nosey, though this time I'd be hard-pressed to shake the questions off. If our mate bond snapped into place, Giselle would be required to protect Meredith, too. No doubt she took that responsibility as seriously as I did.

And Giselle didn't seem to be the only one watching us as we crossed the room to two chairs in the middle of the long table. Shay's eyes twinkled with curiosity, and Benedict, who perched on the table in front of one of the empty chairs, glared at me with narrowed eyes. I had a feeling that when Giselle pulled me aside, the nephilim and Benedict would do the same to Meredith.

"Now that everyone is awake and given a clean bill of health," Miriam Black started, "we should discuss how to proceed."

I pulled out Meredith's chair, pushing it back in when she sat down next to Shay. As Benedict slipped into Meredith's lap, I took my place between my mate and my sire. The table seemed divided into halves, with those in the *Abscondita* Coven sitting on one side and S&S members, Giselle, and Tana on the other.

"Aya and I took advantage of the light and performed yet another sweep of the woods earlier." Stuart rested his hands on the table. "No one was hiding, and there were no more bodies to be found."

"Thank the Goddess for that," Olga muttered. The old fire witch had been up half the night, burning bodies. "I'm not ready for another night like the last."

"But you are anticipating it, correct? Preparing?" I leaned forward.

Claire, the steel-haired Irish witch, nodded. "Of course, we are. The Ringmaster might have failed, but why wouldn't the OA want a seeker of their own to find the other stones?"

"Agreed." Meredith pursed her lips. "We can assume that the OA will want the stones, now that the Ringmaster told them who has them. Eventually, the princes and their Darkborn might even start working with the OA against us. Their aims align well enough."

"The Court of the Blood as well," Giselle added lightly.

"How so?" Gloria's voice turned raspier than normal.

Her injury appeared healed, though I suspected she'd stayed up most of the night, replaying how to repay the person who'd injured her. The woman was a spit-fire if I'd ever met one.

"As I mentioned before, I spied on the OA for the Blood." Giselle sighed. "Now that my cover is blown, I will have to report to my kin. Which brings us to one important matter." My sire leveled the witches of the *Abscondita* Coven with her gaze. "This was brought up earlier, to no resolution, but I have to reiterate that it would be foolish for you all to remain here. You need to find a new place to conduct business and train the *Vindix*. If the King of Vampires wishes, he can see into my mind—see this very place."

Each *Arcacusto* flinched, but Miriam recovered first. "Our decision has not changed. We will remain."

"Do you have a death wish, old woman?" Giselle asked. "Surely, you have heard of the Blood. If the king sees this place, he will come. He will not hesitate to take your knowledge or the *Vindix* to find the stones."

"The *Vindix*? What would he do with us?" Tana, who sat at the far end of the table, leaned forward, eyes wide with terror.

"First, he'd use you to find all seven stones. Then, once he had them, and you, in his possession, he'd make you wield their power in his name. Perhaps you'd be a blood slave too." Giselle shrugged. "The vampires of Isila are a different breed than those here, child. More savage by far."

"I'm not a child," Tana retorted, which only made Giselle smirk.

"Either way, you do not want any of my royal bloodline to come here." Giselle's voice darkened in warning.

"Then, we'll further enhance our wards." Miriam swept her hand around the room. "We spent part of the night and much of the morning doing so, but with time we can put even greater protections in place. The more varied, the better. Perhaps the nephilim can help?" She looked at Shay.

Shay leaned forward. "I can. And Hans and I have an even better idea. Two, in fact."

"Go on, then." Miriam waved for her to continue. "I'd rather not die here waiting."

"First off, you allow the necromancer to leave and become a spy for us. Hans and I already spoke with Josiah and our coven master. Josiah has agreed to spy on the OA, but you have to release him."

The members of the *Abscondita* Coven shared glances. They didn't trust the necromancer. After what he'd done, I didn't either, but I also knew Josiah.

He'd done terrible things but was not bad at heart. If given a chance, he would work to right his wrongs. For me, the biggest issue was how he'd hurt Meredith.

The idea of him getting close to her again made me want to punch a wall. I wasn't sure I'd be able to get anywhere near the necromancer without having a strong desire to rip his throat out.

But use him as a spy? Yes, I'd do that.

"Was anyone going to ask me about this?" Meredith spat out. "You know, as the only surviving person Josiah basically *hunted*? You don't think I deserve a say in this? Because I do and I'd much rather him go to trial and have someone related to the victims deal with him."

"Rooms," Shay whispered. "It's not what we'd typically do, but it *is* a good plan."

Meredith glowered at her friend, but Hans interjected. "It was my idea. If you want to be mad at someone, do it here. But I stand by my choice because as long as Josiah complies, this is the only thing that could give us an advantage." Hans's gaze shifted to me. "I bet Tobias thinks so too."

Meredith turned. The apples of her cheeks were still red with anger. "Do you?"

"I am inclined to agree that this will give us an edge." I reigned in my ever-simmering anger at the necromancer. "But if you wish for me to stand with you, I will. Always."

Her soft lips pursed and, though I did not think she was aware of it, her fingers floated up to her collarbone. The line the necromancer cut into her skin was barely visible. In a few more days, it would be gone, but the pain of that moment would stick with my mate forever.

"Meredith?" I whispered.

"Fine," she replied. "A spy is useful, but I swear if he puts one toe out of line. " Her eyes narrowed as she let an unspoken threat hang in the air.

"What if we let him go, and he vanishes?" Olga asked wisely. "Even if he does not want to work for the OA any longer, why would he wish to put himself in the middle of what's to come? The Princes of Hell have risen, young ones. A war will follow."

"I have that covered," Hans said. "We make him swear a Vow of Intent so he can't betray us without losing his power." He rubbed his neck. "And someone escorts him to the Ordo's headquarters."

"Which looks like a job for me." Giselle leaned back in her chair. "I cannot get too close, but I can go with him to a point. Scare him into submission."

I doubted that was necessary, but I wouldn't deny my sire the privilege.

"And your second proposition?" Miriam prodded.

Shay folded her hands on the table. "I can help you reinforce your boundaries, but you'll need more. Lots more. I want to invite our coven master here."

"*More people*? Sounds like a bad idea," Gloria muttered.

"He's trustworthy," Meredith interjected. "And a powerful mage. You want his help."

"I need to go see him later today anyhow." Shay tapped her fingers on the table. When Meredith and I gave her a questioning look, she continued. "He wants a luxiter too. I'm taking him to the Coven of Illumination to buy one."

The question of what Luca was bartering in exchange for a valuable luxiter flitted through my mind, before Giselle cut through it.

"Seeing as Shay has already invited someone, I should mention that my daughter will arrive here today."

Each *Arcacusto* stiffened. Aside from the *Vindix*, they didn't want visitors, had balked even when I insisted on staying, and now people kept pouring in.

And more might still, if we get this land protected well enough. This bit of woods might become a haven for many.

I wasn't about to say that out loud, though.

"What use could we have of your daughter?" Claire asked diplomatically.

"Serena is skilled at tracking and hunting. She's a vicious fighter and extremely intelligent too. She would be excellent protection if anything else were to befall this land."

"Would it be necessary with an enhanced ward system?" Miriam challenged.

Shay shrugged. "You can't be too careful. That's already been proven."

And it had. No matter how well Shay and Luca wove their magic with witching magic to protect this manor, land, and any *Vindix* who might arrive, there was always a chance someone more powerful would strike and tear their protections to pieces.

"If the other *Vindix* arrives unprepared, like Tana has," Olga spoke up, "then you're correct. We will need the help to protect them until they're ready."

The question of when that would be hung in the air. Tana, at least, knew how to use fire, but she wasn't an elite fire-wielder. Nor did she understand how to use the Ruby yet.

"It's best to assume you will receive untrained witches," I said. "Meredith, too, did not know of her heritage until she joined S&S. If you start from there, then you can create a plan to educate them as rapidly as possible."

"Which means you'll be busy and require Serena's help," Giselle dug in again.

No one argued. No one even spoke, though I could guess by the twitching of Miriam's left eye that she wished to argue. Instead, however, the old witch stood. "It's settled then. We're staying at the manor. The necromancer will leave, and more will come to assist. If that's all?"

No one looked inclined to piss the *Arcacustos* off any more.

"I believe that's all." I nodded.

Without another word or a glance at me, Miriam left the room.

The others of her coven followed until only the members of S&S, Tana, and Giselle were present.

Meredith let out a long breath. "I feel bad. We're making them bend to our will."

"Times of turmoil require people to bend or they break. The elder witches had better get used to it." Giselle turned to Shay and Hans. "Now, why don't you introduce me to that necromancer, so I can get moving?"

<hr>

SEEING AS HANS NO LONGER HAD ACCESS TO HIS WIZARD MAGIC, we had to recruit a caster to perform the Vow. Luckily, Gloria seemed to want to do anything but rest further and jumped at the chance.

The members of Shadows and Secrets and Stuart helped her down the stairs. Stuart, aside from being the dominant air elemental in the coven, was also the second best warder, after Miriam.

When we reached Josiah's door, Stuart turned. "If I lift all the wards now, the magic will take better. Is that what you want?"

"The Vow has to stick, so yeah," Hans said. Though he

cringed anytime he mentioned a Vow of Intent, he also seemed to have taken up the mantle for the effort.

Stuart got to work at undoing the wards and the air filled with the faint scent of honey. Hans watched the wizard, a forlorn expression on his face, and I was glad when Stuart finished. I felt bad for the bloke, but Hans needed to get his shite together and lean into the powers he still possessed. Who knew what time we had before we met with another opponent?

The door swung open and the necromancer himself jumped off the bed and his eyes locked on my mate.

"Meredith! I'm so sorry! I—"

Before I could even consider stopping, I shot forward and grabbed Josiah by the neck.

"Tobias!" Meredith shouted. "What are you doing?"

But I couldn't answer her, couldn't do a thing except glare down at the necromancer who had tried to take my mate's magic—the creature who had been willing to risk her life.

"If you want to live, don't talk to her," I snapped. "Don't touch her. Don't look at her. Don't think her name. Don't even bloody *breathe* in her direction. Do you hear me?"

"*Breathe*?" Shay whispered, her tone incredulous. "Oh, shit. Tobias is going all mate-protector."

"Stop!" Meredith tried to place herself between me and the necromancer, who gasped for air. Wisely, Josiah averted his eyes. "Tobias! He's going to pass out and we need him."

I snarled. "Josiah, do you understand? Blink twice if you do."

Two quick blinks followed, and because I did not wish to upset my mate more, I released the necromancer.

He drew in a wheezing breath and turned his back on my

mate, but not before Meredith's fist shot out and slammed into his stomach.

I smiled darkly. "Don't we need him, love?"

"Of course, we do," she retorted, "but it was *me* he was going to kill and I deserved a shot, too."

"Okay, okay." Shay stepped closer to Josiah, who bent over with his hands on his knees, struggling to pull in air. "He did something horrible, but no more beating on him—at least for now. We need to get this Vow done and move on to other things."

"Like?" Meredith placed her hand on her hips.

"Training Tana. Which I assume will include you." Shay shrugged. "Hans has to work through some things, and I need to go to New Haven to pick up Luca."

"Right." My mate rolled her shoulders back. "Big day. Let's get on with it, then."

Shay walked over to Josiah. "Hey, we need you to make a Vow of Intent so we can be sure that you won't screw us over."

Josiah coughed a few more times before he straightened. For the briefest moment, his eyes glanced at Meredith but quickly snapped away.

Behind me, Giselle laughed so softly I was sure the others hadn't heard, but I had. I'd meant every word of my threats, too. If he so much as took another step closer to Meredith, I wouldn't be liable for what I did.

"What does that entail?" Josiah asked.

"It's a promise that you won't screw us over," Hans snarled. "If you do, you forfeit your magic."

Josiah paled, his gaze still on the ground. "I don't think—"

"Well, too fucking bad!" Meredith shot back before he could finish. "I don't think I wanted to have my magic stolen, but that nearly happened. Your power won't go aways unless you betray us—*again*. You have a choice in the matter, so be a man and make the right one this time."

The necromancer winced. "Fine. I'll do the Vow. But who is gonna take on that responsibility? Most people wouldn't want my magic."

Gloria cleared her throat, and Hans stepped forward. "Gloria is casting, but I'll be the binder."

Questions entered Josiah's eyes, but he was either too scared or too smart to ask why Hans wasn't taking care of the casting himself.

"You'll have to walk me through it." Josiah allowed Hans to lead him a few paces away from me and Meredith. The Hellblooded wizard then gave a brief explanation to Gloria and Josiah and the pair linked hands. Hans placed one of his on top of theirs and the binding promise began.

"Goddess, hear me." Gloria spoke loud and clear. "Bind Josiah's word to Hans Novak. Ensure his intention is true. That his promise is of the light, not the dark. Should he go against his promise, tie his magic within him to be released only at Hans's will."

Light funneled around the trio as Gloria chanted the words again and again. My hair lifted and the skin on the back of my neck prickled. I'd never witnessed a Vow before and was surprised to feel so much. It must have been even more intense for Hans, because his eyes closed.

When he opened them again, they glowed a brilliant gold. I sucked in a breath.

"The Goddess has accepted the bargain." Giselle sighed, as awed as me. "Do you, Josiah, agree to spy on the Ordo Aeternum, on behalf of the Coven of Shadows and Secrets? Do you swear to do nothing to harm any coven members and work only for them and their aims?"

"I agree," Josiah said without hesitation.

A brighter light wreathed their hands. The illumination seeped between their fingers and then began to pulse.

Hans tilted his head back, as if experiencing some type of miracle. I had to admit, though I was no witch, as the light swirled around and the power of the Goddess encompassed us, it was the closest bloody thing I'd ever felt to a divine moment.

The moment that power vanished into the air, Hans's eyes met Josiah's. Josiah's no longer glowed.

"Forsake us," Gloria said, "and you will live forever without your magic."

Josiah shook his head. "I have no intention of betraying anyone."

"We'll see about that." I grabbed Meredith's hand and walked toward the door. "Get cleaned up. My sire will take you to the OA when you're ready."

We entered the hallway, but before we even got up the stairs, Giselle's heels sounded on the wood floor. "Tobias? A moment?"

I tightened my grip on Meredith's hand, a gesture my sire did not miss. Her eyebrows arched high. "I'm afraid I'd prefer to speak with you alone, my son."

Meredith nodded. "I need a moment alone anyway, before I go to the library. Tana needs training, and I should study more too."

Right, the forbidden library. Only the *Vindix* and the *Arcacustos* earned the privilege of entry. Already, that rubbed me the wrong way; now, I wouldn't be allowed to be near my mate when our bond was so close to being set. That put me on edge. And yet, she had to go.

"Good luck today."

"I'll see you later." Meredith kissed me on the cheek and then left. With every step she took, the urge to run after her grew.

"My dear, you are in trouble."

I exhaled, turning to Giselle with considerable effort. This was only getting worse by the minute. "I know."

"It will be less pressing once the bond is in place. Not immediately, but eventually. Within weeks."

"It's difficult to believe."

"In a way, the bond reassures you. Don't get me wrong, Tobias, you'll still be protective and always want her, but it won't be so overpowering. Which brings me to why I wanted to speak with you."

I nodded, urging her to continue.

Giselle cleared her throat. "After I drop off Josiah, I must seek the Blood. They will interrogate me and call for you and I've been thinking—"

"You already told me this," I interrupted her as the irritation of being away from Meredith grated on me. How was I going to deal while she studied all day?

Giselle chuckled delicately. "Let me get to the point before you do something hasty." She exhaled. "When the Blood calls, Tobias, you must either be bonded to Meredith or have left her. For good."

My stomach sank at those words. Just the idea made me feel wrong—empty. The only other emotion was the violent urge inside me rearing up to challenge anyone who even suggested such a thing. I quelled it quickly. Giselle might look delicate, but she was my sire, stronger than me, and could control me in a second.

"Why?" I asked, tension riddling my voice.

"If you have forsaken her and truly mean it, the Blood will take no action against her. If you are with her and do not take her to Isila, the Blood will capture her. Expect them to *always* find a way. Of course, I do not expect you to leave her, but it is an option." She squeezed my shoulder. "I only wanted to bring it up because I care for you and wish for you to be safe. Now, that extends to her too. No matter what you choose, I will be there for you."

There was wisdom in my sire's words, but I'd never be able to leave Meredith. If the Blood demanded I take my mate to their violent court, I wasn't sure what we'd do, but I knew one thing: separating would tear my soul to bits.

CHAPTER TWENTY-ONE

SHAY

THE DAY HAD LASTED A YEAR, AND IT WAS ONLY MID-AFTERNOON.

And somehow, I still haven't gotten the hot goss, I thought, swinging by the corridor where the exclusive, fancy-pants library was located. Meredith and Tana had been hidden away there since Josiah took his Vow, but I had it on Stuart's authority they'd soon break for lunch. So, I leaned against the dark wooden wall, content to wait. As it turned out, I didn't need to wait long.

At the end of the hallway, the door swung open and Meredith, the very witch I wanted to corner, walked out. She stretched her arms and blinked, as if she'd been reading since the elder witches shoved the *Vindix* in that room. Maybe she had, and maybe I should have been more chill and waited to talk to Rooms, but I couldn't. I needed to hear what was going on between her and Stiff.

"Rooms." I pushed off the wall.

Meredith jumped and spun my way. "Jesus, Shay! You almost gave me a heart attack."

I gestured to the wide-open hallway. "Not like I was hiding."

Meredith shook her head and walked toward me. "My eyes are all blurry from reading." She paused before adding. "And I'm so freaking hungry."

"Wanna get lunch?"

"For sure," she said, and we fell into step.

"What are you doing today?" Meredith asked before I could investigate about the vampire. "I thought you'd be going to get Luca already."

"He needed the morning—New Haven time—to get some stuff in order. I'm going to leave in a couple of hours and swing by the house first since I don't have anything packed. Need something while I'm there?"

"I do have a couple of things I want. We'll be here longer than I expected." Meredith clicked her tongue. "I'll make a list. Thanks for asking."

"You're welcome. I wanted to talk to you about something else, though."

My roomie cut me a glance. "Oh?"

That had sounded way too innocent. She was playing dumb. Too bad for her; I wasn't about to take the hint. The world was going to the shitter, and I needed to hear something good. "You and Stiff. Are you getting it on?"

Meredith snorted. "You're about as subtle as Tana."

"What's that supposed to mean?"

"The whole time we studied, she kept trying to slip in questions about Hans. She doesn't know who he is, or his powers, and I didn't tell her 'cause that's his business, but she tried to get any tidbit she could out of me." Meredith sighed.

My stomach rolled. A memory of Tana flirting with Hans when I arrived in the infirmary early that day filled my mind.

"Luckily, Miriam and Hannah are task masters," Rooms added. "They only allow so much chit chat before they tell us to get back to work."

"Don't avoid my question," I said, partly because I wanted to forget about Tana and partly because I wanted to know what was up with my bestie and the vampire. "You and Tobias? He called you his mate . . . But does that mean what I think it means? " I arched my eyebrows.

Meredith smirked. "We're together. And soulmates."

"I called it!" I shrieked.

Down the corridor, a door swung open. Gloria poked her head out and scowled. "Keep it down, will ya? I'm resting."

"Sorry." I continued only when the older witch shut her door again. "I totally thought you were soulmates!"

"You did?" Meredith asked. "How?"

I shrugged. "It's weird. You're not the same magical order, but I felt like something was off about Stiff. Like, when you disappeared in New York, I just felt like he could find you."

"That's why he didn't think it should be possible either." Meredith shrugged. "But we both sense the bond growing. Giselle is certain it will snap into place soon."

"Damn, girl." I exhaled sharply. "How is he? In bed?"

Meredith's cheeks turned pink, drawing a gasp out of me.

"Don't tell me that you haven't yet?"

"Ohmygod. *Calm down*, Shay!" Meredith hissed and slapped my arm. I must have squealed again without realizing it. "No, we haven't. We've done other things, but not that."

I let out a low whistle. Honestly, Stiff was, well, *stiff* and usually grumpy, but he was also undeniably gorgeous. That the girl had such willpower was impressive. Or crazy.

"Do you think he'll bite you and not be able to stop?" I

asked, recalling how Tobias had seemed crazed by Meredith early on. "Are you scared?"

Meredith turned down another corridor, and I was glad she knew where she was going because I sure as hell didn't. Nor had I even been paying attention, now or earlier. Basically, since Giselle left with Josiah, and Tobias had offered to train with Hans, I'd been wandering and checking in on Luca.

"I guess a little." Meredith bit her lip. "When Denz bit me, that hurt like a son of a bitch. Tobias won't be so violent, but—"

"It's traumatic," I said, not wanting her to go down that route for a second longer. She already looked uncomfortable enough. "How will the bond snap into place?"

For my kind to solidify a soulmate bond, we encompassed each other in light magic. For vampires, it was a blood exchange —and usually sex. For fae, it was getting it on and recognition of the other person being your other half. I didn't know how the soulmate bond materialized with witches, though since all the rituals took some type of intention, I'd guess a spell or something.

But Tobias was a vampire and Meredith was a witch, so what would happen?

I'd only known one other couple to claim someone outside of their order as their soulmate—Kora and the fae Prince of the Spring Court. Kora was a witch, a friend, and a former coven member.

"We're not sure." Meredith stopped walking. The scents in the air, broth and freshly baked bread, told me that we were near the kitchens. "But our bond is growing stronger. It might be intimacy. Or him drinking my blood. If I have to do some-thing witchy, I don't know what the hell that is."

"Ask the witches here. Or Hans?"

"Are you fucking kidding me?" Meredith barked out a laugh. "I'm not asking Hans! I'll try Hannah. She's the most approachable out of the *Arcacustos*."

Mentally, I identified Hannah as the only female member of the *Abscondita* Coven who wasn't old. She was also the healer who'd seen to Hans. I nodded. "You should check with her. Might soothe your nerves."

My roommate nodded. "Yeah, you're right. I'll talk to her when I go back to the library." She nodded to the kitchen. "Can we drop all this and eat? I want to let my brain be mush for a few minutes."

I wished I could ask more, but could tell that Meredith needed a break, so I nodded. "For sure. Let's chow down, Rooms."

ARMS HEAVY WITH BAGS THAT WERE FILLED WITH MY CLOTHES AND a few other items Meredith had requested, I strode into S&S's tomb, finally feeling myself again.

Just being in my own clothes would have felt nice, but I'd also showered at home and sprayed my own perfume. There was something about being put together in the way I liked that helped me focus.

The coven headquarters was busy, as usual for the middle of the day, and a few people tried to stop me to question me. Naturally, they were curious about how my mission in DC had ended. I wasn't sure how far the news of the princes had spread yet, so I played coy. Luca shared information strategically, and I didn't want to mess that up.

"Can't say yet." I shook my head, and though I could tell

they wanted to press, they didn't. We were all trained not to push if it was coven business.

After being stopped a few more times, I made it to Luca's office and knocked.

"Come in!" he called from inside, so I did.

The moment I laid eyes on the coven master, my stomach sank. The poor man had been to Hell and back.

"Luca." I shut the door behind me. "Are you okay?"

"I am." He stood from his desk, which was littered with papers. "It's been a busy morning, preparing to leave. And what with the news of the Princes of Hell and speaking with the Covenant."

"Have they told the world the whole truth about New York? And the rising?" I asked, meaning only the supernatural world, of course.

Humans would only learn about the princes if shit really hit the fan. Though it was looking bad, we hoped that it wouldn't come down to that.

"They're going to release the news soon." Luca scrubbed a hand over the back of his neck. "Today, most likely. They're preparing, too."

"For what?"

"The Princes of Hell will claim territory. All rulers do," Luca said. "And others will realize that and want a safe place to land."

"Has the Covenant started to put together safe zones already?" My eyebrows rose in question.

He swallowed. "Not yet. It's difficult to know where to put resources when the princes have been lying low. But the Covenant is mobilizing supply chains and alerting their army."

I shuddered. My mother was a Covenant Seat and had

always been involved in politics, so even when I was very young, I heard about the going-ons of the magical community. I couldn't recall the Covenant Army ever being mobilized.

"Who will run things while you're gone?" I asked. "Gunner?"

"He's in California with Harper."

"Oh. She's back home?"

We hadn't been in contact. For now, it was smart to minimize calls from the *Abscondita* land. Still, I was shocked Luca hadn't mentioned it earlier.

"Darkborn attacked her father, and she was called to his side. Gunner went to support her." Luca exhaled a long breath, and I felt bad for the mage. All three of his head guys were elsewhere, taking care of real-world issues. "Lisha will hold things down here."

"She'll do a great job," I assured him. "Did you pack anything? Will you be staying at the manor house for long?"

We'd already texted about reinforcing the wards, but Luca might not want to stay after that.

"For as long as I need to feel up to speed." He pulled a ridiculously small Italian leather duffle bag out from under his desk.

"Uh, I think you're going to need more than a single pair of jeans."

Luca laughed. "It's charmed. I have enough for a week."

Dang, that was handy. If I wasn't a nephilim, I would want to be a mage. They had the most versatile power.

"And the thing you're going to barter?" I asked cautiously.

He hadn't revealed to me what it was yet, and I dared not ask if it was one of the many dark objects that S&S had collected and stored over the years. I trusted Luca more than that, but I was curious as to what he had that would be valuable enough for a luxiter.

"In the bag." Luca strode across the room to join me. "One more thing and, then, I'm ready when you are." He veered toward the bookshelf dominating one entire wall of his office and picked up a box. "New phones. These were secured by Gus. They each already have my new number programmed in as well as Meredith, Tobias, Gunner, Harper, Hans, and you. I shared those numbers with Harper and Gunner earlier too, so if you call, they'll know who it is."

"Perfect! It's getting old having to borrow a phone from the Brits." I took the box and opened it.

Basic smartphones were inside, but if the techy bear shifter Gus had played around with them, they were sure to have unique features.

"I'll add my mom, too."

Luca nodded his agreement. So, I added her personal cell and business phone, and then texted her that it was me before slipping the device into my pocket. From another, larger cardigan pocket, I pulled out the luxiter.

Nicolas Flamel had enchanted the luxiter so that it would only be bright and obvious when called upon. It was an advanced bit of spellwork that I appreciated. Sooner or later, I'd be in a dark place, sneaking about, and need an escape. I didn't need the light to give me away.

"That's it?" Luca examined the luxiter.

"Yup. Looks like a little ball, until you use the magic word and let it know you need it." I squeezed the grape-sized orb.

"I'm looking forward to trying one out on my own."

I offered my arm, which he took, and then I secured my bags. "Hold on to your teensy bag! Luxiter, take us to Nicolas Flamel!"

Light forced me to shut my eyes, and Luca yelped in shock as we became weightless. There was a sensation of being made small and traveling super fast. Then, suddenly, we slammed into the ground so hard my knees buckled. I braced, and Luca seemed to as well, because he didn't fall.

When I opened my eyes, I grinned. We stood outside the headquarters for the Coven of Illumination. I hadn't been sure if the luxiter would let us inside. Apparently, it did not. I suspected Nicolas had powerful wards in place—maybe even ones specific to luxiters, but I still got the satisfaction that this baby worked like a charm.

"That was a ride." Luca placed a hand on his stomach as if to calm it.

"Each time gets easier," I assured him. "Now, let's talk to Old Nick." I approached the door, but before I could knock, Luca spoke.

"Shay, if Nicolas accepts my offer, you're about to learn something about me that I do not share with others."

My eyes widened. "Should I let you go at it alone?"

"No." Luca shook his head. "It's time that I confided in a few people. My sister—"

"You have a sister?"

For a moment, he furrowed his eyebrows in confusion, but then his dark eyes cleared. "That's right. You weren't with them. Meredith, Tobias, and Harper already met my twin in New York. Should anything happen to me once I hand over the object I intend to barter, ask them to find her and to tell her what happened. Also, I will avoid mentioning her to Flamel. I'd appreciate it if you'd do the same."

What the actual hell was he going to give Flamel?

"Shay?"

"Of course." I nodded. "I won't say a thing—to anyone."

He gave a weak smile. "I'll tell Meredith, Tobias, and Hans when we see them. That way, if my worst nightmare comes to pass, you can speak to them. Make a plan."

I nodded. "Okay." A pause passed between us. "Are you worried about Flamel? What if he uses whatever you're going to give him inappropriately? Like for the dark? He has demon blood and other dark objects, you know."

"The holder of such an object would be wise not to brag about it. Someone as old as Flamel will understand that." He turned to the door, as if to say that was that.

It sure didn't answer all my questions, but Luca clearly wanted to move on, so I knocked. It took a minute before footsteps sounded. When the door opened, the old man stared back at me. Circles and bags ringed his wrinkled eyes and his thin hair was sticking out every which way.

"You—it hasn't been enough time," Flamel said.

"I know," I replied. "Although I do hope that you have at least one more luxiter ready. I understand if you don't. Really, I'm here because my coven master," I gestured to Luca, "wanted one too."

"Luca Moretti." The mage stepped forward and offered Flamel his hand.

The old man shook it but still did not seem at ease. "You cannot create luxiters with mere money. Creating them is taxing. It strips me of life-force, and though I have a way of replenishing it, I do not take on more work lightly. Shay and her friend had to pay dearly. What they gave me was much rarer than riches."

"I understand." Luca said. "I can provide something of great use. An item I think you will find a need for soon."

Flamel's eyebrows pinched together. "You're the Coven Master of Shadows and Secrets?"

"I am."

The Alchemist studied Luca for another second before opening the door to allow us inside. "Then, I assume you're correct in thinking you have secrets I know naught of. Follow me."

We trailed the old man through the headquarters, passed a lounge area filled with books and tabletop games, and into the workshop at the back of the building. The scents of sage, rosemary, and earth hung in the air. This time, the shelves and many items on them did not threaten to overwhelm me, though they appeared just as jumbled as before. A cauldron bubbled away in the back glowing with a soft light. I wondered if parts of the luxiters were being made in there.

Flamel went to a workbench and opened a drawer. "Here are two more luxiters that I've had the time and energy to create." He exhaled. "I'll need the night to recover before I begin working again. Perhaps longer."

My lips parted in surprise. I'd hoped to get one more luxiter and return at the end of the allotted week for the other six. To have created two since Hans and I left Paris was pretty miraculous.

I smiled at him. "Thank you. And that's fine. I can tell that you're working hard to uphold your end of the bargain."

"One does not go back on their word. Not in this world," Flamel replied, correctly. In the supernatural world, things ran differently. You didn't break a promise, or not deliver on a deal, and expect not to pay dearly for those actions. Often with blood.

"Now, Luca." Flamel gazed at him. "What is it you brought?"

Luca stared down at the luxiters, inert at the moment, but full of potential. From his pocket, he pulled out a gold coin.

"This is a talisman from the Mage Court of Isila. It will keep its holder safe. I have kept it on my person all my life and it has never failed me."

Flamel held out his hand, and Luca deposited the coin into it. Only then did I see the markings on the metal. I didn't recognize them, but they resembled runes.

"What are its limits?" Flamel asked.

"It has none."

Gray eyebrows rose, and even I grew skeptical. "Impossible."

"I'm certain," Luca said, no hesitation in his tone.

"How can you be sure?" Flamel asked.

"Because my mother, a woman who has every reason to keep me safe, gave it to me. A subject of the Mage Court gave it to her at my birth. It was the only thing that would hide me from the people that will surely come hunting when King Tyra dies."

"Why would they hunt you?" I blurted out, unable to help myself.

Luca drew in a breath. "I am a bastard son of King Tyra of the Mage Court and I have a claim to that throne. As do all of my many siblings. Other bastards included. Once the king dies, it will be all out war to see who can take the throne and I—even here—am a threat to them."

My stomach plummeted. Holy crap! Luca was part of the royal line of succession in Isila! The Mage Court too . . .

I shuddered. Most of the courts in the other realm weren't known for their kindness, but the mages were among the worst—second, or maybe just tied with the Court of the Blood.

"You're saying this talisman has the magic to hide you from all mages? Even your father?" Flamel examined the coin closely.

"It hides you from any danger, which, for me, does include my father. It is always on me. Or close by." Luca paused. "There is great danger in the world right now. That talisman might be your best hope at surviving."

The old, the weak, the sick, and those unable to defend themselves would soon walk the razor's edge of death.

"Take it," I urged. "You'll—want that to help."

"Will it work on others?" Flamel asked.

"Anyone who holds it."

The old Alchemist nodded. "I've had a long life. Full too. But I have kin." He closed his hand around the talisman. "And you have a deal."

Luca's shoulders lowered, the only hint that he'd been uncertain if Flamel would take the talisman or not.

"I will make your luxiter after I complete the ones Shay and Hans ordered," Flamel said. "It's only fair."

"That's fine." I handed one luxiter to Luca. "We will share until the others are ready. What do you say we come back in a week and a day? Will they all be ready then?"

Flamel inclined his head. "They will."

I looked to Luca and the coven master nodded. "We'll leave you to it, Mr. Flamel. Keep that talisman safe."

The Alchemist dropped the magical artifact in his pocket and showed Luca and me to the door. The moment we were outside, I wheeled on him.

"How are people always hiding their royal ties? First Tobias! Then Hans! Now, you!"

Luca smirked. "We seem to find one another, don't we?" Then, the smile fell from his face. "Though for most of us, it seems like a curse." He patted his pocket absently, and I sensed that was where his talisman was usually stored. He seemed to realize what he was doing and met my eyes. "Shall we journey to the manor? And tell the others?"

I wouldn't get over this news so fast, but it would be best to be back in England, in relative safety. Plus, Luca and I had wards to erect. So, I extended my arm, linking us, and pulled out the luxiter.

"To the *Abscondita* Coven," I whispered and light took us once more.

CHAPTER TWENTY-TWO

HARPER

My stomach twisted into knots as I exited the car and gazed up at my family home. The modern mansion did not fit the California forest that surrounded it, but Dad had built their home here because Mom loved this land.

The scent of redwoods and sun-warmed dirt filled my nostrils. After a red-eye flight and way too much time in San Francisco trying to get a last-minute car rental, I was on Midnight Pack land.

My pack dominated the outskirts of a supernatural town, tucked right up against the Santa Cruz Mountains. And though the town was mostly inhabited by wolves, almost all of them lived here, in this wooded suburb area Father had designed for our comfort.

"Nice spot," Gunner drawled as he assessed the area. "I was thinkin' there'd be more people around the pack, but nope. It's secluded. Perfect."

"The Ferenz family has held this land for over a hundred years." I admired the way the morning sun played on the yellow and orange leaves. "Even though Dad only built and relocated the pack here twenty years ago, no one could encroach. Try as they might, my ancestors had the area on lock."

"That's awesome." He took in the woods that lined the drive.

I bet that he wanted to shift and run. After so much travel, I itched for it too. Wolves weren't made for planes or being too cramped. But first, I had to see my father.

"You'll need to pay your respects before doing anything else," I reminded my partner. If he was going to insist on joining me, he needed to abide by the rules—wolvea blooded or not. "At least to Mom. I'm not sure if Dad will be up for visitors who aren't family. Mom will let you know."

Alphas hated others seeing them at their weakest, but honoring their mate honored them. It would be a suitable substitution.

"Sure." Gunner pointed to the row of cars lining the drive-way. "Looks like your family has visitors. Or do you just have this many cars?"

"These aren't all ours," I said, though we did have a lot of cars. Dad had hobbies, two of them being collecting vehicles and wine, but these belonged to someone else. "They belong to his betas."

"They're watchin' over him?"

"I—I guess so. Come on." I forgot all about getting my bag as I beelined it for the mansion. It took him a second, but Gunner jogged to catch up behind me. It was a good thing he did, too, because, before I reached the front door, two wolves rounded the house.

Their hackles rose and growls slipped from their lips. I stopped, allowing them to take me in—to recognize who I was.

The moment they did, one shifted, and I groaned. I hadn't recognized him in wolf form, but before me stood my high school sweetheart, Aspen. He'd grown larger since I'd seen him last; his chest muscles filled out the white t-shirt to perfection, but the changes didn't end there. Aspen had grown a beard, and on his hip he wore a belt that held a blade. He'd become a man while I'd been away. A man with the obligation to protect his pack—not a young adult who only had to study at the nearby college and work a part-time job to pay rent.

"I've got this," Aspen said to the other wolf, who ran off around the house. He turned to me again and approached in a business-like, stiff manner, only intensifying my fear for my father. "Your mother has been waiting."

"How is he? Any changes?"

Aspen swallowed, and his face softened. "I'm glad you're here."

Behind me, Gunner took a step, which broke the spell between me and Aspen. My ex looked up. "And you are?"

"Gunner Ray Bryant, Heir to the Blood Moon Pack, in North Carolina." He set something down and stuck out his hand. Only then did I notice Gunner had grabbed his bag, mine, and my purse.

Aspen took it, eyebrows arched high and shoulders tight. "I've heard of that pack and the alpha." The tone in his voice indicated he knew Gunner held the blood of the most powerful wolves in Isila. "Your pack is respected, but now I wonder why you're here?"

"He's part of my coven," I answered. "A partner, and given what's been happening, he wanted to come with me to make sure everything was okay."

"Bad things have been happenin' everywhere," Gunner added. "Can't be too safe."

"Partner? You mean you're mates?" Aspen's eyes widened.

I blinked at that, but recovered quickly. "No! Platonic."

Besides my family, I hadn't told anyone here much about S&S or how we worked, and I would not start right now. All they needed to know was that I was a part of an organization.

"Right, then." Aspen's attention turned back to me. "I guess you want to see the alpha."

"Yeah." I marched around him. "Good seeing you—"

Aspen turned and walked alongside me. "You won't be able to get in without me."

"I have a key."

"After what happened, your mother put new precautions in place. Blood magic. Only your mother, father, other family members, and the alpha's betas can get in now. Other pack members are having their homes protected soon, too. I'll show you how to work it."

Mom had brought a witch onto pack lands to perform magic? She was far more terrified than she'd let on.

"Okay, show me in." I was tired of futzing around. I needed to see Mom and Dad, needed to learn what had happened and what they thought might come to pass. If they were protecting their home, they thought something big was going to go down.

Then, what he'd said earlier clicked. "Wait a minute! You're a beta now?" I slapped Aspen on the shoulder and the air of a tough-guy wolf evaporated. For a brief second, a goofy grin lined his face, but it disappeared, like he wasn't used to smiling much any more.

"Alpha named me beta a month ago. I think your dad wanted young blood in the core group."

"Aspen, that's remarkable."

Usually betas were older, more seasoned wolves. The

exception being if the pack named an alpha young and chose their friends to stand at their side. My father had kept the same three betas—Rikard, Aura, and Crystal—close for my entire life. I wondered if he was grooming Aspen to be the lead beta when I took over, but that would be presumptuous. Depending on when that day came, I'd prefer to have the guidance of older betas, not just those my age.

"I was honored," he said as we approached the door of the mansion.

They had placed a black pad below the doorbell. Aspen pulled a knife from the belt he wore and poked at his thumb. Blood welled, filling the air with a metallic tang as he pressed his thumb to the pad.

A beep sounded, and the door clicked. Reaching out, Aspen opened it. "That's all there is to it."

Simple enough. I thanked him and stepped inside. Our home would have been better placed in the Hollywood Hills, but Dad never would have been able to live somewhere like that. Somewhere with so many humans around.

Most packs would die for such a setup, and I was lucky to have grown up in this environment. Even if it was like living in a small town within a small town. All the wolves in the Midnight Pack lived here. Growing up, it had been too close for comfort sometimes.

"Your mother is around," Aspen said. "Probably upstairs. In your parent's wing. Or—"

A clatter rang out, coming from the right. "Or the kitchen. I'll find her."

"I can put your bag in your room? Yours too, if you want? They have a guest room that they use." He looked at Gunner.

Gunner set the duffles and my purse down. "Sure, man. I appreciate it."

"Thanks, Aspen," I added.

He grabbed the bags and headed upstairs, leaving me alone with my partner.

"Nice place," Gunner said as I led him through my home.

It was airy and light, with glass walls from floor to ceiling, letting in sunlight and a view of the woods. To soften the modernity, Mom added hints of home. A green throw over a wing-backed chair. Photos of our family lined the walls. Candles rested on every surface—all unscented, of course.

"Mom loves decorating it."

"She's talented."

"Whoever that is, I love him!" Mom called out, and I rolled my eyes as Gunner grinned widely.

"She loves *everyone*," I said before he could let it go to his head.

"A good woman." Gunner grinned, not at all brought down.

"Harper, honey, who is this?" Mom appeared, her hands covered in flour with a bit in her red hair too and a sparkle in her green eyes. Mom was in her late forties, but looked years younger and full of life. Her nose twitched. "A wolf, handsome and charming too! Where have you been keeping him?"

"Mom, please don't encourage him." I stepped into my mother's arms.

She squeezed me tightly. "I'm so glad you're here and safe, baby."

"Me too," I said, though I remained still conflicted about this. Not about supporting my family. They were everything to me. But the threat of the Princes of Hell loomed everywhere, and if I was here, I couldn't fight where I was needed. And yet, Luca had been so sure that this was my place, and I had to trust that. I broke away from my mother. "This is my partner in S&S."

Gunner held out his hand to my mother. "Gunner Ray Bryant of the Blood Moon Pack, Ma'am."

"Blood Moon Pack, you say . . . Oh, by the Old Ones." Mom shook his hand. Her eyes widened for a moment before she caught herself.

This had to be the first time someone from the Blood Moon Pack stepped foot on to our lands, and it shook even my mother, one of the best diplomats in the Midnight Pack.

"It's good to meet you, Gunner. How has your pack been faring?"

Dad would have been more worried that Gunner might challenge him, but not Mom. She was the softness to Dad's hard core.

"Good. I hope you don't mind, but I told them there was trouble out this way. Nothin' specific, of course. I just wanted to keep them safe."

"That's fine," Mom said. The only reason she was okay with it was because she'd barely told me anything at all. Anything important would be said later, without Gunner around. If it had implications to weaken the pack, Father would forbid me from sharing it with Gunner.

"I can't fault you for wanting to keep your own safe." Trouble clouded Mom's eyes. "I only hope that we do the same. And perhaps it's best that you not mention your pack right now, Gunner? No disrespect, but we're rivals."

"Your alpha is injured. I get it." Gunner made a motion of zipping his lips. "Won't say a thing."

"Where is Henley?" I asked, realizing that the house was way too quiet. "And Ethan?"

My other brother, Elijah, should be at UCLA right now, but the other two still lived at home.

"Henley's at school. She'll be back this afternoon. Ethan is working today. You remember the glass blowing shop in town?"

"He works there now, too?" Ethan wasn't into higher education, but he was a hard worker and had another job at a restaurant so he could build his own place on pack land.

"Until five tonight."

I paused. "Mom, do you think it's smart for them to be going about their normal life? I mean, I don't expect them to sit over Dad, not that he'd allow it anyway, but someone tried to convince Dad to join the Darkborn. What makes you think they won't go after our family to convince him again?"

"That came up." Mom sucked in a deep breath. "But a lot of Henley's teachers are in our pack. And Ethan . . . he won't let anyone tell him what to do."

Out of the twins, Ethan had a harder time with authority. Still, he had to listen to the alpha.

"We also have people going to check on him," Mom added after a moment. "He doesn't know."

Ah, that made more sense.

"We'll go see him later." When we did, Gunner and I would perform a sweep of the shop. We'd make sure Ethan knew where his best weapons were and that he wasn't doing anything stupid, like blocking the exits. I loved my brother, but he didn't think strategically.

"First, you need to speak with your father," she said. "He's in our room. Gunner, would you like to keep me company? I'm making scones."

"I'd love that," Gunner drawled. "I'm not much in the kitchen but—"

"You're a guest. I'll get you a plate." Mom turned and, for a moment, left me alone with Gunner. His eyes, silver with flecks of blue in them, leveled me.

"You gonna be okay?"

"I'll be fine." I nodded. "You should go on. Mom isn't one to wait for long."

"You look a lot like her," Gunner noted.

"Thanks." I smiled, taking the compliment. My mother still stunned crowds, and I did indeed get my red hair and green eyes from her. Just like Henley did. "I'll find you once Dad and I are done."

"Don't rush. I'm in good hands." He took a deep breath as a whiff of cinnamon and nutmeg rolled into the hall.

We separated, and I walked to the opposite side of the mansion and climbed the stairs. When I reached the top, I was shocked to find a man sitting outside my parents' door, my father's oldest and most trusted beta.

"Rikard," I said. "Is everything okay?"

"Of course, Harper." He stood and clapped a fatherly hand on my shoulder. "A beta has been out here at all hours."

And outside too. I swallowed down my rising panic. "My father wanted that?"

"Your mother. Your father is, I'm sorry to say, powerless to persuade her."

Maybe Mom was just being overprotective? "Were you there during the attack?" I gestured to where a long thin cut ran the length of his forearm. It was healing, but still red —fresh.

"I was. We were in San Francisco speaking with a wine distributor."

Wine distribution was only one part of my father's busi-ness portfolio. The other part, I suspected, was not legal, but he'd never confided it in me and I didn't ask. When I became the alpha, which had always been the plan, I'd learn—and decide if I wanted the pack to continue in that direction.

"And they approached you there?"

He scowled. "They did, but the bulk of the attackers waited until your father was alone. Cowards."

"How many?"

"A dozen on the alpha. Just three on me, but enough to delay me in getting to him." Rikard shook his head, regretting that he hadn't been right at my father's side. "We're lucky he's alive."

"Thank the Old Ones," I breathed, my heart thundering. "I guess I should go in? Mother says he wants to see me."

"Of course." He stood aside, allowing me to pass.

I steeled myself, the anxiety mounting. Dad had been in many fights, but I'd never seen my father grievously injured. Never seen him as less than a powerful wolf.

When I opened the door, I realized how right I was to be worried for him. The scent of blood, old and dried, hung in the air, mingling with the stench of old bandages. Under it all was my father's smell, but not. He was unwashed, unmoved—ill.

I went to the bedside to find him sleeping, but the moment I laid a hand on his shoulder, Alpha Ferenz's swollen eyes opened and latched on me. They, at least, were the same; bright blue, but surrounded with blackened skin just turning purple.

"Daughter. Take a seat."

There it was, a piece of him that was not injured and broken. His proclivity to get down to business remained intact, and that gave me some reassurance. I pulled a chair over, taking him in more slowly this time.

Bruises marred his face and his nose had shifted, broken.

One arm hung in a sling and the fact that his shifter healing abilities hadn't taken care of the broken bones already meant that they had to be badly broken. Shattered to pieces, even. I didn't see the bandages I smelled, which made me think they were wrapped around his body and hidden by blankets. Had the Darkborn stabbed his internal organs?

At the thought, my wolf reared her head, howling at the injustice of it all.

"This is no time for our other aspect." Dad faintly smiled and it looked painful. I yearned to reach out to him, to lay a comforting hand on his, but knew he wouldn't have it. "I need you like this, Harper, level-headed. Calculating. We have much to discuss."

Forcing my wolf into submission, I leaned forward. "Yeah, like how are you?"

"I'll be fine. I need to talk to you about the future of the pack."

What? He was bedridden and wanted to talk about the pack? "Dad, I came here for *you*. Not the pack."

"Always the pack first."

I let out a long exhale. "But look at you."

He grunted. "I'm aware of how weak I appear, how weak *I am*, but I will not allow something similar to happen to my daughter and heir. Harper, you need to return to the pack lands. For good."

"Dad, I have obligations with the coven." Ones I didn't want to release. Not yet.

I had always assumed I'd succeed my father as alpha. Of course, someone could challenge me, but I was strong and smart and well-loved here, so it always seemed unlikely. Still did. And yet, I simply wasn't ready. Being an alpha meant the life I'd built was over for good.

"They are nothing compared to those of your people."

He didn't understand that the coven was my family, too. Especially Shay and Meredith. It hurt my heart just to think about leaving them.

I blinked several times. "But you're alive and strong, Dad. Once you heal, you'll be fine."

"I need you here to learn, Daughter. Need you to prepare."

I paused. "You think they're going to come back, don't you?"

He nodded, and that one gesture sank my stomach to my knees.

"They wanted our pack to side with them. I denied them— would that I could have taken all their lives too." His face hardened.

"What did they look like?"

Dad's eyes closed. "I didn't get a clear look at them."

"Why not?"

"They wore masks and hoods."

I swallowed. They could be anyone, even a person living in town.

My father's gaze leveled at me. "They're not taking no for an answer. They'll be back, and I might not be able to stand up to them. Which means you'll have to. You must keep the pack strong. Protect our lands. Say you'll do it. For me."

I stared into my father's eyes, unable to believe what was happening—that I wasn't here to show support and help him heal. That today, I dipped a toe into a new role, one I wasn't sure I was ready for, but that didn't matter, did it? I *had to* be ready. "I promise, Dad. I'll protect the pack."

"Good. Start immediately. Call the betas together today, and as soon as you can, gather the pack for a barbecue. I need you to put your foot forward. To claim your right, before someone else does." His jaw clenched.

"Are you worried about that?"

Not once had either parent mentioned they worried about a new wolf rising to challenge our family.

"When leadership is weak, so too becomes others' moral fabric. Remember that, Harper." Dad coughed, and though I was dying to learn if he suspected anyone in particular, I stood.

"I'll let you rest."

"Get your mother to send out a notice for the gathering," Dad said.

"I will." I walked to the door, feeling conflicted over what I'd just promised.

CHAPTER TWENTY-THREE

GUNNER

By the Mother Wolf, I'd died and gone to heaven.

"More jam?" asked Harper's Mom. "I have an amazing organic strawberry one."

"This is perfect the way it is, Ma'am."

"Diana," she corrected, as she'd done a few times before.

I was a grown man and pretty chill, I liked to think, but when you were talkin' with an alpha's wife, you showed them the same respect you'd show their mate. My pa had drilled that practice into me, and lived by it himself, no matter that he was usually the bigger wolf when alphas got together. One day, I'd do the same with my mate, and I wouldn't want some young man from another pack—a rival pack, no less—on a first name basis with my woman. Not so quick, anyway.

"No jam needed." I stuffed another scone into my mouth. She'd been feedin' me since the moment Harper left, and I wasn't complainin' one bit. The woman baked like an angel.

"What else are you two going to do today?" Mrs. Ferenz asked.

"Not sure. I'm here to support Harper." I shrugged.

"You're not doing work for the coven?"

Ah, she was fishin', and by the nonchalant tone she used, I was bettin' that this she-wolf was a master at hookin' what she set out to catch.

"Depends," I said. "I—"

"Mom, quit trying to get secrets from him. We can't say anything." Harper breezed into the room, fillin' my nose with the scent of apples and sun-baked hills.

"The Covenant should make an official announcement." Her mother's nose wrinkled. "It's not as if I don't know some of it. A group called the Darkborn hurt my mate. I deserve more information."

Harper stopped to stand next to me, and her teeth dug into her bottom lip. Her ma was right. It stunk that we couldn't be more open, but my partner was also right not to say a thing.

"I bet they announce it tonight." I gave Harper an out. "They had a hell of a time cleanin' up a mess, but they should be done now."

Mrs. Ferenz shook her head. "I swear to the Old Ones you're too good at keeping secrets."

Harper laughed lightly. "Comes with the gig." She turned to me. "My dad wants me to call a meeting with his betas. I already spoke with one upstairs and he suggested that we meet in town. The pack has a clubhouse there. It's secure, and apparently there is paperwork Rikard thinks I should see."

"I'm guessin' I have to fend for myself?"

"Yeah." Harper nodded. "They won't let you in, but there's a brewery nearby. You could relax there."

"And the glass blowing studio," Mrs. Ferenz added with a megawatt smile. "You should stop by there. Get your mother something. They do lovely work."

I didn't have the heart to tell her that my ma didn't care if I ever showed my face in our pack—let alone if I got her a present. "That the same one your brother works at?"

"Yep." Harper smiled. "He might let you watch him work and we can do the sweep of the shop afterward to make sure it's safe."

"Sounds great. I'll do that. I'd like to run the woods later too, if the pack wouldn't mind?"

"I'll go with you. That way, the wolves know you're okay on our land."

"Be careful when you do, Harper Mace. The Darkborn might be lurking and you two aren't mind-linked."

"We will, Mom," she assured. "Also, Dad wants to have a barbecue."

Mrs. Ferenz threw up her hands. "That wolf has got to be joking! And I'm guessing that he'll want to attend?"

"Uh, he didn't commit either way," Harper said, and they shared another long look.

I had a hint why her pa would want his daughter to throw a shin-dig and officially meet with his betas. Pa would do the same thing if someone had beat the tar outta him.

The alpha was puttin' things in place for when Harper took over. The question was, what did she think about this?

I stood and stretched, cutting down the tension that was building between the women. "Ready whenever you are."

"Let's go now." Harper pointed to the door. "The sooner I get this done, the sooner we can take a run. You're going to want one to chill out. Once Henley comes home, she'll talk your ear off."

I laughed. "I can handle that."

My partner let out a dry laugh. "Let me get my bag. Meet you in the car?"

"Sure thing."

She ran upstairs, and I headed outside. Though wolves had been patrolling before, I wasn't worried that they'd come at me. Aspen was a beta, and by now had alerted the whole pack a stranger was around.

I pushed the door open and walked to the car, full in my belly and with pep in my step. I hadn't even made it back to the vehicle when Aspen himself appeared out of the woods surrounding the home.

"Did you speak to the alpha?"

"Naw. Just Harper. That's how it should be, right? She's family and family comes first."

Aspen looked me up and down. "You're really not together?"

"Nope." Though as I spoke the words, my inner wolf lifted his head.

That was weird. I'd been around Harper hundreds of times, and the wolf had never been possessive of her before. Then again, this guy was givin' off major jealous vibes. "You don't gotta worry, brother."

"Maybe not," he said, "but if you get any ideas, this pack stands with her."

"As they should."

For a moment, Aspen looked like he wanted to say something more, but instead looked at the house.

I listened hard. Footsteps from inside approached.

"See you later." Aspen slipped back into the woods as Harper exited her home.

"I'd kill for a coffee right now," she said, oblivious to the fact that her ex had tried to wolf me up. "You want one before I drop you into town? I know a brilliant spot."

I got in the car. "Sure."

She turned the key, and the engine roared to life. I waited

until we were out of the driveway and down the road that led away from the pack land before askin' what I wanted to know.

"Your pa wants you to take over, doesn't he?"

She exhaled. "I figured that wouldn't get past you."

"Not when I'll be in the same position one day."

Harper pursed her lips tightly. "You're right. He wants me to talk to the betas to get things for succession in place, and the barbecue is to remind people who I am."

"Like they could forget." I snorted.

From the corner of my eye, I caught her lookin' at me.

"I mean, you'll be a great leader," I pivoted. "But do you want to do it now? Considering what's going on?"

"The problem is they don't know what's going on. When the Covenant finally makes the announcement, I think it will be easier."

"You didn't answer my question."

She paused and kept her gaze on the road.

"That's because I'm not sure if I'm ready or not. I haven't been myself lately, and I'm beginning to wonder if it's because of what's happening. Because of the princes." The she-wolf sighed. "Want to listen to music?"

I took the hint. "Sure, chica. You pick. I'm along for the ride."

COFFEES IN HAND, HARPER AND I WALKED DOWN THE TOWN'S sidewalks. It reminded me a lot of the town near where my pack lived, small, with many local shops and places to eat. The scenery with the mountains and the nearby ocean was different, but other than that, they were pretty similar.

"Okay, so I'm meeting the betas right there." She pointed to an unmarked home, one of those that looked like a small-town lawyer's office. "You're just going down there. Do you see the glasswork studio's sign?" Her finger drifted down the street, and I followed.

About four buildings away, a sign covered in bright blues, purples, golds, and greens popped out at me, vibrant and fun. They made me think of my little sister, Kate. Ma wouldn't like a trinket but maybe I'd find something that Kate would love in the studio.

"Mom said Ethan is working alone today, so you should be fine." She sipped her coffee and cut me a glance. "Sorry I have to ditch you, but Ethan is pretty talkative, and I told him you were coming by. He's always been interested in S&S, and I think you two should get along fine."

"Bet we will." I rolled my shoulders back, relaxin' a bit. "You'll stop by when you're done and we can go for a run? Or should we look into this Darkborn thing first?"

"Run first, research after."

"What about the barbecue?"

Harper shook her head. "That won't be tonight—the pack is too big to throw something together that fast—and I want to learn more about who assaulted my dad. Where they might be now."

"Sounds good. I'll be ready." I lifted my cup and let her get on with her duties, strollin' down the quiet street toward the glasswork shop.

When I got there, I let myself in. A bell tinkled, alerting anyone at work that they had company. A moment later, a young man of about nineteen or twenty exited a back room. Blond and so tall he was gangly, the young wolf held himself like someone finding their way in life, whereas his sister's stance always screamed confidence.

"Hey, what can I do for you?" Harper's brother asked.

"I'm Gunner. Harper's partner in the coven."

"Cool, man." His face split into a wide grin. "Heard you were part of the Blood Moon Pack, too! We don't see many wolves from that pack around here."

"I'm pleased as moon punch to be the representative," I said, and meant it.

Not everyone in my pack wanted to reach out to other large packs and make alliances. Harper's dad and my pa were prime examples. Something about the other rubbed them the wrong way. But I didn't feel the same. If I could smooth relations when I became alpha, I would. This was a nice start.

"Why don't you come to the back? I'm starting a new piece."

I followed him to the back of the studio. Immediately, heat bowled me over. I'd figured it would be hot back here, but this was like steppin' into an oven. "How do you handle the heat?" I motioned toward the fire burning in a furnace.

"You get used to it." He shrugged, but I doubted that I'd ever get used to such a thing.

I'd grown up in the south and already I was sweatin' bullets. There wasn't any humidity in the shop, but this was hellish all the same.

"You can sit there, if you want." Ethan gestured to a bench far from the heat source.

"I'm good. Long flight and we've been in the car a lot."

"Bet you want to run, huh?"

"We got plans to, later."

Ethan smiled. "The pack has plenty of land for that."

"It's real pretty around here. Can't wait to explore."

CHAPTER TWENTY-THREE

"You're her partner in the coven?"

The change in topic threw me for a loop, but I recovered quickly, and took in how he was lookin' at me. Maybe I was more than a partner.

"Yeah, we work together." I nodded.

"Too bad. You look like her type."

I thought back to Aspen. We were both wolves, but that was about where the similarities ended. Plus, I'd known the she-wolf for a while now and she'd made it clear many times that I was not her type.

"We're better this way." I turned and assessed the back of the airy room. Glass-blowing instruments rested on shelves, sorta scattered and disorganized. Long rods that I was sure had some sort of fancy name and huge-ass tweezers lie on worktables. A big fan stood at the back of the room too, notably off.

"Can't turn it on until I'm done here. It'll mess up my work," Ethan said. "Want some tunes, though?"

My attention had lingered on the fan too long, but could anyone blame a guy? I'd been here about two minutes and the back of my shirt was already gettin' soaked.

"Sure."

"You cool with reggae?"

"One of my favorite types of music." I beamed at him, liking his vibe. "What are you making?"

"A vase." He picked up his phone. Suddenly, music blared through speakers in the ceiling. Then, the wolf grabbed a long rod. "Someone in town commissioned a certain design and I'm the best at it in the studio. The color is my fave, too. Reminds me of the lake near my pack's land."

"Cool, man. Well, don't let me stop you. I'm going to look around, though."

"Stay clear of the furnace, 'kay?"

"Will do." I took a sip of my black coffee as Ethan got to work.

Though I meant to start checkin' out the area for items that could be used as a threat against Ethan, I couldn't help but watch him. Soon enough, he had the rod in the fire and the beginnin' of a vase on the end. How he'd get it out of there was anyone's guess, but there was one thing I could tell by watchin' this wolf. He loved what he did. I could relate. I loved my job too.

And on that note, I'd better get to doin' a sweep. I didn't want to be loungin' about when Harper got here. Plus, the sooner I got this done, the sooner we could run the woods.

Steerin' clear of the furnace, I walked along the edges of the room, taking in the tools with a critical eye. Unfortunately, a ton of glassblowing tools could be used to harm a person, and there was no way Ethan or the studio would be gettin' rid of them. But there were other items that were probably optional. I made a list of them in my head as I moved deeper into the studio.

I swung around a line of five furnaces, and was examining the back of the vast space when the bells on the front door tinkled. Wonderin' if Harper got done with her meeting faster than she expected, I made my way back to the front, doin' a full circle of the studio and bobbin' my head to the Caribbean jams Ethan played. The young wolf sang along, and he was pretty damn good, too.

But when I rounded the final furnace, all the levity in my heart vanished and my pulse began to thunder. Ethan must not have heard the bells 'cause he was still engrossed with the furnace. He didn't realize a man stalked toward him, shoulders tight in a way that promised trouble, and magic in his hands.

Aw, hell no.

I sprung into action, dropping my coffee and lunging for one of the rods. My fingers wrapped around the cool metal, and I sprinted around the many dangerous items toward the person closing in on Ethan.

For his part, Harper's brother still had no idea that someone was comin' for him. He was too caught up in his art, and singin' along with a song. And for the magic-worker's part, he was so focused on the wolf that he didn't see me comin' from behind.

In fact, he never saw me 'cause I closed in quick, and knocked him right over the head with the rod. The magic disappeared, and the man fell to the floor.

"The wind flying—what the fuck, man!" The tune Ethan had been singin' fell from his lips, turning into a roar that ended in the shattering of glass as his creation fell from the rod and broke.

"This man nearly attacked you." I dropped to my knees.

"Shit! I didn't even hear anyone come in."

"The music. Keep it lower?" I suggested as I pulled the man's shirt collar down.

"What are you doing?"

"Looking for this." The Sigil of Lucifer was branded on this guy's chest, the same as it had been on Hans's sister, Nicoleta. "He's Darkborn."

"Aw, crap." Ethan ran a hand through his long blond hair. "Mom is gonna flip."

"She already is." A voice came from behind, and I turned to see Harper standing in the doorway.

"What happened? Why are you here so soon?" I asked,

shooting to my feet and taking in the way her chest heaved. "Is someone chasing you?"

"This attack coordinated with another." Harper swallowed, her eyes locking with Ethan's. "Someone tried to break into Henley's school and take her. The betas are going there now and extracting any pack pups."

Ethan's growl filled the room, but there was no time for wolfish posturing. We needed to get the Ferenz kids on pack land—all of them. Independent, full-grown wolf of not, Ethan could no longer claim that he was safe, or capable of dealing with the threat of Darkborn coming after him.

"There's more." Harper pulled her gaze from her brother and looked at me. "The Covenant made their announcement as I was running here. Word that Wrath was specifically responsible for New York's attack, and the princes' rising is going to spread and fast. Since this one got cut short because of the break in at the school, there will be another meeting tonight." She paused. "I know you're not part of the pack, but you've seen what I've seen. I need you there."

The way she said it made my chest puff up with pride. "I got you." I turned. "Ethan, close down the shop. You, and this guy," I gestured to the man still knocked out on the floor, "are comin' with us."

CHAPTER TWENTY-FOUR

HARPER

The Darkborn scum was just starting to stir when I pulled up to the house. I glanced in the rearview mirror. His eyes were still closed. The ropes that Ethan had found in the glass studio still wrapped around the man's hairy wrists. Behind our captive, my brother's car followed. It was only now that we stood on pack land that I could breathe freely, knowing that he was safe.

"You guys got a secure place for him?" Gunner arched his eyebrows. "Magic proof too?"

"Of course we do," I replied.

Smaller packs wouldn't have invested in a holding place warded against many types of magic, but the Midnight Pack wasn't your typical pack that could fly under the radar and never attract opponents. This wasn't even close to the first time others attacked my pack.

It was, however, the first time that we'd been attacked by a group of zealots who wanted demons to rule. Well, second, if you counted the attack on Dad. What a bunch of psychos.

"Best be gettin' him in there." Gunner opened the car door

as I killed the engine. He didn't even make it to the backseat when the man groaned.

"What the fu—hey!" A thud told me that our captive had kicked the side of our rental.

Still in my seat, I twisted. The man stared back at me, eyes open and full of anger, but I just scowled at him. "Don't do that again. I'm not paying for damage."

The man kicked the door, harder this time, and struggled to sit up, only to fall back on his side with a moan.

"Aw, hell." Gunner growled, and a scuffle ensued in which the man tried to fight Gunner off, but my partner wasn't having any of it. He punched the guy across the jaw, and again, our hostage went limp. "Sorry. Might delay questioning."

"Whatever. He deserved it." I got out of the car and rounded it to help, but Gunner waved me off.

"I got him." As if the full-grown man weighed nothing more than a small child, Gunner hefted the man's weight over his shoulder with ease. The muscles in his biceps flexed, drawing my eye, and my inner wolf made an appreciative sound.

"Thanks." I turned my back on my partner and closed the car door, forcing my wolf to chill as I did so.

Both Gunner and I were primed to become the next alphas of our powerful packs. So, even if we wanted to be together, it was fated to fail. Neither would give up that leadership role. Not willingly, anyway.

"Follow me." I led Gunner around the back of the home, only to be met with three wolves. They stopped and lowered their heads to me. "We need the Black Hole."

Gunner snorted. "That's what you call it?"

"We're sci-fi nerds in this house, okay?"

The other wolves escorted us the rest of the way, and when we arrived, one shifted. I didn't recognize her, but that wasn't unusual. New members joined the pack regularly—liking the stability and protection that a large, established pack brought.

"Here's the key." She handed the key to me. "You're the alpha's daughter?"

"Yep. Harper. And you are?"

"Felicity. Joined two months back." She eyed Gunner appreciatively, but he was shifting the man on his shoulder and didn't notice.

"You can continue your patrol. The betas will be back soon, but we're going straight into a meeting, so you'll need to stay here for a while longer."

Felicity nodded, and sure that she'd relay the message, I opened the door to the cellar we used as a holding room for threats to the pack. Feeling around inside, I flicked the switch. Lights blazed in the space large enough to hold ten comfortably. Twenty, if we had to cram people in—which we never had.

"Over there." I pointed to a futon that we kept in here, along with a few wooden chairs.

"Nice dungeon," Gunner murmured as he stooped to enter.

"Hardly a dungeon. They even have water because we're not total animals." I pointed to the sink and paper cups on the counter.

"Only half." He winked, and my lips twitched. "Still, Harp, I can smell the blood."

I cringed. Okay, there was that. Aside from the obvious wards, the scent of spilled blood from when my father and his betas required answers and our captives were not forthcoming never quite left this room.

"Holding room," I insisted, because even if unspeakable things happened here, I disliked the term dungeon.

"Whatever you say, chica." Gunner deposited the man on the futon and wiped his hands on his jeans. "He sorta stinks like sulfur."

I tilted my head. "I don't smell it."

"I don't think it is *him*, but as if he touched someone with that scent." Our eyes met, and he didn't have to say what he was thinking. Demons reeked of sulfur, so this guy could have a direct connection. "Might be high up in the Darkborn."

"You're not thinking Wrath, are you?"

"Naw. Maybe a lower level general or whatever." Gunner studied the man. "Don't know much about Wrath, but I doubt he makes himself accessible to the many."

"No." I exhaled. "Well, let's wake him up and see, shall we?"

The betas would be here soon, and I wanted to have as many answers for them as I could. Even though I'd just spoken with them, with the Covenant announcing that seven demon princes roamed the earth right as we'd disbanded and my brother had been attacked, we had things to talk about again.

It's getting real all too fast. I grabbed a paper cup and turned on the water. Once the cup was full, I returned to the man and poured its contents on his head.

The man shot up, sputtering for air. When he saw he wasn't alone, he glowered.

"Let me go."

I laughed. "We'll get right on that. After you tell me why you attacked my brother?"

The man's eyes narrowed. "You're Ferenz's blood?"

"Alpha heir."

"We should make a deal."

I scoffed. This guy had balls, I'd give him that. But he didn't know how loyal wolves were. "I'd never betray my pack."

"We can strengthen your pack beyond your wildest dreams." He leered at me as if he seriously believed I'd be happy about such an offer.

A snort escaped me. "I doubt that. Now, why did you go after my brother?"

"We require your pack."

"My father already got his ass kicked for telling your master no." I gestured to where the Sigil of Lucifer was branded into his skin, letting him know I knew what organization he belonged to.

"The word of one wolf means little to my master." The man shrugged. "He will get what he wants."

Like hell he would. "Which Prince of Hell do you serve?"

The man blinked. "How do you—"

"*Which*?" I pressed.

"I intend to bow to Lucifer."

"And what order are you?" Gunner asked. I didn't see why, but I was sure he had his reasons. When the man didn't answer, my partner took a menacing step closer.

"Wizard," the man blurted and leaned back, as far away from Gunner as he could get.

"Type?" Gunner pressed.

"Caster."

"How many of your kind are with the Darkborn?" I sensed that this was where Gunner was going.

"Dunno. My coven joined up earlier this year. Things only recently started picking up . . . " He trailed off as my stomach sank over the idea of whole covens of witches joining the Princes of Hell. "Wait a minute . . . what's happened?"

"Was something supposed to happen? Besides them appearing in this realm?" Was it possible that he knew the Princes of Hell's plans? Did all the Darkborn?

"No." He swallowed and looked at the ground. What a liar.

Our questioning continued, but we had zero luck getting anything important out of the wizard. So, when my phone buzzed, I read the text and looked at Gunner.

"Everyone is here."

"Just as well. Feel like we're wastin' our time." Gunner glowered at the man. "I don't like wastin' time. Makes me mad. Think about that while I'm away." His voice dropped to a low growl.

The man swallowed. He'd been oscillating between fearing Gunner's hulking form and being cocky during our interrogation, but maybe a threat and a nice long time alone in this room would help loosen his lips.

Time in one's own head often brought out our worst fears.

I backed away, moving to the door, and Gunner followed. The man didn't speak as we let ourselves out. The wards sealed around and behind us. Once outside, I locked the door and sighed.

"Well, it was something. At least we learned that whole organizations are siding with the princes."

"Still wasn't enough." Gunner grunted. "I don't wanna hurt the guy but . . . "

"Force might be necessary," I finished, disliking the idea. We were dark artifact hunters and sometimes our missions necessitated a show of strength, but not too often. Few in our coven liked the idea.

Felicity darted out of the woods in her wolf form, dashed

straight to us, and shifted. "Would you like me to watch the door?"

"Yes," I said, pleased that she had such foresight. I'd have to ask my father about her. "I'm keeping the key, but watch it just in case."

"Okay." She cast a glance at the door. "I'll stick to this area."

"Thanks. Gunner?"

We fell into step, and I led him into the house, using my blood on the back entrance pad this time.

It wasn't often that the pack leaders gathered here. My family preferred to keep the house for just us, and meet in town, but seeing as we had an enemy locked up in the cellar, it felt right. Also, I'd have to speak with my father after the meeting. I had a hunch that he didn't know about the rest of the princes yet, and as alpha he should. Though, I preferred to have a plan on how to keep the pack safe before I met with Dad.

We walked through the door to Wolf Den, a small meeting room, and found that we were the last to arrive. Mom was there too, asking if anyone needed refreshments. The moment we entered, the light chatter between the betas, Mom, and Ethan stopped.

"Is Henley okay?" I asked.

"We extracted her, and she's in her room," Rikard, Dad's senior beta, answered.

"And the person who tried to take her?"

"We lost the trail." Rikard grunted. "What about the magic-user who attacked Ethan?"

I pointed to the general direction of the cellar. "He's in the Black Hole. We just spoke to him. He's a Darkborn wizard, and not very forthcoming. I got the sense he's hiding something big."

"Same here. We learned his entire coven joined the Dark-born" Gunner shook his head. "That ain't good."

"Why is *he* here?" Rikard stared at Gunner.

It was a fair question, though the sharp tone of my father's oldest beta made me cringe.

"He's my S&S partner, and I want him here for what I'm going to share with you. He knows things I have no experience of." I took my seat at the head of the table.

"But he's Blood Moon Pack," Rikard retorted on my right. "This is *our* business."

"Probably not for long." Gunner took a seat at the long table that dominated the room. Wisely, he took one at the periphery, far from the head of the table.

And yet, three other betas didn't relax. They just watched him with their eyes narrowed in distrust. None were as senior as Rikard, and while they might feel the same at Gunner's inclusion, they weren't about to voice it.

"Who's at Father's door?" I asked Mom.

Now that she was here, she wasn't taking care of Dad like she had been when I met the betas in town—before the attack on Ethan and Henley. Before the Covenant announced their news.

Damn. A lot had happened in just a couple of hours.

"Rikard's sons," she replied, which eased some tension inside me. The best option was that the betas took turns watching their alpha, but a family tie was a close second. Rikard had four grown sons, all as brawny and devoted to the pack as their father.

"Okay, good. Then, let's begin."

"We've started," Aura said, her Mexican accent thick

despite having lived in California for twenty-four years. "Ethan has been regaling us with his tales of the attack since the moment he entered the house—loud and clear—like the pup survived a war or something."

Crystal, a tall, muscular blonde of about forty, sniggered, which made Ethan turn red.

"If you had someone break into your work, you would tell others about it too."

"Didn't break in," Gunner drawled. "They used the front door, but yeah, it wasn't cool."

Ethan leaned back and a sour expression crossed his face.

So, I got the meeting back on track. "If the Darkborn dared to attack Alpha Ferenz's children, that means no one is safe. The pack has to be on high alert. No one leaves our land without a reason."

"Some of us have jobs." Crystal pointed a finger at herself. "Other than pack duties."

"I get that," I replied. "But the risk is too great. If the Darkborn took you, or anyone, the pack would do whatever they could to get the missing person back. And that involves risking even more people." I let out a long breath. "We're going to set up a fund for those who need the money until this is taken care of . . . Which might be awhile."

Rikard's lips pulled tight. "Why do you say that? Why can't we just find this group and attack? Teach them to leave us alone."

Attack. That was the way of the Midnight Pack. But now, I just wanted these people to stay out of what was to come. To stay safe.

Something big was about to happen. We needed to be ready and to fall back on the way of the wolf. To stick together, because if wolves did that, the pack always survived.

"You haven't heard the news still?" I asked. I'd half imagined that they'd hear the news on their way to rescue Henley. Or maybe after they saved her.

The others shared glances, and it became clear that they hadn't been online since our meeting. I knew without asking that Mom hadn't either. I only knew because I had an alert on my phone and had looked at it after my first meeting with the betas went to hell.

"Tell us." Crystal tapped the table, as if unable to handle the pause.

"The Covenant just made an announcement, and it's something Gunner and I are connected to." I cast a sidelong glance at my mom, who sat across from Gunner. "There's a reason this group, the Darkborn, are trying to form alliances. They're working for the Princes of Hell, and those royals just broke through the barriers of Earth a couple of days ago."

Mom leaned forward, her face pale. "Are you saying that Hell's Royals are here?"

"I am. All seven." I swallowed deeply. "And we think it's only a matter of time before they do what prince's do—build kingdoms. For that, they need alliances." I nodded down to my partner. "Between the two of us, we can answer many of your questions. Gunner traveled to Hell for something, so he might know even more than me."

"Doubt that," Gunner said. "But I'll help in any way that I can."

For the first time, the betas didn't look upon him with a cast of skepticism. No, their faces were full of horror. As each one leaned forward and put their hands on the table, I prepared to handle their queries and set up a plan to keep my pack safe.

CHAPTER TWENTY-FIVE

GUNNER

MY SHOULDERS LOOSENED AS I WALKED OUTSIDE AND BREATHED IN that sweet California air.

The meeting with the Midnight Pack's betas had lasted well over two hours, and I was ready to shrug off this form and run my tail off.

"Sorry, I kept you waiting." Harper stepped out of the doorway to her house and closed the door behind her. "Mom wanted to ask a few more questions before she told Dad what was going on."

"She's doin' it alone?" Usually, a beta would inform the alpha of bad news.

"I planned to help, but Rikard cut in and said he wanted to go with her to tell my father. They've been friends all their lives. He thinks he failed Dad somehow, by not knowing what was happening in the world—not that, that was possible."

"He's devoted."

She blew out a long breath. "I can only hope to have that kind of beta one day."

"You will." I smiled. "You'll be a good leader, Harp."

Her lips curled up slightly, and I got the sense my vote of confidence meant something.

"Have you spoken with your father?" She strolled alongside me and passed, urging me to catch up with a wave of her hand.

"Not yet. My phone is in the car. I was plannin' on doing it after our run. Need to clear my head first."

And plan on how to tell my pa he needed an evacuation plan. If the Darkborn came for the Midnight Pack, eventually, they'd come for mine too. Unlike Harper's pack, my people had an out. Father's blood ran through me, that same blood of the wolvea. We had distant kin in Isila and they'd find a way to bring us over. Maybe the whole pack too, if Pa could swing it.

"Same." She tossed me a grin. "Let's quit yammering and get running."

She broke out into a run for the trees surrounding her home. Heart rate kicking up, I followed, my legs eating up the ground, catching her in a few long strides. She pushed harder and the thrill of competition sang through me.

"Race you to that oak!" Harper pointed and kicked it into high drive.

"Damn girl!" I laughed, straining to catch up.

"Some of us aren't a mountain of muscle, so we have to be fast!" She let out a yelp of joy when she reached the tree and spun. "By the Old Ones, that felt good!"

I was there the next second, my cheeks hurting from my big ass smile. "Beatin' me or runnin'?"

"Both."

I snorted. "Let's not stop, then. Your bro said you got a lake in these woods?"

"Due north. About one and a half miles that way." She

extended a hand. "As kids, we used to go for a swim and then play in the caves not too far from the water. We didn't even care that we were sopping wet and stinky."

I knew how that felt. My pack had places where the kids loved to run wild and play, too. Some of my best memories featured a river runnin' by our land.

"Race ya there," I said, wanting to see the place that made Harper smile so wide.

Her eyes brightened. "You want a rematch? Even though I know the way and you don't?"

"Girl, I can smell water. And hell yes, I wanna rematch. Shift."

Magic shimmered in the air as we shifted. Suddenly, a wolf with reddish brown fur and mischievous green eyes stood in front of me. With my black fur, silver eyes, and much larger form, we looked as different in this aspect as we did as humans.

Harper let out a growl. The she-wolf grew impatient.

I barked and turned toward the woods. She did the same with a gleam in her eyes that had me wishin' that we were mind-linked.

But wolves had been runnin' with those who weren't in their packs for years and we had a system.

Harper barked, marking the second signal.

A low growl left me, telling her to be ready. When the third bark left my muzzle, she took off.

Dang, this girl is fast, I thought as I chased her.

For about two seconds, we raced neck and neck, but then the trees grew thick and we separated. Harper sped up and even though the trees were dense, she wove through them without a problem. For a bigger wolf like me, that wasn't easy, but I'd never give up so fast.

We ran through the forest, the wind whipping through our fur, the smell of nature fillin' our noses. California was green, like my part of the country, but it smelled different here. The ocean was closer than where my pack lived. The vegetation differed. I soaked it all in, having been in cities for too long.

As I allowed my other nature to take over, the pounding of paws filled my ears. Harper was just ahead, her ears flicking back—listening for me, judging the distance.

I grinned. The she-wolf was worried, and as the smell of lake water flew at me, I put on more speed. It was about time I really gave her somethin' to worry about.

I bore down, paws slamming into the ground, my pace increasing. I was hot on her heels, and Harp sensed it. She sprinted harder.

My tongue lolled out as breathing became more difficult. At that moment, in the distance, I caught a hint of blue. The lake. At our pace, it was only a couple of minutes away. I broke out into a dead sprint and overtook her.

A howl of frustration left Harper's throat, but I wasn't about to look back, not when the lake opened up before me with the water so invitin'. I ran harder, pushing my legs to the limits, and the beach appeared beneath me, rocky and rough.

A second later, I plunged into the water, victori—*Splash*!

A weight landed on my head, and I plummeted deeper into the lake. I twisted, doggy-paddling to the surface and gasping for breath.

Laughter hit my ears, and when I opened my eyes, I found Harper in the lake shifted back to human form.

"I got you!"

I barked and shifted.

"I won fair and square!" I called back, unable to believe she had the balls to claim the win.

"No, you didn't. I leapt and was above you the whole time. I landed right in front of you. I won!"

That sneaky she-wolf.

"That's air, this is water." I splashed her, only to have the gesture returned right away.

"Fine." Harper stuck out her tongue. "Tie?"

I stared her down, my alpha nature rising, demanding she back down. She felt it too, 'cause her lips pursed.

"I'm alphablood too. It won't work on me."

I wasn't so sure about that. I was a wolvea, closer to the strongest wolves. Harper was a powerful wolf, but nothin' topped the wolvea. And yet . . .

She never made herself smaller, never backed down. Even now, she paddled closer to me, wearing the serious expression she usually kept on her face.

I missed the smiles. The laughter. I wanted to hear that again, and what the hell did it matter who won? We had bigger battles to fight.

"Tie," I said, barely keeping the growl from my tone.

She winked. "That's what I thought."

With that, she swam back to the shore. I trailed behind, takin' in the blue lake and the Santa Cruz Mountain range that framed the water. I'd never seen anything more pretty. That was until Harper exited the water.

Whoa, baby.

Her clothes clung to her every curve, revealing more of the wolf than I'd ever seen. My heart skipped a beat and down below, my little wolf stirred.

Down, boy.

Sure, the girl looked good, better than usual, and typically she looked pretty hot. But was it that my wolf was so close to the surface? Or . . . I sniffed the air. Was she turned on, too?

Harper turned, and with the California sun beating on her cheeks, she looked like a drenched goddess. "Wanna walk back?"

"What?" I asked, too stunned for words.

"Want to walk back? Take our time?"

I shook my head under the guise of drying my hair, as I tried to get my head on straight. It worked. Kinda.

"Yeah, sounds good." I climbed up the lake's bank and onto the pebbled beach. My shirt stuck to my chest, and I didn't miss how Harper's eyes dipped down, takin' me in as I had done with her.

The moment was brief, though. Harper caught herself, and her attention turned to the sky. "A falcon." She pointed, and I turned in time to see the bird, larger than any I'd ever seen.

"They're not usually in this area this early," Harper said. "Hawks come here in the winter."

"Well, things are changin'." I took off my shirt and rang it out. As I did so, I cut her a glance and couldn't help but smirk.

Oh, yeah, now the girl was really starin'. Pride ran through me. An alpha wolf couldn't help it, but I also didn't need to be cocky about how the females looked at me. Pa had taught me better.

I put my shirt back on. "Maybe we'll see more on the walk."

"Right." Harper's voice sounded slightly strangled. "We'll have to keep our eyes open." She turned and walked toward the woods, her hips swayin' in a way that called to me deep in my soul.

Oh, I sure as hell would be keepin' my eyes open.

We didn't walk straight back, which I didn't mind one bit. Goin' back to Harper's family home meant back to business, and a brief break was what we needed.

Instead, we wandered the woods, and she told me stories about things that happened when her pack ran in them.

"That's where I first shifted. I was eight," she said, pointing to a clearing we passed by. "Mom and I had been picking mushrooms and—*poof*—I shifted!" "That's where I took my vow to the pack," she said when we came upon the biggest damned tree I'd ever seen.

When we reached a stream, Harper laughed. "That's where I had my first fight." Her lips had curled up at that one, which made me think she won.

We veered back to the mansion when I caught her staring at a tree with markings etched on to it. I nudged her playfully. "You get your first kiss there?"

"Uh, yeah. Something like that." Her cheeks had colored, and something inside me roared with jealousy.

Whatever had happened here had been formative for her. Had it been Aspen? Suddenly, the guy seemed even less likable than before.

I blinked. *What the hell, man?*

I wasn't this guy. This weird jealous wolf. Even with my few steady girlfriends, I was laid back and Harper wasn't a girlfriend, just a partner.

Though it kinda felt like the lines were blurring there.

"They're good woods," I said as we exited the trees and found ourselves on her family lawn. "Your pack chose well."

"There aren't many natural wolves in California, so owning this much acreage is key. It keeps us safe."

I was about to say that no matter where shifters were, hiding from humans was important, when a scream cut through the calm of the afternoon.

"What the hell?" I asked. "Is that comin' from the Black Hole?"

Harper swallowed. "The betas said they were going to give the wizard a while to stew before they tried to make him open up. I bet Crystal is in there now. She's the . . . ummm . . . "

"She extracts information," I finished. "Pa has a wolf like that, too. It's not pretty work, but sometimes it's necessary. Like now."

Harper nodded as another scream bit through the brilliance of the day. "There's no need for us to check on her. If she learns something, she'll tell me. Let's go inside."

"I need to call my pa. Can I have the car keys?"

She fished them out of her pocket and handed them over. Once we reached the house, ignoring the screams the whole way, she turned to me.

"I'll leave the door open so you can come inside when you're done. I'm sure Mom will have a late lunch ready for you. I'll text Luca while you're on the phone, too. Give him an update."

"Sounds good, partner," I said, and we split. I grabbed my phone from the car and saw that in the time between the glass studio and now I'd missed three calls from home.

My heart rate kicked up. Had something happened to them already? I'd thought we'd have more time.

Nervous, I dialed Pa's direct line, and thanked the Old Ones when he picked up on the first ring.

"My boy. We just got the news from the Covenant."

"Hey Pa." I exhaled. "I wanted to talk to you about that."

"This has to do with your coven?"

"It does." I told him what I could, only a smidge more than what was public knowledge, and once I was done, he remained silent.

"Pa, I think you need to be proactive about this. Take the pack to Isila."

CHAPTER TWENTY-FIVE

"That's over two hundred wolves."

"Wolf Island is a big place."

"It's a huge favor, son. I don't know how much sway I have."

That was the rub. For certain, my family could find refuge in the other world, but Pa would never leave his pack behind. More than anything, I wanted them to go, to be safe. I hoped that the wolves in the otherworld would be open-hearted and help their kind.

"What about you, Gunner?"

I inhaled. "I gotta stay. I'm too close to the heart of the matter."

"That's not what I wanna hear."

"It's the truth." I swallowed. "There's more."

"Tell me."

I'd hesitated on this bit before. It wasn't public knowledge, and it had to do with Harper's people, but I couldn't let the same happen to my pack. My family. "My partner in S&S is a wolf and demon followers propositioned her pack. Darkborn, they call themselves. I already told you they attacked the alpha and now they went after his kids. I think they're gonna try again."

He blew out a long breath. "Why are they doin' this, though?"

"They want wolves to fight for their cause."

"We would never." Though I couldn't see him, I could picture Pa's chest puffin' up.

"I don't think they plan on leavin' people alive if they deny them too much." I turned and leaned against the metal of the car, warmed from the sun. "You and Alpha Ferenz are equally influential Pa. That's another reason you have to go."

Silence followed. He knew Ferenz's name, knew that they

were equals, and if something could befall Alpha Mace, then Pa wasn't safe either.

I was about to press harder when my father sighed. "I'll speak to the royals. If they allow it, we'll be gone within the week. Are you sure you won't join us?"

"No, Pa. I can't come. But I'll stay safe. I promise."

"Don't make promises you can't keep, boy." His voice softened.

"I'll do my best."

"I love you, Gunner. We'll call if we leave this realm."

"Love you too, Pa."

CHAPTER TWENTY-SIX

TOBIAS

I waited by the village pub, alone, save for the rising moon that battled with the sun's dying rays.

Serena, not knowing that Luca had arrived with new mobiles, had sent a text to Claire's phone just an hour ago. Giselle must have gotten the witch's number before she left. My sire always had been an excellent planner.

Though I anticipated my sister's arrival, I was also using this time to be on the lookout. It was unlikely that the Ordo would strike *Abscondita* lands so soon after their first assault, but until new wards were up, those at the manor needed to remain vigilant. As Shay and Luca were working on the wards at that very moment, it would take hours still for them to be in place.

I exhaled a plume of white breath that filled the chilled autumnal air. In the tavern that claimed to sell the 'best fish and chips in the village!' humans laughed and conversed over pints of ale that warmed them from the inside out.

In mere weeks it would be All Hallows Eve. Where would I be then? In Isila—kneeling before the Blood King? Scouring the world for the remaining five *Vindix* with my mate? Still in England puttering about and trying to be helpful as Meredith trained and learned of the *lapis caelesti*? Still lost as to where we'd go next?

No. I could not believe that last one.

The minutes had begun to build and were ready to explode. Something big would soon happen, though what, no one knew. The idea drew a shiver down my spine, one that stilled as the sound of an engine cut through the quiet night.

I leaned closer to the road and took a peek from behind a bush. Judging by the speed and the vehicle's profile, a sports car drove down the narrow country lane, too fast. Hidden in the bushes, I waited.

The car maintained its pace. Just when I thought it might be a country bloke out for a dangerous spin and nothing more, the driver flashed the car lights four times.

My lips tugged up. Serena did always enjoy making an entrance.

I emerged from the foliage just as she brought the car—a Ferrari—to a sudden stop.

"Brother!" My sister's French accent called out as her face appeared, as stunning as ever. The only difference from when I last saw her was the natural way she wore her black hair. "Am I following you?"

"I ran here," I said. The exertion had been necessary, and I'd taken it as yet another chance to survey the area as I traveled.

"Then, get in!" She nodded her head to the Ferrari.

"You seem to be in a hurry." I rounded the car and let myself into its plush leather interior.

"Giselle mentioned you would need help, and I saw no

need to delay." Serena's slim fingers trailed over her red seat. "You like? I bought it when I arrived at Heathrow."

I rolled my eyes. Both of my siblings had a penchant for the finer things in life. Castles, jewels, high-end fashion—you name it, Serena and Raphael loved it. Giselle too, come to think of it.

"You could have rented a car."

"Tobias!" Amber eyes glinted, striking against her glowing ebony skin. "I thought you would appreciate this bit of beauty."

"I do. Hans will too."

"Who's that?"

"A S&S member. He's an amateur mechanic."

"Can't wait to show Francesca off!" She revved the engine and threw the car into gear. Before I knew it, we drove far too fast down the country lane.

"Slow," I murmured.

"I can stop her on a euro."

Of course, she could. With vampiric vision, Serena would see any oncoming vehicle, person, or animal long before they saw us. And yet . . .

"Secrecy, Serena."

"*Oh, fine.*" Her foot lifted off the gas. "I thought after your break in at *Le Bastion* you'd be less of a stickler for the rules."

I snorted. "What else has Giselle told you?"

"Not nearly enough. Like, nothing of your witch! Spill, brother!"

"Her name is Meredith Stone. She's a keeper of one of the *lapis caelesti* and a seeker."

"A seeker is once in a generation, and yours holds the sacred stones?" A whistle parted her lips. "Tobias, she seems out of your league. Can you handle this woman?"

I laughed. The question might have offended the old me, but perhaps my sister was correct. Meredith was turning out to be nothing like I originally thought.

"You smell like her," Serena added. "Like she's claimed you."

"She wouldn't know how."

Serena arched a dark eyebrow. "Are you sure about that?"

"I only meant that she's a new witch. She's been training and learning nearly every waking moment, but I doubt that something so innate about our world has come up."

"Maybe her magic did it and you didn't even notice." My sister cleared her throat. "I can't wait to meet her."

"No stories from the past."

"Like you're going to stop me."

I huffed out a breath. Giselle always claimed that Serena was the smartest of her children, and it was true. Serena held many advanced degrees. Her IQ was off the charts, and she had a past that gave her a degree of street smarts that took Raphael and I years to accumulate.

Intelligence aside, my younger sister was also the most stubborn. It was an annoying trait she shared with my mate.

We caught up on the last decade as she drove down the country lane toward the manor where the *Abscondita* Coven hid from the world. When I pointed out the turn, Serena's eyebrows shot up.

"They are well hidden. I didn't even see that turn until you pointed it out. I bet it's a misdirection ward."

"Only those who are told it exists can see this area. And after tonight, it will be even better concealed. As we speak, Luca and a nephilim in my coven are putting up new wards."

She knew Luca was a mage and nodded. "Powerful."

Overgrown ferns pummeled the Ferrari, which made my

sister curse under her breath. We were nearly to the house when I spotted a stain on the gravel. Blood.

"Is that from the fight?" She slowed so that her headlights caught the dark splotch.

"It must be. I didn't see it on my way to meet you. I ran through the woods."

"Someone should clean it up. Blood isn't just telling of violence."

If the person who'd bled lived, or someone had a vial of their blood—which I would not put past the OA—a powerful mage might use a blood spell to transport here, rendering our new wards useless.

"I'll tell the *Abscondita* fire witch she should burn the gravel to be safe."

Not only would that get rid of the blood, it would also set Tana with another task. Olga, Tana's mentor, said the young witch needed as many as she could handle to control her magic before she began working with the Ruby of Flames.

"That'll do it." Serena clicked her tongue.

"Park there." I pointed to my rental car.

Serena parked, and by the time we got out of the car, the front door to the manor flung open. Meredith appeared, and my heart gave a single hard *thunk*.

My sister turned and smirked. "Positively besotted."

"Bite me," I said, exiting the car to meet the witch who'd stolen my heart.

"Hey." Meredith waved. "I just got done studying."

"I apologize that I couldn't tell you where I went before I left."

The blasted witches of the *Abscondita* Coven still wouldn't let me in their precious library. No matter that I was trained in research and preservation and had been dying to get my hands on more books about the *lapis caelesti* for years.

"Luca did. They're still in the woods working on the wards." She stopped and threw her arms around me. "I'm glad you're back. It's weird that I can miss you so much when it's only been a few hours."

I squeezed her tightly, inhaling her honey scent as I slipped a finger beneath her chin and brought her lips to mine. Aware that we had an audience, the kiss was softer, more chaste than others we'd shared. When I pulled away, I smiled down at the witch. "We're mates. We will always want to be near one another."

From behind, a soft cough came.

"Serena is here and impatient as ever." I pulled away. "Ready to meet her?"

"Of course."

I waved my sister over. Wisely, she'd stayed back until I'd greeted my mate. We weren't even fully bonded, and I was already inclined to be ferociously protective over Meredith. A vampire needed to get my approval first. At least, until I'd taught my mate how to best protect herself against my kind. A matter I planned to attend to tonight.

"Meredith, this is my sister, Serena."

Serena beamed, and though Meredith held out her hand, Serena did things the French way. She gripped my mate by the shoulders and kissed her cheeks in the European manner of greeting.

"Oh." Meredith exhaled and then let out an airy laugh.

"I'm so pleased to meet you, Meredith." Serena smiled. "Tobias told me a bit about you on the way here, but I can't wait to get to know you on my own. We're sisters!"

My mate's eyes widened. For someone with her past, I

imagined the idea of collecting people who would be friends with her, even love her, was odd. Then again, she did fine with Harper and Shay.

"That's wild. But in a good way." She grinned at Serena, who beamed back. "Is your last name Laurent too? I'm still not entirely sure how this whole vampire family thing works."

"Serena Aurore Liis Laurent. I use the Liis when I do not want to garner attention. Much like Tobias often goes by Aston." My sister shot me an amused look. "Though, I'll say I do not hide my vampire lineage nearly as much as my brother."

"You were French before being turned?"

"Giselle found me in Paris, where I was born and raised."

She omitted the dire circumstances under which our maker had found Serena and for that, I was grateful. The tale was grim, and I despised thinking about it—even if the perpetrators had been thoroughly handled. May they rot in Hell.

"One day we can all take a trip there," Meredith said. "When this is all over. I've been to Paris, but on a job. I'd love to explore it with a local."

My sister's smile broadened, and my insides warmed. The pair was already getting along swimmingly. It was better than I imagined.

"Sounds perfec—" Serena's words choked out and her body grew limp. I caught her just before she reached the ground. With a curse, I lowered her gently, keeping my hands on her.

"What's going on?" Meredith asked, kneeling beside us. "Is she having a seizure?"

One glance at my sister's amber eyes, now glazed over, told me the truth. "A vision."

"Excuse me? How is that possible?"

I held my sister tightly to keep her stable and explained. "In her human life, Serena was a witch—although she did not know it. She had visions of the future, and that gift did not leave her when she changed. It's not common for vampires to retain gifts from their past life, but she cannot control them. This is how she looks when they take over, and this one appears to be a strong one."

Meredith's jaw tightened, and as the tremors wracked my sister's body, I grew more worried too. Alas, the fear left me just as suddenly as the vision left my sister, and her eyes became amber once more. They locked on me.

"I already knew that you smelled like her, and I scented you on her the second I got out of the car, but now I . . . "

"What?" I asked, my mouth dry.

"Your mate bond will solidify soon, brother. And when it does, be ready for the Blood to call."

"I already planned on going. Eventually."

"With her. They will *demand* it."

I swore. Of course, we'd considered this but I still held some naïve hope that maybe, just maybe, I'd be able to attend court without my mate. That way, I could keep her safe. "Are you certain? Is Giselle there?"

"Not yet, but she will be and the king will tunnel through her mind. He will want to see Meredith and he will not take no for an answer. He will also try to keep her for his own means, but your mate will fight it and make a dangerous deal with him. Prepare her for our kind."

Meredith let out a shaky breath that resonated deep in my core. "A deal?"

"You will see no other choice," Serena replied.

"But can't visions be wrong?" Desperation thickened in my mate's voice.

"Not mine." Serena shook her head. "Mine are *always* right."

I swallowed and helped my sister to stand, not wanting to think about what would happen soon. We'd considered that she'd have to go to Isila, that the royals would want to meet her. My mate had claimed that she'd go anywhere with me, but this was different now. To be summoned by the king, to make a deal with him, and for him to try and keep her there by force was another matter. One that made my insides boil with rage.

CHAPTER TWENTY-SEVEN

HANS

"You can go harder," Serena said. "Push yourself."

My stomach roiled. "I don't want to hurt you."

The vampire scoffed and, with two fingers, gestured for me to come closer. "Don't flatter yourself. I can take it."

I pulled in a steeling breath. As much as I hated it, she was right. Serena had been on manor land for two hours and since then, she'd embroiled herself into business here. Even the kind no one else wanted—especially not the elder witches. Knowing full well what I was, Tobias's sister had signed up to help me train my dark powers. Rolling my shoulders back, I squared off with Serena. "Prepare yourself."

"Get on with it."

The words were barely out of her mouth before I did as the vampire requested and struck again.

My demon magic hit her square in the chest and Serena curled inward on herself, jaw tight. I clamped down, though, feeling that she fought back. It wasn't the first time Serena had done so, though it still surprised me that people could break free of my powers to cause pain. No one had before.

Then again, until recently, I'd only ever tested my magic on humans. Back when I was a child and teetered on the edge of darkness, I'd used my magic to inflict pain on them whenever I felt they deserved it. In those days, they'd only been able to scream in agony.

Magical orders, however, were a different story, which Serena had proven. And she was about to do so again. I recognized the feel of her strength, fighting back.

Attempting to stymie her bid for freedom, I leaned in a bit more, but to no avail. Serena cast off the curse and ran at me. A millisecond later, her fangs scraped at my neck. "Not enough," she hissed. "Wrath would be free faster."

"I tortured him before."

The vampire pulled away, amber eyes shining in the moonlight. "You caught Wrath unaware once. Now that he knows what you can do, you cannot count on it again. If I can throw your magic off, if I learned that quickly, he can, too."

I frowned. Though I despised putting Serena—anyone—through this, I recognized the value she was giving me.

"Have you tried tapping into other magics? You said your sister uses tendrils to do her bidding. And Prince Orien smoke-travels?"

"Correct. I've also used tendrils in the past, though not on purpose." I paused, thinking of the day dark ribbons had burst from me to save Shay. I still had no idea how I'd done that. "Nicoleta can smoke-travel too."

"Have you tried that?" Serena crossed her arms.

"I've not."

"Well, you should! You've been involved in smoke-travel so you should even know what it feels like." Tobias had called out from thirty feet away, where he worked with Meredith on fending off vampires.

Beyond them, Olga and Tana practiced fire magic. Under my gaze, the old fire witch turned. She scowled.

Only an hour ago, I had come clean and told the *Arcacustos* the truth of what I was. Considering they'd believed me to only be a wizard before, they hadn't taken it well, but Tobias, Luca, and Meredith stuck up for me. Much to my surprise, Tana and Shay had too, and the *Abscondita* Coven had been forced to allow me to stay on their lands.

I smiled at Olga, hoping to win her over a touch, but the Russian witch turned her back on me. Tana, on the other hand, grinned, even as Olga barked at her to encase her entire body in flames. As if reflexively, fire shrouded her, but only for a few seconds.

The girl had powerful raw magic, but the control of a novice. That made me think Tana's ability to burn her home down had more to do with her unregulated emotions that seeped into her magic and perhaps the Ruby of Flames, rather than her brute strength. Still, she was making progress. As was Meredith.

It was exciting to see my once-student try new variations of hedge magic. I wished that I could provide more help than spouting off the occasional tip on energy manipulation and hand motions, but with my wizard powers gone, I was not that useful. And I had to admit, Tobias was doing a good job.

The vampire did not know how to wield magic, but he'd studied up on witching offensive tactics so he could defend himself. Meredith had fended him off twice in thirty minutes —with magic, a marked difference to when she'd tried the human tactic of gouging his eyes out in the S&S tomb.

The memory pulled a chuckle out of me and I felt lighter, a welcome reprieve. Using my demon powers sent darkness surging through me and that bogged me down with unpleasant emotions, so any levity was welcome.

"Do you think you could?" Serena asked, pulling me back to the moment. "Smoke-travel?"

"I passed out during the actual traveling. I had also just lost my wizarding magic, so a lot was happening." I pushed back the memory of that awful night in DC. "But if Nicoleta can do it, I don't see why I couldn't. I'll try."

"It would be useful to have another means of travel," Serena said. "We don't know when we'll need to move."

She was right. We had three luxiters on hand, but the others wouldn't be ready for a few days. In the meantime, if I was separated from one of the luxiter holders, and I needed an escape, this could be a good option.

I cringed, hating the idea that I was about to delve deeper into my darker side. "I'll give it a shot. On myself first."

"If you manage, I'll join you."

After a few rounds, I added mentally. The youngest Laurent was not scared of pain or discomfort.

"While you're waiting, can you come here, Serena?" Tobias asked. "I'd like to try a double-pronged attack on my mate."

Meredith smirked. "He needs help, 'cause I'm rockin' it!"

"That you are!" Benedict cheered her on from where he perched on a tree branch at the edge of the lawn, like a cat overlord. "No vampire, be they royal or normal, will attack my witch!"

Serena laughed. "Yes, I'll help, if Hans is okay with that?"

I nodded, preferring it that way. After hearing that Meredith would be required to visit the Blood Court of Isila, and they would put her in harm's way, she needed more help than me. Or maybe that was wishful thinking.

Serena joined her brother and Meredith and I turned,

feeling less on display with my back to them. It took no effort at all to call my dark magic so that it pooled under my skin, shading my already gray veins closer to black. They would return to normal in time. Yet, I still hated seeing them. Would I ever get to use magic and not be physically altered?

It didn't seem that way, so I needed to man up and get on with things. When the next conflict came, people would depend on me. I could not fail them like I had failed Shay when Nicoleta and Wrath abducted us.

Inhaling sharply, I pulled my power into my fingertips. I had no idea how to smoke-travel, but among witches and wizards, I was an expert caster. When a witch first started casting, their intention was as important as knowing the right spell, and it so happened I knew a few demon spells. Regular words that I'd never heard spoken as spells too.

My mother had taught me spells that might help me survive should Prince Lucifer or his minions seek me or Nic. At times, Lilith also spoke in a demon tongue, teaching me random words by proximity.

As I grew up in the rustic mountains of Romania, it was often cold, requiring fires. I'd learned the word demons would use for smoke. I suspected if I paired that with an intention of teleporting a small distance, I might succeed. That was, if I had the talent for this at all.

I raised my hands, pooling my dark power in my palms. "*Kono.*"

The veins of my palms grew black, stark against the pale skin there, but no smoke appeared. I tried again, this time envisioning the smoke, and yet again, nothing happened.

It stayed that way, until the fifth attempt, when the faintest puff of black smoke arose. The stench of it filled my nostrils, acrid and rotten.

CHAPTER TWENTY-SEVEN

That was the scent of the underworld, but it was so small. Worthless.

Though I'd just begun, I dropped my hands with a huff.

"I'm surprised there is a single thing you can't do," a voice said from behind.

I spun, startled, and found Tana standing there. How long had she been watching me?

"Olga needed the loo, and I wanted a break," she said, reading my expression. "How are you doing?"

"Fine."

"Your neck too? Did the bite heal?" Her eyes raked over my face, lingering on the scar along my jawline.

Then, she batted her eyelashes.

Oh . . . I had not really believed Shay earlier, but she was right, Tana was flirting. I met her gaze. She was young, perhaps twenty to my twenty-seven years. Too young for my taste. I needed to make sure Tana understood.

"My neck is good. Thanks for asking. You're not in S&S, but I consider us a sort of professional team, and I appreciate you looking out for me."

Her face fell at the word professional, but she recovered quickly and smiled. "Of course." One glance over her shoulder told me that she wanted an out. I was happy to oblige.

"I should get back to practicing."

"Right. Me too." She gave an awkward jerk of the head and returned to where she'd been working earlier.

I exhaled, hoping that would work.

"You always were so diplomatic with the ladies," another voice said.

I turned back toward the woods to find Shay walking out of the trees. Twigs had lodged themselves in her long, brown hair and leaves clung to the sweater she wore, and yet, she still looked attractive.

"That's nice to hear," I said.

"All the girls you dated in New Haven would mention it when your relationships ended. You played the field, but you were always respectful."

My nose wrinkled. "I did not play at anything."

"Don't deny it."

"I prefer to think of it as dating widely."

She laughed. "Okay, sure." When I smirked, she shook her head. "How's the training going?"

"I've learned a few new things about my abilities. Namely, that if someone is powerful enough, they can throw the pain off. But right now, I'm trying to smoke-travel."

"Do you need another pair of eyes?"

I stared at her, confused.

"I was passed out in DC, but I saw your sister smoke-travel in New York, remember? I smelled it, too. I don't know if I can actually help, but if I can, I will."

A pause passed between us. Why was she volunteering to help with dark magic? "Are you sure? What about the wards? Are you and Luca finished?"

Shay pressed her lips together for a moment before a long exhale parted them. "I've behaved badly around you, but I meant what I said earlier. I want to work on my prejudices. And specifically, I want to help *you*. You've always been willing to help me, Hans. And, besides, you don't deserve what's happened to you. If that means telling you what I see is similar to what I saw in New York, then that's what I'll do." She paused and drew in a long breath. "But honestly, a part of me thinks if I can help you with your dark powers, then maybe I'm doing something deeper. Maybe I'm helping you accept them yourself."

I snorted. "I'm that obvious, am I?"

A soft smile pulled up at her lips. "Sometimes we're our own worst enemies. I'm a prime example."

"You're not," I assured her.

She shrugged. "Agree to disagree, but I would like to help. If you'll let me." She gestured to the woods. "Luca is putting the finishing touches on his part of the new wards, so I have time."

What could I say to that besides 'yes'? Shay was fucking right on the money. I needed to work on self-acceptance, and she was putting herself out there, too.

"Sure," I said. "I'll try again."

She took a couple of paces back to better observe as I pulled the dark magic to the surface again and spoke the word for smoke. As I did so, I envisioned the smoke wrapping around me, and then blinking me out of existence only so I could end up on the other side of Shay.

As if it were waiting to show off, the smoke appeared and this time it was *a lot*. It wrapped around my body, and I held my breath, wondering if it might really be that easy.

But no. I stayed in place. The smoke dissipated into the wind, obscuring Shay's face for a moment. When the air cleared again, she looked thoughtful.

"So?" I prompted.

"That smelled and felt the same as when your sister used it," she said.

"Felt?"

"I didn't consider it before, not until it materialized, but your sister's smoke was charged. Like walking onto a steel bridge when there's a storm brewing, you sense the electricity.

Yours was the same, so that tells me you might be on the right path."

Interesting. I hadn't noticed that when I smoke-traveled.

"You're also making me think I need to light-travel, too."

"Isn't that what the luxiters are for?"

Shay shrugged. "For now, but my father said that some angels can light-travel, and if I can do so without a tool that frees up my luxiter for someone else. I just haven't had time to try." A yawn escaped her. "Maybe I'll have to ask Mom about that, but tonight isn't the time to start. After ward-setting a whole freaking forest, I'm beat."

"You and Luca have done a lot." I grinned at her. "Anyway, you should rest. Thanks for your help, but I can take it from here."

She looked put out, like I'd dismissed her earlier than she thought was appropriate. Perhaps I had. Though we were mending fences, I didn't need Shay around my dark powers.

She opened her mouth to reply, but before she got a word out, her phone rang. The sound echoed through the quiet woods.

"Speak of the nephilim, that's my mom's tone," she said. "Her ears must have been burning. Hold on." Shay grabbed the phone from her pocket and answered it. "Hey, Mom. What's—"

Shay's mouth snapped shut as a voice on the other end replied. Even from where I stood, the tone was frantic. Terrified, even. When Shay's light brown skin blanched, I tensed.

What was going on?

"Are you sure? Mom, are you safe?"

What the hell?

"Okay . . . okay, *yes*. I'll tell Luca" Shay swallowed thickly. "Get out of there, Mom."

My pulse was pounding as Shay and her mother exchanged a few more words. When she hung up, she looked as if she'd seen a demon prince.

"What happened?"

"My mother is on the run, escaping Los Angeles on wing."

My eyebrows pinched together. "On wing?"

"It was her only out." Shay's hand trembled as she put her phone back in her pocket. "She doesn't know who or how, but one of the demon princes has taken LA. It's overrun with their followers and people are fleeing for their lives."

CHAPTER TWENTY-EIGHT

MEREDITH

WE SAT AROUND THE LARGE TABLE. THE AIR VIBRATED WITH terror. The hours of training with Tobias seemed like they'd happened years ago when, in reality, only twenty minutes had passed since Shay shared the news.

LA was under the control of the demon princes.

Angelina Ramos had fled the city on the wing and was certain that that was the only way out. The roads were blocked and the most populous part of the city had been barricaded with dark magic. From her bird's-eye view, she'd seen hundreds of people march toward a dome of magic before disappearing into a dark cloud that rolled over the city.

Tobias squeezed my hand. He hadn't let go since Shay shared the news in the yard, and as his presence stabilized me, I didn't want him to. This was another big strike on our world, and no one was stupid enough to think this would be the last, so I wanted my mate close to me. As close as he could be. I cast a glance at Tobias's face as he spoke with Hans. I was more certain than ever that I wanted to form our full mating bond before more destruction occurred. I swallowed as the seriousness of the world's situation crashed over me again.

Would more cities fall tonight? Why LA? Were all seven princes living there, or would they take separate kingdoms, as Shay's father had suggested?

My stomach churned.

"She's on the verge of a panic attack," Benedict murmured, drawing Tobias from his conversation and pinning his attention on me.

"Breathe," Tobias whispered. "Luca will have more information."

The moment we'd found the coven master in the woods and Shay told him the news, he'd leapt into action. Since then, he'd been calling every contact he knew, including Covenant Seats. Surely, the Covenant would have a plan in place for this already. Right?

My questions were dashed as the door opened and Luca appeared, his cell clenched in a whitening fist. He rounded the table, passing the elder witches and Tana, and stopped only when he got to the free seat between Tobias and Hans.

My mate scooted closer to me. The table holding the tree with the gems that represented the *lapis caelesti* was large, but not big enough for this many. I wondered if Gloria knew a spell to make it larger.

"What news?" Tobias asked as Luca settled into his seat.

"The Covenant tells me that two Seats still live in the city—a wolf and a siren. They've heard nothing from them. As far as we can tell, Angelina got out one of the last calls. The entire region appears to have gone black."

"Black?" Hans's tone sounded strangled.

"Either phones are no longer working or people are not answering them. We have no way to pass or receive information about what is happening there." Luca shook his head. "Our only information has come from people who fled quickly."

He trailed off, looking ill. Angelina had seen people marching toward a dome of magic. She'd said they looked mindless, like zombies. What if they'd been possessed, but were now dead? Did anyone in the city still live?

"This is the worst possible scenario," Luca said. "We do not know what the princes are doing or their next steps."

"Another city will fall." Tobias shook his head. "It's just a matter of time."

As much as I hated it, I agreed with him, and yet, I also couldn't fathom what that meant for the world. Where did we begin?

Luca turned to me. "Finding the other *Vindix* has just become much more important. By claiming a city with millions of people in it, the Royals of Hell have not only put people at risk, but they've announced to everyone that magic is real and thriving."

I drew in a sharp breath. I hadn't even considered that, but of course he was right. New York had seen magic recently too, though the Covenant had covered up that shit show. But with one major city under demonic control, there would be no way to hide it.

"Meredith? Do you have any more clues regarding the stone keepers?" Luca asked.

I felt like a failure. I hadn't even found Tana, the other *Vindix* present at the manor. She'd been drawn to this place, not me to her. The books I'd been studying told me that the *Vindix* would be drawn to one another, so that made sense. But with such an enormous world to search and danger lurking around every corner, how would I find the final five?

Especially if they did not have their talismans. I twirled my moonstone ring around my finger. The talismans were the key to recognizing the others. I really needed the other *Vindix* to have them . . .

Then, there was the matter that some might not have their sacred stones or even know that they were magical. Oh, god. Too much rode on this. *On me.*

With one hand, I gripped the side of the table and tried to take a deep breath. "Nothing. It would be helpful if I had *anything* to go on. A place to start . . . "

"Maybe if we got our hands on the Pearl of Hell or the Opal of Heaven, it would be easier?" Shay gazed at me. "Don't the stones, like the *Vindix*, want to be together?"

Hans leaned forward, head nodding. "It's a common thread in magic—that like calls to like."

"We can use mine?" Tana held up the Ruby of Flames, which was never far from her hands nowadays.

"It's a possibility." Miriam tilted her head thoughtfully. "But no one is keen on letting you roam free, being untrained as you are."

Tana scowled. "Meredith doesn't know how to use her stone."

"I've never even seen it in real life!" I replied, somewhat indignantly. I liked the girl, but sometimes she said things that annoyed me. "Nor do I see how useful the Opal will be, but that's beside the point. I should just work on finding it first."

Tana shrank back in her seat. "Sorry. I just want to be in on the action."

"There will be plenty of that," Miriam assured her. "And you won't be the only *Vindix* who needs lessons."

"Fine." Tana sighed and fell silent.

"Do you think the Opal and the Pearl are on the loose in

LA?" Hannah asked Luca. "Was there any sign of them? Madness, perhaps?"

"I'm not sure," the mage replied. "I'm still hoping to hear from a few contacts, though there's a good chance the Princes of Hell are sticking together. If they are, that means Wrath is there and the stones will be too."

"We need to go there then," I said, already hating the idea. Benedict did too, because that comment earned me a derisive hiss.

"Yes." Luca nodded. "But not right now. We should wait through the night, see what news arises in the morning, if any. I want to have as much to go on as possible before we act."

"Goodnight, Benedict." I stood outside the door to my room with my vampire right behind me. At Tobias's invitation, my familiar had taken to using my mate's old quarters so that he could be as close as possible while still allowing Tobias and me privacy.

"Call if you need me," the familiar replied.

I nodded and shut us in, only to question myself a second later. I turned to my mate. "Should I be training again? Hans is out there. Luca is calling people all over the world to get information. Shay too. I should do something other than trying to get some sleep, right?"

"Hans needs to train," Tobias replied. "Demon magic and all its possibilities are new to him. You have but one job and that is *to seek*. You already know it well. As for Luca and Shay," he sighed and his eyes grew weary. " . . . they will need to exhaust all of their contacts before rest finds them. You have few contacts in this world."

Actually, aside from S&S members and those at the manor, I had zero contacts. Supremely worthless, I kicked off my shoes and pulled off my socks before perching on the edge of the bed. My fingers wrung together. "What do you think they're doing to LA?"

Tobias shot me a look. "Do you really want me to answer that?"

No. I didn't, and my gut told me I'd see firsthand soon enough. We might have to wait until morning, but we'd go there. If the *lapis caelesti* were hidden in the City of Angels, it was the only place on Earth worth going to.

"Meredith, you must relax."

"I don't think I can." I swallowed. "We're going into danger tomorrow, Tobias, and I can't have it end like New York."

"It won't," he growled. "I would never let anyone take you again."

"And I feel the same."

Shock rippled across his face at the idea that I could be worried for his well-being, but that was what it was to be mates. Even if our bond was not completely in place, I knew in my soul that Tobias and I would be bound for life.

"If we go, when we go, I don't want to separate from you. In fact . . . " I paused, but the idea had been playing in my head in the background for most of the meeting. It was because it was what I wanted. What I needed. "I want to seal our mate bond."

"We will. When—"

"*Tonight.*"

Tobias stilled in that preternatural way only vampires could manage, not even the slightest twitch moving a single muscle. Not even the pumping of blood producing a pulsing artery. I stared in awe at what he was before he turned his evergreen gaze on me. "Are you quite certain?"

"Positive."

"You know—"

"Yes, Tobias, there's a risk. You'll need to bite me. I know no matter what we do together, neither of us can be sure what will snap our bond in place." I inhaled slowly. "And, despite all of that, I want to be with you. I want to know you completely before we go to war—and I think that will be soon."

"I might feel the urge to have you drink from me too," Tobias replied. "Some say the bloodbound bond requires it."

When he'd given me his blood before, it had been to save my life. I'd been grateful, but still grossed out by the idea of drinking from the vein. While the thought of drinking from him still wasn't natural, it no longer made me recoil. It was a part of him and that was what I wanted. This vampire standing before me was who I wanted. "I'm fine with it."

He reared back and then recomposed himself. "The Vampire Court—"

"—will call for me no matter if the soulmate bond is in place or not," I said. "Giselle and Serena have made that clear. So, I want to do what I want to do. As long as you're ready too. I'm over my moment of fear. Are you?"

He swallowed, the sound of it filling the room, before he prowled my way. The intensity in his eyes, his gait, and the way his muscles coiled made my breath hitch.

Oh god, was I ready for this?

He licked his lips, and I swore my panties dampened, giving me a firm answer.

Oh, yes, I was ready. Overdue—even if I was a little terrified.

What would it be like, making love to a vampire? Would anything besides the bite hurt? How would the bond feel when it snapped into place?

"Stop thinking," Tobias rumbled. "I can see a million thoughts running around in that pretty head."

That struck me as hilarious and I snorted out a laugh. "I learned all about vampires today, and that is not one of their strengths."

"When it comes to me and you, it is."

"Oh." I exhaled as he hooked two fingers under my chin and lifted my face. Our eyes locked and the air between us turned to fire that rushed over my body, igniting every single part of me.

"You are exquisite," he murmured, and there was no holding back. I was his. Arms trembling with anticipation, I wrapped them around his neck and pulled him close.

Slowly, his lips explored mine, and as his tongue swept into my mouth, I pushed back in a heated dance of our own, perfect rhythm. Tobias inched closer, pressing his body between my legs and the impressive length of him against my thigh.

"On the bed," he demanded. "I need you on the bed."

Pulse thundering with anticipation, I broke away from him and scooted back. I hadn't gone more than a few inches when his deft fingers found the hem of my shirt and pulled it up and over my head.

A hiss left my mate, his eyes on my chest which was agonizingly restrained by my bra. I slipped it off and his expression grew feral before he pounced, lips locking around one nipple. "By the gods—every single one that has ever existed—you taste amazing."

My back arched, my lower half pressed into him and then

the words I never imagined that I'd utter slipped through my lips like air. "Drink from me."

He stilled. "If you invite me, I cannot deny my urges. Are you absolutely sure?"

"I don't want you to deny a single desire. Not when it comes to me." I panted, wanting every single bit of him.

Deep inside, a thrum built within me—one I'd only ever noticed when my blood had sung around him. Was that the bond? Was it saying to get on with it already?

"Do you hear it?" Tobias whispered.

"I do." I pulled his lips to mine, took them, and sighed with pleasure. "Now, don't keep me waiting, Tobias."

He chuckled as his mouth trailed my jaw and his fangs brushed my skin. A warning.

"Mmmm," I sang, a welcoming, and Tobias's fangs slid into my skin.

For a moment, sharp pain radiated from the bite, but it was only a second before a warmth rushed through me. I gasped as my sex clenched. What was going on?

Tobias drank deeply, and each gulp of blood brought me closer to the climax.

Then, it struck. My body tightened, and I let out a gasp, shocked at what was happening.

He released, brought his lips to mine before smiling down at me. "A perk for vampire lovers."

"Does that always happen?" I gasped.

"Not always."

"And why not mention it?"

"If you were more frightened than impassioned, it would not have come to pass. But you're not scared, are you, little witch?"

My head swam with questions as he dipped and peeled off

my pants. His shirt and pants followed, and soon enough we were bare before one another.

I took him in, both intimidated and excited. All I wanted was him, our joining. I wanted the vampire and me to connect in the most intimate ways possible.

As if he could hear my thoughts, Tobias climbed over me, pressing himself against my opening. His eyes met mine, giving me one last chance to say I wasn't ready, that this had gone too far.

"Please," I whispered, and he thrust in; the full length of him filled me.

A gasp of ecstasy ripped up my throat as my fingers wrapped around his neck and tangled in his dark hair. Effortlessly, we found a rhythm and our hips rolled together. Our fingers explored the other's skin, leaving tendrils of fire in their wake.

"Meredith," Tobias whispered. "I love you."

"I love you too." As the words left my lips, tears filled my eyes.

For someone like me, a thief with barely a friend in the world, love had always flown out of reach. A thing for others that I'd never thought I'd have because that meant bearing all of myself—the good, the bad, and the super ugly, too.

But now, love was here. I held my love and explored his muscles rippling beneath my touch. We were worshipping one another.

Instinct had me pull myself tighter to Tobias, strengthening our connection and pulling a moan of pleasure from his perfect lips. As long as I breathed, I'd never let this man go.

As if he felt my desire for more connection, more pleasure, just *more*, he increased his pace. I met him, our bodies moved to a dance of their own making, and my core coiled with a delicious tension.

I whimpered, which drew a rough chuckle from the vampire. His gaze met mine and his eyes twinkled with a glimmer of pride that he was bringing me so much pleasure.

"More." I sharply exhaled. I was so close now, so ready to release again.

Tobias gathered me to his chest, thrusting hard and so deep that my orgasm exploded through me—explosive and burning through me, tearing at my very soul.

I let out a cry of pleasure just as he did. Suddenly, his wrist rested firmly at my mouth and a metallic taste exploded on my tongue.

The bloodbond. He craved it, so I drank.

This time, I was aware of what I was doing, not on the verge of death. The blood filled my mouth, not revolting in the slightest, but rather sweet, rich. A nectar.

I drank deeper, enjoying it, and Tobias tipped his head back, his eyes closing in ecstasy. A thrill ran through me that I could give him this, that we were taking this step in our relationship.

Another sip slipped through my lips, and I moaned. Before my greedy lips I could take another, he pulled his wrist away, and brought his mouth to mine.

My hand found his cheek, and I pressed my magic into him, not even realizing I was doing it until he glowed. I gasped, sure this would be going too far.

But then, something inside me shifted. His eyes widened, showing me that he felt it too.

Wholeness, complete bliss, and knowledge I would do anything for this man overcame me. My limits held no bounds, not even burning the world.

CHAPTER TWENTY-EIGHT

Nothing.

He stared into my eyes. His burned with a million emotions and his chest heaved, though he didn't have to breathe to live.

"Meredith?"

"It happened," I assured him. "The mating bond is in place, isn't it?"

"Yes. Look." He held up his wrist, and my eyes narrowed.

A glowing band of light encircled his wrist. It looked a lot like the tattooed swirls that had appeared on my body after I took a dip in the Enchanted Pool, though much simpler. This was just a band with two small lines cutting through it on the thumb side of his wrist.

"What does that mean?"

"It's a symbol." Tobias took my left hand, and I gasped. I had the same thing. "Ours are identical and it tells others that we are bound."

My mate pulled me to his chest, and we held one another. We were ready to take on the world together.

CHAPTER TWENTY-NINE

HARPER

Sounds came from the kitchen, indicating that I wasn't the first to wake. I followed them to find Mom, my little sister Henley, and Gunner gathered around the island, eating pancakes. Henley's hand was clamped over her mouth as she laughed at one of Gunner's jokes.

I hung at the threshold of the room for a moment, watching them. I loved the way the corners of Mom's eyes crinkled when she laughed and how Henley smiled so wide that you could see nearly all of her teeth. I even enjoyed how Gunner seemed so at ease with them—comfortable enough to claim a stack of pancakes at least ten high.

My insides warmed. My family was everything to me, and I didn't get to spend as much time with them. Though the circumstances were dire, being home was a blessing.

"Harper!" Mom caught me watching. "There are more pancakes warming in the oven."

"And I made the smoothies!" Henley lifted a glass filled with green juice. "They're so good, right Gunner?"

"Excellent." My partner took a sip. I noticed the way his

nose wrinkled as he did so, but Henley didn't. He was sweet to pretend for her.

"Thanks." I set about making myself a plate stacked with pancakes and a big glass of green juice. "Did anyone get anything out of the wizard yet?"

Mom shook her head. "He passed out and there's been nothing new. Crystal will try again today." She cleared her throat. No one liked to think about what Crystal did to get the answers she wrangled out of prisoners.

"How's Dad?" I asked to change the subject.

My mother's face softened with love. "Better. Actually, he would like breakfast. Henley, since you're done, be a dear and take your father a plate. The juice too."

"He doesn't like green things." Henley scarfed down her last three bites of pancakes. She was a growing, ravenous wolf.

"Sometimes we have to do things we don't like," Mom said. "Tell him it will make him get better faster." She paused. "And that I insist."

My sister didn't question that. Dad loomed large as the Alpha of the Midnight Pack, but in this house, Mom called the shots. If she wanted our father to eat or drink something to make him heal faster, he'd choke it down.

Henley gathered breakfast for Dad and dashed out of the room with such speed that Mom had to yell at her to slow down.

"She reminds me of my sis when she was that age," Gunner said, his eyes crinkled at the corners. "Always moving."

"Kate, right?" I sat down across from him.

"Yeah." His eyes widened. "I'm surprised you remember that."

He *loved* talking about his sister. I'd heard stories about the girl many times.

"You talk a lot." I winked at him. "And I listen well."

"Harper Mace!"

Gunner snorted. "It's alright Mrs. Ferenz. It's true."

"Gunner, *please*. I told you to call me Diana."

"I'll try," the alphablood said. "It's kinda beaten into me to use respectful titles. My pa insists."

"How charming," Mom said, and I got the sense that though she was very informal—especially for an alpha's wife —she meant it.

"How are preparations going for the shindig?" I asked. Aura had been in charge of doling out jobs to other pack members, but Mom liked to be involved in those kinds of things, so I assumed they had talked.

"Great. It will be a lunch-time thing." Mom took a bite of a pancake on her plate. "We have a few hours to prepare you."

"Prepare?" I arched an eyebrow. "I'll shower, if you're insinuating that I stink."

"You don't." Gunner smiled at me. "You smell nice."

Mom and I stayed silent for a moment, and I caught a glint of mischief in her eyes before she continued. "If you're up for it, I'd like to do a Calling. You're stepping closer to your role as our leader and it feels right to reach back to the past for guidance."

I didn't want to think about stepping into my role as alpha because that would mean my father was dead or too weak to rule. But there was also no way I could resist calling the Old Ones with Mom. I'd met a lot of wolves in my life and only my mother had ever successfully spoken to the ancestors.

"I'd love that." I nodded.

"You gals talkin' about calling the Old Ones?" Gunner's tone was riddled with awe.

"Yeah. Mom has done it a few times."

Gunner set down his fork with a bite of pancake still on it. "That's unique. I've never heard of a wolf in this realm doin' that. Just one in Isila."

Not for the first time, I was jealous that he had been to the otherworld. That he'd laid eyes on Wolf Island, the land the first wolves claimed after the fae opened a portal to another world. A land where magic was in the open, and wolves didn't have to hide.

"You can watch." Mom sat her fork down and met his gaze. "Henley wants to as well. Ethan will want to come too."

I squirmed. Mom rarely invited anyone outside of family to Callings. "He might not—"

"I'd love that." Gunner exhaled.

"Great." Mom stood and grabbed her plate. "You two finish up and meet me in the Moon Room in, say . . . Thirty minutes?"

<hr>

After breakfast, I dressed in a green maxi dress. No one wanted to look bad with the possibility of an Old One coming to visit.

Once ready, I walked to the Moon Room, a sacred space Mom used for Callings and other spiritual practices.

Ethan, Henley, and Gunner waited outside.

"You look nice." Gunner eyed the dress for a second longer than normal.

"Thanks. Seeing as this Calling might work, I wanted to look good." I gestured to the door. "Did Mom lock it?"

"No." Ethan shook his head. "She's in there and knows we're waiting for you."

I chuckled lightly. "I'm sure she wouldn't mind if you went inside."

"It feels wrong." Henley pursed her lips. That didn't explain it to me. "We need to be invited, and that means by both of you."

"Uh, okay." I didn't see what they meant. This was more their house than it was mine. I hadn't lived here full time in years.

"It's just a sign of respect," Gunner added. "Not everyone can Call. And that you can sure shocks me. In fact, I was thinkin' back to the Calling I witnessed in Isila. The wolvea performing the ceremony was covered in magical symbols and had been known to call the First Wolves a time or two. He was powerful as all get out, but even he said sometimes no one came."

I let out a dry laugh. "I've never succeeded on my own. Mom has, and I've seen it, but not done it alone."

"Still. You have the gift, Sis," Ethan said. "We can feel it. There's something different about you."

Okay, that was enough with making me feel a little like a freak. "Let's go inside."

I opened the door and found Mom lighting the three candles on her altar, which was at least twice the size of mine. Water and earth adorned her gleaming table. She took her earth from the pack graveyard hidden away in the woods. Maybe that closer connection to the ancestors' resting place was why her Callings worked and mine didn't?

I tucked that away for future consideration. I'd have to see if there was a shifter graveyard in New Haven.

"Need help?" I swept across the cozy space. Aside from the

altar, there wasn't much we kept in the Moon Room, just a few cushions for meditating, blankets, and plants.

Mom smiled at me. "Someone turn down the lights. Hen, Ethan and Gunner, you three can sit in those chairs." She pointed to the wall by the door where three of our dining room chairs now sat. "You must stay quiet during the Calling."

The spectators took their places, each studying the Moon Room. Gunner's gaze snagged on the spherical moon that hung from the ceiling and lingered on it with appreciation.

The design was one of a kind, a play of sculpture and water and lighting that bathed the space in an otherworldly glow that mimicked the real moon's light. To make it even more special, on the full moon, Mom placed the sculpture outside to charge so that she could feel the moon's effects, even if she chose to do a Calling during the day. She claimed it helped but wasn't essential, so I noted it as something else that might be holding me back. Did I need to commission one?

"Do you want to Call anyone in particular?" I asked. When I tried, I put out a general Call. But since Mom was better at this, sometimes she requested specific people arrive—ancestors of her line, or of my father's blood, were the most common.

"I was thinking your grandfather Ferenz would be a good wolf to Call."

"Any particular reason?"

"He led as alpha for fifty years. He was the youngest wolf to take up the post. I know that your accession won't happen today, baby, but he might have words of advice."

"That sounds great," I said, and I meant it. Becoming alpha wasn't on my top list of things to do soon, but wisdom was wisdom.

"Kneel with me." She dropped to her knees, landing lightly on a pillow in front of the altar, and offered her hand.

My heart beat faster as I joined her. I loved these moments between us. Loved that Mom and I shared something so special, so unexplainable.

My hand slipped into her dry and warm one and she squeezed it. "We call on you Mother Wolf, Guardian Alpha, guiding pack—hear us, your descendants seek your wisdom." She pressed one hand to her heart, and I did the same. The air in the room shifted and my breath hitched along with it. Already, this felt different from the rituals I performed. Mom was something special.

"We offer our blood and our breath to bring a wolf beyond the veil to this world." Mom removed her hand from mine and slipped it under the altar, where she kept a small blade. Daintily, she poked at her thumb and waited until the blood welled. Then, she dripped a bit of blood over the earth, into the water, and over a candle. The flame sizzled when the liquid met it. Finally, Mom held her thumb up, offering it to the air, before placing her palms together at her heart. "Alpha Liam Ferenz, please, grace us with your presence, your light, your wisdom."

She bowed, and knowing this was the moment, my breath stuck in my chest. The ritual was static, rarely deviated from, and this was where we'd know if Mom had succeeded.

Excitement trickled through me and the seconds ticked on. It was so quiet in the Moon Room I could hear the others breathing behind us and could sense their anticipation.

Would my grandfather come? And if so, would he be a fully formed ghost? Or just a head? Mother had seen both.

As if she could feel my anxious nerves and wanted to calm them, Mom's hand found mine once more. She squeezed and exhaled, eyes trained on the altar on the flickering trio of flames.

I tried my best to mimic her serenity, my attention landing on the flames in time to see the one on the far-left grow. My pulse jumped. That one represented the Mother Wolf.

"Mom," I whispered.

"Hush." Her eyes widened.

By the Old Ones, it was happening! More than anything I wanted to whip around and beam at my siblings and Gunner and tell them the good news. But somehow, I held my shit together and thanked the ancestors. Suddenly, a mist materialized to my right.

It gathered slowly, but gained speed. Soon enough, a body formed, followed quickly by a face. After a full minute of my heart nearly beating out of my chest, it became clear that this ancestor was not my grandfather.

This wolf was a female, and I didn't recognize her in the slightest.

"Old One." Mom spoke with reverence. "Thank you for gracing our home. I'm Diana and this is my daughter, Harper."

"I am aware of who you are and who you called. I apologize for taking his place." The female's voice sounded ancient and full of wisdom, though she couldn't have been over forty. "I came in his stead, for I have news."

"And we are the willing recipients of whatever news you wish to tell." Mom inclined her head politely.

My heart thundered so hard I could hear it in my ears. Old Ones, I was so glad that this hadn't happened to me on my own. I didn't think I could even form words. If I could, I definitely wouldn't sound as refined as Mom.

I rolled my shoulders back and sat up straighter. Just in

time too, because the Old One turned her luminous eyes on me.

"Harper, my girl, you must prepare."

My heart sank as I thought of my father, stuck in bed. "For what?"

"Upheaval. Danger. The shattering of your life as you know it."

I swallowed. "Can you be more specific?"

The Old One's gaze drifted to my mother, and then back to my siblings and Gunner. "I cannot. But I can say that you will soon learn to step into your true self. Use what love you have around you during this troubled time."

"I—who are you?" I asked.

"An ancestor. One who threw your mother's line into a similar upheaval and changed the course of history." As if saying she was done, the white glow of her dimmed and the mist fell.

"Do you have any advice?" I asked, frantic. What did this mean? Could I avoid it? Upheaval now . . . When the Princes of Hell were here. That was not welcome, and I feared I wouldn't be up to the task.

"Fall inward. Accept every piece of yourself." The wolf's words rang in the air as she vanished from sight.

I knelt there, rigid for a moment, before the tremors began. Mom's hand fell on my shoulder.

"Breathe, baby. Breathe."

"She had to have meant Dad. He's going to die," I whispered. "I need to go check on him."

"Harper! We need to close the ritual!" Mom cried out as I leapt to my feet and ran to the door.

Footsteps followed me down the hallway, and I knew without looking that it was Gunner. My siblings would stay for our mother and Mom would never leave the ritual space open. Just two minutes ago I would have said the same thing about myself, but the fear surging inside me, the possibility that my father was slipping away at that very second, overpowered me.

Crystal, the blonde beta, was at his door, and when she saw me coming, her eyes widened. "What's wrong?" Her hand landed on her hip, where she kept a dagger. "Is it the prisoner?"

Old Ones, things were going to hell here if wolves needed to walk around armed.

"I need to see my father." I reached the door, only for Crystal to place a protective hand on the knob.

"And him?" She inclined her head, and for the first time, I turned to Gunner.

"Harper? Are you okay?" His expression was worried, full of reproach.

"Fine. You need to stay out here."

"But what was that about?"

"Later, Gunner." I shoved by Crystal, who appeared far more inclined to let me through now that she knew an alphablood of another pack wouldn't be around her leader.

The beta stepped aside, and I pushed through the door, recoiling at the scent of old blood and healing. There was a fine line between healing and rot.

"Daughter?" My father sat up in his sickbed and stared at me. "What happened?"

I rushed to his side and perched on the bed. "How are you?"

"Healing. The nurse said I should be able to leave my bed today. As long as I remain sitting."

"No infection? No illness?"

His eyebrows knitted together. "No. Where is this coming from?"

"I-I—" Not sure of what to say—especially to the man who did not approve of Calling Old Ones or anything mystical—I turned away from my father, only to find another person watching me. Gunner's bulk stood in the doorway, just beyond Crystal's muscular arm stretching over the threshold.

"She heard something. It scared her," Gunner said softly, but not softly enough for wolf ears.

My father leaned forward, an action that required an effort he wore on his strained face. "You're the Blood Moon Pack heir?"

"I am, sir."

"Come in here."

"Are you sure, Alpha?" Crystal called out. "This is inadvisable."

"Don't question me, Beta."

Crystal's hand retracted, but the sour expression on her face remained. Gunner walked into my father's chambers, not a flicker of discomfort on his face from the smells that lingered when someone was confined to a sickbed for long periods.

"What did my daughter hear?" Dad asked when Gunner approached the bed. "What sent her running to my room like she thought I was dying?"

"That might be what she thought," Gunner said. "We got news from a spirit who made it sound that way."

My father scowled. "A spirit, is it?" One sidelong glance made me shrink back. He no longer considered this matter urgent. "Harper, you know better than to play at Calling. It's pretending. A wolf is no magic worker, and it's a disgrace to pretend."

"Dad, I—"

"If I may," Gunner interrupted, "I saw the spirit. It was as real as you and me, sir."

"*Alpha* Ferenz," my father corrected him. "And what is your name?"

"Gunner Ray Bryant."

"Alpha *Heir*," Dad added. While posturing, he preferred titles and he was certainly posturing now.

"Sure, Alpha Ferenz."

"You work with my daughter? At Yale?"

"I do."

"You attend the university?"

Gunner shook his head. "I don't. I'm too old to blend in there."

Dad studied him carefully. "Your father, he's a powerful wolf. You mean nothing against my pack by coming here, do you?"

"Never. Harper is a colleague and friend." Gunner's eyes and voice held nothing but respect in them. "In fact, I asked my father to mobilize our pack and find someplace safe."

I'd known that he called his family, but he'd told them to leave the pack land? To where? Wouldn't their land be the safest spot?

"Yes, my wife told me what happened with my children and the Covenant's announcement. What happened to me makes more sense now. The attack." Dad scowled down at his broken arm, clearly pissed that his shifting abilities hadn't already healed him.

"If your pack has a hidden place to go, I'd recommend it. My pa is getting as far away as possible." Gunner swallowed. "Do you have connections in the other realm?"

Ah, so that was where Alpha Bryant would try to hide his people.

"We don't. We would have to take sanctuary with another pack in this world." It shocked me how open Dad was being about this notion. Then again, Gunner was being equally vulnerable, admitting a retreat, and maybe that was why. They were both two alphabloods, worried about their people. "That's something that you might need to consider, Harper. Finding a safe place. Our home no longer qualifies."

"Wh-oh-yeah," I said. "I can look into places we can go. Just in case."

Dad nodded. "Good. I need to re—"

Loud, running footsteps came from the hallway. Before I stood, Rikard rushed through the door, and Mom trailed behind him with tears in her eyes.

"What happened?" My heart launched into my throat.

"We just received word that something happened in LA," Rikard said. "The entire city has been without power since last night. No one in our circle has gotten a phone call in or out."

"What does that mean?" I asked, confused. Surely, a blackout in a city wasn't so serious? Even one that lasted hours. "Did they record an earthquake?"

"No" Mom shook her head. "The Covenant released a message that came from a nephilim Seat. They believe it has to do with the Royals of Hell."

I cut a glance at Gunner, my stomach sinking. Were the princes already staking their claim?

"My son," Dad whispered, and another horror washed over me. Elijah, Ethan's twin, attended college in LA. "No one can reach him?"

"No." Mom's voice broke. "I tried."

Dad turned to me. "Harper, I need you to research now. Find a place for the pack to relocate and hide. Announce it at the barbecue."

"It hardly seems time for a barbecue now, Alpha," Rikard said. "Should someone drive to LA to retrieve Elijah?"

I agreed, and I got the sense that my father did too, but he just shook his head. "No one leaves. LA is five hours away, and that puts too much distance between a rescuer and the pack. When we don't know what's happening, that would be foolish. My son is smart and strong. He can take care of himself." The tone in father's voice wasn't so sure, but he couldn't just think of our family now. He had hundreds of wolves to consider, and he had trained us to be strong.

And Elijah *was* smart. I had to trust Dad's opinion that my brother would be okay. He'd seek out other wolves, they'd band together and watch each other's backs.

"The wider pack remains ignorant to this, correct?" Dad asked.

"The Covenant only released the news to pack, clan, and coven leaders."

"Keep it that way until the gathering. Let the wolves have a few more hours of normalcy," Dad said. "Once you tell them to move, they will have only a few hours to pack up their lives for tonight, we must flee."

CHAPTER THIRTY

MEREDITH

THE DAY AFTER MY MATE BOND SNAPPED INTO PLACE, I WORE A long sleeve shirt. Not that it helped. Even with my new magical band hidden, everyone noticed the difference between Tobias and me.

That made me uncomfortable. Not them knowing we'd slept together, or even that he'd bitten me—which was plain to see because, despite Tobias's application of magical vampire blood on the site, the fang punctures still hadn't healed.

No, it was more that others somehow sensed I'd changed and become someone I never could have imagined. Yesterday, I would have done a hell of a lot to keep Tobias safe. The same went for Shay, Harper, Luca, Hans, and Gunner; the members of S&S that I was closest to.

Now, though, he was on a different level. I'd burn the world to keep my mate from pain, and it appeared I wore that intensity on my face. Of course, there was Shay, wanting to know *every* single detail.

"How did it feel?" she asked when I left the *Abscondita* Coven library for lunch and an update.

Little news had come in during the night and Luca remained slow to act. To be safe, he insisted we remain in England, at least until the afternoon. He hoped that someone would call back, that they'd have more information, but I wasn't so sure. So far, everyone he and Shay had spoken to was as fearful and ignorant as to what was happening in the black hole that was now Los Angeles.

"Girl, are you serious?" I asked, eyebrows arched as I took her in.

Shay was always stunning, but right now, she looked like hell. Dark circles ringed her eyes and her hair hung limp, hinting that she hadn't even showered since she'd helped Luca put up the wards in the forest.

"You need a nap."

"Can't." Shay held up her phone. "I need to be here if someone calls."

"The ringer would wake you up."

"Not after the night I had."

"I can watch the phone." I felt somewhat guilty that while I made love to my mate and slept like a baby afterward, everyone else had been stressing.

"Just answer me, Rooms! I need something nice to think about, and none of my other close friends ever had a soulmate bond snap into place."

"What about that fire witch who used to be in the coven?"

Shay rolled her eyes. "I need more data, okay? Please, don't be a prude."

Unable to help myself, I laughed. "It's not common with nephilim?"

"It's not common *at all*. And definitely not with my order. Sometimes nephilim know their soulmates for *years* before they feel the pull to bond with them! Like, *why*? I think our souls must be stingy or something." The thought looked like it pained her and now that I knew how it felt to have a mate bond in place, I understood. I hadn't known what I'd been missing, but if someone severed my mate bond now, I'd break.

"Well, the sex was amazing," I said, knowing that I would not get out of this. "Unlike any I've ever had."

She held up her hand. "Okay, sure, but Tobias has had, like, five hundred years to get good at sex, so I'd hope he was decent."

"He's only one hundred and sixty-seven."

Well, that was a sentence I'd never thought would come out of my mouth.

"Whatever." Shay rolled her eyes. "I mean, I'm happy that you got some, and normally I'd be all about that goss, but this is so much more intriguing. I want to hear about the *bond*."

"It was bliss." I exhaled, trying to recall every aspect of my emotions at the moment, but it was impossible. There had been too much, and it had been too intense. "I felt complete, like I hadn't been before, even though if you'd have asked me, I would have felt fine."

"Was magic involved? I think you two might be the only vampire-witch soulmates ever."

"There was." I nodded. "And blood. I guess we combined what our orders would do?" I held up my wrist, exposing the band I'd been hiding.

Her eyes widened. "That's a mark!"

"It kinda showed up. I didn't even notice it until Tobias pointed it out."

Shay sighed. "That sounds amazing."

"It was. *It is*."

We chatted about lighter topics until we reached the kitchen. Luca, Tobias, Tana, Miriam, and Gloria sat at the table, eating lunch and discussing what was happening in the world outside. Benedict lounged in the kitchen too, slyly stealing bits of meat off of Tana's plate whenever she wasn't looking. The poor girl needed to bat that cat away or she wouldn't have any lunch left.

The moment my mate saw me, Tobias broke away from Luca and stalked over.

"I better make myself scarce." Shay darted off, taking the seat Tobias had occupied as my mate swept me into his arms and kissed me.

My toes curled as the spicy scent of him rushed over me, all consuming, and when we broke apart my head swam.

"You alright there, love?"

"Yeah." I tried to smirk like he hadn't gotten to me, but I failed. "Is it always going to be this intense?"

Tobias shrugged. "When Giselle spoke of her mate, which wasn't often, she said the first few days after the bond forms were the most intense. But he was a vampire, and we're not normal, so who's to say?"

I wasn't sure if I wanted the sensation to dim or not, but dang if it didn't make keeping my head straight difficult.

"Where's Hans?" I asked, trying to switch gears.

"Practicing smoke-travel with Serena."

"He managed?"

"He only traveled about two feet, but it's a start."

Considering Hans had only been attempting to smoke-travel for less than a day, I took it as a huge win.

"Good news." I snaked my fingers between Tobias's, relishing the chill of his skin against the warmth of mine as we approached the others.

"I'll get you lunch," Tobias said. "A sandwich? Chips?"

"And cucumber on the side," I requested. This coven grew

the best produce. Probably because one of them was gifted in the powers of earth. "Thanks."

"Of course." He landed a kiss on my cheek and strode to the island, leaving me with the others.

"Strange to see Tobias like this." Luca kept a hand on his phone as he awaited a call or text from one of his many sources.

"In a good or bad way?" I tried not to feel guilty about the wan hue of his skin or the bags under his eyes.

"Oh, very much an improvement. The man needed something to focus on besides his work." The mage shot a sly glance at my mate. "A social life will improve him greatly."

"I can hear you." Tobias didn't even look up from the sandwich he made me.

Luca winked at me. "Perhaps he'll loosen up and be a bit of fun now."

I smothered a laugh as Tobias glared at the mage. "You never complained when I was around for a mission, mage."

"Anyway." Luca's Italian accent rang through the kitchen. "How was studying? Tana told us she's learning quite a lot."

"Fine," I said.

Tana was catching up and still into the interesting bits of studying, whereas I was learning about the varied histories of the stones—in the rare instances they popped up in history at all. "I think I'll work on my magic after lunch, though. I can't keep sitting for the rest of the day."

"That you will," Luca agreed. "In a practical manner."

I gaped, and the others fell silent. "Does that mean—"

"We're going to Los Angeles," Luca replied.

"You got more info?" Shay asked.

"No, and I'm not sure any will come. I'm resigned to the fact that we will have to be the ones to witness what is happening there." Luca sighed. "Perhaps we can save some of the stranded too, with the luxiters. How many can they transport?"

"As many as can attach themselves to the person controlling the luxiter," Shay said. "So, a lot. Not that I think we'll have people flocking to us if the city is a war zone."

Or if they were all zombies. No one mentioned that, though. The thought was too terrifying and no one knew how to handle it.

"But even saving a single person from a city ruled by Hell is a win," Luca said.

I agreed, and more than that, I was ready for action. Scared down to my bones, of course, but ready.

"So . . ." Tobias appeared at my side with my lunch in his hand. He set it down in front of me. "When do we leave?"

"In a few hours, once the sun is well up in California, we'll travel there." Luca gazed at his phone. "I'd prefer to have the light on our side. Some texts claim that certain species of demons cannot handle sunlight, so it will thin their ranks. We must seize any advantage we can get."

I thought back to the fields of demons in Hell. Many types of monsters roamed the underworld.

"In the meantime," Luca stood from his seat, "I should get some rest. You too, Shay. Everyone should." His dark brown eyes hardened. "We have no details on the city, but whatever is happening there, it's more dangerous than walking into a den of lions."

<hr>

The hours passed slowly and, with each minute, my tension grew. When the appointed time came, Tobias and I left our room and walked to the manor's front door. I patted the dagger at my side the entire time and wished the coven possessed guns, too. Of course, I could defend myself with magic, to a point, but firepower wouldn't go amiss either.

The other S&S members, Benedict, and Serena stood at the ready, though half of the *Arcacustos* and Tana were there, too. I shot Tobias a look, which Miriam caught and interpreted correctly.

"Don't worry, girl. We're not coming, and neither is the fire witch." Tana scowled at that, but Miriam did not notice. Even if the elder did, she probably would not have cared. "We're here to wish your lot luck."

Thank the Goddess. Not that the members of the *Abscondita* Coven weren't capable—after all, I'd seen them fight with magic and they'd helped protect their property from the OA— but we did not know what we were walking into. What if we had to run for miles?

"We appreciate it." Luca inclined his head to Miriam, who gave the mage a warm smile. Out of everyone here, including me, she had taken a shine to Luca the most. "Once we get the lay of the city, and hopefully our hands on the *lapis caelesti*, are we welcome back here?"

Luca did not plan on returning to New Haven soon. That shocked me, but then again, our undertakings were pretty important and he'd left the coven in responsible hands.

"You are." Miriam nodded. "Especially if you retrieve the sacred stones." Her eyes gleamed with the possibility, making my chest tighten.

Miriam and the other *Arcacustos* had known about the *lapis caelesti* for far longer than I'd been alive. They'd educated themselves on the enchanted stones and hoped that one day, they'd see the *Vindix* rise. Seeing their efforts come to fruition, albeit slowly, had to be both terrifying and exhilarating for them.

I could relate, though differently. I wanted the hope and the power of the stones. I wanted to learn how to wield the Opal of Heaven effectively. Most of all, I wanted to bring the *Vindix* together and obliterate the Princes of Hell.

Today, we had a real chance at making headway. If the demons didn't murder us first.

"Wonderful." Luca inclined his head to the coven and turned to Shay. "You know where to land us?"

"My mother's home overlooks the city. She saw destruction coming her way, but as far as she knows it did not reach her place. We'll go there." Shay pulled an unlit luxiter from her pocket. The sight of it made me squirm.

I held another, and Shay had given the final one to Tana. That the *Abscondita* Coven and Tana had an out and an additional layer of protection eased my nerves. As for me, I'd tried to refuse the orb, but Luca and Tobias had insisted. I was a *Vindix*. If I had to make a fast escape, I was to do so. With or without them.

I had no intention of following those orders. I'd never leave my mate behind, nor my coven. Even Serena would be unthinkable. She was Tobias's sister and now a part of my family too.

"We'll know quickly if the home isn't standing, the luxiter won't work." Hans cast his gaze at all of us. "We'll have to try elsewhere."

"In that case, I have a place we can go," Luca said. "Though Angelina's home would be best. A view, a chance to take in the destruction from afar, is preferable."

"Then, let's hope Mom's place is still standing." Shay held out her hand. As I was closest, I took it. Tobias linked with me and went on down the chain. At the end, Benedict leapt into Luca's welcoming arm.

"Everyone ready?" Shay glanced down the line.

We all assured her we were, and I looked at Miriam.

The old woman's eyes softened. "Best of luck. We hope you return soon."

"Thank you," I said as Shay whispered the password and the luxiter began glowing.

"To Angelina Ramos's Los Angeles home," Shay declared.

Light exploded, and a constricting sensation smothered and ripped me off my feet and through space.

My teeth ground together as the light enveloped us. I had no idea how long we traveled for. All I knew was that it felt longer than the last time I light-traveled. Was that because we were traveling so much farther? The moment my feet slammed against the floor, I forced the questions from my mind.

I pulled myself together, forced down the bile rising in my throat, and scanned the area. We stood in an opulent home decorated with angel imagery. Clean, modern, and creamy white.

And still standing.

I swallowed. No demons jumped out at us. No evil presence overpowered us.

"We're safe." Shay sighed in relief.

For now, I added mentally as I pulled out my phone. I needed to see if it worked, or if they had killed millions in the city to keep the secrecy. Four bars of service stared back at me, making my stomach sink.

"I have cell service," I said.

Shay sucked in a breath. "Millions of people either simultaneously lost their phones, died, or zombie-walked into Lucifer's territory."

"Where can we see the city?" Luca asked. "I need to get a sense of how much destruction we're talking about."

Shay dropped my hand and waved for us to follow up a flight of stairs and into an entertaining space that was the size of our entire New Haven home.

Windows dominated the entire far wall, and outside, the night shrouded the city.

No. Wait. That couldn't be right. We'd left England after seven in the evening. With the time change, it would be past eleven in the morning here. Where was that famous California sunshine?

My blood turned to ice and, with each step closer to the window, I froze a little more. But that was nothing to what I felt when I reached them and looked outside.

The valley below was indeed shrouded in darkness, but not a natural kind, a kind of darkness brought on by evil. Only torches lit within a two-mile radius around a single structure gave us any indication of what had happened.

Three dozen city blocks were leveled, leaving only smoke and ash in the wake of an obsidian castle.

CHAPTER THIRTY-ONE

TOBIAS

ACRID WIND WHIPPED AROUND ME AS I RACED DOWN THE HILLS toward the castle, the most likely location for the princes, and hence the *lapis caelesti*. Above, Shay and Hans flew, barely visible thanks to the thick, black smoke Luca had conjured to obscure them in the darkened sky. At my side, Serena raced with the coven master on her back, just as my mate and her familiar clung to mine.

While Angelina's home had been perfect for viewing the city, it was too far away for us to have any idea of what was happening below. Aside from the palace, all that we could make out was destruction and a shimmering magical barrier that domed over most of the city.

Whether that ward had been set up to keep the princes' minions in, or others out, we weren't sure. Our first order of business was to pass through the enchantment.

With the help of vampire speed and flight, we'd covered a lot of ground, seeing much as we raced forward. Parts of the city that were far away from the castle were still largely intact, if under a veil of darkness. However, as we got closer to the castle, all that changed. Glass, metal, and other rubble littered the streets. Traffic lights had collapsed and street signs had been flung into the middle of roadways. Buildings had caved in and those that stood were covered in ash and filth. The electricity had been cut off too, leaving a void where an electrical hum would normally fill the world with sound.

As far as people went, we hadn't come across a single living soul outside the barrier. Nor had I smelled anyone hiding in their homes.

I swallowed, remembering the zombies Angelina Ramos spoke of. Had the princes called them into their territory like some dark siren?

A shudder ran through me and, immediately, Meredith's soft lips met my cheek.

"We'll be okay," she whispered, though it sounded to me a lot like she was trying to convince herself.

I squeezed her thighs where they wrapped around my middle and kept racing into the darkness, unsure if what she said was true. We were heading into a rising kingdom, one created in a mere day's time and ruled by the vilest evil to ever walk the Earth. Being *okay* didn't seem in the cards, but I would not squash her hope.

Hope was often the difference between life and death.

As it stood, my priority was to get us in and out of the city alive and with the *lapis caelesti* in tow. Any other information we learned, any lives we might save, would be a bonus.

"We're closing in!" Serena called out. "Be on the lookout for demonic or Darkborn attacks."

"Indeed." I studied the city as we blurred by. Still no sign of a human or a magical being.

Knowing Meredith and Benedict would not be accustomed

to traveling at such speed, I kept a keen eye out until the wards loomed only a block away.

"Here." I stopped within a block of the pearly-black shimmering dome that separated what remained of the city of LA from what was now the dominion of Hell.

"Let me down," Meredith said, and Luca requested the same from my sister.

Though I'd rather not, I did as my mate asked. I did not sense a nearby threat, but I would not hesitate to scoop her up if one approached. Capable witch though she was, Meredith was also my mate, and I'd protect her at all costs. She wobbled when her feet touched the ground. Benedict shook as well when he landed. He'd been squished between my back and Meredith's front the entire time, and as such, did not see much at all. Between that and the speed with which I ran, the cat would take time to center.

Shay and Hans dropped from the sky to join us a moment later. Immediately, the angel vanished her wings, but, as discussed, Hans kept his out. They looked like Wrath's and therefore might convince an enemy that we were not hostile long enough for us to attack. We needed to seize every opportunity we could get.

"What did you see up there?" Serena asked.

"You can't see inside it," Shay said. "I mean, you *can*, because we all saw the castle, but you can't see very well. It's blurry—as if I needed strong glasses. The castle is the only thing that stands out."

"No one was guarding the barrier, then?" I pressed.

"Not a single soul in sight." Hans looked shaken by the concept.

If no one guarded the barrier, it was because the magic was strong. Would we be able to penetrate it?

"We need to get closer to assess it." Luca pointed up ahead. Now that Hans no longer had wizarding powers and did not know the full extent of his demon magic, the mage would be the one to take care of getting us inside. We fell in line behind him, each person on the alert for an attack.

"My stomach hurts," Shay said as we stepped up to the dome, close enough to reach out and touch it. She ran a hand over her arm, rubbing it softly. "Skin too. Actually, all of me aches."

Hans shot her a worried look. "I bet that's coming from whatever is inside. Hell feels different from this world. I'm guessing that the princes will try to mimic that sensation."

Shay nodded, and Meredith laid a soft hand on her friend's shoulder. Leaving my mate to comfort Shay, I turned my attention to the barrier and Luca. The mage was already assessing the dark magic by reaching out with his own powers. A soft blue magelight crawled across the gleaming black surface, and where the magics touched, blackened liquid oozed across the shield, like oil and water fighting to mix.

A few moments later, Luca withdrew, wiping a bead of sweat from his brow as he did so. "I think I can get us through. But it might hurt to cross over. That's part of the magic here. It not only will keep people out—repelling them—and trap them inside, but it will hurt anyone who tries to push through the repelling magic."

"It won't dissolve us or anything?" Meredith chewed on her lower lip.

"I don't think so." Luca narrowed his eyes at the black surface.

"That doesn't invite total confidence." Serena studied the barrier. "But we have to try. I'll go first."

I opened my mouth to argue, but before I spoke a word,

my sister held up a hand. "Of those orders present, vampires are the most indestructible. If anyone can withstand the pain or anything else this ward throws at us, it is us, Brother."

She was not wrong, and yet, I hated the idea that my sister was going to risk harming herself. I looked at Luca. "Is there a way to thin it first?"

Again, the mage studied the ward with his power, though this time for a shorter period, before he nodded. "I think I can spread out the effects, to thin it, as you said. Let me try before you do anything, Serena."

"Fine."

I rolled my eyes. She sounded as if she wanted to get on with it, as if we weren't trying to save her from experiencing a lot of pain. My sister was so impulsive sometimes.

Luca got to work, pummeling the barrier with magic that lit up a circle ten-feet in diameter. It took a few minutes before his power worked, but when it did, I was sure we were on to something. The shimmering blackness was being pushed to the edges of Luca's magical circle. Slowly but surely, every speck of light separated, inching outward. When there was a portion of the barrier that was still opaquely black, but with no sparkle, Luca stopped and cast a glance at my sister. Sweat trickled down his tanned face. "If you wish, I'll keep my powers flowing to maintain a small portal."

Serena stepped forward and, without hesitation, walked through the circle created by Luca's magic. She winced, sucked in a faint inhale, and took a step back.

"Serena," I started, "you can come back. We'll—"

"Shut it, Tobias." She gritted her teeth and her voice sounded so raw that she had to have been hiding the pain better than she let on. She moved forward again, leaned into it. "I just . . . need . . . argh!"

Suddenly, she stood on the other side, her chest heaving with effort. Everyone waited, and when she composed herself, she shook her head.

"It hurts, but thanks to Luca's modifications, it's bearable. So, you're aware there's a lot of crap over here. And bodies."

I winced. Of course, we'd imagined that many people had died, but to know corpses were in the streets and we'd have to pass on by and go about our mission was rather disturbing.

"On a scale of one to ten, how painful?" Shay didn't look like she believed Serena, probably for good reason. Of anyone here, demonic powers would affect the nephilim the most.

"If you wish, we can go first and try to pull you through?" Luca asked. "I think it might affect you more, and that way you don't have to make such an effort."

Shay cocked her head, considering that. "I guess that's what we'll have to do. I can't stay here." She gestured to the desolate cityscape.

Turning, I scooped Meredith up in my arms.

"Hey," she yelped. "What are you doing?"

"I'll be able to pass through as fast as my sister. Faster than you, and I won't have you in pain for longer than necessary."

A little of the fear clouding her eyes cleared. "Benedict. In my arms."

The familiar leapt up and Meredith caught him, pinning the cat against my chest.

"Brace yourself, Meredith. Benedict."

She drew in a sharp breath, nodded like the warrior she was, and I stepped into the ward. Pain sliced through me, making my still heart stutter and Meredith released a strangled gasp, barely stopping more noise by slamming a hand over her mouth and using the other to grip a yowling Benedict tighter. It felt like trying to walk through a wall of solidifying cement—if that wall were filled with thorns and spikes that pierced every inch of your flesh.

I marveled at my mate's strength. Even when she was hurting, she recognized that we could not announce ourselves and endanger the mission. She wasn't making even the smallest sound. Still, I wanted nothing more than to get her out of this magical horror.

The seconds ticked on, and my every muscle strained. On the other side, Serena urged me forward, and when she reached out, I did not hesitate. I shored Meredith up with one arm, trying not to notice the tremors wracking her body, and took my sister's hand.

Serena yanked me through, and my mate and I slammed into her before I caught myself.

"Meredith, are you okay?" I asked, looking down at her.

"W-w-will be," she stuttered.

"That was bloody awful," I whispered, holding my mate as her trembling died ever so slowly. As I comforted her, I took in our new surroundings.

As Serena had said, rubble and corpses reigned. Only the most well-constructed buildings remained standing, though with notable damage to their roofs or with a wall or two blown in. Other homes and offices were nothing but piles of debris on the ground. Littered amongst the wood, metal, and plastics were bodies, some intact, some in pieces. The moment Meredith saw one that had been brutally torn in half, a shocked cry left her lips. Again, I held her tightly. It would only get worse the closer we got to the palace.

"Steel yourself, love."

Her face pressed harder into my chest, and one arm held the cat as she gathered the strength to take in the surrounding horrors. Slowly, she loosened her grip.

CHAPTER THIRTY-ONE

Benedict looked up and his amber eyes widened. "It's awful."

Meredith inhaled and took in the scene a second time, her face grim and mouth tight. She said nothing, but as I set her and her familiar down, I felt her struggle to center herself.

Hans was next, and he shocked everyone as he stepped through. When he got to the other side, his eyes were wide.

"I—didn't expect that to be so easy."

"It must be your demon blood," I replied. "Perhaps you can help Shay and Luca?"

The coven master could make it on his own, but he was already expending considerable energy to dull the ward's effects.

"Try it with your smoke!" Serena said. "It's cloaking, right?"

"I think so. At the very least, I can try," Hans said. "I'll go back." He shifted back through the barrier as though it was nothing and relayed the information to the other two. Shay nodded vigorously, and Luca agreed to try it, too. Hans instructed them to hold hands so he could lead them through one by one with Luca last, as he would still need to be siphoning magic into the barrier for anyone to pass through.

The next thing I knew, smoke poured from Hans's hands. He still hadn't mastered traveling more than a few feet, but was improving at calling the smoke. Once it covered Shay and Luca, Hans took Shay's hand and stepped back through the barrier.

Again, I waited for a snafu, but none came and when Shay and Luca stood on the other side, blinking at their good luck, I exhaled loudly.

"Thank you." Shay sighed. "I felt it, but I think it would have been so much worse without you."

"No problem." the Hellblooded wizard smiled. "I'm glad that my magic could do some good for once."

Shay looked like she wanted to say something more, but Luca released his magic from the barrier and stepped deeper into the rubble that was once a bustling city.

"The chances are good that people are hiding in the buildings that are still standing." Luca pulled out his phone. He let out a long hum. "As we suspected, there's no service here. So, even if people are alive, that's why no information is getting in and out. We need to learn what has happened before we infiltrate the castle for the stones."

"That office looks promising." I pointed to a structure a few blocks up. It was as dark as all the rest, but considering there was no power in this part of the city, that did not mean no one was inside. "Intact and about as far from the castle as you can get. I'd hole up in there."

"Let's check it out," Luca agreed.

Our group prowled forward, ever on the lookout for an attack but, again, none came. All we saw were more ripped apart bodies and downed buildings. If anyone was alive, they were deep in hiding.

When we reached the building I'd spotted, we stopped at the door. Someone had boarded it up, which if you took away the doom and gloom of the hellscape, certainly did not fit the aesthetic of the area.

"There has to be people inside," Meredith said. "This place looks almost normal."

"Yeah, these boards likely weren't there before Hell rose. They're a line of defense." Shay shook her head. "As if they would do anything if the demons wanted inside."

"Or against us." Serena ripped the outermost board from

the doorway. The nails pinged off and landed somewhere on the concrete.

"Perhaps we should be quieter?" I gazed at her with a lifted eyebrow.

Serena scoffed. "Brother, if you think that anyone hiding inside hasn't been watching us approach, then your brain is glitching."

She had a point, so I let her continue on until the boards lay on the sidewalk and we faced a door.

"Vampires in front." I joined my sister.

"What if they have a stake? Or a sword?" Fear laced Meredith's voice.

"Far more likely that they have a gun, love."

"But if they discharge it, that would give away their location," Serena mused. "Knives seem to be a better option—swords, well, where would they get them from?"

"Be prepared for anything and everything." Luca nodded to the door as if to say 'get on with it already.'

I extended my hand, pausing as my fingers graced the door, and listened. I was 90% certain that no one lurked on the other side, so I swung it open, ready to strike should I have been wrong.

But I wasn't. Only an empty hallway stared back at me.

Meredith exhaled, the sound so full of relief I couldn't help but give her a reassuring smile that died almost as soon as it was born.

Footsteps sounded, fast and heavy. I twisted again to find a wolf racing down the corridor, two magic users at its back.

"Aside!" Luca hissed.

Serena and I parted, allowing the mage to throw up a shield as the wolf shifter launched into the air. The beast hit the shield with a hard *thunk* that vibrated through the hallway.

The wolf slumped to the ground, unconscious. Behind him, his partners stopped in their tracks.

"Who are you?" Magic blazed in the palms of one young man of about twenty, lighting up the otherwise dark hallway. "And what are you doing here?"

"Luca. I'm a mage, and we're part of a group sent to scout the city. Hopefully, we can learn how to free it."

"How did you even get through the dome of terror?" the other magic worker, a young woman, asked.

"My magic is quite varied and strong," Luca said. "I didn't dismantle the ward, but merely weakened it enough to slip through."

"How do we know we can trust you?" the woman pressed. "You might be with the devils."

"Would I be here for any other reason but to help?" Shay stepped forward and her white wings released from their magical hiding place.

The magic workers dropped their attacks.

"Nephilim?" The female gaped at Shay.

Shay nodded. "Yeah."

"But what about him? He has dark wings like some demons I've seen." She gestured to Hans.

"He's with us. Part demon, part wizard, and all-around good guy." Shay's tone turned hard. "You can trust him."

For a moment, the witch didn't seem certain, but then she turned back to Shay. "How can you stand it out there? I can't even sleep, the magic in the air is so vile and I'm a witch."

Before Shay answered, the wolf stirred. Thanks to his quick healing abilities, when he opened his eyes, he was alert. The wolf leapt up and growled.

"No, Elijah!" the young man shouted. "They're okay. They have a nephilim."

The wolf stopped growling, but the hackles on his back remained. He still didn't trust us.

"They're here to scout and help the city." The girl stepped closer to the wolf, but her attention did not waver from us. "Do you think you can sneak us through the ward? I want out of here."

"When we leave," Luca replied, and the magic workers' faces fell.

Though making them wait seemed harsh, I understood. We couldn't leave the mage at the barrier while the rest went to the castle in search of the stones. Luca possessed the most varied magic, and we'd all agreed that foremost, we needed to get our hands on the *lapis caelesti.*

Before anyone could say anything, the wolf shifted into a young man with short blond hair and a tan that spoke of hours in the California sun.

"I recognize you," he said to Shay. "You're one of my sister's friends."

Shay's eyebrows pulled together. "We've met?"

"No, but I've seen your picture. You know Harper Ferenz?"

Shay gasped. "You're one of the twins! Oh, crap!"

"Let's hope you don't have your sister's attitude." Benedict sounded peeved.

"Elijah." The young wolf huffed out a breath at the cat's annoyance. "Does my sister know about LA?"

The way he looked at us told me he knew of S&S, but wasn't mentioning it around the other two.

"We haven't been in touch in days," Shay said. "But maybe? I take it you didn't get a message out before communications were cut off?"

"No, we were out getting tacos and the darkness fell so

fast. It was the one time I left campus in weeks." Elijah shook his head. "Shitty timing. I should have stayed put and ate at the dining hall."

"What do you know of the fall of the city?" Luca asked, clearly wanting to get back on track.

"Demons took it." Elijah gestured down the hall. "We should move deeper inside the building to talk. The devils have been doing random rounds, and we don't want them to hear."

We followed his lead and traveled deeper into, what appeared to be, a modern office building. As we walked, the magic workers introduced themselves as Laura and Dean. Both were witches who happened to be nearby when the castle exploded from the ground.

"We weren't acquainted with Elijah before," Laura said. "Crazy to think after all that we've been through."

"Were you alone when the palace rose?" I asked Elijah.

"I had a friend with me." Elijah's voice sounded clipped. "He's gone." The look on his face said it all, and I didn't push.

Other people were in the room they led us to, and naturally, I wondered if any of them were humans.

"Should we speak freely?" Luca asked, clearly on the same page as me.

Elijah snorted. "Two are humans, but what does that matter anymore? They saw a castle pop out of the ground, monsters take to the streets and kill hundreds, and some freaky smoke brings others to the castle like zombies."

"Valid point," Luca said and our group spread out, ready to listen and learn what we could before diving deeper into the parts of LA that the devils now controlled. "What do you know of what's occurring in the city? Has anyone been to the palace? And what of the smoke that worked outside the barrier?"

Elijah perched on the edge of a desk covered in crisp packets. His arms crossed his broad chest. "Like we said, demons are searching for people to bring in. At first, they killed a bunch because they were fighting."

"What about the zombies?" I asked.

"I don't understand why they did that, but it was like they made the castle, fought those who resisted, and then brought more docile people into the city." He scowled. "My theory is that they didn't use the zombie-smoke in here because it would make their own followers zombies too." He cast a glance at Laura. "You got anything to add?"

The witch nodded. "We've been trying to learn more. Recently, I was out and wound up close to one of the ranging parties. I overheard them talking about Lucifer. Apparently, that's his castle, but the other demon princes are there too—at least until the end of today."

"Why today?" Luca asked.

"There's a wedding happening at the palace tonight," Laura shrugged. "Who the hell would be getting married now, I have no idea, but the soldiers ranging the rubble said she'd be a princess."

"Are you fucking kidding me?" Hans bellowed, which caused the other people in the room to duck and look around nervously.

Those in our group watched him, confused. All except for Shay, who laid a hand on his shoulders.

"Breathe, Hans. We'll stop it."

"She doesn't want it stopped." Hans shook his head.

"The rest of us would bloody love to know what you're talking about." I crossed my arms and stared at him.

Hans glared at me. "My sister intends to wed Wrath's son, Rikel, and give him heirs. She bragged about it in Italy, though I'd hoped the day was in the distant future." Hans took a deep breath and his face turned redder with the effort it took to calm himself. "But it seems my hopes were in vain and today is her wedding day."

CHAPTER THIRTY-TWO

SHAY

Since stepping beyond that vile ward, I'd been feeling sick to my stomach. The energy in this bubble was so off, so *horrible*.

Of course, I tried to hide my inner turmoil to get on with our mission, but I wasn't doing a great job. Hans couldn't stop casting me glances or laying a comforting hand on my shoulder. He'd proven time and time again that he might be half demon, but in his heart, he was a good guy.

"This is the best way to get there?" With a glowing finger, Luca pointed to a road on a map of LA that someone had found in the office building. The map wasn't up to date but without cell service, the old map proved the best we had to go on.

"Yeah," Dean, the wizard, replied, holding a candle as close as he dared. "Laura and I came from that direction earlier. Thank the Goddess we weren't there anymore 'cause that's the same street we took. It should lead you right to the palace."

It was after two in the afternoon, not that anyone could tell by looking outside, and for the last four hours we'd been strategizing on how to get into the castle. Unfortunately, no one in this building was a fae, so a glamour was out. Luckily, we had devised one other way to get in.

According to Elijah, it wasn't only the demons from Hell who roamed the streets. Darkborn did too, many of whom flouted their Sigil of Lucifer brand. We would pose as one of their cult members. Lucky for us, it just so happened one of the humans hiding in the office building was a true-blue Hollywood makeup artist.

Another person held a flashlight aloft while Shelly, our miracle worker, was putting the finishing touches on Meredith's Sigil. Like every single false brand she'd created before, her work looked like a *real* branding, but Shelly's skills didn't stop there. The makeup artist had also contoured all of our faces to the point that we were unrecognizable.

The girl had mad skills.

"That's all done for you." Shelly leaned back from Meredith's brand. "You think it's good enough?"

"Perfect," Meredith agreed. "We'd have been so screwed without you."

"That, we would have been." Luca packed up the map. When he'd have a chance to pull it out, I wasn't sure, but if it made the guy feel better, then so be it. "Thank you all. We'll do our best to return this way and, if we can, we'll get you through the barrier to safety." He looked at our team. "Ready?"

I stood from the seat I'd been chilling in, as did every other S&S member. Benny leapt off the windowsill and shot toward Rooms.

Elijah stood, too. "I'm coming with you guys."

I nearly groaned. I'd been wondering why Elijah had

insisted on getting 'branded' by Shelly. Now, we understood the young wolf's motives.

"That's not the best idea," Luca said.

"My sister works with S&S, so I can trust you. And I have to know what's happening out there. My family's pack is so close . . . " he trailed off.

Luca looked like he wanted to dissuade Elijah, but after a few seconds of contemplation, his shoulders loosened. "You're trained to fight?"

"Since I was fourteen. Harper needed someone to spar with who wouldn't go easy on her cause she's Alpha Heir, and my twin and little sis suck at sparring."

Luca nodded. "Let's get moving, then. Shay, are you ready to play your part?"

While I'd opted for my face to be contoured because Wrath had seen me, I'd chosen not to have the Sigil of Lucifer painted on my skin. It wouldn't make sense. As a nephilim of a certain power level, it was likely that any semi-observant demon would sense my angel magic and question why I was present. Therefore, I was acting as a random nephilim captive who had been in the wrong place at the wrong time.

I held out my hands and let my wings release from the magical bindings that kept them hidden in my back. "Ready."

Luca worked a band of magic around my wrists, making it loose enough for me to move, but tight enough to be convincing. Once we were sure I could also still reach into my pocket for the luxiter, he moved on to my wings and pulled them together too.

"That's not uncomfortable?" he asked, pulling on the wing bindings.

"I'm good."

"Okay, everyone, game faces on." Luca led us down the hall and out the door.

The moment I stepped outside, the stench of sulfur filled my nose, making me recoil. Though I was certain that it stank in the office building we'd taken temporary refuge in, too, somehow it was *so* much stronger out here.

"Oh dear, will you look at that," said a disembodied voice that belonged to the now-invisible Benedict.

"What?" Meredith hissed, peering around. "No one else is out here."

"The castle! Yeesh, you guys need to open your eyes or I'm not sure we'll survive the day."

Everyone turned, and when I saw what Benedict was talking about, I gasped. The central castle tower was now alight at the top, like it was the world's biggest candle or something.

"That must mean something," Hans stated what I was sure we were all thinking.

"Let's assume it's a bad omen," Meredith muttered, "like everything else in this freaking bubble of doom."

Had I been anywhere else and the stench and rot of this place wasn't making me ill, I would have laughed. The girl wasn't wrong.

"If anything puts us in danger that we can't escape, we use the luxiters right away," Luca said. "Back to Angelina's first. Especially if we're separated."

"Why didn't you use those things before?" Elijah asked. He'd been told about the luxiters, but not exactly how they worked. We didn't need to spread that knowledge around.

Hans let out a humorless laugh. "Teleporting right into the castle would have been genius, no?"

"Obviously not," Elijah muttered. "I was curious."

I shrugged. "My mom has a house outside the ward and that felt safer. Once we got there, we decided to hoof it down here until we had the lay of the land."

The gang started walking down the street. I positioned myself in the middle. For a few tense blocks, nothing happened. We were met only with the dead lining the streets. I wished we could have helped them, but who in the world could have guessed that when Lucifer claimed a city as his, it would be this one?

I focused on the back of Luca's head, and tried to feel safe between Hans and Rooms even though I was about to walk straight into a pit of vipers. I focused so hard, in fact, that when four demons appeared after a curve in the road, I nearly pooped my pants.

The beasts loomed at least seven feet tall and four hundred pounds, larger than any demon I'd ever imagined. With their leathery faces and prominent horns that extended above their noses, they looked like rhinoceroses.

What the actual fuck? How did they breathe with that thing above their nasal passages?

"What are those?" I hissed.

"No idea." Hans shook his head, and even though I should have been happy that he knew so little about the Hellborn, I found myself exasperated. Pretty damned terrified too. Were we doing the right thing?

Yes, of course. If Nicoleta married Rikel, Wrath would be in attendance. That meant the *lapis caelesti* were here too. There was no way he'd let those stones wander too far from his side.

"Hans, if your Mom is in that castle, you better keep your cool this time," Meredith said softly.

He glared at her. "I won't screw up again."

"Shut up," Serena hissed in the front with Luca and Tobias.

We did, and not a moment too soon because one of the rhino demons, the largest of all and likely the leader, took an interest and lumbered over.

"Who are you?" He grunted, shocking the crap out of me. This one was bipedal, but with his horn and tail and leathery skin, he definitely didn't appear remotely human. That they'd be able to speak hadn't occurred to me.

In answer, Luca rolled up his sleeve, revealing the Sigil of Lucifer Shelly marked there. "Darkborn. We were patrolling and found a nephilim."

The rhino's beady eyes widened, and he looked past the three in the front. His attention caught on my wings, and he smiled, revealing blackened teeth and gums.

I shuddered and fought not to look away when Hans's hand brushed my own. The touch lasted only a second; any longer and we might have blown our cover, but it was what I needed to keep my strength up.

My coven supported me and wouldn't let me fail. I needed to be there for them, too.

I rolled my shoulders back and stared the demon in the eye. He growled, but I didn't falter. Even when plopped in the center of the literal worst place in the world, I needed to project strength.

"I can take her," said Rhino Face. "I want to."

"Are you of proper station?" Luca's tone was more subservient than usual; a smart move. No matter how high a Darkborn might rise in the prince's ranks, they almost certainly weren't more important than those born in Hell.

The rhino monster snarled, but didn't press, which gave Luca his answer.

"We'll take her, then."

"To the fire cells," the rhino added.

CHAPTER THIRTY-TWO

Fire cells? That sounded menacing.

"That's what I thought too," Luca agreed smoothly.

Appeased, the monster stepped aside, as did all the others in his group. We continued down the street, now within a direct line of sight to the palace. As we walked, other demons questioned Luca, but he told them they were leading me to the fire cells and no one pushed harder—just smiled those cruel, cold smiles.

"What's going to happen when I get inside?" I whispered as we passed another group.

My presence would get us into the castle, hopefully with ease, but I doubted the second half of the plan. How in the world would we enter and find me a place to luxiter away? There were so many more demons than we'd imagined.

"Too bad you can't go invisible," Benedict commented.

"Or that we don't have any invisibility potion." Fear laced Meredith's tone. "I wouldn't mind some right about now."

"We'll find a place." Luca replied without looking back. "Even if you have to teleport away from the cell. It will work."

Nicolas Flamel had assured us that the luxiters would work anywhere. I exhaled a long breath to calm my racing heart. Luca was right. This would work.

I held that belief tightly to my chest as we approached the wide-open gates. That they weren't closed hinted that the Princes of Hell had nothing to fear.

I swallowed, but kept on walking, ignoring the stares of demons. The jeers. The insults. When we reached the door, another rhino-faced monster stopped us, gripping a war-hammer in his hands.

"Marks."

Everyone except me revealed their falsified Sigils of Lucifer.

As we'd hoped, they were good enough to trick demons, and the guard lowered his hammer an inch.

"What is this?" He pointed the war-hammer at me.

"A nephilim. We captured her. She was trying to help others escape." Tobias's dark tone was convincingly rough and uncaring.

"Idiot scum," the demon said, but a light had turned on in his eyes. One that didn't bode well for me.

The monster turned and waved to a demon with the face and tail of a snake and the body of a man who'd spent decades lifting weights to get swole. "Zark! Come 'ere! I'm going to take this one to the fire cells!"

I stiffened. I wasn't supposed to be separated so soon! I needed a spot to light-travel away.

My inner panic shut down as Luca turned. His dark brown eyes told me to chill, that I could still escape. Though I knew that, and was putting on a convincing show, inside, I was still freaking out. What if they did something to me before I got to the cells? What if they assaulted me? My heart raced so hard I thought it might explode out of my chest.

"I'm the daughter of a nephilim Covenant Seat," I blurted out as Zark joined the rhino-faced demon. "A good bargaining chip."

I could practically hear Luca's groan—but *honestly*! I wouldn't put it past these monsters to rape or maim me on the way to the cells! As a valuable hostage I might stay in one piece long enough to use my luxiter.

"The Seat, you say?" The demon grunted and the light in his eyes dimmed. "Your sire would pay for you?"

"Whatever you want."

Rhino Face scowled. "The princes would want to see you."

Oh, shit. I had not counted on that. What if I was alone and somehow Wrath recognized me?

"But they're busy celebrating the upcoming wedding." Zark spoke up this time. "Which you Darkborn are commanded to help with. That blonde bitch wants it perfect."

At my side, Hans stiffened, but caught himself before the demons noticed.

"You'll have to sit there 'till tonight," the Rhino guard finished. "Come on. I'm takin' ya."

"We can," Tobias ground out. "We want the recognition for bringing such a valuable hostage."

The demon barked out a laugh. "Too fuckin' bad, bloodsucker." He reached out, hand shooting past Luca and Tobias, and grabbed my shoulder. "Come on, angel scum."

I jostled forward, dreading my future as I separated from my friends and was led deeper into the castle.

CHAPTER THIRTY-THREE

MEREDITH

My mouth went desert dry as I watched an ugly ass demon pull Shay deeper into the black halls of the palace. Already, our plan was falling to pieces.

"She'll be okay," Hans whispered as Luca began walking, putting on a show of confidence, even though I suspected he was as worried as I was over Shay's fate. "They won't hurt a valuable hostage."

"The princes will. And your sister."

Hans winced. "They're too busy with the wedding to see to her. She has time and the luxiter. Shay is smart. She'll be okay."

"What will happen if she disappears before we do and someone finds out? Won't they immediately be suspicious of the people who brought the nephilim here?"

Luca turned. "Do *not* spiral, Meredith. Focus. I'm going to buy us as much time as possible, but you have one job right now. *Seeking.*"

Shit. Right.

I called my magic to life, allowed it to fill me, to find what I was looking for—my stone, the Opal of Heaven—and the Pearl of Hell. Wrath would keep them safe and likely together, right?

My heart thundered in my chest as I pressed my magic out, allowing it to guide me, to find the Opal and claim my birthright. The others formed a loose sort of cage around me, allowing me to follow the flow and seek until I struck gold. Luca led the group deeper into the dark, gleaming palace, careful to stick to the hallways that were filled with demons.

Though I was seeking, I also couldn't help but notice how elaborate the palace was for a castle that had just been . . . well, I wasn't sure how the demons had made the structure. I pictured it as being pushed out of the ground, a jagged, menacing daisy.

Paintings lined the wall, most depicting the same seven domineering figures, one of which was Wrath. The others had to be his brothers. They appeared tall, handsome and looked mostly like men—if hard, brooding ones, with a few beastly quirks.

Where no paintings hung, tapestries represented scenes of Hell. One, I was sure, was of the Field of Punishment, a torturous part of the underworld I'd been unlucky enough to traverse. Seeing it again brought back the smell of burning flesh, making me want to vomit.

"Any luck?" Hans whispered after passing a group of demons that struck me as different from those we'd passed by earlier. They were smaller, less dirty. Not warriors. No, these demons and demonesses wore formal attire—gowns and elegant pants and tunics.

"Nothing yet." I tilted my head to one female in a sleek black gown. Shimmering onyx wings veined with red spread across her back. "Who are these people?"

Hans knew what I meant. "I think feudal lords and ladies. No one is as powerful as the royals in Hell, but there are lesser nobilities. Or perhaps they are Darkborn with power in this world." He nodded to a different woman in a red gown. I cringed as she drank blood from a docile man's neck.

A vampire, then. Surely Darkborn.

A thought struck that made my blood freeze.

Would Denz be here? Or even Tobias's brother? The makeup artist brilliantly disguised my mate and Serena, but vampires had a great sense of smell. Would Raphael recognize his siblings' scent? Or even Hans and Shay? They'd been his captives.

The question tipped my tongue when a female demon with black antlers and a three-pronged tail entered the corridor, spotted us, and strode straight for us.

"Uh, does anyone recognize her?" Serena hissed. "'Cause she sure seems to know someone here."

No one did, and my anxiety only grew as the demoness stopped in front of our group and crossed her arms over her chest.

"I thought that idiot simply wouldn't send more workers." She pointed to the door she'd come out of. "We're setting up chairs now. Do your job."

"Of course," Luca replied smoothly, as my own brain glitched. What the heck was this demoness going on about?

The answer became crystal clear as she ushered us into a courtyard being set for an event. The wedding. Hell-style.

My lips parted as I took in the decor. Somehow, lush plants grew in the space, most of them blood red. Black roses lined an archway at the end of an aisle that was covered in black petals. People had set a few rows of chairs up, but judging by the pile of chairs along a far wall, there were still many more to go.

"What are you waiting for?" The demoness pointed to the chairs. "Get to work, Darkborn!"

Tobias snarled, but I brushed by him on my way to the chairs, ripping him out of his fury.

"Chill," I hissed. A scene could easily spell our death, and while this wasn't ideal, we could work with it.

"This is unexpected," Benedict said from somewhere around my feet as I took one chair and shifted it under my arm. Again, I wished the rest of us were as invisible as my familiar.

"Bloody hell." Tobias joined me and grabbed two chairs in each hand. "They treat their cult like servants."

He had a point. The room was filled with other Darkborn—not a demon in sight, aside from the one ordering us around. The Darkborn were all working their asses off to get the wedding perfect, but why? Did they think they'd be rewarded if they were a good peon? I supposed it wasn't too far-fetched. Nicoleta was Darkborn and she was marrying a prince. Maybe the others thought they'd get lucky like Nicoleta.

"What if Shay escapes?" I whispered again; the fear clung to me. "They might come looking for us for an explanation of why Luca's bonds didn't hold. There's nowhere to run out here." I gestured to the enclosed courtyard.

"Then, be fast." Luca grabbed a chair. "Meredith, Seek."

"We have an hour until the guests file in," the demoness barked. "Get to work, all of you!"

An hour and those of great power would be here watching the wedding. It would be the best time to grab the stones and run.

So freaking find them, I thought, and called my powers. Slowly, I pressed my magic out of the room and down the halls, venturing farther than I'd ever done before. Not only was I growing stronger, using my powers felt more natural, easy even.

My confidence boosted even more when I struck gold after only a minute of seeking. Not having expected that, I damned-near dropped the chair I carried. Thankfully, Tobias was there and his quick reflexes kept it from clattering to the ground and drawing attention.

Luca, who stood next to me, arched an eyebrow in question.

Before I answered, though, I focused. That pull of my magic, that tug right behind my breastbone told me that I was near the *lapis caelesti*. But there was something more, too.

My ring had warmed as it had done the night Tana and I first met.

Did that mean that this menacing castle hid another talisman—and another *Vindix*?

CHAPTER THIRTY-FOUR

SHAY

"In there, angel scum." My demon jailer grunted and shoved me into a cell.

I tripped past the bars, relieved to find a normal dark, dank cell. Righting myself, I turned back to the monster in time to watch his hand raise, middle finger and thumb pressed together.

"Hope you like it hot." He snapped his fingers and suddenly flames erupted, lining each wall.

A strangled sound left my throat as an oppressive heat filled the small space. So that was what they meant by a fire cell.

Fuck my life.

The demon cackled and slammed the gate shut behind me. "Better tuck in your white wings. Wouldn't want to burn those feathers."

I didn't even give him the pleasure of a response, just lifted my chin defiantly. We stared each other down and as much as I didn't want to look at his ugly, horrible face, I didn't flinch, didn't look away. When the monster snorted, I knew I'd won this battle. He turned and walked away, muttering something about entitled angels under his breath. The moment he lumbered out of my sight, I let the tears that had been gathering in my eyes fall.

The entire walk to the fire cell, I'd been harassed. Threatened. The deeper I strode into this palace, the more my instincts screamed to get the heck out and run. Run far, far away.

It was a lot, especially considering that my friends were in the castle looking for sacred stones. I feared for them as much as I'd been freaking out for myself. What if their cover got blown somehow? What if *I* blew it by disappearing too soon?

The questions tumbled out of my head as I caught sight of the flames along the edges of the room. Were they . . . moving inward?

Another minute passed before the flames moved again. One inch closer. Goosebumps rose along my arms.

I spun, taking in the space. It was about seven feet wide in both directions. How long would it take the fire to reach me? *Would* it reach me? Or was this screwing with my mind? Demons weren't above physiological torture. To hear tales of Hell, they enjoyed doling it out—practicing their vile methods on their own kind.

The fact that I was a hostage of value had not been lost on the demon who had brought me here. That made me think I wouldn't be burned alive, but this could make me very, very uncomfortable. It could hurt. Disfigure.

I needed to time this right and give my friends enough time to find the *lapis caelesti* and escape, *and* I needed to get the heck out of here before the fire burned me.

I swallowed and sent luck to my coven as the flames crawled another inch closer.

CHAPTER THIRTY-FIVE

HARPER

Since the news of LA's fall, my mom, the betas, and I had taken turns calling Elijah, but not a single person had gotten through.

I felt helpless to save my brother, and I hated that, but I couldn't sit around and cry about it. So, I put all that frustration and fear of doing what my father had commanded me to: finding a place where our wolves might hide.

Unlike Gunner, the Midnight Pack had no connections to Isila, so that was out. However, I did find correspondence between Dad and an alpha in the San Juan Islands off the coast of Washington State. The islands were remote enough that it unlikely a leader of Hell would claim the territory around them as their own. And we could drive there in just a day. As long as boats ran to the island, getting there wouldn't be an issue. Our pack might fly under the radar there, and when I called the alpha, he'd agreed to house us. But he insisted that we move fast. Leaving tonight would be best. He did not want anyone trailing us to his safe haven.

I'd already passed the information along to Dad, who'd agreed with the other pack's leader. In my first real act as alpha heir, I'd make the announcement at the gathering that some pack members were currently setting up for. Since the barbecue was in the middle of the afternoon, there would be enough time to pack and move out under the cover of dark.

The idea made my stomach ache, and I gripped it with a groan. "Can't have that at the barbecue."

In front of the pack, I had to do my best to appear pulled together and strong. Medicine would be needed.

My personal bathroom proved bare of antacids, so I left my room to search the hallway one, keeping my ears open for Gunner, who'd decided to rest for a while. He planned to help the pack move out, which meant a long night for everyone. Judging by the loud snores coming from his room, he was still asleep. Searching through the second bathroom proved fruitless too, and I shut the medicine cabinet with a sigh.

The girl in the mirror looked exhausted and worried. It would take a ton of work to radiate like the confident alpha heir I wanted to portray tonight.

"Maybe Mom hoarded them." I turned away from the mirror and searched for my mother.

Unlike the antacids, I found my Mom easily. She was in my parent's chambers, getting ready for the barbecue while Dad slept. My gaze raked over him as I walked around the bed.

Dad still looked bad, but he was determined to make an appearance at the gathering, all to support me. He'd even ordered a wheelchair to be brought in. Word had it Rikard had found one and would be back with it soon.

"Mom?" I breathed as I joined her in their walk-in closet. "Do you guys have anything for a queasy stomach?"

My mother gave me a soft smile. "Nerves?"

"Yeah."

"Let me get them for you, baby." She slipped into their en suite and emerged a minute later with two tablets smelling of chalk and peppermint.

"Thanks." I popped the antacids in my mouth.

"Of course, baby. Have you decided what to wear? You have less than an hour to go." She gestured at the leggings I'd changed into after the Calling.

"I've been busy trying to find a suitable place to relocate the pack."

"Every leader needs to look the part, Harper." Mom studied me with a critical expression.

"I was going to wear jeans and a sweater," I grumbled. "It is cashmere. Is that good enough for you?"

"It will do. But I have something else in mind." She opened her jewelry box, an extravagant wood box with six levels, and plucked out two earrings. "These. They're simple enough, but will give you that polish. Perhaps a boost in confidence, too."

These earrings weren't just gorgeous two-carat gems. They were family pieces, and my mother's pride and joy. They'd been passed down from mother to firstborn daughter for as long as anyone could remember. I'd always known one day they'd be mine, but I had not expected that day to be today. I'd always pictured receiving these on my wedding day. Or the day when I became alpha. While today was a first step in that, I still had a long way to go to fill the role.

"Are you sure, Mom?"

"They're yours now, baby." She took my hand and pressed the earrings into my palm. "I want you to wear them when you step into your new role. To honor both sides of your family."

"Thanks." My hand closed around the earrings. "They're beautiful."

"Put them in. I want to see."

I did so and once I had the backings secured, Mom's eyes crinkled at the corners. "Lovely. Look at them."

Inhaling deeply, I shifted to face the mirror and my own lips curled up as I admired the way they sparkled. How seven smaller diamonds haloed the larger, centered ones and caught the light perfectly.

"Thanks, Mom."

"You're welcome, baby. Now, go get ready. The barbecue will start soon."

I refrained from saying how I still thought it was ridiculous that we were continuing to call this a barbecue and walked out of the closet to find Dad sitting up in bed.

"Hey," I said. "Did we wake you?"

"I can't sleep anymore. Have you heard from Rikard?"

"Yep. Your chair should be here any minute."

"Good. You're ready?"

"I am."

He cleared his throat. "Your partner, he seems like a decent wolf."

"He is. Even if his family is a rival pack, Gunner is a good guy. He's never been territorial or tried to dominate me to prove a point."

"Hmmm. Keep him close then. We might need more connections than I ever imagined."

I wasn't sure what to say to that, so I kissed my dad on the cheek and left to get changed for the gathering that would hurl me into a new phase of life.

I STOOD AT THE WINDOW THAT OVERLOOKED THE BACKYARD. Outside the mansion, pups played. Older wolves in my pack milled, laughed, and chatted as if today were a regular day. To them, it probably was, and I was about to spoil that. Soon, their lives would be upended, and they'd be sent into hiding.

"No time like the present," Gunner's drawl came from behind. "Or you just gonna look out the window all day?"

I turned. "Almost ready."

"Feels weird, huh? Taking on tasks that others have done your whole life?"

I nodded with pursed lips. "It does."

"Want me to hang with you? I can crack a mean joke to break the tension."

That got me to laugh, because it was true. Gunner was the best at that in our coven. And while I was more stoic, right now I appreciated his levity. "Sure. Let's join the others."

Gunner gestured to the hallway. "I'm right behind ya."

Rolling my shoulders back, I led the way outside, and the moment I opened the door and that California sun shone in my eyes, the conversations outside stopped. People stopped to stare. My heart began thudding wildly.

"Hey y'all," Gunner drawled. "I know this shirt is a tad tight, but Ethan assured me I was very West Coast. Don't go makin' me feel self-conscious."

Laughter fluttered over the lawn and people turned back to their conversational partners. They still stole glances at me, and at Gunner, but it wasn't so much all at once.

I exhaled. "Thanks."

"They know somethin' is up."

"And they're not wrong. The pack will caravan north tonight." I exhaled sharply. "I worry about leaving Eli down here."

"'Course you do. He's family."

"Yeah." I gave Gunner a soft smile. "If news comes in that might otherwise persuade me to go to LA, let me know."

"Will do, boss." He fake saluted, and I laughed, glad for the moment of levity. It somehow eased so much tension in my shoulders, and as I descended the stairs and placed my feet on the lawn, everything seemed much more doable.

Dad was present, in a wheelchair and already looking exhausted, but he was still there—supporting me. Mom milled about, too. Her role was to ease anyone's tension, and it was obvious by the smiles she left on faces that she was doing so to perfection. Neither Henley nor Ethan knew about LA yet, but as the alpha's children, they too understood they were to help our parents, and they were doing a great job. Henley assisted in small ways, like playing with smaller children. Ethan entertained by juggling and generally making people happy.

The betas were in fine form too, each in their own sphere of wolves, assuring them that the alpha was well. It was the first time that most of the wolves of the Midnight Pack had seen Dad since his attack.

I exhaled again, long and low, trying to calm my racing heart. Trying not to think about Eli or what was happening a few hours south.

Right now, I needed to do my part. Schmooze. Get these wolves to trust me so that when I told them the plan, they wouldn't question it or my father's choice to give me this task. I needed the people I'd grown up with to see me in a different light. As a leader—someone capable of taking on the role of alpha someday. Someone capable of assisting the alpha and giving him good counsel *now*.

I needed them to see me as that person, to trust me as my father did.

"Go on, chica. Get 'em," Gunner whispered.

I tossed him another smile before diving into the crowd that I was dead set on winning over.

CHAPTER THIRTY-SIX

GUNNER

Beer in hand, I watched along the edges of the barbecue as Harper wove through the throngs of wolves. At first, she stuck to those who looked about her age; her comfort zone, I was guessin'. Aspen clung to her then, and I had to bite back the growl rising in my throat, until she moved on to an older group of female wolves. The she-wolves weren't so sure at first, but within minutes they were smilin' back and noddin' at whatever she was sayin'.

The girl was killin' it, and that was sayin' a lot.

Yeah, Harper had been born to this pack and meant to lead it all her life, but she wasn't around these parts too often. Wolves needed to know the person who led them would *always* be there, that they could trust her. For Harper and the Midnight Pack, this was the first step in closing whatever gaps there might have been between the pack and the alpha heir.

As if she felt my eyes on her, Harper turned and connected with me. She gave me a nod, as if to say 'I'm doin' alright'. I lifted my beer to her.

My partner and I had had a couple of good days—great days, actually—but I couldn't think too much about that. She'd been stressed and, until recently, I'd been one of the few people who knew the truth of the evil in the world. Of course, she would lean on me. We were colleagues, and this was business.

"You're going to lurk on the edges?"

I twisted to find Aura, the beta, walkin' my way. "Sure am. Shouldn't you be with your alpha? Or the heir?" I shot Harper a glance and smiled. "Actually, she don't need help. She's a natural leader of wolves."

"That's debatable." Aura shook her head.

"Why would you say that?"

It grated that she wasn't supportin' her heir. Even if Harper didn't pick Aura as one of her own betas, Aura should respect Alpha Ferenz's decision and his bloodline.

"She's alphablood certainly," Aura replied, sensing the edge in my voice. "But there's something different about that wolf."

Most wolves in this realm couldn't Call ancestors, wouldn't dream of it, but somewhere in Mrs. Ferenz's family line, they'd learned. It made me wonder if she wasn't wolvea deep in their bloodline. But they would know 'bout that.

Matter of fact, I would too. My lineage was common knowledge, and my family made it a point to meet the few other close wolvea descendants that resided in this world. "Different isn't bad," I said.

"No, different isn't bad." Aura watched her alpha heir. "It's unsettling."

I took a swig of beer, a nice California craft brew. "Any news on the city?"

My voice dipped as I asked the question. There hadn't been anything more from the Covenant for hours. I hadn't heard from S&S either, but things might change on a dime. I was bettin' Alpha Ferenz wanted his betas to be checkin' their phones often for updates.

"No one has gotten word in or out since the nephilim that allowed the Covenant's PSA." She sighed. "We might send a small task force down to check it out tonight."

"What about the move?"

"It would be very small. Ten strong wolves. The rest will retreat."

Poor choice, but I held my tongue. This wasn't my pack, and no one understood what was goin' on five hours south. Only that the city had gone dark and there were demons there. That wasn't promising, but there were also about a million variables at play.

"You disapprove," Aura said.

"My opinion doesn't matter much here, though, does it?" I took another swig of my beer.

Aura shrugged. "While I would love to agree, our alpha does not."

I cast her a glance. "What's that supposed to mean?"

"He wants to talk to you."

Ah, so that was why she'd sought me out. "Took you long enough to tell me."

"I wanted to make sure his judgment was sound."

"That's not your job."

Aura motioned left. "Follow me."

As if I wasn't completely aware of Alpha Mace Ferenz's location in the crowd, Aura parted the wolves. Their eyes followed me with a burning curiosity.

"Privacy," Aura barked as she neared her alpha. Immediately, everyone below the rank of beta took a dozen steps back, leaving only Rikard at Mace's side. Aura joined her alpha so his betas flanked him, a protective gesture if there ever was one.

"Want Crystal and Aspen to join?" I asked, a joking tone in my voice. "You know, in case I go for him?"

Ferenz's lips curled up wolfishly. "You're not that stupid. But then again, neither are my betas. They're as clever as they are loyal. You understand?"

I did. The alpha was injured, and the betas had only left his side on his orders. I didn't expect them to do so now. "What can I help you with, Alpha Ferenz?"

"I want to speak of the relationship between you and my daughter."

"We're colleagues and a current team for the coven. Surely, you've heard about how S&S operates? We work with partners."

"I don't know as much as I'd like about that organization, but Harper is firm in her secrecy. You are too, I expect?"

No way in hell I'd give up coven secrets. Not even to Pa, so I wasn't about to share them with Alpha Ferenz. "Loyal to the end."

"Too bad," Ferenz muttered. "I expect there is much in the Shadows and Secrets archives that would interest me."

The items we held for safekeeping would interest any person who desired power. It was why they were best kept with us, under the protection of a mage of great magical ability —and who sought no wider influence in our world. Luca was a man in a million, and I'd never betray his trust. I kept my lips shut and waited.

Ferenz exhaled. "That's not why I wanted to speak with

you, anyway. I'm more interested in your *personal* relationship with my daughter."

"You mean . . . If we're datin'?"

"Precisely."

"Unfortunately for me, I'm not her type."

Harper's father scoffed. "The girl is a genius and I'm proud to call her my daughter, but she doesn't know what her type is."

I found that hard to believe. Harper was one of the smartest, most perceptive members of S&S. When you had people like Toby and Luca in that group, that was sayin' a hell of a lot. She was younger than them by centuries and yet she still kept up. Outpaced them, even. "I think you're underestimatin' her."

"Did she tell you that she dated Aspen? It was a high school romance, to be sure, but still . . . " Ferenz tracked a wolf in the crowd. I followed him and found Aspen, still hovering near Harper, and occasionally casting glances her way.

My inner wolf growled, but I told him to shut the hell up. He was being absurd, and probably egged on by Mace's questioning.

"So? What's wrong with the guy?" I forced out

"Nothing. I admire him, in fact. That's why he was named my newest beta. But is he right for my daughter?" Ferenz pulled his attention back to me. "Absolutely not. Harper needs a strong wolf who will pull her out of her shell. Someone on her level." He paused. "Someone who, like her, isn't like most wolves."

I didn't reply.

"You're not like most wolves, Gunner."

Ah, there it was. Ferenz had seen a way to merge the blood

of the wolvea with his own bloodline. In doing so, he willfully ignored the practicalities of the situation.

"And what about the fact that our packs, our territories, are on opposite sides of the country?"

"Our packs have created something amazing. Something most wolf packs couldn't do. What's saying one of you couldn't live bi-coastal?"

Only a thousand years of wolves ruling—kingdoms and packs. If the alpha wasn't in residence most of the time, unrest set in. Inevitably, someone rose to challenge him or her. And I couldn't hide from my own desires. Whoever I married, be it a mate I found for myself or my fated mate, I wanted them with me.

"It's an idea." I shrugged. "But we have some pretty important issues on our mind right now."

Even as I spoke the words, the memories of yesterday came rushing back: our race through the woods, how my body had reacted to Harper when she got out of the lake. How she'd taken her time in showing me her woods on the way on our walk. That hadn't been all business. No denyin' it, though I didn't need to mention it to Mace.

"Mull it over," Ferenz said. "It's clear to me that things are changing and wolves will have to as well." He looked up at me. "You're a powerful wolf. And I saw the way that you watched my daughter when you ran after her to my chambers. You care for others, for her. I want that for her."

She was my S&S partner, and we were friendly, but before I got the words out, a scent caught my attention.

Rot. Eggs. Fire.

My shoulders stiffened.

Sulfur.

I twisted and took in the crowd. No one else had noticed,

not even Harper, who joked around and laughed with a crowd of elder wolves—still intent on doing the job her father had set out for her.

"Alpha Ferenz, there's something wrong," I said. "I smell—"

A scream cut through the crowd. In unison, Aura and Rikard spun, and the surrounding air shimmered brilliantly as their wolves threatened to explode from their skin to defend their alpha. They held the inner animal back, though, showing impressive restraint.

"What was it?" the alpha asked, still calm and collected, and rightly so. A scream could mean many things. Maybe someone pulled a prank, someone saw a snake, or someone had shrieked with joy.

Or that an enemy approached, and I was becoming pretty damned sure that was the case. The whiff of sulfur had grown stronger, sticking in my nostrils.

As wolves constricted inward from the outskirts of the gathering, the truth revealed itself. A young wolf in his twenties sprawled on the ground, a knife sticking out of his back.

"There's sulfur in the air," I said. "That means demons."

"From that direction." Rikard pointed toward the man who'd been stabbed.

As if the beta summoned the devils, twelve darted out from the woods, three hurling knives with terrifying skill. Wolves shifted, ready to defend. I spun, hunting for more and spotted twelve other foes approaching from the house, and another dozen from another direction.

Shit. Where was Harper?

I twisted again to find that she was already coming our way, sprinting with fear in her eyes. Behind her, the fight began as the wolves lashed out at the demons. Blood sprayed and children cried, their mothers pulling them to their chests, trying to shield the youth from the horror.

"Dad!" Harper cried out when she reached us. "We need to fight."

"Let the others," Alpha Ferenz replied. "Harper, you need to—" a choking sound left his mouth and his hands flew to his throat.

"Dad! What's going on?"

More choking sounds came, and they weren't from the alpha. Rikard and Aura were choking, too. Heart racing and the sounds of Harper yelling in my ears, I turned to take in the pack.

The shifted wolves were still fighting, unaffected, but those in their human forms weren't. They were choking, but why? Had the demons poisoned the food and drink?

I didn't get it, couldn't fathom what was happening, but then I saw something that made my pulse quicken. A very faint cloud of darkness approached one of the gals in the middle of the crowd. She held her kid and looked terrified and didn't even see the cloud comin'. Didn't seem to notice it form around her head and then . . . it disappeared.

She began to choke, dropping her kid as her fingers splayed across her neck. Then her eyes flashed crimson.

I blinked as everything clicked into place.

"Non-corporeal demons. They're like little black clouds," I said.

"I-I think I saw!"

"They're possessing them. Harper, we need to run!"

Harper's mouth had fallen open, and she took a step back as Rikard began to growl, his eyes glowin' like rubies. My heart leapt into my throat when I saw that Alpha Ferenz's were too.

"Oh no . . . Rikard?" Harper cried out. "By the Old Ones . . . Dad? Are you—"

Still in human form, the alpha lunged, fallin' from his wheelchair and collapsin' on the ground, all the while snappin' wildly at his daughter. Hair grew on his arms and his nose elongated as he tried to shift and my heart rate spiked. The alpha was already possessed and trying to turn into a wolf. What if he succeeded? What would the demon inside him do with a shifted alpha wolf? Nothin' good.

I grabbed Harper's arm and pulled.

"No, Gunner! I have to help!"

"You're no nephilim and they're possessed and soon they'll all be tryin' to shift. Can you take on your pa and all his betas and anyone else who joins in to protect the alpha?"

The terror in her eyes said it all. And as strong as I was, I couldn't take on that many powerful wolves. Didn't want to either, not when they were my partner's family.

"So, run, Harper!"

This time she did, and it was then that we saw we weren't the only unaffected people. Ethan and Henley sprinted back to the house, two corporeal demons at their backs.

Harper's face fell. "Henley can't fight. Ethan is not so great either."

"Then we do it for them." We spun to chase down the demons and gained on the younger Ferenz kids.

A roar came behind and, though I didn't look, I was pretty damned sure the solid-form demons were coming for us. We had to get to her siblings and shift. Those who had shifted to wolf form before they were possessed seemed to be safe from the clouds. I had a feeling that the animal nature protected them from bein' taken over in the first place, and thank the Old Ones those wolves were still fighting.

CHAPTER THIRTY-SIX

But they weren't just fightin' the demons anymore.

The possessed humans had started to punch and kick at their own pack members, their family. Though our kind was weaker in our human form, there were far more possessed humans than shifted wolves.

And what if all the possessed people tried to shift like Alpha Ferenz? Then we wouldn't just be dealin' with possessed shifters in their human forms, but a whole pack 'o wolves with no control over themselves.

There was no way to take on so many. Even though my alpha instinct kept yellin' at me to fight, with this number of adversaries, this was a losing battle. Our only option was to grab those kids and run. And we'd best do it in our wolf forms, just to be safe.

"Harper, shift. We'll kill the demons after Henley and Ethan, then you mind-link to your siblings and we get the hell out of here."

She did as I said, and suddenly, we were two wolves chasing her brother and sister. In this form we were much faster and we closed in quickly, each leaping on a demon that looked like a rhino and a man had one ugly-ass baby. I wasted no time in going for the tender parts, ripping out the neck. To my side, blood gurgled, assuring me Harper had done the same. A short distance away, her siblings had stopped and watched.

Henley trembled so violently that I was surprised the poor girl could stand. She sure as hell didn't know what to do, and neither did Ethan. The pair needed direction, and Harper was still demolishing her demon.

I shifted. "Take your wolf forms. And listen to your sister!"

The pair did as instructed, and I was faced with one brown wolf and a reddish-brown one. I returned to wolf form too, and let out a bark. My S&S partner lifted her head from her kill, saw that her siblings were safe, and sprinted for an open bit of woods.

Another bark got her siblings to move their asses, and I took up the rear, hopin' to lose the demons in the forest.

CHAPTER THIRTY-SEVEN

HARPER

I KEPT MY EARS TRAINED BACK, LISTENING FOR MY SIBLINGS AS WE sprinted through the forest on all fours.

Henley ran right behind me and then Ethan. Gunner was supposed to be taking up the rear, but I could barely hear him. Careful to maintain my speed as we raced through the woods, I chanced a glance back.

My heart lurched. He had stopped to take on two rhinoceros monster demons.

I loosed a howl to get his attention and Gunner's head snapped my way. He howled back, his intent clear even though we weren't mind-linked.

Go. I have them.

Inside, my instincts roared. Members of S&S did not leave their partners behind, and I'd already done so once with Gunner. I'd hated every second of it, but it had been the only way to save Sara. In this instance, I was in another pickle. If I stopped, Henley and Ethan would too. And despite Dad's training, neither were skilled fighters.

Unless . . .

Henley, Ethan! I tapped into our pack's mind-link. *I need you to keep running! Go to the other side of the lake. Up the mountainside to those caverns. Wait there for me and Gunner.*

No way! Ethan shot back. *I'm not leaving you behind.*

It's a command.

You're not my alpha. You're not even a beta, sis.

That little shit! He knew darn well what I was, and though I wanted to rage and storm at him, I also understood why he denied me. He'd left Mom and Dad behind already. He couldn't do the same to me. Plus, we both recognized that Henley was a real liability.

Tossing one more glance back at Gunner, I exhaled. One of his attackers was already dead, and I'd caught him as he lunged at the second. His jaws connected, ripping out skin and muscle. Blood spurted, and the demon fell as Gunner's victorious howl filled the air.

Thank the Old Ones. He'd catch up, and we'd all live.

Trying to convince myself of that, I kept sprinting. Kept listening for other demons approaching. I was certain they were in the woods, but they didn't know this forest like me.

Not the corporeal kind, anyhow. Images of the black smudges of smoke, clouds as Gunner had said, engulfing the faces of my pack members and possessing them came rushing back. It had been so subtle that had he not seen it too, I would have thought I was crazy. But I had seen them. Those smoke demons—whatever the hell they were called—might have been fast enough to catch us.

I picked up my pace. Loud panting at my back announced that my siblings were close to their limits, but I didn't let up. We couldn't—not if we wanted to live.

Minutes later, the lake came into view. We burst through

the treeline to hug the shore as we raced around it to the mountains rising just beyond the blue waters.

We ran so fast that soon the lake spread out behind us and we entered the woods again, our paws carrying us up a steep incline. My pulse raced. These caverns were where young wolves played, so each of my siblings knew them well. Every wolf who grew up in Midnight Pack land did.

But they also weren't secret. What if the demons had assembled here and then approached the pack land? Where had they come from, anyway? How did they know the pack would be together and the barbecue would be the best time to strike?

Was there a traitor in the pack?

I shook off the dread dripping down my spine. No. My father wasn't always a law-abiding citizen, and he'd done some horrible things to protect his status, his family, and his pack, but no one in the Midnight Pack would betray him. Everyone loved him.

I kept telling myself that until the caverns in the mountainside came into sight. I couldn't lead my siblings in there without being certain.

Ethan, Henley, stop, I ordered them and slowed down because there was no point in sprinting into a possibly occupied series of caves. *I need you to wait here.*

Like hell, I will, Ethan replied.

I was about to get into a fight with my brother, when Gunner raced up alongside us, carrying with him the scent of demon blood, and shifted.

I followed suit, hating that because we weren't in the same pack, we couldn't mind-link. It had never been an issue before, but now it was plain dangerous.

"No sulfur in the air," Gunner said. "I think we're safe. For the time bein', anyhow."

An exhale parted my lips. He was right. If that many demons had been here in the last twenty-four hours, this place would smell horrendous.

I turned to my siblings. "Shift. We're going inside."

This time, they followed my directions and, together, we made our way into the cave. As Gunner predicted, the first cavern was empty. As the caves were interlinked through the mountains, I walked in deeper, checking the second and the third caverns. No one was there and my sensitive nose did not detect a whiff of sulfur.

Confident that we were safe for the time being, I walked back to my siblings and Gunner, only to find Henley kneeling before the wolvea, wrapping something around his leg.

"This should work," she said. "Once your healing kicks in, you'll be fine."

"Oh, crap, Gunner! How did that happen?" I ran forward, taking in the blood streaming down his jeans. How had I not seen that before? I'd scented blood but assumed it had been from the demons.

"One of 'em got in a good swipe. But I'm fine. I'm already healin', and Henley here is a great nurse."

"Doctor in training," she corrected him.

"Shoulda known with brains like yours in the family."

"I'm so sorry, Gunner." I shook my head. "I should have helped you."

"No." His tone was firm. "You did what you had to do, protectin' your family."

"S&S code," I reminded him.

"I'm fine, Harp. Really, I am." He looked so genuine that my pushing back felt ungrateful.

I sighed. "Thanks for helping get them out of there."

"Yeah, thanks, man," Ethan said. "I'm not a fighter, not like Harp and Eli anyway, and Mom told me to get Henley out of there." His voice tripped when he spoke of our mother.

"What happened to her?" I asked.

"She shifted and fought," Ethan said. "She even saw Dad lunge at you and said we needed to leave."

"And she said we'd be fine." Henley's red eyebrows screwed together. "I guess she meant if we outran the demons doing the possessing?"

"Can't be it." Ethan frowned. "One of those black clouds got all up in my face! But it didn't possess me. Mom saw too . . . That was when she looked relieved and then told us to run."

I cast Gunner a sidelong glance. "What do you think?"

"Guardian spirits?" he asked. "Your family can Call. Has your ma ever talked to you about those?"

"She taught me about them," I replied. Guardian spirits were when a Caller bound a protective spirit to another. Usually, a loved one.

"She didn't give you one?"

"No. At least, I don't think so." My teeth dug into my bottom lip. "Wouldn't I feel it if she bound a protective spirit to me?"

"I can't say." Gunner looked around the cave, as if lost in thought. "Your ma seemed pretty good at Callin', though, so I expect if she didn't want you to know, you wouldn't."

That struck me as true.

"Not Dad, though?" Henley sounded wounded, and I reached out to clasp her hand.

"She'd have to ask Dad. He's alpha. He's never liked her Calling the Old Ones."

Tears filled in my sister's eyes. "What's going to happen to them?"

"I'm not sure," I said. "But we need to get somewhere safe."

"This is safe." Ethan gestured around.

"For now," Gunner amended. "Some of those demons might have a wolf's sense of smell. Or better, even. There are lots of types of demons we don't know a thing about. I saw 'em in Hell."

"You went to Hell! Whoa, man!" Ethan's eyes widened.

"Not right now, Eth," I said.

My brother rolled his eyes. "Yes, master."

I was so going to clobber that kid.

"Anyway," I put on my most authoritative voice to reroute the conversation. "We can't stay here. But seeing as our home is no longer safe, we have to figure out where else to go."

"Let's check the coven." Gunner pulled out his phone. "Looks like I have a couple bars of service. I'll give Luca a ring."

I hadn't brought mine out to the barbecue. I'd wanted my pack to see me as present with them, but I was glad that Gunner had his.

He dialed the coven master, and I heard the phone ringing. It rang and rang and rang, and eventually a message machine picked up.

"Luca, it's Gunner. Man, there's trouble and we need to talk to you. Give me a ring as soon as you can." Gunner hung up. "Nothin'"

"What are they doing?" I exhaled sharply, frustrated, worried, and scared.

"I dunno. I'm gonna shoot Toby, Stoney, and Hans texts too. Just in case. Tell them we need them." His fingers raced over the keyboards as he sent off the text messages. All the while, I sank deeper into despair. When Gunner met my gaze again, I nearly shattered. He came closer.

"Harp? You okay?"

"People I love are in trouble." Tears pricked in my eyes and, suddenly, an elephant sat on my chest. I leaned against the rock wall, trying to calm down, to control my breath, and as Mom used to say, therefore my life.

What wishful thinking. It was all too clear now that I controlled nothing. Nothing in here, and certainly nothing beyond the rocky walls that sheltered us from the dangers outside.

CHAPTER THIRTY-EIGHT

HANS

WE'D BEEN HELPING SET UP FOR MY SISTER'S WEDDING FOR LESS than an hour, but it felt like a fucking lifetime.

Since Meredith sensed the *lapis caelesti*, and maybe even a *Vindix* talisman in our midst, each person in our group had been working double-time. The sooner the affair began, the sooner we could act.

And yet, conflict riddled me. As much as I wanted to get the stones away from Wrath and his brothers, I also wanted to see my sister, to stop her from this horrible fate. She'd chosen her path, yes, but she was so young. So unstable.

I cringed, hating to think that about my blood—even if it was the truth. Nicoleta shouldn't be marrying *anyone*, let alone an Heir to Hell. She needed help.

But today, I couldn't give her that. So many times before, I'd tried to get her to see the light, always risking others as I did so. Today had to be different. Too much rode on us being here and finding the stones.

I kept that in mind as people wearing ball gowns and suits started entering the courtyard, searching for their seats.

Around the edges of the opulent space, workers put the finishing touches in place. Not far from where I lit black candles along the outside aisles, Tobias and Meredith littered the ground with black and red petals. I stood to move on to the next candle when Raphael Laurent entered the room alongside my mother.

All the air left me as the pair swept up the center aisle, chatting like they were old friends. Forgetting my disguise, I twisted, keeping my back to them and trying not to freak out.

Lilith looked the same as she had when I was growing up. Stunning with her red hair and a flawless complexion, she held herself with an air of power that few could match. Easily the strongest of the demon queens, my mother's magic was on par with the Princes of Hell. The issue was there was only one of her and seven of them and the brothers would always choose each other above anyone else.

Did mother know the vampire she walked alongside had kept me captive? Did she know he would have killed me? I didn't think she'd be able to stomach such a thing. More questions came as they took their seats, and I thanked the Goddess so many scents filled the courtyard that Raphael didn't detect his siblings.

But our safety might not last forever. We needed to get out of here, and fast. I shuffled over to Tobias and Meredith, who hadn't been watching the guests obsessively.

"Stiff," I murmured, the name Tobias hated, if only to keep his real name off my lips. Vampire hearing was excellent, and Raphael wasn't too far away. "We need to get you and your sister out of here. Your brother is a guest."

Tobias stilled. "You're certain?"

"He only held me captive in his castle, so yeah, I'm sure," I shot back. "Third row."

With a preternatural air only vampires could manage, Tobias turned. The moment he spotted his brother, his eyes blazed with heat.

"Hey," Meredith whispered. "Let's slip out. The others—"

"If you do not hold an invitation, *leave now!*" The demoness overseer swept around the edges of the room, clapping her hands. "Line the corridor for our procession!"

Internally, I groaned. We wouldn't watch the wedding, but they expected us to add to the pomp. I'd still have to see Nicoleta make the biggest mistake of her life.

"Come on." Meredith hissed at us and pushed me toward the door.

Within seconds, the hallway outside the courtyard brimmed with people bearing the Darkborn brand. Luca shepherded us to the back, and once there, he threw magic around us.

"Silencing bubble," he said.

"Serena, did you see that our bloody brother is in there?" Tobias leaned closer to this sister.

"What? That asshole!"

"Indeed." Tobias eyed the door, and Meredith placed a hand on his shoulder, trying to keep him from running.

"Did you sense the stones?" Elijah asked.

"And a *Vindix* talisman," Meredith replied, which made the wolf's jaw drop. Apparently, no one had told him the news while we set up.

"Are we going to wait until the procession files by and find the stones and the talisman as fast as possible?" Elijah glanced about nervously.

"Hopefully the *Vindix* will be with their talisman," Meredith added.

"That's the plan," Luca said. "We'd leave now, but it would draw too much attention."

With so many demons and Darkborn around, we needed to be careful not to draw attention. As much as I wanted to get this shit done, Luca was right. We needed to wait.

"I'm still worried about Shay using her luxiter," Meredith whispered.

"As am I," the coven master replied, "But no alarm has been raised yet, so she has stayed put. Knowing her, she'll buy us as much time as she possibly can, though she can't stay contained forever. Which is why when we can leave, you must be ready to seek."

Tobias slipped his hand into Meredith's palm and the witch nodded, resolve plastered on her face. Before we could conduct more business, music swelled.

"Here we go," Benedict muttered from somewhere near my feet. What the cat had been doing as we decorated for my sister's wedding was anyone's guess, but he was still with us.

The song was sinister and the following procession left no doubt as to why. One by one, male demons filed in.

I recognized them from the paintings lining the corridors. Though they all looked mostly human, some had horns or tails and all possessed an air of cruelty that screamed these males were the Princes of Hell. Each royal had wings just like mine too, and that made me squirm. Seventh in the column of devils was Wrath and the heir came next, looking very much like his father and smug. I wanted to claw Rikel's eyes out, to hurl my magic at him, but that would give us away. As much as I wished to stop my sister's wedding, I could not risk my coven.

The music took a slightly lighter tone, though it was still far more dramatic and darker than the normal bridal wedding tune. Everyone straightened, and a lump rose in my throat.

When Nic appeared in a glimmering black ball gown, Luca wrapped a hand around one of my arms, and Meredith seized the other. The fact that they were holding me back told me I wasn't hiding my emotions well.

That was my sister, beaming as she walked by with a gleaming tiara of ebony moonstones on her head. My gut clenched so hard I nearly doubled over.

Nic looked elated, and that made me want to die.

The moment she disappeared into the courtyard, I slumped.

"I'm sorry." Meredith released my arm.

"Me too."

"I'm dismantling the silencing bubble. Say little as we move. Meredith, you lead," Luca said as our supervisor demoness waved the crowd away and the doors to the court-yard shut.

I yearned to glimpse inside one last time, to see this moment for my sister even if I disagreed with it, but Serena took me by the hand.

"Come." The vampire pulled me along.

We followed Meredith down the corridor, trying to put on the air that we belonged in the castle. Stopping briefly at an intersection of hallways, she took stock of her magic and turned left, down a way we had not yet gone. Looking back, Meredith assessed the crowd. I mimicked the gesture. No one had followed us, but that didn't give me much peace. They might have been busy, but equally, we could have been entering a forbidden part of the palace.

"Both the stones and the talisman are close, I think." Meredith kept moving, kept seeking. "Here." She stopped five doors down, and our entire group tensed as her hand landed on the doorknob.

"Careful," Tobias murmured. "If there is an alarmed ward on this door, we aren't that far from the ceremony. Those in the courtyard might hear."

"My ring is leading me here, so this is where I should find the *Vindix* talisman. We have to go inside. Do you sense anything on the door, Luca?"

Luca shook his head. "No magic, no wards." It shocked the shit out of me for a moment until I realized, why should it?

In the palace at this very moment were seven Princes of the Underworld, at least one Queen of Hell, an heir, and my sister. All powerful people. Who knew what *other* creatures lurked the hallways and were loyal to the royals? Why would anyone try anything stupid when the punishment for said actions was sure to be painful and wicked? Possibly deadly, too.

With a shaky hand, Meredith turned the knob. The door opened without resistance and a collective sigh ran through our group.

We rushed in to find the spacious bedroom, decorated for the height of dark luxury, empty. A vanity stood by an arched window, overlooking the dark city of LA, and atop it was an item that I recognized.

Lit by candles, the blue-black stone I'd so often seen hanging around Nicoleta's neck gleamed in the center of smaller ones. A pit formed in my stomach.

"Nicoleta." I hung my head, heart sinking. "This is her room."

"What?" Meredith paled. "There is no way your sister is a *Vindix*."

"This is hers. My father gave it to her." I strode over to the vanity and picked up the necklace. The metal was hot to the touch, and I dropped the damned thing. "Ah! It burned."

Meredith stiffened; her stare locked on the jewelry. "Nicoleta wore that the night we emerged from Hell, right?"

"It's a gift from my father. She rarely takes it off . . . though I suppose Wrath did not want her wearing anything from her witch line during her wedding."

"Holy shit." Meredith stepped closer to the necklace. "My ring grows warmer the closer I get to it. Hans, *that's* the talisman." She paused, eyes wide. "And I don't think it works for Nicoleta, but it burns *you*. It's trying to tell you, *us*, something." She picked it up and studied it. "The central stone. It's surrounded by seven smaller ones."

"Bloody hell," Tobias murmured.

But I just stood there, unable to believe what she was implying. It couldn't be true. I would have known, right?

The necklace was my sister's and while I'd seen it all my life, I'd never touched it. Why would I? It wasn't my style to wear a girly necklace, and Father had always intended it for her.

"Hans," Meredith stared at me with widened eyes. "I think *you're* a *Vindix*."

"Impossible." I staggered backward, shaking my head in disbelief.

"It's not! You're half wizard! Witching blood is the only thing all *Vindix* must have in common. And the family who owned the Pearl of Hell died off!"

I blinked. "How can you be sure?"

"What do you think I've been reading about in that damned *Abscondita* library? Fate, or whatever, has chosen you to be the new holder." Meredith shoved the necklace into my hands.

Again, it burned, but she kept it there and slowly the heat dissipated to nothing, as if the necklace had said its piece.

"This necklace is reacting to you. It belongs to you." Meredith spoke with authority now, convinced. "*Not* Nicoleta."

"We can't be sure," I retorted. "Maybe my sister had it warded so no one would steal it."

At that, the witch rolled her eyes. "Wait until we get back to England. I'm going to toss your ass in the Enchanted Pool and when your tats all turn white, I'm going to say I told you so."

I stared at her, stunned, unable to form words.

"Whomever is the *Vindix*," Tobias butted in. "Meredith's ring tells us that the necklace belongs to them. Take it and we need to mo—"

The door burst open, and everyone spun, ready to attack. The moment I saw who it was, my heart leapt.

"My son," Lilith whispered, fear lacing her voice, "what are you doing here?"

"Mother!" I ran to Queen Lilith as she shut herself in Nicoleta's room. "You left the wedding?"

"It's over. Demonic ceremonies are quite short."

Meredith swore. "If these are Nicoleta's chambers, we need to leave!"

"She won't be back for hours. No one is coming this way," my mother replied. "You have a little time—though I would not suggest you linger longer than you must."

"Where do they go?" I asked. I didn't know what happened at a demon wedding, nor after.

Mom looked uncomfortable. "The bedding ceremony is public and taking place in Rikel's chambers. All the princes will be present—as will many guests. I begged to leave because I did not wish to see that part of our tradition. My Lord Husband granted my request."

I sucked in a breath as another dire matter rolled over me. "Lucifer knows about Nicoleta and me now."

"He does." Mom took my hand. "His anger was horrible to behold, but Prince Orien made a deal with my husband. He will not harm Nicoleta now that Prince Rikel owns her."

"And me?"

Mom's expression broke me. "You, my sweet boy, must be *very* careful. Which is why I'm here. I sensed you in the courtyard, knew why you risked your life to come, and used my powers to track you." She glanced at the necklace in my hands, brow furrowed.

I was certain my mother did not know what it was. Considering her proximity to the Princes of Hell, it needed to stay that way.

"You're here for the stones," Mother said. "I am not aligned with the princes on the matter of destroying this world. I will help you get them."

"I can feel them." Meredith's tone rose with excitement. "If you provide a distraction—"

"I'm going *with* you to help. It will be faster this way," my mother interrupted her.

"Lead the way, Mother." I was not about to argue with her.

I trusted my mother. Since the princes and those they ruled had been imprisoned in the underworld, she had entered this world many times and then left peacefully. For her, ruling Hell had always been enough, but it wasn't that way for the seven princes.

"Hans," Luca hissed.

"Trust me. And her," I said.

The group stood stock still for a moment, but then Meredith stepped forward. "Queen Lilith saved our asses once. I trust her."

My mother smiled. "We must go."

As quietly as possible, we left the room and traveled down a series of deserted hallways. Everything was so empty, so quiet, that it felt wrong. This unnatural quiet was because the entire palace was off watching Rikel bed my sister. Vomit rose in my throat.

"Mother," I whispered as she marched down another corridor. "Is there any way to help Nic?"

The queen cast a sorrowful glance at me. "Not now, Hans. Maybe not ever."

Silence struck me until she stopped in front of a set of unguarded gilded double doors. "Why are there no guards in this part of the castle?"

"No one would dare steal from the princes," Mother said. "Besides, where would they go? I don't know how you got through the ward around the city, but very few can manage that type of magic."

"We barely did." Meredith shuddered. "Jeez, this is giving me déjà vu. I can feel the Pearl so strongly—and more—I guess that's the Opal."

"You know how it feels?" Mom raised an eyebrow.

"I'm the person who set it free on the world." Meredith looked guilty. "Though I didn't know what it was then, of course."

My mother took her in for a long moment. "Well, this is your chance to erase that wrong." She opened the door to an opulent chamber filled with books and random objects standing on pedestals.

"What is this place?" Meredith asked, walking past a pedestal topped with a glass box. Inside, a polished stake gleamed. "This says someone used it on Napole Laurent?"

Tobias got closer. "Napole was not just any Laurent. He was a born vampire, *an original* and a powerful prince. This must be sacred wood . . . Any stake would kill a normal vampire, but something stronger is required of those who were born this way."

"It was made of ash blessed by the Goddess of Witches herself," Mother answered. "This is Lucifer's trophy room. Orien was allowed to place his pretties in here until he found a palace of his own."

I shuddered. A palace of his own—in his own kingdom.

"Any idea when that might be?" Luca asked, and my mother turned to him.

"No. Nor where. I will remain here and Prince Orien has always been quite secretive when it comes to sharing with my lord husband. He only kept the stones in this room because it is warded—wards that can be crossed by, or alongside, those of royal demon blood."

"Won't they suspect you helped?" Luca asked.

"My son is royal, too. Now that my secret is out, and Wrath has met Hans, he will be Orien's first guess."

I drew back. I'd always known the fact that had Lucifer allowed me to live, they would consider me a bastard Prince of Hell. But to hear it spoken out loud did not sit right.

"It's in here." Meredith stopped before an elaborate ebony box inlaid with gold etchings of a king on a throne of skeletons.

"Here," Mother reached out and pressed her hand on the box. It clicked open and two gems gleamed up at us.

Immediately, the Pearl drew my attention, which only seemed to strengthen the claim that I was a *Vindix*. I shook my head, unable to fathom such an idea.

Meredith reached out, touched the quarter-sized Opal, and her eyes closed momentarily. "Wow."

"You keep that one close," Mother said. "Always on your person."

Meredith looked at her. "I don't understand its purpose. Why would Wrath even want it?"

"It's not that he wants to use the Opal," Mother replied. "He wants to be sure others—*you*—cannot spread its effects. Take away free will and sow fear with the other stones and the prince's rule becomes that much easier."

Meredith's lips parted as the truth washed over her. "Okay, yeah . . . that tracks."

Mother grabbed the Pearl from the box and handed it to me. My palm warmed when it touched my skin. "You must go. Now."

"Agreed," Luca said. "The sooner we leave, the better. Shay might escape the fire cell at any moment."

Mother whirled on him. "Fire cell? Someone in your group was taken there?"

"Yes," Luca said. "But she has a device that allows her to light-travel. She can get out."

"No, she cannot. Only smoke-travel is permitted from the palace."

My stomach dropped. If that was true, Shay was trapped! "Are you sure?"

"Quite."

"Fuck." I swore again and stuffed the Pearl of Hell into my pocket. "We have to save her."

The Queen of Hell exhaled. "Can you smoke-travel, son?"

"I've tried, but can't manage to go far yet."

"Then, I will have to go with you to ensure you escape the palace." She turned to the vampires. "You will not want to join us. Fire might already consume the cell, and I cannot guarantee a landing free of flames. A blaze of that size will be deadly to your kind."

Tobias cast a glance at Meredith, who shook her head.

"I'm going after Shay."

"You're my mate—" he retorted, his eyes burning from within.

"Tobias, use your super speed to run back to the office building we found earlier. We'll meet you there." Meredith turned to my mother. "We need to get Shay. Now."

The group ran to the door and left the room, only to find a trio of horned but otherwise human-passing demons and one vampire waiting just outside.

"Meredith," the vampire hissed. "So good to see you again."

"Can't say the same, Denz."

I stiffened at the name. This wasn't the first time Denz had seen Meredith since he'd been turned from human to vampire. Recently, he'd tried to rip out her neck and from the positioning of his body—like a tiger ready to pounce—he was going to do so again.

The vampire snarled. "For someone who threw me to the wolves in Egypt, you have a high opinion of yourself." His arm snapped out, striking Meredith in the middle, and she went flying back into the trophy room.

Tobias roared and leapt at the younger vampire, but the demons behind Denz struck too fast. Magic blasted Tobias backward, and suddenly, we were pushed deeper into Lucifer's trophy room.

"Mother!" I shouted as she hurled herself in front of me and fell from a blast. I hauled her back up as one demon tried to strike her again.

"You must be the bastard of Lilith," he hissed, eyes glowing red. "Her blood is no match for that of Prince Levi."

Levi, the Prince of Envy. This must be his son. Before I could process any more, glass shattered behind me, and Levi took that moment to attack.

His magic hit me, a bullet to the chest. This demon was powerful, but my dark magic fought back inside, demanding to be released. I let it fly and when the power of pain hit him, the heir fell to his knees screaming.

"Silence him!" Luca called out, battling somewhere beside us.

Before I could follow through, a wolf ran at the heir and tore out his neck. I exhaled, nodded at Elijah, and glanced down at my mother. Her eyes fluttered open, thank fuck.

"Mom? Are you okay?"

"Fine, darling. Help me stand."

Because the coven was engaging Denz and the other two demons, I could do so. The moment Lilith was on her feet, she looked around.

Meredith had the ashwood stake in hand and drove it toward Denz, who fought Tobias. My eyes widened as the moment the stake struck, the new vampire let out a hiss and whirled on her, knocking her to the ground—but not before Tobias finished what his mate had started and ripped off Denz's head.

Another demon fell a moment later, a victim of Serena, leaving only the one who battled Luca.

"That's one of Asmodev's heirs," she explained.

Asmodev, the Prince of Lust. I swallowed. "Should we knock him out?"

Elijah and I had already killed one heir. Perhaps the third

demon was an heir too? What would be the repercussions of their deaths?

"We can't." Mother shook her head. "He's seen me. Not to mention, he's a swine. He tried to tempt your sister. To entrap her."

There was fury in her voice, and as this demon heir came from the Prince of Lust, I could imagine why. Anger built inside me. I was about to strike, when Mother, quick as a flash, decapitated the final heir with a tendril of magic. Luca spun, chest heaving.

"Thank you."

"Of course." My mother straightened, leaving no sign that one heir had bested her. "I should tell you, however, that those demons were related to the princes. Two bastards and one trueborn, but to demonkind they are all equally important and powerful, so now you must truly hurry. Once their bodies are found, an alarm will sound." Smoke swirled at the Queen of Hell's feet. "Vampires run swiftly. We will save your friend from the fire cell and then meet you outside."

"The office," Luca reiterated before Tobias could argue again. "Do as I say."

"Benedict!" Meredith called out, racing our way. "Get in the smoke!"

"I'm with you! Hold out your arms!"

The witch's arms jostled as a cat landed and became visible in them, his amber eyes wide with fear.

For once, Mother appeared astonished, not having known that Benedict was present, but she said nothing, just waited for Meredith, Luca, and Elijah to gather closer to her. Once they were in place, she sought Tobias's and Serena's attention. "Vampires, go. We will be there soon."

"Go, Tobias," Meredith urged. She was the reason he was still here, the reason he might risk his life to follow.

"You can't protect her if you're dead," Serena added, to which her brother snarled. "Stop it. Come with me."

Though Tobias looked like he wanted to argue further, Serena finally succeeded in pulling him out of the room. The next second, the vampires disappeared, and the smoke thickened.

The last thing I saw was the three demon bodies and what remained of Denz, before the smoke overtook us.

CHAPTER THIRTY-NINE

SHAY

Sweat dripped down my face, as fast and fierce as a waterfall.

I'd waited as long as I could for my friends, but at that point, I had ten minutes, max, before I became nephilim toast. Hopefully, they'd gotten their hands on the *lapis caelesti* and were outside the dome of terror that hung over LA.

If not, I would feel like such a piece of shit.

Luca's magic bound my wings and hands, but he'd worked the bindings to look constricting while still giving me enough wiggle room to reach my pockets. I took advantage of his genius loophole, and my hands slid into my pocket to grasp the luxiter. Carefully, I pulled it out. If I dropped it in here, and it rolled into the fire, I'd be so pissed at myself.

Inactive, the luxiter was dull, but after checking that no guards were coming, I brought it to my lips.

"*Volar*," I whispered, and at the magic word, it lit up, ready to do my bidding. "Take me to Angelina Ramos's Los Angeles home." I squeezed my eyes closed, preparing for the rush that was light-travel.

But nothing happened. No extreme blast of light tried to penetrate my eyelids. No swooping motion told me I was no longer standing on solid ground. Heat from the fire continued to wash over me.

No . . . Was this real?

I opened my eyes. Yep. The fire was still there, circling me, mocking me.

My mouth went dry. This couldn't be happening. I pulled the luxiter closer, determined to be more precise. "Take me to Angelina Ramos's home on Prato Drive, Los Angeles."

I remained in a cell, surrounded by fire.

"Oh, shiiiiiit."

The luxiter wasn't working. Nicolas Flamel had told me it would work anywhere in this realm, but apparently, this vile castle didn't qualify!

I was tempted to hurl the orb into the flames, and scared enough to even consider throwing myself in after it, but that thought vanished quickly. Shay Ramos was a fighter, not a quitter.

"Help. Let me out of here! I have information for your princes."

The guard hadn't been back since he'd locked me in here, but that didn't mean he wasn't lurking around. Shit, if they knew the fire was going to torch a nephilim alive, they were probably sitting down the hall with popcorn just waiting to hear my screams, the evil little shits.

Confirming my suspicion, someone laughed.

"Gettin' too hot for you, angel scum?"

"I can give you information that will make your masters happy. Let me out and I'll tell you what it is!"

"In a few." The same rhino-faced demon who met us at the

castle door appeared, and his beady eyes went straight to my hands. "Hey, what's that?"

Oh, crap. In my panic I'd forgotten to pocket the luxiter again. It didn't work in this cell, but the luxiter was invaluable everywhere else in the world. If I got out of here, I'd need it to escape. Quickly, I shoved it in my pocket.

"Nothing."

The monster grunted and held out a hand. "Give it."

"No."

"Fine. I'll take it from ya, 'den." He pulled a set of keys out of his pocket and stuck one in the door.

I shuffled back, but flames nipped at my heels and singed the bottom of my wings. I yelped and leapt forward an inch.

Rhino Face laughed humorlessly. "You ain't goin' nowhere." Without a worry, he stepped into the flames. "But I can chase you. No problem. I—what's dat!?"

Smoke, thick and black, plumed from nowhere to materialize around me. My rising panic soared into overdrive. I was cornered in a flaming cell by fire and smoke and a demon the size of the Hulk.

I still had no answer as to what to do when a red-haired woman appeared—followed by Rooms, Luca, Hans, and Elijah, all of whom let out yelps of pain as they landed smack dab in the flames. They leapt toward me into the small fire-free space I had left.

"Who the hell are you?" I directed my question to the ginger I didn't know.

"Queen, Lilith!" The demon at the door fell to his knees. "What are you—"

A whip of darkness struck from Lilith, severing the demon's head from his neck. I gaped, but my questions remained lodged in my throat as Lilith spun and spread her arms wide. Quick as a flash, the fire in the cell surged backward a foot, allowing us to stand unhindered.

My shoulders slunk, and for the first time since stepping foot in this cell, I took a full breath. "Wow. Thank you."

Lilith nodded. "I'm sorry we weren't here sooner. I had no idea this cell would have progressed so quickly. Usually, it takes many hours for the fire to reach the captive."

"Guess I'm lucky." I craned my neck to look at Hans, who was paler than I'd ever seen him. Eyebrows knitting together, I returned my attention to the Queen of Darkness. "What's going on? Why are you all here? Where are Tobias and Serena?"

"I knew this cell would have fire in it and this much fire, particularly hellfire, is deadly to vampires. They had to run."

"Why?"

"Your group has stolen the *lapis caelesti*," she said, making my heart leap with joy, but not before she added, "Wrath and his brothers will soon know. And as you've likely learned, you cannot use light magic in this castle." Lilith gestured to the binds around my wrists. "Release her. Once you're out of the palace you will need all the help you can get."

Luca stepped forward and with one wave of his hand, the bindings were gone on my hands and wings. I stretched the latter out, relieved to have the usage of them again. They'd be useful in escaping.

"I can smoke-travel you out of the palace," Lilith said, "but not beyond the dome surrounding the city."

"That's great," Meredith piped up. "But we need to land in a certain spot. Where Tobias and Serena are. Can you get us there?"

"Of course. Show me." Queen Lilith held out a hand to Meredith, who took it. "Think of the place."

I assumed that Meredith did and, soon enough, Lilith released her. "I have enough of an idea to get you close. Is everyone ready?"

Okay, so this was happening here and now. I nodded, and everyone else affirmed that they, too, were ready.

The Queen of Darkness wasted no time. Smoke filled the cell again, and the floor fell away. This felt almost identical to light-travel, just as constricting, just as disorienting, only dark, a little stinky, and vaguely electrical feeling.

I was thankful when my feet touched down on concrete and the smoke cleared so that we found ourselves in the city outside the castle once again.

Elijah spun. "We're only two blocks away."

A blur came from that direction and, suddenly, both Tobias and Serena were in front of us. Meredith threw her arms around her mate.

"We're okay," she whispered. "Everyone is okay."

"You must run. Get beyond the barrier." Lilith pointed, as if we could miss the freaking dome of terror. "There's little ti—"

A roar sounded from behind, and as one, we whirled around. A few blocks away demons rounded the corner, charging right for us. I cursed my white wings, which surely acted as a beacon to them.

"Mom, go! Before they recognize you!" Hans called out.

"I love you, son." Smoke filled the air and she disappeared.

"We need to run!" Meredith yelled.

"There's no way we'll make it." Hans's eyes darted around. "They're too fast, and it took us too long to get through the barrier the first time, but . . . " He trailed off and his eyes landed on a massive Mercedes SUV.

"Do it!" I yelled, recalling our auto theft in France. "Luca, open the doors on that Mercedes!"

The mage clearly had no idea why, but he performed an unlocking spell. Hans ran to the SUV, shoved himself inside, and his hands worked beneath the wheel. Within seconds, the beast of a vehicle was roaring.

"Get in," he commanded.

I jumped in and felt an invisible weight land on my lap. Benny appeared, looking up at me with wild eyes. For once, the cat seemed scared speechless.

"Luca, you'll need to create a hole in the ward that's big enough for this tank." Hans gripped the steering wheel tightly. "We'll be mobbing toward it at full speed."

"I'll do my best." Luca hopped in the passenger seat.

"Winged monsters are approaching from the palace, and the flame has turned red. The alarm has been sounded." Tobias pointed upward as he shoved Meredith into the car. "Serena and I will ride on top. Fight them off."

Not only did we have an army approaching from the street, but flying demons were coming our way too? If we got out of this hellscape alive, it would be a damned miracle.

"Stay alive or I'll kill you." Meredith hissed.

"Of course, love." Tobias shut the door after Elijah hopped in last. "Three knocks after an assault will tell you that we're fine. Now go."

Hans revved the engine, and the two vampires landed on the hood of the vehicle before we took off for the barrier.

CHAPTER FORTY

MEREDITH

The Mercedes roared down the street, shaking as three winged demons hit the side of the vehicle. The small tank had barely righted when we began jostling over . . . well, I tried not to think about what Hans drove over as we raced toward the boundary ward.

"Bumps ahead! Hold on!" Hans's voice rose over the rev of the engine.

I gripped the seat in time to save myself from being hurled into the ceiling. Above, a hard *thunk* made my heart stop. Was Tobias still above us? Serena?

If anyone can survive that chaos, it's a vampire, I told myself right before someone rapped on the metal above us three times in rapid succession. I exhaled at the signal. They were fine—or there, at least. Thank the Goddess.

"I see the ward!" Hans yelled. "Keep fighting them off and we have a chance."

"When should we roll down the windows all the way and bring them inside?" Shay cried out as one of the rhino-faced monsters slammed into the side of the vehicle. She thrust her sword through the crack in the window, stabbing the monster through the throat.

"Do it now!" Hans grunted as we jolted over yet another large object.

Shay rolled down the window and checked that no one else was coming before sticking her head out. "Stiff and Serena, come inside! I need to touch you to use the luxiter!"

Two hands appeared and like a damned ninja, Serena slithered her body through the window and into the backseat. My mate followed, his motions not as sleek, but that he could even fit through the window was miraculous enough.

"Are you okay?" I asked, shifting closer to Shay to accommodate the vampires.

"Fine." A gash on his cheek healed before my eyes. "The flying ones were troublesome, but there weren't as many."

"We're at the barrier in ten seconds," Hans informed us. "Do you got it, Luca?"

"Getting there!" Since the barrier came into view, the mage had been blasting magic at it, thinning the ward. Now, he reached as far as he could out the window and another spray of magic left his hands.

"Keep it going." Hans jerked the wheel to steer the vehicle to the left, around a pile of rubble.

We hurdled over a few more items, but our speed never slowed. The barrier came ever closer. Soon, we were twenty feet away and then ten. I sucked in a breath and closed my eyes, preparing for the pain.

A wash of hot magic flowed over me. Like last time, there was resistance and a sharp onslaught of pain. As if someone had taken a hundred knives and dug them into my skin, but as fast as we struck it, we blasted through the other side. All the pain vanished, leaving me gasping for air.

Luca screamed as he pulled his arms back inside. Blood dripped down it, and the reason why became apparent as one of the flying demons shrieked outside. It must have flown in at the exact same time the vehicle burst through the barrier.

Tobias lunged into the front seat, grabbed the demon's head, and twisted. Bones snapped and, with one hard shove, my mate pushed the body outside.

"Let me see," Tobias insisted, as Luca doubled over from the pain. It took the mage a second to right himself and show us the arm.

I gasped. A sizable chunk was missing from Luca's forearm and blood spurted from the wound. Had the monster torn open a vital artery?

"Compress it," Serena instructed, and Tobias ripped off his shirt to wrap it around Luca's wound. Immediately, blood soaked through the shirt. I swallowed down the panic rising in me. Was Luca going to make it?

"Everyone, grab on to me," Shay said.

"Go to your Mom's place," I said, worried that the disorienting effects of light-travel might harm Luca more. It usually left me feeling off and I'd never been injured while light-traveling. "Don't risk going farther with his arm."

"For sure," Shay's eyes darkened. "I need to ask Flamel a lot more about these before I take big risks using one again. I'm pissed that it didn't work in the palace."

With my free hand I clutched her hand, and as soon as we formed a chain, Shay spoke the magic word and the luxiter glowed.

"To Angelina Ramos's Los Angeles home!"

Light blasted, and the Mercedes disappeared as, once again, the luxiters pitched us back out of the tunnel of constriction and light, and I landed in the same home as before.

Shaking, I hauled myself off the floor and went to Luca. Blood was starting to leak from his makeshift bandage, and Luca's face had lost some of its warm tone. "We need to clean that. It—"

"If you want any chance of that closing properly you need vampire blood. Now." Serena bit into her arm. "Get him in that chair."

Hans and Tobias did as she said, and Serena stood over the mage, offering her arm. "It will be less weird if you take blood from me."

For a moment, Luca looked uncertain, but my mate stepped forward.

"You need it, and we need to get out of here once we're sure you're not hemorrhaging blood."

"We can leave now." Luca's head drooped.

Oh, no. We weren't moving an inch until he drank and was well enough to hold his head up. At the moment, we were safe, and I would not allow him to die because we were scared.

"Luca, please," Shay urged. "Do it."

The coven master gave a weak nod. Standing off to the side, Serena brought her arm to his lips and Luca drank. Though there was nothing between them, my own memories of drinking Tobias's blood when we sealed our mate bond came rushing back and I looked away.

Shay caught my eye and exhaled. "That was a close one."

"It sure was," I said. "But we got them." I patted my pocket, where the Opal lay hidden. "You'll never guess what else."

She arched an eyebrow.

"I think Hans is a *Vindix*."

"Shut the fuck up!" She cast a glance to the side of the room. Hans stood there, alone and holding his sister's necklace. His face was pale, his eyes locked on the piece of jewelry.

Shay stared at him. "I can see you told him? Is that his talisman?"

"I think so. We won't know for certain until we get back to England, though. He—" My phone vibrated in my pocket, and I stopped. We had service again, and three more phones in the room buzzed, making my stomach clench. "I need to check that."

Shay's eyes widened, and she nodded.

I pulled out my phone and saw Gunner had texted me. It was short and direct. They needed help. Pronto.

My stomach sank. They were in California, not too far from here. Could the same thing be happening where they were?

"Did you get a message from Gunner?" Tobias's tone was tight.

"I did. Hans?"

Hans fished his phone from his pocket. "He said it's urgent."

I drew in a sharp breath. "What if they're hurt?"

Shay turned to the coven master. "Luca? Can you travel?"

He finished drinking blood and already looked to have more color in his cheeks. Of course, the wound on his arm wasn't healed yet, but it had stopped spurting blood, which meant that the arteries or veins had sealed themselves. I knew from experience now that he wasn't about to keel over, the vampire blood would continue to work on him.

"I can." He had his phone in hand, too. "Gunner called me as well. I haven't listened to the message yet, but it doesn't bode well."

"Four messages," Tobias murmured. "No, that can't be good." My mate approached the coven master. "Serena and I will help you stand until the healing powers of her blood finishes working."

The vampires assisted the coven master, and the group circled up again as Shay pulled out her luxiter. "Unless you want to try yours, Rooms?"

"Nah, let's just get to them." I scooped up a fried-looking Benedict.

"You sure?"

"Positive." I positioned myself between her and Tobias. I could practice with the orb later, but Luca was frail and the tone of Gunner's message rang ominous. I didn't want to waste time.

Everyone attached themselves to Shay, and she ignited the luxiter with the magic word. Once it was good and bright, she said Gunner's name. For the third time that day, I tunneled through a constricting tube of light. This time, however, it wasn't as bad as the other experiences. Maybe Shay was right and I would get used to this.

I thought that until we landed on uneven ground and I fell over.

"Steady." Tobias was there in an instant, righting me as Serena supported Luca.

I threw him a thankful look and then turned to the coven master. He didn't look any worse, or better, but at least the light-travel hadn't blown his arm open again. What a relief.

"I'm fine." Luca grunted. "Set me down for a moment. I need to breathe."

Serena sat him down as the rest of us spread out. I wasn't in a home, or the woods, or anywhere I'd expect wolf shifters might wait, but in a cave. What the hell? Why?

"Woods are outside." Serena detached from the group once Luca was settled. She explored one way before she turned and lifted her nose to the ceiling. "The cave system goes deeper. Maybe they moved back?"

The question of why hung in the air, but the luxiter had brought us here for a reason, so she had to be right.

"Let's explo—*shit!*" Shay leapt back, hand flying to her chest and nearly giving me a heart attack too as a creature emerged from the depths of the cave, eyes gleaming in the darkness.

The creature, a giant black wolf, let out a whine and shifted into Gunner. "Didn't mean to scare y'all," he said, straightening his shirt. "Thought you might be demons. You smell like 'em."

His nose wrinkled, and I tried not to take offense. After where we'd been, we probably reeked.

"It's fine." I sighed in relief. "Are you okay? Why demons?"

"We're fine and lucky for it. Demons attacked Harper's pack. Possessed lots of wolves, maybe all of 'em by now. As far as we know, we're the only ones who got out unscathed."

"Are you certain?" Luca ground out. "The Midnight Pack is large and strong."

After what we'd seen in LA, it shouldn't have been surprising, bone-chilling, or anything but what we should have expected, and yet, a now-familiar cold dread gripped me. It wasn't just the city that the demons were occupying. They crawled across the state. How much further would Lucifer's reach extend?

Gunner nodded. "We saw these smoke-beings do most of the possessin'. They were real sneaky, and I don't think anyone saw 'em comin'. Now, a couple hundred wolves are being controlled by the demons. The monsters saw us leave, too. They might still be hunting for us in the woods, but Harper knew this place and guessed it would be safe for a bit. We ran here with her sis and brother. Been lookin' for escape routes since. You know, in case we need another way out."

At the mention of his family, Elijah let out a strangled sound that caught Gunner's attention. His eyebrows furrowed, as if he slightly recognized the wolf. "Who are you?"

"Eli!" A young man who looked like a long-haired, surfer boy version of Elijah burst from the depths of the cave.

"Ethan!" The men ran at each other, hugged, and Gunner stepped back, clearly having heard of Elijah before even if he had never seen him.

"Harp, Henley, come out!" Ethan yelled into the depths of the cavern.

Sounds of shifting rock came from the darkness behind the men. Seconds later, Harper appeared with a teen version of herself.

"Elijah," Harper whispered, relief sweeping her face as she took a step closer. "Thank the Old Ones! I—" Her hand flew to her ear. "Ow! It burns!"

Harper tried to take out an earring, and Shay ran forward to help, but I remained frozen in place. My ring had begun to heat up.

I swallowed as my heart began to beat faster, a war drum sounding in my chest.

No. It couldn't be.

Barely daring to believe it, I shot a glance at Hans, but he was no longer holding the necklace we'd found in Lucifer's palace. Vaguely, I recalled him putting it in his pocket right before we light-traveled to the cave.

He wasn't touching the necklace, and yet *my* moonstone ring warmed on my finger.

Another talisman was here.

Blood Moon Magic

Faerie Blood

The Bonegate Series - A Fanged Fae sister series

Hawk Witch

Assassin Witch

Traitor Witch

Illuminator Witch

The Royal Quest Series

Dragon Prince

Dragon Magic

Dragon Mate

Dragon Betrayal

Dragon Crown

Dragon War

The Starseed Universe

Prophecy of Three

Souls of Three

Rising of Three

ABOUT THE AUTHOR

Ashley lives in the lush and green Pacific Northwest with her husband, their dog, and the house ghost that sometimes makes appearances in her charming, old home.

When she's not writing fantasy novels she enjoys traveling the world, reading, kicking butt at board games, and frequenting taquerias.

For all the latest releases and updates, subscribe to Ashley's newsletter, The Coven. You can also find her Facebook group, Ashley's Reader Coven.